**WELCOME TO**

In your hands is a one-way ticket to the Old School.

It is a literary world that is shadowy and unknown. A fiction few today remember or have read.

This original "pulp fiction" represents an edgy and extreme chapter of black literary history. It is at once dangerous and deeply transgressive, gritty yet bold and experimental.

Your tour guide—a lost generation of black authors with street credentials born of hard times and tough luck.

Your destination—the charred remains of urban America. Places like Flatbush, Hell's Kitchen, South Philly, and, most ominously, a federal warehouse for repeat drug addicts. But in the Old School, even suburban tree-lined streets can play host to violence, and a perfectly nice young man can become a twisted psychopath thanks to one small problem: his Mom.

It is an era whose time has come and gone. It begins as early as 1958 and leaves off about 1975. But this is not a sentimental journey. Get on board and you will visit a world inhabited by original players and hustlers . . . mack daddies and racketeers . . . police and thieves . . . cops on the take and girls on the make. Flawed little men with big dreams, bad guns, and no hope for redemption.

It is a world of the desperate and the deranged; the doomed and the damned; a world where the sun never shines.

You get the idea.

America wasn't ready for these hard-boiled dispatches when they first appeared, and they were lost to history. Reclaimed in the Old School they join Stax Records, 70s gangsta chic, and the blaxploitation flick as cultural artifacts to be embraced by a new generation.

These books deserve a second chance, and in the Old School, they get one. So get on board.

Marc Gerald and Samuel Blumenfeld, Editors
Old School Books

# Portrait of a Young Man Drowning

# OLD SCHOOL BOOKS

edited by Marc Gerald and Samuel Blumenfeld

CHARLES PERRY

# Portrait of a Young Man Drowning

Old School Books

W · W · Norton & Company
New York · London

Copyright © 1996 by Marc Gerald and Samuel Blumenfeld

*Portrait of a Young Man Drowning* copyright © 1962 by Charles Perry

First published as a Norton paperback 1996 by arrangement with Simon & Schuster.

Printed in the United States of America.

The text of this book is composed in Sabon, with the display set in Stacatto 555 and Futura.
Composition by Crane Typesetting Service, Inc.
Manufacturing by Courier Companies, Inc.
Book design by Jack Meserole.

Library of Congress Cataloging-in-Publication Data
Perry, Charles, 1924–1969.
    Portrait of a young man drowning / by Charles Perry.
        p.   cm. — (Old school books)
    ISBN 0-393-31462-6 (pbk.)
        1. Young men—New York (N.Y.)—Psychology—Fiction. 2. Mothers and
sons—New York (N.Y.)—Fiction. 3. Brooklyn (New York, N.Y.)—Fiction.
4. Violence—New York (N.Y.)—Fiction. I. Title. II. Series.
PS3566.E6949P67   1996
813'.54—dc20                                                              95-39541

W. W. Norton & Company, Inc., 500 Fifth Avenue, New York, N.Y. 10110
http://web.wwnorton.com
W. W. Norton & Company Ltd., 10 Coptic Street, London WC1A 1PU

1 2 3 4 5 6 7 8 9 0

# CHARLES PERRY

CHARLES PERRY'S ONLY published novel is the one you are holding. This is a tragedy, for it is a work of breathtaking originality and unbearable suspense.

Perry was born in Savannah, Georgia, in 1924, but moved to Brooklyn when he was still in grade school. During the 1940s, he was a co-star of the hit radio series "New World A-Coming." A jack of all artistic trades including painting and music, the theater was Perry's first—and truest—love. Several of his plays, including "Luck of the Becketts" and "Mr. Marlowe's Race Problem," were successfully launched in the 1950s.

*Portrait of a Young Man Drowning* draws heavily on Perry's firsthand research of gangsters and juvenile delinquents in his own Brooklyn neighborhood. A homage to Joyce's *Portrait of the Artist as a Young Man,* it is a novel without precedent—astonishingly unique and shockingly bold. It is also among the few novels of its day by a black author to draw on an almost exclusively white cast— a decision, says Perry's daughter Chrissie Rivera, made not with an eye to the market, but out of fear that issues of race would cloud the fundamental humanity of the story's characters.

Despite unsettling, controversial themes, *Portrait of a Young Man Drowning* dropped like a bomb when it first appeared in 1962, leading author Kay Boyle to call it "one of the most powerful and disturbing novels I've read in years," and one *Times Literary Supplement* reviewer to remark, "This is not a pretty story. . . . Mr. Perry has written a fluent, graphic talk of tragic quality, all the more alarming for its being so firmly integrated with the everyday world." Believe the hype. Thirty-odd years have done nothing to diminish its shock value.

Perry soon began work on a semi-autobiographical account of the mysterious real-life murder of his eleven-year-old son, Charles, Jr., with the working title *I Wake Up Screaming*. Tragically, he was stricken with inoperable cancer, and died in 1969, when he was just forty-five.

The unfinished manuscript is believed to have been lost in a Perry family flood.

To a quick brown boy now still
and to Harry Guardino, of course

# Portrait of a Young Man Drowning

**I** AM MYSELF AND MYSELF IS MYSELF. I am me. I am here. I am something. I am somebody. I can reach high, high. I can jump, skip, hop, run like the wind. I can holler loud, walk, talk slow or fast. I can fight . . . Arnie shows me how. I am somebody. Everything is for me. The sun shines on me. The rain wets me. The snow comes for me and I go sledding and sliding, throwing the balls. I am round and quick. I have hands that can take, scratch, hold open, close, hit. I have feet that can walk, run, jump, kick. To roaches and flies and bedbugs I am a giant. I can pick them up in my fingers. I can squash them or step on them. Nobody hollers.

## 2

Hap, he is my father. He is so big. Not strong, but so big. He sits at the kitchen table, eating onions raw. He watches me. He says nothing, just watches me. I feel scared and run to Ma. She picks me up in her arms. Hap watches me . . . chews onions, watches, watches. I do not care. Ma holds me. I am safe.

Ma's name is Kate. Hap calls her Katydid sometimes. Everybody else calls her Kate. I call her Ma because she is.

We got a dog. His name is Rags. He is Hap's dog but he likes me. We play together all the time. I got two friends—Arnie and Charlie Trolley. We call Charlie "Ding Dong" because his name is Trolley. Arnie and Ding Dong are older than me, but they are my best friends.

I live at 170 Myrtle Avenue one flight up. I can look out of my front window and see pushcarts by the curb all the way down Myrtle for three blocks. On Saturday nights the Avenue is crowded with shopping people because there are no pushcarts allowed on a Sunday.

In our house we got lots of rats, roaches, bedbugs, but I must not say this. Roaches always come out when Ma's friends visit and make her ashamed. Hap's friends do not come to the house. In the summertime the flies and mosquitoes come to visit. Ma rubs my body all over with some kind of stuff so they will not bite. They bite me anyway. I got bumps all over from mosquitoes and bedbugs. Ma uses a Flit gun but it does no good. She says the bedbugs are in the walls. I can't see them. We will move soon anyway.

## 3

"What do you want to be when you grow up, little boy?"

"A man," I say.

He laughs and shakes his fat German head. Pohndorff, the butcher, does this. "And when you are a man what will you want to be then?"

What a question! "A doctor," I say. Everybody knows that.

He puts his hands on his hips and says, "And why do you want to be a doctor?"

I bite on the piece of baloney he has given me and wonder why he is so stupid. "Because I want to make my mother well. She cries all the time."

"Then you'd better hurry home with the meat or you'll be crying from what she will give you!"

I run out of the store to the street.

## 4

I stop to watch four girls in pink and red dresses, jumping rope in the warm sunshine. One is waiting, one is jumping and the others are turning. I like the sound of what they are saying as they jump.

> *"I'm mad at you,*
> *I'm mad at you.*
>
> *"Why? Why?*
>
> *"Not because you're dirty,*

*And not because you're clean,*
*But just because you kissed your fella in a magazine.*

*"Pepper, salt, mustard, cider, vinegar!"*

The girl who is jumping trips and falls down. Her dress flies up and her drawers are dirty. The other girls laugh and shake their fingers at her.

"Shame, shame, I know your name. Iris wears dirty drawers!"

I do not understand. What is so funny about that? My drawers are dirty, too. Girls are crazy. I don't like them any more and go skipping off.

An old Italian man with a great big mustache and a feather in his cap is grinding an organ on the crowded street. Nobody pays any attention, but I like the music and stop to listen. Where is the monkey, I wonder? Maybe if he had his monkey people would stop to listen and fill his tin cup with pennies. But I like the music even without the monkey, and if I had a penny I would give it to him. I go up close to listen. Suddenly he looks down on me and frowns.

"Show's over," he says.

He picks up his box and goes on down the street. I watch him and water comes in my eyes. Maybe he had a monkey and it died. I feel so, so sorry for him because his monkey died.

At home Ma says to me, "What happened? What kept you so long?"

I tell her about the organ man and his monkey what died.

"Nonsense," she says. "Why feel sorry for him? Feel sorry for us—you and me. We're alone and hungry in the world whenever your father gets the notion in his head to go running around."

"Running around what?"

She does not answer me. I go back to the street again to look for things.

## 5

"Where are we going?"

"Shush!"

Ma is pulling me by the hand. She is mad. She is rushing. We go sailing down the stairs, through the streets, down into the subway. The train goes screaming through the dark—a station—up onto the street again. It is a strange place. Strange houses, strange stores, strange people. I want to stop and see everything, but Ma pulls me along fast with her. Whe-e-e! We go like a kite in the wind, passing houses, stores, a church, a beggar. Now Ma stops and looks at a paper in her hand and at a house. Everything is so new and strange. Is this a different country? There is a johnny-pump in front of this house, and it is skinny and taller than me. Our johnny-pumps are all fatter and shorter than I am. Ma pulls me up the stairs and we go into a hall. There is a soft rug on the floor. We stand in front of a door and Ma knocks. It is dark in here but I am not afraid because Ma holds my hand very tight.

The door opens and a lady with white hair is standing there. She looks like a nice lady and she is smiling and she says to Ma, "Yes?"

Ma says, "I am Mrs. Odum. I am Hap Odum's wife."

The lady looks scared, but I know Ma will not hurt her. Ma points to me.

"This is our son. Can't you see what you are doing to him?"

What is she doing to me? I can't see her doing anything but standing there looking at me. Ma is talking loud and scolding her. She tells Ma to come inside and we go in and she closes the door.

"I am sorry. Let's sit down and talk nice."

"Can't you see what you are doing to him?" Ma asks again.

"I'm sorry—I didn't know."

I did not know, either. I still do not know what she is doing to me. Maybe she is magic and she is doing things to me I cannot see or feel. Ma is very angry. She tells Ma to sit down. A little, brown dog comes in from another room, laughing at me and wagging his fuzzy tail. I go to him and sit on the floor and rub his soft back. He licks me all over. We play as Ma and the magic lady talk. I am so happy with the dog I can hardly hear what they are saying.

". . . my husband."

"I didn't know. . . ."

"... for three weeks."

"... your husband."

"How could you? ..."

"But I didn't know."

"... kind of people."

"I'll tell you—"

"Shush—the boy!"

"Wait."

The lady is standing over me, smiling. She smells nice. She kneels beside me and pets the dog with me.

"You like the puppy?"

"Yes, m'am."

"Her name is Pixie. Do you know what a pixie is?"

"A brownie."

"Yes. You're a smart boy. How would you like to take Pixie in that other room over there? You can close the door and play as much as you like while your mother and me have a talk. Would you like that?"

Ma says, "Go on, Harold."

I pick up the little puppy and go into the room.

"Now close the door," the lady says to me.

I close the door. I am in a bedroom. It is just like Ma's room, clean and pretty. Me and Pixie, we play on the bed. We wrestle, we bark, we bite each other. She chases me and I chase her, under the bed and over the bed, knocking the shoes all around the room, under the bed and over the bed again. We do this for a very long time and get very tired. We stop to rest. I lie across the bed and Pixie curls up in my arms. I hear Ma and the magic lady talking in the next room. I wonder why they are talking so long? I get tired of waiting. I do not hear them talking. Maybe they are finished. I get off the bed and tiptoe to the door. I crack it open and look into the room. They are still talking. The magic lady is giving Ma a drink of water. I close the door soft again and go back to the bed. I pat Pixie and her tail waggles. I look around. I put the shoes back under the bed. It is a very pretty room and smells so nice and sweet. There is a dresser just like Ma has. There are pictures and other things on it. I go over to see what they are—a hairbrush and comb, keys, Vaseline, powder—and a bright red box with a picture of a man kneeling with a big ball on his back. It is a pretty box and I wonder what is inside. I open the box and it is a surprise—balloons! A box full of white balloons, and I will have some fun with them. I take them back to bed with me. I take one out and blow. It does not go up good. I try others, all of them. They are not very good balloons. I will have fun with them anyway. I take a handful and throw them up in the air and see how many I can catch before they fall to the bed again. It is a lot of fun. I throw them up again and again. Pixie barks at them and grabs them. She rips them with her sharp teeth. We jump up and down, up and down with the balloons. I get tired again. I lie down on the bed to rest. Pixie sits down beside me and licks my face. Her tongue is too wet. I turn my face away from her. I feel sleepy. My eyes won't stay open. The bed feels so nice and soft and warm and . . .

*"Harold!"*

Ma's voice wakes me. Pixie jumps off the bed. I sit up and rub my eyes. Ma is in the doorway and the magic lady is behind her. They are looking at me with eyes big and scared.

"What have you got there?" Ma asks me.

"Balloons," I say, picking them up again. "But they are not good ones. They won't blow up."

The magic lady's face is very dark.

Ma slaps the balloons out of my hand and jerks me off the bed and out of the room. The magic lady is trying to say something to her, but Ma pulls me across the room and we go flying out of the magic lady's house.

Ma puts me to bed early.

Hap comes home. He is very mad. I hear him yelling at Ma in the kitchen. I hear chairs banging, plates breaking. He is mad because we went to the magic lady's house. He has lost his job.

He is saying, "You had no right to butt in."

Ma says, "Think of your family."

"My family! Well, what will you do now? I got no job. She owns half the business."

"You can find something else."

"We're in a depression, my darling girl!"

"No job at all is better than that."

"No job at all is better than thirty dollars a week in a depression?!"

"Yes, if you have to lose your respect for it!"

"Oh, Kate! You make it sound so filthy."

"What else is it?"

"All right, can you eat this 'respect' of yours?"

"It's better, Hap, yes it is. You'll get another job."

"Where? Just you tell me *where*?"

"Somewhere. You'll find another one."

"Oh no I won't—because I'm leaving you right now!"

"Hap!"

"Get out of my way!"

"Please, don't, Hap! What will we do? Oh, my God, what will we do?"

"You've got respect now—Find a way to eat it!"

"Hap!"

The front door slams. Hap has gone. I hear Ma crying in the kitchen. Did Hap lose his job because I played with the balloons? I am scared. I pull the covers over my head and shiver.

I wake in the morning. The lamp is next to my bed. I know that Hap will be gone a long time. I am glad because now I will have light.

I go to the bathroom. Ma is there vomiting in the toilet bowl.

"What's the matter, Ma?"

"Nothing, nothing. Go back in the kitchen and sit down."

I go. Ma comes into the kitchen, wiping her mouth on a towel.

"Are you sick, Ma?"

"No. My stomach was a little upset, that's all. Come. Ma wants to talk to you."

I go to her. She picks me up in her lap.

"Harold, we are all alone now. Your father has gone away."

"Where?"

"I don't know."

"Will he come back?"

"I don't know. Now we have no one to bring the money home, no one to take care of us. Do you understand?"

I get scared and start to cry. Ma squeezes me tight.

"Don't cry. We will look out for ourselves, yes we will. I must get a job so we can have food to eat, and you must act like a little man and take care of yourself while I'm working."

I stop crying.

"That's better. And you must promise me you won't play with bad little boys like Arnie while I'm away."

"I promise."

"If you ever need help when I'm away, go to Pop Carlson upstairs. He will be sort of watching out for you."

"Okay."

Ma gives me a hug and a kiss. "That's my angel! You are the man in the house now. You won't betray Ma's trust in you, will you?"

"No, Ma."

I love Ma. She is a good lady. From now on I will hold her hand tight when we go in the street so she will not get lost.

# 7

I am playing in front of the house with Rags. Ma has gone to look for work, and I must stay in front of the door until she comes back. I see Frank, the cop, standing on the corner. He is a nice cop. All the kids like him and he likes us. Frank gives us dimes and nickels sometimes. Me and Rags run down to the corner.

"H'ya, Frank!"

He smiles. "Hello there, Harry. Say, what kind of a dog you got there?"

"I don't know."

"Well, why don't you ask him?"

"*Ask* him? Dogs don't talk."

"Why, sure they do."

"They *do*?"

"Sure. Watch me. I'll ask him for you. What's his name?"

"Rags."

Frank bends over and holds Rags by the neck. "Rags, tell me, what kind of dog are you?" Rags makes a little noise and Frank smiles and lets go of him. "See? He told me."

"What did he say?"

"He said he's a 'just as soon' dog. . . . He'd just as soon eat as to sleep."

Frank laughs. He gives me a nickel and walks around the corner still laughing. I do not understand.

I look at the nickel in my hand. No, I do not feel like eating candy now. I go upstairs in the house and put the nickel on the table. I see a piggy bank there and it makes me think of something swell to do. I will get some more nickels and fill that bank up. I will be rich then because I will have money in the bank.

I put my nickel in the piggy bank and run downstairs to the street again. I think of all the good things I will buy for me and Ma when I get rich. I want to hurry and do it. I look all around until I find Frank again. He is standing in front of a candy store on Prince Street. I go to him and ask for another nickel.

Frank says, "Why, Harry! I just gave you a nickel. What'd you do with it?"

I tell him how I am going to get rich. He laughs and says it will take me a long time to get rich. I will have to grow up first and do a lot of hard work and other things.

This makes me sad. I sit down on the curb and feel like crying. Rags licks my mouth. Anyway, he likes me. I go back upstairs to the house and shake the nickel back out of the piggy bank. I buy a bar of Oh Henry candy for me and Rags. We sit in the doorway and eat it. Rags looks at me and wags his tail. I feel much better.

I play on the floor in the kitchen. Ma sits quiet at the table. We did not eat supper and it is very late. I feel dizzy and my stomach hurts.

"Ma, I don't feel good."

"What's the matter, my precious?"

"I don't know."

"I'll give you a spoonful of Moreland's bitters. It will make you feel better."

"I don't want tonic. I'm hungry."

Ma looks sad. "We'll have to wait until Pop Carlson comes home. I'll borrow money from him for supper."

"When will he come home?"

"I don't know. Soon. Come—take sugar and I'll sing to you."

I go to her. She pulls me up in her lap. She holds me tight.

"Who is a boy's best friend?"

"You are, Ma!"

"Yes and I'll sing you a song about mothers. It's about what my mother meant to me when I was small. It is the way every child should feel about his mother. . . ."

"There's no milk."

"Make believe. Now sh-h, listen. . . .

> *"One bright and guiding light*
> *That taught me wrong from right*
> *I found in my mother's eyes."*

I feel better.

> *"Those baby tales she told*
> *. . . I found in my mother's eyes."*

She rocks me. I am sleepy. . . .


## 9

I look at the big bottle of tonic on the bathroom shelf. On it is a picture of a little girl with yellow hair and a blue bonnet. She is smiling. She is holding up a bottle of tonic. The bottle she is holding up also has her picture on it in which she is holding up another bottle of tonic. And on that bottle of tonic there is another picture of the girl holding up the bottle. . . .

I wonder. It is funny. How many pictures of the same thing are there in this one picture? I look close. I can only see two pictures good because they get smaller and smaller. But there must be many, many more.

Now I study it hard: on the first picture there is a girl holding a bottle of tonic with the same picture on it, and in *that* picture there is a picture, and in *that* picture there is a picture, and in *that* picture there is a picture, and in the next and next it is the same, and I guess it will go on for the end of the world.

It makes me dizzy and dreamy. I am scared. I stop quick and run out of the bathroom.

## 10

In the classroom the teacher asks, "What is bread made from?"

"Flour," someone answers.

"That's right," Teacher says. "And who will tell me where eggs come from?"

"Chickens!" a girl shouts.

"Very good. And milk? Who will tell us where milk comes from?"

I know. I raise my hand.

"Yes, Harold?"

I stand up. I say, "From tits."

Some kids laugh. I am surprised. Some kids look at me like I am dirty.

"From the tits of what animal?" Teacher asks me.

"No animal. From my mother."

After school the boys make fun of me. They call me a baby. They say I said a nasty thing about my mother. I am ashamed and mad. I cry. I fight. I kick, scratch at them. I wish they are all ants so I can crush them under my foot.

## 11

Today I learned about Abe Lincoln in school. He freed the slaves when he was the President. He was a good, kind man. I would like to be like him when I grow up and help the horses. The peddlers on Myrtle Avenue treat the horses mean. They work them hard all the time, never give them rest, and they are beaten. When I grow up I will free all the horses like Abe Lincoln freed the slaves.

## 12

When I say words Arnie always says, Ma slaps me.

Ma asks, "Where do you learn such words?"

I tell her the truth.

She tells me, "Stay away from that brat. Don't play with him. He's a nasty, filthy kid."

Almost everything that is fun to do Ma says it is bad or nasty. But I will do what she tells me because she is my mother and I love her.

## 13

Uncle Frank, big like a mountain, sits stiff in the kitchen chair, looking down at me over his fat belly. I play on the floor. He talks and talks. Uncle Frank just watches and watches me like Hap.

"He needs shoes, Katherine. Let me buy shoes for the boy."

"All right, Frank, you can do that. And don't think I'm not grateful for a brother who . . ."

"I'll come by tomorrow and take . . ."

"No, it's just that . . ."

"You're too prideful, Katherine, you've always been too . . ."

". . . the whole family . . ."

"Not me, Katherine, not me!"

". . . love and affection for your own!"

"Okay, I don't want to argue, Katherine. Here, boy!"

"Harold?"

"What?"

"Your uncle called you."

"Come here to me, boy."

I go to him. He smiles a little at me.

"Can you spell?"

"Yes sir."

"Spell cat for me."

"C-a-t, that spells cat."

"Dog."

"D-o-g, dog."

He smiles and pats my head. "Smart little towhead! He's got Mama's chin, Katherine. Ever notice that?"

"Yes."

"Can you spell house? I'll give you a nickel if you can spell house for me."

"No," I say, "that's too friggin' hard."

"Harold!"

Uncle Frank's face is dark. He looks mean. He does not like me any more.

"Go play," he says.

I go back to my marbles on the floor.

"Katherine, I wish you would let me and Lucy keep him. This is no place for . . ."

"Never. I would never . . ."

". . . be reasonable . . . for the boy's sake . . ."

". . . have her throw it in my face? Never!"

". . . only till you get on your feet. After all, we have none of our own. . . . We can give him much more."

". . . a mother's love?"

"Be reasonable."

"I won't hear it!"

"This is no way . . . a boy . . . language . . . niggers, kikes, wops . . . filthy neighborhood . . . after all, he's my blood, too. I won't stand for—"

"You can't frighten me with . . ."

". . . force you . . . give him up . . . report you to . . . unfit mother . . ."

What is going on? There is a big fight. Ma is screaming at Uncle Frank standing in the doorway with his hat in his hand. Ma grabs me up in her arms.

"Get out! Get out!" She screams at Uncle Frank.

"Yes, I'll force you to give him up. You'll see!"

Uncle Frank goes, slamming the door. Ma squeezes me tight, tight, tight. She cries.

"What's the matter, Ma?"

"Oh, my baby, my baby, my baby!"

## 14

I wake up in the morning. The lamp is gone from my room.

I dress for school. I go down the hall to Ma's room. The door is closed. I knock.

"Ma, I'm all ready for school!"

Ma calls from inside. "Fix your own breakfast this morning, honey. You can do it. The corn flakes are on the table."

"Okay."

I fix my breakfast and eat very slow. I cannot swallow so good. I finish and put my bowl in the sink. I go back to Ma's room and knock on the door again.

"I'm finished, Ma. Ain't you taking me to school this morning?"

Ma says from inside, "No. You're getting big enough to go by yourself now. Run along now, sweet, and be careful."

"Okay."

I get my books and go downstairs to the street.

I feel sad. One thing I know; Hap has come back home again.

MA AND HAP SIT AT THE KITCHEN TABLE, playing cards. It is raining outside and I cannot go out to play. I stand by the table and watch them put the cards down.

Ma slaps me hard on the face. "Stop picking your nose! How many times do I have to tell you?"

"Oh, leave the boy alone, Kate."

"But he never picks his nose when you're away, Hap. Only

when you're home. It disgusts me. It looks like he's just trying to make you think I don't teach him manners."

"Picking his nose isn't bad. He'll outgrow it."

"Harold, stop that crying at once or go to your room!"

I turn and go.

I lie across the bed in the dark room. I stop crying. I don't care. I wish I could catch cold or something and die. I will eat something smelly and maybe I will die. I feel like jumping out of this window. Maybe tomorrow I can get run over by a big truck and be crushed and smashed by the big, heavy wheels. Nobody would holler because nobody cares.

## 2

It is late at night. Ma gives me my supper. It is not much: bread and milk from the can. Ma did not have money for food because it is payday and Hap has not come home yet. Ma does not look at me, but I know there are tears in her eyes. I eat very slow because the dry bread is hard to swallow.

Someone knocks on the door. Ma runs to open it. Two ladies wearing pants bring Hap in between them. Hap is drunk-sick, the way he was last payday. They sit him on a chair and his head falls on the table and he is asleep. The ladies tell Ma they found Hap laying downstairs in front of the door, but Ma looks like she thinks it is a lie. She thanks them and they go. She searches Hap's pockets. She sees me watching.

"Go to bed," she tells me.

Ma washes Hap's face with cold water, and I go to bed. I hear Ma yelling at Hap. Now she is crying. Now she is yelling. I stop up my ears with my fingers and put my head under the covers.

## 3

I finish and flush the toilet. I turn to wash my hands at the sink. I see the brush with all the long hairs that Hap uses when he shaves. He puts soap on it and makes a foam on his face. I take the brush and wet it. I will make foam, too. I rub the brush on the soap. It foams up. I rub harder, harder, and make a lot of it all over the sink. It is pretty and white. It is just like bubbly snow. I will make a snowy bathroom and fool Ma and Hap. I will put foam all over, and when Ma and Hap come in they will wonder how all the snow got inside. What a cute and funny trick to play on them! It will be like April Fools' Day. They will laugh and see how smart I am.

I make a big soapy foam in the sink and throw a lot on the floor and walls. I soap up the brush and paint foam onto the toilet seat and around the bowl.

The door opens sudden. I jump. It is Hap. His eyes get big as he looks at all the foam. I get scared.

"What are you doing?"

"Playing."

He comes closer, grabs me by the shoulder.

"Is that my shaving brush you have there?"

"Yes, I was just painting—"

"Why, you little—"

I scream. He takes off his belt and beats. I scream, scream, scream. I hold on tight to it.

"Now, you listen to me—"

"Yes, Hap, yes. Please don't hit me any more!"

"Shut up."

"Please don't . . ."

"I'm through beating you. Shut up!"

"Yes, Hap, yes."

"Now, you listen to me—"

"Yes, sir. Yes, sir."

"That brush is not to play with. Don't you ever touch it or anything else of mine again. Do you understand?"

"Yes, sir."

"If you ever dare touch anything of mine again I'll give you something worse. Have you got that through your head?"

"Yes, sir. Yes, sir."

"All right. Now clean up that mess and wiggle your little ass back off to bed!"

I get busy quick to clean it up.

*   *   *

I lie very quiet in bed. The room is dark. The tears have stopped and my behind does not sting any more. Someone comes into the room.

"Harold?"

It is Hap! I tremble.

"Yes, sir?"

A hand pets my hair soft.

"Are you all right?"

"Yes, sir."

His hand reaches for mine and puts a cold circle in it.

"Here . . . put it under your pillow."

"What is it?"

"A quarter."

"For me?"

"For you."

"What for?"

"Nothing, damn it! Go back to sleep. Good night."

He goes.

# 4

I come in from play. The light is on in the kitchen but I see no one.

I call, "Ma?"

She answers, "Is that you, Harold? I'm back here—in my room."

I go to her room and stop in the doorway. She is in bed. Her eyes are wet and red. Her hair is all sloppied up. She has a handkerchief in her hand.

"What's the matter, Ma?"

"I don't feel well, Harold. I have a cold."

"It makes you cry?"

"Yes. Darling, I don't feel like getting up. Can you be a little man and fix your own supper?"

"Yes. What have we got?"

"Meat balls. You know the way Ma does—first the potatoes,

the gravy on top, and you take a meat ball. There are some green peas on the back of the stove, too, in a little pot."

"Okay." I start away.

"Harold . . ."

"What?"

"Be sure you scrub very hard in the bathroom before you touch one bit of food."

"All right. Ma, can I have two meat balls?"

"Yes, you may, my dear pet."

I finish eating. I am full and tired. I get ready for bed. Ma calls me. I go to her room door again.

"What?"

"What are you doing?"

"Getting ready for bed."

"Come get in bed with Ma. Your father won't be home until late tonight."

I am scared. I step back. "No."

"No? What's the matter . . . don't you love me any more?"

"Yes, I love you."

"Then come get in bed with me. You'll be company and a comfort for Ma in her misery."

"But I *can't*—"

"What do you mean you *can't*? You mean you don't want to?"

"Yes, I want to, but—"

"But what?" She sits up. "What is it, Harold? What's the matter with you? Why are you looking like that?"

"I'm afraid."

"Afraid? What nonsense! What's come over you, Harold? Afraid of what?"

"I don't know. Please, can I go back to my room now?"

"Oh, all right, go on."

I hurry and get into bed. I pull the covers over my head and squeeze my legs tight around it.

## 5

"They don't!" Arnie says.

"They do!" I tell him. "Everybody has."

**30**

"They don't!" Arnie shouts. "You don't know from nothin'."

"They do, they do." I turn to Ding Dong. "Hey, don't they, Ding Dong?"

"Gee, I don't know myself, nudder, Harry."

Arnie says, "Okay, I'll prove it to youse. Come on."

"Where?"

"Up my house. My aunt's visitin' there with my little cousin. Come on."

We race down the street and around the corner on Hudson Avenue. We follow Arnie into a house and up the dirty stairs. His front door is open. Inside a man is talking to a lady and a little girl. Me and Ding Dong wait in the hall as Arnie goes in.

Arnie says to the lady, "Aunt Jenny, can I take cousin Geraldine out to play?"

"Yes, yes—but don't go far."

"Okay. Come on, Geraldine."

Arnie takes the little girl by the hand and we follow him downstairs.

"Where you going?" I ask.

"In the cellar."

We go down in the cellar. We stand around Geraldine.

Arnie says, "Watch! Geraldine, pull up your dress and pull your drawers down."

She does. We look. I am surprised.

I ask, "What happened to it?"

Arnie says, "Nothing happened to it. She was borned that way. I told you so. All girls are borned that way."

Me and Ding Dong kneel on the ground to see it better.

"Does it hurt you, Geraldine?" I ask.

"What?"

"Your thing there."

"Nope, it don't hurt."

"What does it feel like?" Ding Dong asks.

"Nothing much," she answers.

"Can you pee through it, Geraldine?" I ask.

"Sure. Want to see me?"

"Yes."

She stoops over. We watch her close.

"Wow!"

"Ain't that something, Harry?!" Ding Dong says.

"It sure is! I never seen nothing like that before."

"It's a real pisserroo!" Arnie says. He goes over and sits on an old carriage and looks at Geraldine.

She stands up straight. "I do that all the time," she says, smiling.

"Boy, that sure is something!" Ding Dong says.

I am tired of watching. "Okay. Come on, let's go back out and play."

Arnie says, "Youse guys go on back. I'm gonna stay down here a while. I want to watch Geraldine some more."

Ding Dong says, "Can I stay and watch Geraldine with you, Arnie?"

"No," Arnie says. "This time I want to look at Geraldine by myself."

"Come on, Ding Dong," I say.

We come up out of the cellar and start down Hudson to Myrtle Avenue.

"What'll we do?" Ding Dong asks.

"Want to go begging on Fulton Street?" I ask.

"Naw!"

"Let's steal some apples off the pushcarts."

"Don't feel like it."

"We could go to City Park."

"Friggin' park."

We walk along slow. I don't know what to do. I try to think of something.

"Geraldine sure can pee good through that thing," Ding Dong says.

"Yes. I never saw anything like that in the whole world before!"

We reach Myrtle Avenue and stop. We look up and down. Nothing is happening. The el train goes by above.

Ding Dong says, "Harry, I think I'll go back down that cellar and look at Geraldine some more."

"But Arnie won't let you. He said he wanted to look at her alone."

"Maybe he'll get tired. If he gets tired he could let me look at Geraldine while he rests up."

"Okay, I want to go home and eat anyway. See you tomorrow."

"So long!"

"So long!"

He goes that way; I go this way.

I buy a pound of frankfurters from the butcher for Ma. I go the long way back home. It is so much more better and I see so much more. It takes me through Hudson Avenue where Ma does not want me to go because it is so tough. The poolroom is there where Louis Varga and Jerry the Wop hang out. They are the toughest guys in the whole world. There are girls there, too, who stand in the hallways and windows and call men inside. But I do not go there just to pass the poolroom or watch those girls. I go there because I hope I will see Arnie. He is three years older than me and smart and very, very tough. But I like him and he likes me.

"H'ya, Harry!"

"Arnie!"

He puts his arm around me. "Let's go stealing on Myrtle Avenue."

"I can't. Somebody might tell Ma like the last time."

"Friggin' somebody!" he says and spits through his teeth. We sit down on the curb and watch people and autos go by.

"What you got in that friggin' bag?" he asks.

"Meat," I tell him.

"For your old lady?"

"Yeah."

"Friggin' meat!"

"Yeah," I say.

We want to do something. We do not know what.

"Let's go peep on the who-ers," Arnie says.

We walk along Hudson Avenue until we come to a house where a lady is sitting in the window on the first floor. We go through the alley and hop over a fence to the back of the house. The shades on the back windows are down, but there is a little crack in one of them and we can see into the room. There is only a bed there, and a girl is sitting on it, playing cards with herself.

Arnie frowns. "They ain't working yet," he whispers. "It's too early."

We hop back over the fence. Arnie snaps his fingers.

"Hey, let's go hitching out to Prospect Park!"

"Okay, but I can't carry this."

He looks at the meat. "We'll hide it. Gimmie."

He takes the package and sticks it behind a garbage can against the wall in the alley.

"It's safe now. You can get it when we come back. Come on."

We come out of the alley. The lady sitting in the front window calls to us.

"Hey, you kids, wanna make a nickel?"

We say sure and run over to her. She is wearing a pretty red dress. She hands Arnie a wrinkled dollar bill that smells like face powder.

"Go around the corner to the drugstore," she says, "and buy me a small-size can of alum. Alum, can you remember that?"

"Sure, alum. I know what the stuff is."

"Hurry back," she says, "and maybe I'll give you a dime apiece."

We run down the street. When we turn the corner, Arnie stops and we start walking slow.

"The old bag!" Arnie says. "She ain't got no more walls."

"What?"

He pokes me with his elbow and talks out of the side of his mouth. "That's what they use that stuff for, you dope. To make walls, to make walls."

"Oh," I say.

I do not know what he means, but I make believe. I want Arnie to like me and I want to be smart like him.

We go right past the drugstore. I tell Arnie.

"I'm gonna keep this dollar," Arnie says. "Who wants a friggin' dime? I gonna treat you to the movies. Come on."

I laugh with joy. We run.

It is a good picture. Helen Twelvetrees and Philips Holmes are in it. Helen Twelvetrees is Ma's favorite movie star. Ma looks just

**34**

like her, too. Everybody says so. I love the movies. I know all the names of the stars—Bob Steele, Richard Dix, Walter Huston, Hoot Gibson—I know them all. In this picture there is a big fight at the end with everybody in the picture fighting. Ricardo Cortez gets killed with his own knife. We jump up and down shouting while the fight goes on. The boss comes down and tells us to shut up or he will throw us out. We keep still but not for long. Arnie buys me all the candy and peanuts I want. All my pockets are filled with chewing gum and candy. A comedy comes on next, with Charlie Chase. He is a dope in this picture. A man tells him, aw, go fly a kite! He gets a real kite and flies it. Another man tells him to go jump in a lake and he does it. He is a real dope. We laugh, laugh, laugh! We sit through the main picture again just to see the big fight at the end. We shout and jump and yell. The boss comes down again and tells us to get the hell out. We go. We don't care. We have seen everything.

Outside in the street it is getting dark. I remember that Ma sent me to the store.

"I'm gonna get hit," I say. "I shoulda brought the meat home first."

"Friggin' meat!" Arnie says. "Come on, let's go get it."

We go back to the house on Hudson Avenue. We are careful to make sure the lady who sent us to the store is not in the window. We slip into the alley. Arnie takes the meat from behind the garbage can, but there is a big, wet hole in the bag. Some of the meat is gone.

"A cat must've found it," Arnie says, "but most of it's still there." He hands me the bag. "Come on, let's get out of here."

We come out of the alley. A woman starts shouting.

"There they are! Run, catch them!"

It is the lady who sent us to the store. A man starts after us. We turn and run as fast as we can. Arnie is way ahead of me and ducks around the corner. A hand grabs my shoulder and pulls me to a stop. I am scared. I know I will go to jail or get beat up.

The man has on a red shirt. He holds me tight with two hands and looks down at me. I know I am going to be killed and my heart beats faster and faster. The man shakes me.

"Where's that dollar bill?" he asks me.

I tell him I do not have it. I tell him what happened to it. The lady in the red dress comes up to us.

"They spent it," the man tells her.

"What's that other boy's name? Where does he live?" she asks me.

"I don't know."

The man looks at her. "What'll I do with him?"

"What *can* you do with him? He's too small. Kick him in the pants and let him go. I'd like to get my hands on that big one, though."

The man shakes me again. "Listen, you little bastard, you tell that friend of yours if I ever catch him I'll kick his ass all over Hudson Avenue, understand?"

"Yes, sir," I say and wait for the kick, but he only shoves me away. I am so glad to be free I go running like the wind before the man can change his mind and grab me again.

I get a beating from Ma and no supper.

# 7

I am tired and hungry from playing hard all day. It is after dark, and I know I will get yelled at for staying out so late. I try to think of a good excuse to tell Ma but I cannot. I come to the house and the hall door is closed. I open it and go in. Two people are there and they scare me. Now I see it is Hap in the hall with a friend. They are playing and stop when I come in. I am not afraid any more. Hap does not look at me, but the friend jumps and drops something on the floor that makes a funny *plinny-ninny-ninn* noise. I say hello to Hap. He does not answer me. I run upstairs.

Ma says, "Go wash."

As I come out of the bathroom she is putting my supper on the table.

"Did you see your father?" she asks. "He went to look for you."

"Hap is downstairs in the hall," I say.

"What is he doing in the hall?"

"Playing."

*"Playing?"*

"Yes, with his friend."

"Who?"

"I don't know."

Ma goes downstairs. I finish my codfish, beans and coffee quick. In a little while Hap and Ma come into the kitchen. They are very quiet.

Ma says, "Go to bed, Harold, and close your room door."

I know there is going to be a fuss. I go to my room and close the door. I get into bed. I push my fingers in my ears to shut out the things they are saying.

##

I hate myself. What is the use? No one cares. I wish I was big like a giant. I would smash everything. I would step on this house. I would jump up and down on it until there is nothing left but splinters. And I will not care who is inside when I crush it. I will pay no attention to their cries or yelling. I will just walk away after with Arnie and Ding Dong.

It is still daylight when we come out of the movies. We walk slow along Duffield Street with the parked cars and empty lots. Arnie, my friend Arnie, he spits through his teeth and scratches his balls.

"Tim McCoy is pretty hot stuff. Remember the way he plugged that bad guy while looking in the mirror?"

"Yeah. Who do you like best, Tim McCoy or Buck Jones?"

"Tim McCoy. He's faster on the draw. Nobody can outdraw him. He's a real pisserroo!"

We turn onto Willoughby Street. We come to an empty lot. An old, broken-down car without wheels is sitting there. We go in the lot and climb on top of it. Arnie makes like he has a whip in his hand.

"Geety-yup! This is the Fargo Express. We're riding through Death Valley with crooks on all sides. *Ya-hoo!* Come on, start shootin'!"

I reach for my gun. "Who are you?" I ask.

"Tim McCoy, who do you think? Bang! Bang!"

"And I'm Bob Steele!"

I start shooting, too. Bang! Bang! Bang! We kill thirty or forty bad guys before we get the gold safe through Death Valley. The gun, the stagecoach are suddenly gone now. Arnie stretches out on his back on top of the car. He spits through his teeth.

"Friggin' old car!" he says.

"Yeah," I say. I lie down on the car the way he is doing.

The sun is going down but it is still nice and warm. I feel lazy.

Arnie says, "I know who is tougher than Tim McCoy and Bob Steele put together."

"Who?"

"Jerry the Wop. Even the cops don't give him and Louis Varga any trouble."

"Who is tougher," I ask, "Jerry the Wop or Louis Varga?"

"They're both the same. Jerry the Wop is Louis Varga's bodyguard."

"Gee, I'll bet nobody is tougher than them."

"Nobody. They're a real pisserroo if I ever saw one." He looks around at me and smiles. "You know what some people call me? They call me 'Little Jerry the Wop.'"

"Yeah?"

"Sure. Frank, the cop, says I'm gonna be another Jerry the Wop when I grow up."

Arnie rolls off the top of the car to the ground. He picks up a handful of pebbles and looks around for something to throw at. I jump off the car and pick up some pebbles, too.

"Your father is sure one regular guy," Arnie says suddenly.

"You bet he is," I say.

There is a fence at the back of the lot with a big knothole in it. Arnie tries throwing pebbles through the hole. He misses the first one.

"What's the matter with your father?" Arnie asks.

"Nothing's the matter with him."

I begin to throw at the hole. I miss the first shot, too.

"Is your father a singer or a dancer guy?" Arnie asks.

"No."

"Why is his voice like that?"

"Like what?"

"I don't know—funny, you know, kind of."

I don't know what he means so I shrug. We throw some more pebbles at the hole. Most of them miss. Arnie spits through his teeth and throws his pebbles away.

"Friggin' hole! Come on, let's scram."

## 9

I sit on the curb with Ding Dong. It is a sad day. Arnie has been sent away to reform school. I feel like crying.

"Poor Arnie," Ding Dong says.

"Yes. He was my best pal," I say. "Now I'm all by myself."

"That Arnie! He sure was a swell, tough guy, all right."

"A pisserroo!"

"What did he do to get sent up."

"I don't know."

"It's the second time he's sent up."

"Yeah? What did he do the first time?"

"Hooky, I think. He plays too much hooky."

"I hate cops. All except Frank. I hate all the other ones who sent Arnie away."

"He sure was one swell guy, all right, only—Say, do you remember that little girl, Geraldine?"

"Yes."

"Wasn't that something?"

"Yeah. Did Arnie let you look at her when you went back that time?"

"No. When I go back down the cellar, he's wrestling with her. He chases me off."

I stretch. I get up from the curb. I don't know what to do.

"Where you going?" Ding Dong asks.

"I don't know—home, I guess."

I start down the street. Ding Dong runs after me.

"Hey, Harry, can I be your friend now in Arnie's place?"

"I don't care."

He spits through his teeth. "Thanks, Harry. You're a pisserroo!"

We take a short cut through an empty lot filled with garbage and stuff. I go over to the house next to the lot and pee against it. Ding Dong follows me and does the same thing.

"I wonder why Arnie wants to wrestle with a little kid like Geraldine?" Ding Dong asks.

"I don't know."

I finish and start looking around the lot for things. I find something good. It is big and made of iron. It is like a box and has two iron poles sticking from it. Inside there are a lot of little wheels and screws. It is something like a motor.

"Boy, look at this!" I tell Ding Dong.

He looks. "Say, you found something good there, Harry, boy!"

"Look at all those little wheels and things."

"Bet there's about a hundred of 'em."

"Some have little chains on them, too."

"It's a pisserroo, all right. I wish I found it first."

"I'm gonna take it home. I can play with it in my room."

I try to pick it up. It is a little too heavy for me alone.

"Give me a hand, Ding Dong."

Ding Dong takes one end and I take the other. We carry it two blocks to my house. We sit down in front of the door to rest. We look at it.

"It sure is heavy," Ding Dong says.

"Yeah. I'm sweating."

"After you take all that mud and dirt off, you can shine it up good, Harry."

"Maybe I can get it to work again. It ought to be able to run again with all those wheels still in there. Come on, help me get it upstairs."

We carry it upstairs to my floor. We put it down and I knock on the door. Ma opens the door and her mouth jumps open.

"What are you doing with that?"

"Taking it to my room."

"Oh no, you're not! You take that filthy piece of junk back downstairs this minute!"

"But I *need* it."

"Well, I don't *need* it! You take it out of here. And come right back and wash. You're filthy from it."

Ma slams the door. I look at Ding Dong.

"You can't keep it, huh?" he asks.

"No. Gee, it's too good to throw away. Somebody else will get it. You want it?"

"Sure, but it's too heavy to carry all the way to my house. I'm too tired now."

We take it back downstairs and put it beside the garbage can. We look at it. I feel sorry I cannot have it.

"Now it's going to waste," Ding Dong says.

"Oh, well," I say, "maybe it's not so much."

"Yeah. It's got a lot of dirt and mud on it."

"A lot of those wheels are busted inside there. Maybe I could never get it to run good."

"They're rusty, too."

"Sure. To heck with it. I don't want it. So long, Ding Dong, I'm going up to eat."

"So long, Harry, my pal!"

## 10

Ma sends me to the store for a loaf of bread. I come out of the grocer with the bread under my arm. I go the long way back home so I can see the sights on Hudson Avenue. I turn the corner off Myrtle Avenue and stop in my tracks. Standing up the street, leaning on a johnny-pump, is Jerry the Wop, himself! I stop and look at him. I am scared but I get such a proud feeling just watching him. He is dressed up swell and he is reading a little newspaper. People are passing him on the street, but nobody pays any attention to him. I guess they don't know who he is. If they knew what a tough-guy big shot they are passing they would shiver and shake in their shoes just like I am doing. The loaf of bread slips from under my arm and falls to the street. I stoop to pick it up.

A car comes speeding down Hudson Avenue. I hear a loud sound: *Crack, crack, crack*! The car speeds on past me and around the corner.

What is happening? People are yelling, running into doorways, ducking behind garbage cans and diving into cellars. Now there is no one in sight but Jerry the Wop and me. He is not leaning against the johnny-pump any more. He just stands there looking at me now with big eyes as if he is surprised to see me. He keeps staring, staring. I want to run but I am too scared to move. He coughs once. Blood comes to his lips and rolls down his chin. He reaches out a hand and starts to come toward me. I pee. It rushes out of me, through my pants, down my legs and onto the street but I still cannot move. He comes toward me in slow motion like he is walking underwater. I am weak and dizzy. He falls on his face to the sidewalk. I jump and yell. I turn and fly around the corner.

I run, run as fast as I can, but it is not fast enough because I can feel Jerry the Wop coming after me, getting closer and closer, with the blood running down his chin.

I call Ma as I fly up the stairs. I burst into the kitchen. I run to Ma and hug her tight around the legs.

"What's the matter? What is it?"

I cannot talk. I cry.

Hap pulls me away from Ma.

"What happened? Stop crying and tell me what happened?"

"Jerry the Wop is after me!"

"Jerry the Wop? The *gangster*?"

"Yes!"

"What do you mean, he's after you? What for?"

"Nothing. I didn't do nothing. He just started after me."

"Wait a minute. Just tell me what happened."

"I was going up Hudson Avenue. He was standing there at first. Then everybody started to run from him. I was the only one left so he came after me with blood in his mouth."

"What the devil are you talking about? Why were people running from him?"

"I don't know."

Ma asks, "What were you doing on Hudson Avenue, anyway? I sent you just to the corner."

"I know, but—"

"Where's the bread?"

I am surprised it is not in my hands. I don't know what happened to it.

"Well, where is it?"

"I don't know."

"He probably dropped it. Look how he's shaking—he's scared to death. I'd better go over there and find out what happened."

We hear a lot of police sirens.

"It's the cops!" I say. "They're after Jerry the Wop!"

"Shut up," Ma says. "Hap, you be careful."

"Don't worry," he says and goes out.

"Lock the door, Ma!"

"What nonsense! If your father doesn't find that loaf of bread you will get it good and proper from me."

I run to my room. I crawl under the bed and hide. My heart beats fast.

I hear Hap come back. I listen hard.

"What happened?" Ma asks.

"It was Jerry the Wop, sure enough. He got bumped off on Hudson Avenue. They shot him from a car."

"Who did it?"

"Who knows? Another gang. God, I never saw so many cops at one time before."

"Terrible. Oh, how terrible, terrible!"

"What's so terrible about it? Those hoodlums don't shoot each other often enough for me."

"I don't know—I don't know. . . ."

"No wonder the boy was scared. He must have seen the whole thing. Where is he?"

"In his room."

"Harry!"

I crawl from under the bed. Hap is at my door.

"Yes?"

"Listen, son, did you see any faces of the men in the car?"

"What car?"

"The car they shot Jerry the Wop from."

"No, sir."

"Didn't you see the whole thing?"

"No, sir."

"Well, what was all that stuff you were telling us about Jerry the Wop?"

"He was coming after me."

"He was not. He was probably trying to duck the bullets."

"No, sir. He was coming after me with blood in his mouth."

"Oh, you numskull, get away from me!"

Hap goes back to the kitchen. I crawl back underneath the bed.

"He doesn't realize what he saw," Hap says. "It's just as well."

"You didn't find the bread?"

"No."

"A whole loaf of bread! You ought to give him a licking for it. He had no business being way over there."

"Oh, the poor kid has had enough for one day."

"He'll go without supper, then."


Hap and Ma have gone to bed. I am so scared I lie in the dark with my eyes open. I am afraid to close them. When I do, I can see Jerry the Wop coming after me. Now I can see him with my eyes wide open. I cry and scream out in the night.

Ma comes to the door. "What is it? What is it?"

"I'm scared, Ma!"

"Scared of what?"

"Jerry the Wop. He keeps coming after me."

"Nonsense! How can he come after you when he's dead."

"He keeps coming, Ma. I'm scared!"

"Oh, very well, come—come get in bed with me and your father."

She takes my hand and leads me to her room.

"What is.it?" Hap asks.

"Scared. He dreams about it. Is it all right if he sleeps in with us tonight—down at the foot?"

"Sure, it's okay for tonight."

I crawl between them at the foot of the bed. I feel safe.

Ma says, "Now, try not to think about it and go to sleep."

I pull the covers over my head. I sleep. . . .

Jerry the Wop's face comes out of a cloud of smoke. He reaches for me with a big, bloody hand. . . .

I jump awake! I am scared again. My heart beats fast. I try to hug Ma's legs. She pulls them away. I move closer, reach for them again.

She says, "Stop. Go to sleep."

I turn. I move closer to Hap's legs. I try to hug them easy so he will not notice. He pulls his feet away.

"Now, you cut that out or back to your room you go!"

I curl myself up into a tight little ball between them and hug my shivering self.

## 11

I sit at the kitchen table, eating my supper. Hap has gone out, and Ma is in the bathroom taking a bath. It is a hot night and the front door is open so that more air comes in.

I lick my plate clean and put it in the sink. I have to go to the toilet, but I will have to wait until Ma is through with her bath. I look around for something to do. I pick up Ma's magazine from the chair and sit at the table to read it. I can read the name. It says *Love Stories*. I turn the pages and look at the pictures. Guys kissing girls, girls hugging guys, all smisshy-smasshy sissy stuff. I turn to the back of the book and look at the ads. Automobiles, soap, Camel cigarettes. There is a picture of a lady with a towel around her standing on scales.

"Shame, shame, I know your name!" I laugh. I finish with the book.

I have to go to the toilet very, very bad now. I cannot hold it any more or I will wet myself. I go to the bathroom door and knock.

"Ma?"

"What is it?"

"Ma, I have to make wee-wee."

"Can't you wait? Can you hold it?"

"No, Ma, I have to go in a bad hurry!"

"Oh, all right, wait just a minute." I wait. "All right, now you can come in."

I hurry inside to the bowl just in time. It feels good to let it out. I hear Ma splash in the tub. I wonder.

I come out of the bathroom and close the door behind me.

There is nothing to do.

It is too early to go to bed, but I go to my dark room and lie across the bed anyway. I feel funny. I will sing. What shall I sing?

> *"What are little boys made of?*
> *What are little boys made of?*
> *Frogs and snails and puppy dogs' tails,*
> *That's what are little boys made of."*

I hear a noise. I look around and see a little boy standing in the doorway of my room. I am surprised. I jump up on the bed.

"Hey, what are you doing in here, kid?"

"I came up to see your mother about something? Is she home?"

"Yes. How'd you get in?"

"The front door is open so I just walked in."

"Oh. You live around here? I don't remember you."

"Yeah, I live around here."

"What's your name?"

He laughs. "Damned!"

"Get out—that's no name, that's a curse."

"I know, but that's what my mother calls me. She calls me 'that damned kid!'"

"What's your real name?"

"Don't know. Wouldn't tell you if I did know."

"Want to play some games with me?"

"Play with yourself. I came up here to see your mother, not you."

"You have to wait."

"Why? Where is she?"

"Taking a bath."

"Okay, I'll go in and see her."

He starts for the bathroom. I run behind him. "Wait! You can't go in there."

"Why?"

"Because I told you—she's taking a bath!"

He looks at me and smiles. He winks his eye. "I want to *see* her."

**46**

"Hey, look, kid, you better stop being so fresh or I'm gonna punch you right in the mouth. That's my mother you're talking about. I'll give you a sore lip, I swear!"

"Aw, you ain't so tough. I'm going in there anyway."

I ball up my fists and go for him. He turns around and runs out of the front door. I chase after him. He runs down the stairs, laughing. I shake my fist at him.

"You bum!" I say.

I come back into the house.

Ma calls from the bathroom. "Harold, did someone come in?"

"Yes."

"Who was it?"

"I don't know—some fresh kid. He's gone now."

"Well, what did he want?"

"I don't know. Just some fresh kid. Chased him off."

"Oh."

Some wise guy. When I catch that kid again I will kick his ass all over Myrtle Avenue.

## 12

I go to the butcher with Ma.

She says, "Max, will you trust me for two pounds of stewing beef?"

"Sure, Missus Odum. You want brisket or plate?"

There is another butcher cutting meat on a chopping table. I go over and watch him slice a big piece of meat down to the bone. He takes a heavy thing like a hatchet and chops down with all his might on the bone, *crack*, *crack*, *crack*! until it is cut. It is a wonderful hatchet. I like to watch him cut the bones with it. I wish I could hit something with it. The butcher looks at me and smiles.

"What kind of a knife is that?" I ask.

"A cleaver," he says.

A cleaver. When I grow up I guess I will have to buy me a cleaver.

*T*ODAY I GRADUATE. I Am Way Behind To Graduate at sixteen. Getting left back a lot put me behind a couple of years. But I am not alone. There are plenty of other kids in my class the same age, too. Who would have thought Charlie Ding Dong would ever graduate elementary school? He is almost eighteen! Mr. Burns made a joke about it in class yesterday. He was so happy that Ding Dong is going to graduate this term. He said he was glad because it looked for a while like they would have to burn the school building down to get Ding Dong out of eighth grade. The whole class laughed and hooted at Ding Dong, and I think he was a little sore. Or maybe he just looked that way because he was even surprised himself to be graduating.

I get up early full of excitement and go to the bathroom to wash. I light up a clipper and puff there. I wonder why the first smoke in the morning tastes so good but makes me a little dizzy, too? I look in the mirror. I run my fingers under my nose and around my chin. Nothing is there yet. When will it come? The hair around my dickey has been there since I was fourteen, and I have hair under my arms. Maybe I shouldn't worry about it because Ding Dong does not shave and he is older than I am. He also says he could come when he was twelve. I do not believe him. I cannot even do it now, even though I am sixteen. But I don't care about that so much. All I want to do is grow a nice mustache so people will respect me more and Ma will know I am growing up.

I come back into the kitchen, and Ma is standing over the stove making breakfast of eggs and bacon. The coffeepot goes *blurp-blurp*, and the smell is all over the warm kitchen. Ma looks at me over her shoulder and brushes a strand of blond hair from her eyes.

"Good morning. Happy today?" She smiles a little.

"Sure, Ma."

She turns back to the eggs on the stove. "Your new suit is

hanging in my room." She points at me with a fork. "Put it on and be very careful with it. Don't get any dirt on it. Remember, I must pawn it after you graduate in it."

"Okay."

I do not mind. I know she could not afford to buy it in the first place. I am lucky to have one to wear for graduation. Ma looks a little sad this morning. I feel kind of sorry because I am causing her all this expense and trouble.

I go into her bedroom quietly because I do not want to disturb Hap if he is still asleep. I take the blue serge suit off the hanger. I notice that Hap is not in bed. I come back into the kitchen.

"Where is Hap?" I ask.

Ma sighs as she puts a plate on the table. "God knows where! We went to bed last night just fine. No arguments at all. Nothing, I tell you. We talked of how proud we were of you—all about your graduation today. We laughed and he wooed me. Then when I woke up this morning he was gone. No word, nothing. Gone—just like he always goes."

Why does she look at me this way? What can I do about it? Is it my fault again? I want to tell her I am sorry but instead I say, "But he promised to come to my graduation!"

She shrugs her shoulders. "Maybe he will. Maybe he will get back in time but—" Suddenly she waves me away. "Go—go get dressed and come eat your breakfast."

I dress quickly and sit down to my plate of bacon and eggs. I nibble at my food. I am too excited to eat. Ma sits down across from me. She is picking at her food also. I know she is worrying about Hap. It won't be so bad if Hap does not come to my graduation. He had disappointed me before. But more than anything, I want Ma to come. I want her to see me walk across the platform and get my diploma. I want her to feel proud. Suddenly I wonder if she will be too upset to come because she is worrying about Hap.

"Ma, *you're* going to be there, aren't you?"

She smiles quick and pats me on the hand. "Of course, my darling, I'll be there. Why, wild horses, indeed, couldn't keep me from my lover's graduation."

I feel better and laugh. I finish eating and kiss her goodbye.

"Don't be late, Ma. It starts at ten o'clock sharp in the auditorium."

"Don't worry—I won't be late."

I get to school on time and report to my class. Almost all the guys have on dark new suits and the girls are dressed in white. These are very hard times and only a few people have jobs. All these new clothes must have cost a lot of money, so I guess the parents have sacrificed a lot to get them. It just shows you that most mothers and fathers are very good to their children. But I wonder how many suits will have to go to the pawn shop after graduation, like mine. Mr. Burns calls me up to his desk. He is smiling. He says that I look very good.

"What kind of pattern is that?" he asks. I say I don't know. He holds my lapel between his fingers and looks close at it. "Yes. This is what you call a herringbone weave."

I look close at my jacket. All the time I thought it was just plain black, but, sure enough, there is a design of zigzag lines in it. Mr. Burns opens the jacket and looks at the lining and the lapel.

"Bond's," he says. "That's a good suit. Even in these times you can't get a Bond's suit under twenty-five dollars, I think. Wish you were my size, I'd steal it right off your back."

He waves me back to my seat. I sit down and start thinking on it. Where did Ma get twenty-five dollars to spare just for a suit? Hap is not working and Ma only works part time. I figure she must have saved up for a long time in order to have the money. I get such a warm feeling inside for her that tears come to my eyes. I turn my face away so the fellows cannot see. I love her so much. Because she wanted me to look nice she has worked hard and sacrificed and saved. But I will pay her back a hundred thousand times one day. And I will make her proud of me today, too, when I walk straight across the stage to get my diploma. She will know what a good son she has.

Ding Dong comes into the room, and suddenly we are all embarrassed for him because he is the only one wearing a light-colored suit. It is what they call a salt-and-pepper. It is not a new suit because the cuffs are a little worn. The pants are also too long for him. The sleeves of his jacket cover his hands and he wears a big artificial flower in his lapel. We all pretend not to notice how funny and pitiful he looks, but Ding Dong is making an ass out of himself by parading all around the classroom, showing off with a big grin on his face. It is funny because he looks funny, and pitiful because he does not know it. Right now, Ding Dong thinks he is the sharpest-dressed guy in the whole school. He is even showing off his socks, which are nice, by pulling his pants' leg up and propping his big foot up on his desk. He does not realize that he has a big hole in the toe of his shoe which everybody can see when he does that. He is so happy now I hope no one will tell him how he really looks because it would spoil his whole graduation for him.

Just before ten o'clock we line up and march down to the auditorium. All the relatives and friends are seated in the back. They wave and call at their kids as we go by. I do not see Ma or Hap, but there are so many faces and we are not allowed to stop and examine them. We are marched down to the front. We take seats, boys on one side, girls on the other. The ceremonies begin. At last! I feel very proud of myself. I think of the fellows who did not make it and pity them.

Mr. Ireland, the principal, makes a little speech on welcoming the parents. He has a big smile on his face and he talks in a sweet voice. It is the first time in my life I have ever seen that man smile. And he must be talking in his singing voice because all I have ever heard him do was to growl. I take a quick look in the back to see if I can spot Ma. When I turn my head around again, Mr. Ireland is staring down at me. The smile is still on his face and he is still talking sweet, but his eyes are saying to me, "You rotten brat, if you don't pay attention I'll have you in my office *so fast!*" I sit very still. Thank God, I am getting away from him for good, once and for all!

He finishes his speech and sits down at a table on the platform. Another man is sitting next to him. The man whispers something in Mr. Ireland's ear, and Mr. Ireland answers him without once taking those glaring eyes off me. He has stopped smiling, too. I sit very, very still. I am afraid to even breathe.

Miss Greer, the music teacher, gets up now with her stick and waves us through the song we have been rehearsing for two months,

"There Is a Love." It comes off pretty good, too. I did not think it would because I was almost sure Ding Dong or Slapsie McMan would louse it up with their foghorn voices.

Mr. Ireland gets up again and introduces the man next to him as Doctor Bruce Smith from the teachers college. He is a good speaker, and he makes a speech about all the wonderful opportunities we have for a higher education and why we should take them. I like what he says and will try to follow his advice as much as I can.

Miss Greer gets up again and waves us through "Go Down, Moses." This time Ding Dong and some other fellows really do louse it up by singing in the wrong key. I want to laugh but Mr. Ireland still has his eyes on me. Miss Greer is so mad she turns red as a tomato, but there is nothing she can do but keep on waving until the song is finished. Mr. Ireland makes another short speech and Miss Greer comes back again with her stick. We are going to sing our alma mater song. We begin:

*"Alma Mater Number Five,*
*School ever dear to me . . ."*

The same fellows are lousing it up again. They are singing the words to another tune altogether. Miss Greer stands there sweating and biting her lip but she keeps on waving anyway. She is a very brave woman to see it through like this. The song is finished and she rushes off the platform, straight out of the auditorium. I know she must be crying out there. She is really a very good music teacher and those guys should not have embarrassed her like that. But I guess they are only getting even with her for making us stay after school to practice so much. They know there is nothing she can do about it now.

At last the names are being called, first the girls and now the boys. After each name is called, everyone claps as the boy crosses the platform to get his diploma from Mr. Ireland. My name is called and it seems to fill the whole auditorium, ringing back and forth. I feel proud and light as air as I go up to the platform. It is the happiest time of my life. I feel that I am the only one in the world who is graduating. They clap as I walk across the platform. I know that Ma is somewhere in the back, watching me with tears in her eyes. I stand and walk as straight as I can, my head high up. Mr. Ireland smiles at me, gives me my diploma and shakes my hand.

"Thank you, sir," I say.

"Thank God!" he says from behind his smile of clenched teeth.

The ceremonies are over. I rush to the back of the auditorium to find Ma. Parents and friends are congratulating the graduates. The place is noisy with talk and laughter. I walk all through the crowd but Ma is not there. I start to get choked up inside. I go outside to the street. There are a lot of parents and kids standing in front of the school but Ma is not among them. There is not a sign of her! Now I know it is true. She did not come. She did not see me walk across the stage with everyone clapping. Everybody's mother in the world came but mine. Why did she do this to me? She promised. I know it is on account of Hap. Tears come to my eyes but they are not sissy tears. They are angry ones. I want to hit out at something but I feel too weak. My heart is pounding while my mouth begins to fill with spit. I know I am going to be sick. I rush back into the school and go to the boys' room. I get there just in time. It is a long time before I think it is safe to take my head from over the toilet bowl. I push the wooden seat down and sit on it. I put my head in my lap and cry. . . .

I am like this a long time. I am empty now. I feel better. I get up from the bowl and wash my face. The water is nice and cool. It feels good against my hot face. I straighten my tie and make appearances before I go out because I do not want anyone to know I have been sick. I comb my hair and go out.

All is quiet. I am in the hall just outside the entrance to the auditorium. The people have all gone. The lights are out in the auditorium. I am confused. How could everyone disappear so quickly? Around a corner of the hall a porter comes pushing a broom. He is surprised to see me. He looks at me suspiciously.

"What are you doing in here?" he asks, coming over to me.

I ask, "Where is everybody?"

"Everybody *who*?"

"The visitors, the graduates. I went to the toilet a few minutes ago and people were here. Now they're all gone."

He leans on his broom and looks at me as though he thinks I am crazy.

"A few *minutes* ago? Why, the graduates, visitors and teachers left over two hours ago. The school's all locked up."

"*Two hours?!*"

"Yes, my lad! What'd you do—fall asleep on the john?"

"Yes, sir, I guess I did."

He looks me over close. "You one of the grads?"

"Yes, sir. I have my diploma right here in my pocket."

"Never mind, I believe you." He pulls out a ring of keys. "But let me get you out of here before the super sees you. Them civil servants has got to report and verify everything. He'd probably call the cops on you. Come on this way and I'll let you out."

He lets me out and I go home.

Ma is not home. There is a note on the kitchen table. It reads:

"HAROLD,

*I will be home late tonight. Warm up the beans and pork in the icebox for your supper.*

MA"

That is all. Nothing about the graduation. Doesn't she care? Doesn't she care how I feel? I have feelings like everyone else. I am angry and my eyes get watery again. If she was not my mother I would curse her for doing this to me. I crumble up her note and throw it to the floor.

It is after dark and Ma has not come back yet. The hell with it. I will not sit around waiting for her any longer. I rush out of the house. On the street I do not know where to go. I remember that Ma told me to take off the suit. But I do not care now. I would not care even if it got dirty. I will keep it on as long as I want to. What the hell. I spit.

"Friggin' suit!" I say.

I go over by the poolroom on Hudson, hoping some of the gang are there. I see only Ding Dong. He is leaning in the doorway very sadlike. He has taken off his salt-and-pepper suit and is now wearing dirty dungarees and a torn jacket.

"Hi, Harry."

"Where's all the gang?" I ask.

"Didn't you hear? Arnie's out. They're all up his house. His old man is throwing a big coming-home party for him."

"Arnie!" I shout. "My old pal, Arnie! Well, what are we waiting for? Come on, let's go up."

"I can't go," Ding Dong says.

"Why?"

"Because I ain't dressed up. Arnie says nobody comes to the party unless he's dressed up. Everybody up there is dressed up—guys and broads."

"Where's the suit you had on today?"

Ding Dong looks away from me. "It ain't mine. It's my old man's. It's the only one he's got. He had to stay in the house today while I graduated in it."

I get a funny little sick feeling in my chest. It is pity.

"Can't you borrow it again?" I ask.

"He went bowling in it," Ding Dong says.

"Haven't you got anything at all that looks nice?"

"My old man's got a pretty good sports jacket hanging in the closet, but that's all. No pants or nothing."

I think on it a while. "Come on," I say. "My father's got a pair of summer slacks that ought to fit you. What color is the sports jacket?"

"Kind of a light cream color."

"The slacks are blue. They ought to go good together. We'll stop off at your house and get the jacket, then we'll go over my house."

Ding Dong grins. "Goddamn, we're all set!"

We get Ding Dong spruced up and head for Arnie's. We can hear all the music and laughter as we go up the stairs. Arnie opens the door. His face lights up and he gives me a big grin and a hug.

"Come on in, you son of a bitch! I figured you'd never show up."

"I just heard a little while ago. When did you get out?"

"Yesterday—but my old man wanted me to keep it quiet until he could get some dough to throw me a ball. He went out last night stone broke and came back home this morning *loaded*. He musta pulled off a hell of a burglary somewheres. Come on in the front room and have a drink."

The living room is full of fellows and girls having a good time, talking, dancing and drinking. Most of the guys I know, like Big Nasty Jones and Slapsie McMan. Though I do not know most of the girls, I have seen them around the neighborhood. Arnie's father is standing in a corner, talking to a group of fellows. The music comes from an electric phonograph that sounds like a radio. Arnie takes me to a table where there is whisky, wine and soda.

"What'll you have?" he asks. "I got the works."

"I'll take wine."

He pours me a big glass of red wine. I look around at all the kids with drinks, and I wonder if there will be trouble.

"What's the matter?" Arnie says.

"Aren't you afraid somebody might get drunk?"

"Nobody under sixteen gets a drop. And if anybody gets out of line my old man won't let him come up again. You know how much the guys like to come up here. There won't be any trouble."

"Well!" I say, looking him over. "You look swell. Jail must've been good for you. Where'd they have you?"

"Warwick. Not bad. I learned a lot of things up there. The best thing I learned is not to be a working stiff. I'm gonna hustle—get me a dodge. That's where the money is. I don't mean a thief like my old man, either. A thief is always in and out of jail. And he ends up his life with a cop's bullet in his head. I'm gonna play it safe and cool with a nice little racket like Louis (the Owner) Varga. Maybe I'll have to pull a few hauls for a starter—to get into business. But after that I'm gonna be strictly a racket guy."

"Kids like us can't work the rackets," I say.

"You mean kids like *you*—not *me*. I been around. I'm getting a rep. All I need is an *in* with the right people." Arnie leans over close and whispers in my ear. "While I was up there I made a real *big* contact."

"With who?"

"You know who Abie the Bug is?"

"I know he's around the neighborhood. I never saw him but I hear he's Louis Varga's enforcer like Jerry the Wop used to be."

"Well, I run into a cousin of his up at Warwick. A kid by the name of Karpis. We got to be real tight friends. He told me when I got out to look up his cousin and say hello for him."

"How is that gonna get you in with the rackets?"

Arnie frowns and pours me another drink. I begin to feel good.

"Listen," he says. "I know they ain't gonna say, 'Come on, kid, take over the numbers for us,' just on account of me saying hello for the kid. But it's an in. No matter how small, it's still an in. Look, I say, 'Mr. Abie, me and your cousin was great friends up at Warwick. He says give you regards.' Right away he thinks, 'Oh, so he knows my cousin. He must be a kid who is on the ball.' I say, 'Mr. Abie, if there's ever any little favor I can do for you, any kind of favor at all, I'll be glad to do it free because your cousin sure treated me swell.' So the Bug thinks on that. He keeps me in mind and pretty soon I get to do little jobs for him. I run errands, steal cars and stuff like that. Before you know it, I'm right in solid with them. Then one day maybe he'll say to me, 'Kid, you're a pretty bright boy. You're on the ball. I want you to take over and run this Shylock bank for us.' I tell him it's a pleasure."

Arnie is grinning with happiness as if it has happened already. I laugh at him because he looks so damn silly and it all sounds so impossible to me. I pour myself another drink and we sit down in a corner of the room. The place is cloudy with cigarette smoke and everybody seems to be having a hell of a good time.

"I hear you graduated today," Arnie says. "I'll bet old man Ireland never thought you'd make it."

I laugh when I remember Mr. Ireland's face. "When he gave me my diploma he says, 'Thank God!'"

Arnie laughs. "That son of a bitch!" Suddenly he looks serious again. "What are you gonna do now you're out of school?"

"I'm going on to high school."

"Well, you couldn't get a job anyhow—there ain't none. But what the hell do you want to fart around in school for?"

"Ma wants me to. She says I'll have a better chance for a job later on if I learn a trade."

"Friggin' trade!" Arnie says disgusted. "Nobody ever got rich breaking his back. Listen, I got a idea. I'm gonna get a few guys together and pull a few hauls. Wanna come in with us?"

"No—not now, anyway."

"Why?"

"I don't want to disappoint Ma. I don't want to take the chance of getting in trouble now that her and my old man are getting along pretty good. The least thing happens, he'll walk out on her again."

"Oh, sure."

"But wait a while. And if anything *really* good comes up maybe I'll come in with you."

He pats me on the back. "You bet, Harry, keed!"

I finish my wine. The wine has made me real warm and friendly, but I look around at all the boys and girls and realize I am not happy here. I know almost everybody and I am familiar with all the talk, but I feel as if I am with strangers. I do not belong here. It seems that all these people can think and talk about is stealing something and laying girls. There are lots of other things in this world to talk about, but this crowd just sticks to those two things like they are everything. Arnie's father is on the other side of the room, telling a bunch of guys the different ways to crack a safe. On this side, guys are loving up the girls. At one end of the sofa, Big Nasty, crazy-eyed, is hugging a girl with one hand and trying to put the other up her dress as she giggles. I nudge Arnie.

"Look at Big Nasty. You'd better stop it before your father sees."

Arnie looks at Big Nasty and grins. "Aw, leave him. Pop don't care. He's going out in a little while and leave us the house. You gonna stick around, ain't you? I'll fix you up with Mary Kelly. She's a good piece."

I look over at red-haired Mary Kelly, giggling over drinks with the other girls.

"No," I tell him.

Arnie looks at me a long time as if he cannot believe what he heard.

"What's the matter with you, you dope! Mary Kelly's the snazziest broad on the block."

"Sure she is. I just don't want a girl, that's all."

Arnie looks at me like he is trying to figure it out. He smiles and nudges me in the side with his elbow.

"Say, I bet you ain't even had your first hump yet!" He laughs loud and slaps me on the shoulder. "Sure, that's it! You're still scared of girls, you bum. You friggin' virgin, you! Well, we'll fix that up tonight."

I feel squeamy and filthy inside. I am embarrassed. I jump up angrily.

"Naw," I say. "Cut it out!"

Arnie is surprised. He gets up and puts a hand on me.

"Say, don't get sore, Harry."

"Then cut it out!"

"Okay, okay. I only meant—What's the matter with you, Harry?"

I am burning up inside. I am wobbly from the drinks and want to get out of here and find out what happened to Ma.

"Nothing's the matter with me," I say, shaking.

"Then sit down again and have another drink."

"No, I'm going home—but I'll have another drink."

He pours me a wine. I drink it down quick. He looks at me worried.

"Feel better?" he asks.

"Yeah. I'll be seeing you."

I leave the living room in a hurry. I go through the bedroom in the railroad flat to the kitchen and out the door to the hall. I feel a relief just getting into the hall. I feel as if I have avoided a trap.

The wine is working inside, doing things to me. I start feeling good again with the cool wind in my face.

I get home . . . I am so drunk. I did not know. The dark stairs twist all the way up, up, up to the door. I turn my key in the lock. The light is on. Ma is sitting at the table.

"Hello, Ma."

I stagger in. I stumble over a chair and fall against the wall. I see Ma's face angry, coming to me and all I can hear is:

"Where have you been and what is the matter with you? You've been drinking. O my God! my baby is drunk. Somebody has made my baby drunk. O my God! what is the matter with you?"

Stomach jumping. Everything goes around fast.

"Sick, Ma!"

It comes up and out of me all over the floor.

"Oh, my God!"

Everything spinning, spinning. "Ma!"

"Come sit, sit here."

"Ma!"

"Wait, wait, I'll wash your face. No, take off that jacket. My God, all over the new suit. Didn't I tell you to change? Now it is ruined. Wait I'll get a towel and some water. Oh, I don't know what is going to happen. What did I ever do O God to deserve this? What did I do to anyone? Why must I have all this trouble? Why am I always betrayed? All I ever did was try to live a decent, Christian life. All I ever did. But look at me. Look at us. Struggle, struggle all my life. Tried to make a decent marriage, a decent home. Tried to bring up a child. But what do I get for it? Betrayal and heartache. You will turn out to be just like your father. But who have I to blame but myself? Mama told me. Stay away from that boy, she said. Stay away. He is no good, he will break your heart. Stick to your singing. Leave him alone and study your singing, Mama said. She said you'll be a famous singer someday. Don't you look like Helen Twelvetrees? Stay away from him and you'll be a great singer; marry him and you'll be nothing. It's true—I had a beautiful voice. I did look like Helen Twelvetrees. I still do when I fix myself up, yes I do, and you know that very well. I could have been famous if I hadn't married your father. I could have even married a much better man. Mr. Mizner, my voice teacher, wanted to woo me. He even proposed. Oh, how I use to agonize that man! He had money and he would have given me everything I wanted."

"Imihtondtoubatnawreahot."

"Herenzmsawrmasihtemosdanhooteno."

"Ireahtondottnaw!"

"Actorhcusewomsuoegrogaylruceklkcalbcredluohsriahdaorbdna."

"Listen amotItnawdlottnoduoyi!"

"Harold yhwrettamstahweht?"

"Nothing."

"Yes emerehttasikool. Why emtnodtawoykool? Why suolaejwo-hreuoyteewseveil ebiod!"

"TIaomn!"

"Yeorua!"

"Palmetaispeots!"

"Oh, very well! But anyway I just wouldn't listen to anybody. I only had eyes for your father. That Hap! I would die for him with his sweet talk.

"Now take the rest of your clothes off and get into your bed. Oh, no, there is no light in your room, and I'll need light to put on the cold towels. Go get in my bed. You'll sleep there tonight, and tomorrow I'll put the lamp in your room. Here, I'll help you. Come on, you naughty, naughty boy. What a shame! Did anyone see you? What will the neighbors say to see such a young boy coming home drunk? What a disgraceful thing!

"Iekanekatr ettebruoypeelsrednulliwr eawuoyootffo. Iaeshma? Why yllisdlorahebtnod. I efilevhymrevenlladraehnifoyllisgnihtynaos. I flesruoymawasruoyuoyrehtomerofebymuoyreadwasyobIdnawonkll-Iuoycvah. Nowesnesnonekatruhtrufffostrohseoht. Tthiast. Oh erat-whatllitsauoyybaba. RehtaftubruoyIekelnacdlwbeesecinydaerlaauoy-polev edlliw. You ydoblliwylnamebgnortsgnihtemossihnehthtiwotreh-tafkoolr uoyekil. Keawdnatonuoyera!

"Get under the covers—all the way. Now lay still. I'll go get the cold towels.

"There—how does that feel? Better? Ma will put on a lot of towels and you will feel much better. Perhaps your head will not hurt so much tomorrow. Imagine! I've done this for almost twenty years for your father. Now I suppose I'll have to do it twenty more for you. O Lord, must I bear the cross again?!

"You know what he did? Do you know what your father did today? He left us again. Packed up and gone for good this time. Well, good riddance to bad rubbish. I'm not going to suffer and

**61**

worry and agonize myself over him any more. I know he thinks I will, but he'll be fooled this time, yes he will. He'll come begging to me before I'll go begging him to come back. I'll put a bad-luck curse on him and fix him good. Oh, he hurt me today, Harold, your father hurt me so deep like never before. You know what he did? He came back after you left for school. He was drunk and angry. He called me a—well, never mind. Do you know what it was about? It was the suit. The new suit I bought for your graduation. He wanted to know where I got the money to buy it. I told him I have saved it up. He didn't believe me and called me—I cried. I told him you needed it and he didn't have the money for it, what's the difference where I got it. He cursed poor old Pop Carlson. Then he—he struck me, your father. He knocked me down on the floor. He took the rest of his clothes and left. In a little while I went to look for him. That's why I didn't come to your graduation. Baby, Ma is so, so sorry—But I love that man. God knows I would be telling a lie if I said I didn't. I looked for him, all day long, everywhere I could think of—in the bars, the parks, the hotels—everywhere. I found him just a few hours ago. He was in a bar over on Third Avenue. Standing at the bar with his suitcase at his feet. The place was full of people. I went up to him and I called to him softlike. And do you know what he did? He crucified me in front of all those people. He shouted. He told all those people to look at me. He called me a—a name. He cursed and jeered me in front of all of them. I ran out of there crying, my heart bursting. That man, that terrible man—that's your father!

"Well, what's the use of crying now? What's the use of anything? But I'll never forgive him that humiliation. I'll never forgive him if I live to be a hundred years old. But never mind. We don't need him. We've made out before. I'll get a job and you're much bigger now and can take better care of yourself while I'm away.

"Who made my baby drunk tonight—some of those ruffians on Hudson Avenue? Well, never mind. I know you will not let it happen again now that you have the responsibility of taking good care of yourself and the house while I'm working. I know you'll be a good boy for Ma."

I feel much better now, but I wonder. I look up at Ma and her face is set and sad. Her eyes are red and ringed from crying. The face comes down and kisses me on the cheek.

"Good night, sweet. Now go to sleep." She turns to go.

"Ma . . ."

"Yes?"

"Ma, where *did* you get the money to buy the new suit?"

For a second, Ma looks at me with anger. Now it goes away and her face just looks tired again. She shrugs.

"I see now what it is going to be like," she says sadly. "I'll have to go through the same thing all over again with you. You're going to be just like your father. Go to sleep now . . . I'm going to turn out the light."

She goes to the door and switches off the light.

"Ma . . ."

She turns in the doorway, and I can see her sad face by the light coming in from the other room.

"What is it now?" she asks.

"Ma, I swear to you, there is one thing I will never be—and that is like Hap."

It is funny. She smiles but her eyes look hurt and angry. They look at me as if they could kill.

"Go to sleep," she says and goes out of the room.

It is the strangest thing.

T IS NEARING THE END OF MY SECOND YEAR in high school. I am sitting in the classroom, and a messenger comes in saying that Mr. Robins, the student adviser, wants to see me. I wonder what it is all about. I think I know because I have been absent from school a lot lately and I am not doing much studying.

I go downstairs to the assistant principal's office, where Mr. Robins is seated at a desk. He is a little man with a round, chubby, smiling face. He is studying some papers on his desk. He looks up as I come in.

"Hello, Harold," he says cheerfully. "Sit down."

I sit next to the desk. He studies the papers some more. Suddenly he gives me a worried look.

"Harold, the reason I sent for you, it's about your school work. It's pretty bad. You've failed your mid-term exams, and it doesn't look as if you're preparing to pass your finals. I understand you're not getting your homework done, and you've also been absent quite a few times this month."

He looks at me and I am ashamed to meet his eyes.

He continues, "I have all of your school records here, Harold. Your first-year-and-a-half marks were good. So was your attendance record. But this half term has been miserable so far. Your marks are among the lowest in the school. The thing that bothers me about all this, Harold, is that we know it doesn't have to be. Your teachers tell me you have an unusual capacity to absorb—when you *want* to. They all think well of you and are very much disturbed about this trend your schoolwork has taken. Now, Harold, I want you to tell me something. What is wrong? You must have a problem somewhere. Let's try to find out what it is, and maybe we can straighten it out. That's what I'm here for—to help boys like you who might have a problem. Let's see if we can get to the bottom of this. What is your trouble?"

I want to answer him. I like Mr. Robins and I know he really wants to help me. But how can I answer him when I do not even know what the trouble is, or whether there is really any trouble at all.

"I don't know, sir."

"You have no idea why you're failing in all your subjects?"

"No, sir, not exactly . . ."

"What do you mean, not exactly? You have some idea, then?"

"I don't know. But it's just that—Well, I guess I haven't been feeling so well lately."

"You've been ill?"

"No, that's not what I mean—not *sick*."

I do not know what I mean. I feel silly and embarrassed talking to him like this. I wish I could be off to myself somewhere.

"When was the last time you had a physical, Harold?"

"I don't remember, sir. I think it was a year ago."

He shakes his head and makes a note on my record. "We'll have the school doctor look you over one day this week."

I squirm in my seat. "I'm okay," I tell him.

"Well, there's nothing like being sure, eh?"

He smiles. He leans back in his swivel chair, folds his hands over his fat belly and looks at me very friendly. He looks just like a father should. I like him for this. I want to talk with him.

"Tell me something about yourself, Harold. Do you play baseball?"

"No, sir. I like to watch it, though. I follow the game."

"Dodger fan?"

I lie and say yes because I think he wants me to say yes. I only like to watch baseball. It makes no difference to me who wins, as long as it is a good game.

Mr. Robins smiles and shakes his head. "I'm a Yankee fan myself. Do you play any other sports?"

"No, sir. I don't go in for athletics."

"What do you do in your spare time? Got any hobbies?"

"No, sir, just a dog. I take walks with my dog."

"That's all you do in your spare time? Isn't there something you like to do better than anything else?"

"Oh, yes, sir, I see what you mean. I like to read better than anything else—and the movies. I like to go to the movies—when I can get the money."

"What kind of books do you read?"

*"Horror Tales."*

"What's that?"

"A magazine."

"Sounds kind of gory. Hmm. Harold, what does your father do for a living? Do you suppose he could take a day off and come in to see me?"

"He's not with my mother. We don't know where he is."

"Oh. I'm sorry. Hu-rumph! Ah, tell me, is your mother concerned about you finishing school?"

"I guess so."

"And what about you? How do you feel about it."

"Well, sir, to tell the truth, I don't know."

"What do you mean?"

"Well, once I wanted to—but not now."

"Why?"

"It's so much trouble. It's so much trouble for Ma. I don't want to be a burden on her."

"How is that?"

"We're very poor. . . ."

"Oh. Well—"

Suddenly I am talking before I know what I am saying. It all comes blurting out in a hurry: "Ma has only a part-time job as a housekeeper. She can't even work at that much because she has a bad stomach. She is sick almost every morning. Sometimes there is no carfare and I have to walk all the way to school—twenty-one blocks—and I'm so tired in the classroom that—And sometimes when there is no breakfast or lunch money I get so hungry and dizzy I can't read the lessons, and—" It comes to me suddenly what I am saying and I stop quick. I am so ashamed I wish that I could drop through the floor. I stand up. I want to go in a hurry. "That's not true what I said," I tell him. "I didn't mean to say that."

"I understand," he says.

"It's not my mother's fault."

"Of course not. Sit back down, Harold."

"No, sir. I want to go now. Is it okay?"

"But I haven't finished talking with you."

"No, sir, I can't talk any more. I don't feel like it. Can I go now, please?"

"Well, I suppose so. But how about tomorrow? Will you step in here so we can talk again?"

I know I will not come back to face him again. "Yes, sir, tomorrow will be much better."

"All right, but before you go—Do you have enough carfare for the rest of the week?"

"I don't know. I only know from day to day. . . ."

He goes into his pocket and hands me a dollar bill. I do not want to take it, but if I refuse he will keep me here asking more questions, and I want to get away as fast as I can. I take the money and thank him.

"That will take care of carfare the rest of the week and maybe a little left over for lunch. Harold, will you promise me something? When you don't have carfare to school would you come and see me the day before?"

"Yes, sir, thank you."

"I haven't much, but I will see what I can do. In the meantime maybe you can get a little job after school. That will help out."

"Yes, sir. Can I go now?"

He turns back to the papers on his desk. "All right, Harold, don't forget to come and see me again."

I rush out of there. I am furious with myself. Everything I have said will go into my record. I have embarrassed Ma and myself before the whole world by revealing our awful poverty. I will not come back here again. I will leave school. I will leave school and find a job somehow. If there are no private jobs to be found I will get a public job on the W.P.A. We have been miserable long enough.

**I** GET A JOB ON THE W.P.A. I go down to Columbus Circle where the jobs are assigned. I have no trade or skill, so they classify me as a laborer. They give me a slip of paper showing where I am to report for work tomorrow. It is a real great day for me. I strut like a peacock down the subway stairs. At last—at last I am going to be man of the house. I have grown up.

# 2

Ma wakes me up in the morning with a big smile.

"Get up, my darling workingman!" she says.

She has my working clothes all ready and a nice, hot breakfast waiting for me at the table.

I am all ready to leave. Ma brings in a brown leather jacket from her room.

"Put this on. It's one your father forgot. I think it will fit you."

I put it on. It is a nice jacket, but it is too big.

"The sleeves are too long," I say.

"That's nothing. Roll them up. You'll be out in the open all day and you'll need a nice warm jacket like this."

She tucks the sleeves under for me. It is a little bulky but not too bad. She looks at me with admiration.

"My, but you're growing up! Imagine, you're almost as tall as your father."

It makes me feel proud, then again, I do not like it so much. I cannot figure out this feeling. I brush it from my mind. I take my lunch and start to go.

"Okay, Ma, I'll see you tonight."

"Wait!"

I turn. "What is it now?"

"Aren't you going to kiss me goodbye?"

"Aw," I say and kiss her on the cheek. "Goodbye."

As I go out the door I hear her saying after me: "Just like your father!"

The job is on a great big lot near an old school building. They have a steam shovel going in one section, and there are men digging all over the place with picks and shovels. There is a shack set up at one end of the lot with three men standing in front of it, reading blueprints. I go up to the tall man who seems to be the boss and hand him my work paper. He is a tall, frowning man who looks at the paper a moment and hands it back to me.

"All right," he says. "You're working with Madden. Stand over there a minute until he gets back."

I stand beside the shack and wait. Soon, a short, baldheaded Irishman comes up to the shack. The boss calls me over.

"Madden, here's a new man for you."

Madden looks me over. "Okay," he says. He takes the paper from me and turns. "Come with me."

I follow him to a tool shed.

"Take yourself a pick and a shovel," he tells me.

I take a pick and shovel. He takes me across the lot to a trench about three feet deep and about twelve or fifteen feet long. Two other men are digging in it.

"Get in the trench and start digging just like these other fellers," Madden orders.

That is easy enough. "How deep?" I ask.

He spits out black tobacco juice. "Just dig until I tell you to stop," he answers and walks way.

I get down in the trench and start digging like the other fellows. If this is all there is to the job I know I will make good. It is very easy. The other two men stop to rest a lot, but I keep digging and throwing dirt out. I work hard at it because I want to make a good impression on my first day. Besides, I feel very strong.

The whistle blows for lunch!

We climb out of the hole to eat. I finish my lunch fast. I sit down and relax on a pile of lumber where a bunch of other laborers are sunning themselves, waiting for the back-to-work call. Madden, the foreman, comes over to me.

"Finish your lunch, kid?"

"Yes, sir."

"Okay. I want you to run over to the tool shed and get me a groundkey."

"A groundkey?"

"Yeah."

"What's that?"

He looks at me suspiciously. "What the hell kind of laborer are you? I thought you had experience. Don't you even know what a groundkey is?"

"Oh, yes! Now I know," I lie.

"You're full of tar! Go ask the tool keeper. He'll give you one."

I hurry over to the tool shed. The tool keeper is leaning against the doorway, rolling a cigarette.

"Yeah?" he says.

"Mr. Madden, the foreman, sent me over for a groundkey."

He stops rolling the cigarette and looks at me. "A what?"

"A groundkey."

"Oh, a *groundkey*. Why didn't you say so. We're just about fresh out of 'em right now, kid. Run over and ask the crane operator for one. He usually has two or three extra ones laying around in his cabin."

I go over to the crane operator. He is sitting in the cabin, reading a newspaper.

"Say, mister, have you got a groundkey?"

He looks down at me a second, spits. "Who wants one?"

"Mr. Madden, the foreman."

"Nope," he says. "Broke the last one I had. But do you see them riggers standing over there? Ask them. One of 'em is sure as hell bound to have a groundkey."

I go over to the group of men who are loafing around and talking.

"Hey fellows," the crane operator shouts. "Give the kid a groundkey for Madden."

One of the men looks at me. "What kind does he want—this year's model or last year's?"

"I don't know. He didn't say."

He hands me a shovel. "I guess this year's model will suit him."

I look at the shovel. "What's this?"

"Don't you know what it is?"

"Sure, it's a shovel. But I didn't ask for a shovel. I asked for a groundkey."

"That shovel is the best groundkey there is. It'll open up the ground anywhere in the world!"

All the men begin to laugh. I look at them in bewilderment.

"It's a joke, kid," the man says to me. "Madden's ribbing you. Go back and tell him to take a flying leap for himself."

A joke! I am humiliated and angry. I throw the shovel on the ground and leave them. Why did Madden want to trick me like this? I have never done anything to him. I go back to Madden. He stands there looking up at me. I have the urge to bash in his face but he is an old man. Besides, I do not want to lose my job the very first day.

"Well, where's the groundkey?"

"Listen," I say, pointing my finger in his face, "the next time you want to play a joke on somebody, don't play it on me. If you do somebody is going to get hurt, foreman or not."

"What are you supposed to be—a tough guy?"

"No, I'm not a tough guy. I don't look for trouble. But if somebody wants to give me some, I'm always ready."

He frowns, but there is fear in his eyes because he knows that I mean business.

"Aw, what are you getting so sore about? It was only a little joke."

"Maybe it's a joke to you but to me it's a double-cross."

"Okay, okay—forget it. Come on, let's get back to work."

I take my shovel and get back down in the trench.

Nothing in the world gets me more steamed up than the cross-up. It is just like Ma says. Betrayal is the worst thing you can do to a person.

It is night. My shoulders and arms are sore. They ache from shoveling dirt all day.

I go to bed. I am so tired I go right to sleep. But I get no rest. All night long I dream of shoveling dirt out of a hole.

I wake in the morning more tired than when I went to bed.

## 3

It is evening. I come home very tired. Ma has my bath all ready for me with towels and everything. I get into the nice, soapy, hot water. I lay there and soak a long, long time.

I put on my robe and come into the kitchen. Ma has my supper, steaming hot, on the table. Kidney stew and green peas. I sit down to eat with relish.

"How was the job today?" Ma asks.

"Easy," I say. I do not want to complain. I do not want her to think it is too much for me and that I cannot carry the load.

She kisses my cheek. "My baby. I have something very special to go with your supper tonight."

"What?"

She goes to the icebox and brings a small bowl back to the table.

"What is it?" I ask.

"Sliced Bermuda onions with salt, oil and vinegar—just the way I used to fix them for your father."

I am disappointed. I look at the white, crisp rings in the bowl.

"I don't like raw onions," I tell her.

Ma looks hurt, as if she is going to cry. "But your father *loved* them! Why, he wouldn't have a meal without them."

I do not want to hurt her feelings because she has made them special for me.

"Okay, Ma, I'll try them out."

I hate raw onions. They taste lousy and sting my mouth. I hope Ma will leave the room so I can quickly dump them in the garbage, but she sits down at the table opposite me. She watches me eat with a smile on her face. I know she is waiting for me to eat the onions. There is no way I can get out of it. I eat the onions.

## 4

"Here, Sonny! Here, Sonny!"

I look all over the house for him, but he is nowhere to be found. I go into Ma's room where she is knitting.

"Where's my dog, Ma?"

"Harold, I don't know. I can't understand it. I let him out this morning to do his necessary. But this time he didn't come back as usual."

"*This morning*? You mean he's been gone all day?!"

"Yes."

"Did you look for him?"

She sighs. "Harold, I have more important things to do than running around the streets looking for a dog. Besides, I thought he would eventually show up."

I hurry into my coat and hat.

"Where are you going?" she asks.

"To look for my dog!"

"Oh, my goodness gracious, such a big huff over a dog! You'll never find him after all this time."

I go anyway. I look all over the neighborhood. I do not see him anywhere. I see plenty of other dogs but not Sonny. I suppose someone has found him and will keep him, or he has lost himself far, far away. I feel terrible like I have lost a friend. I start for home again. I am peeved with Ma. She could have at least looked when he did not return. She shows no concern at all. I do not believe she likes dogs. Well, I will get another one in spite of that.

##  5

It is a gray-colored bird. It perches very still on a branch just above my shoulder. It cocks its head to one side and opens its mouth. Slowly the body begins to get bigger as if it is being blown with air. It ruffles its wings and its throat flutters. It begins to sing. It is a beautiful song. I am surprised that such a beautiful song can come from a bird with such dull, gray colors. It is the most beautiful song I have ever heard and I smile with pleasure. Oh, how I would like to have such a bird for my own! I will try to catch it. I begin to lift my hand . . . easy, slowly—Suddenly the bird is gone! It has vanished completely. I begin to cry.

My eyes open. I am in bed. It was all a dream. There was never a bird and I am not crying. I toss. I am a little angry. I feel as if I have been cheated of something.

## 6

It is my second week on the job. I got wise to something: you shovel hard only when the foreman is watching. When he is not watching, which is most of the day, you lean on the shovel and rest. Everybody does this. Laboring is a low, dirty job and the skilled workers treat us like flunkies. There are a lot of old workers who cannot, and do not, work much. There are a couple of crippled guys, too. Now I know why people make fun of this W.P.A. The idea is to do as little work as possible without getting caught. There is no reason to work hard because you cannot advance to a better job. Fifteen dollars a week for three weeks out of four is nothing to make my arms and back sore for every night. I am beginning to hate this job. But, at least, I am a little better off than before and Ma is happier. I will stick it out. There is nothing else to do.

# 7

There is a very quiet, sickly colored man working near me. They call him George. He coughs all the time. Sometimes he coughs so hard I think his lungs are going to come up. He does not talk to anyone and stays to himself all the time. When something is said to him, he only grunts in answer. The other men think he is a little nuts, so they do not try to make conversation with him.

I look around to make sure the foreman is not nearby and put my shovel aside for a breather. I pull out a cigarette. George suddenly stops working and stares hungrily at the cigarette. It is my last one but I know how it is to be hungry for a smoke, so I offer him half. He smiles and says thanks. I light up my half. I am surprised to see him tear open the paper and chew the tobacco instead of smoke it. He puts his shovel aside and begins talking to me. He tells me he is fifty-two and married twenty-five years to a woman he hates. He says he had to marry her because he kept giving her kids and her family objected. I feel embarrassed that he is telling me his personal business. I try to skip the subject, but he does not let me and keeps right on talking about his family.

"I got five kids and they're all bums," he says. "My boy, the only boy, is about your age and he's doing time in Elmira for burglary. There's four girls and three of them are whores. The one that's any good is Lena, my baby. I figure the only reason she ain't a whore is she ain't old enough yet. She's just six years old and smart as a whip. She can sing, too. The people down the Urban League wanted to put her on the radio one time. Never did, though. The time she was suppose to go to the practicing, she took sick. The ambulance doctor said it was malnutrition. Know what that means? She wasn't getting enough to eat." He stops talking and looks hard at me. "Don't think it was my fault. It wasn't my fault."

"I know."

We are both quiet for a long time. Now he starts talking again.

"You see, the relief people don't give a damn about a poor guy like me. Nobody does. I tell them up at the office I don't feel good.

I got misery all the time. But they tell me, 'Go to work or get off relief.' Who the hell wants to stay on relief, anyway? I get off and try to work but no go. I can't get work and everybody's hungry in the house, so I have to go back to the relief office and they give me this Goddamn job. A laborer is treated like dirt. They should have more consideration for the workers. And the government ought to investigate those second-rate snobs who sit on their asses all day long just figuring out new ways to push us around."

"I guess you're right," I say.

"You're Goddamn right I'm right!" he says angrily and turns away.

He begins to dig again and does not say any more to me.

Four thirty we knock off. I say good night to George. He does not even grunt for an answer. He just walks right on by me with his eyes staring straight ahead as if he is in another world.

At supper I tell Ma about George.

She frowns. "The colored are always complaining. You like the job, don't you?"

"Yes."

"Well, see, then? Don't pay attention."

I am treated like a king in this house. Ma treats me so good it makes me proud to be the support. She always has my bath ready and a nice, clean change of clothes. There is always a good, hot supper ready for me. She keeps my room nice, and I have the lamp from her room so I can read in bed every night. She makes everything so swell for me I cannot tell her I do not like the job. I cannot think of quitting, even though I am beginning to hate it almost as much as George does.

# 8

I buy a puppy from a kid for fifty cents. He is a cute little bum and friendly as he can be. He is brown with white markings.

I show him to Ma. He wants to make friends with her but Ma just frowns at him.

"What did you get another one for? He'll only dirty up the house. I won't have that, Harold."

"I'll keep him in my room. I'll clean up after him until I can get him housebroken."

She sighs. "Very well, I suppose, if that's what you want. Really, now, I can't understand why you love dogs so much! Yes, you'll just have to keep him in your room."

I put the dog in my room and close the door. In the kitchen, Ma has taken out her knitting.

"Harold, dear, will you please take the garbage downstairs before you go to bed."

"Okay."

I take the garbage pail downstairs. I trip in the hall and some of the garbage falls to the floor. I stoop to pick it up. I see "Harold" written on a piece of paper among the refuse. I pick it up. It is half of a torn envelope. I look for the other half. I find it and put the two pieces together. It is a letter addressed to me but there is nothing inside. Ma did not tell me about any letter. And why was the envelope torn and thrown away? I am puzzled and curious about it all. I dump the garbage quick and go back upstairs.

"Ma, did I get a letter from somebody?"

She looks at me with surprise. "A letter? What makes you think you got a letter from someone?"

I show her the torn envelope. She is silent a moment. She begins to knit very fast.

"Well, come to think of it—yes. Oh, it wasn't a letter, what you'd call a *real* letter. It was—Well, as a matter of fact, it wasn't intended for you at all, but for me."

"But it had my name on it."

"Yes, but—Oh, I suppose it was because they didn't know my first name so they put yours on the envelope. It was from school— the Board of Education. They wanted me to confirm that you are now working. I sent them a nice little reply to that effect. Does that answer your question, Harold?"

"Sure, Ma."

She sighs, smiles, puts down her knitting. "Come, give Ma a kiss good night."

I kiss her cheek. "Good night, Ma."

"Good night, my darling dear."

# 9

It is a cloudy Friday morning. I am pushing gravel in a wheelbarrow to the cement mixer. George comes in to work a little late and starts digging a brand new hole all by himself.

Two o'clock in the afternoon, George's hole is pretty deep. Suddenly the supervisor notices what George is up to. He rushes over and asks George why is he working in that spot, and who the hell ever told him to dig a hole that deep, anyway? George does not even look up. He just keeps right on digging. The super gets mad and shouts down at him.

"Are you looking for a pink slip? Didn't you hear what I said?!"

Madden and a couple of other foremen hear the super shouting and rush over to assist him. George looks up at them. He tells them to go away and leave him alone. He goes right back to his digging.

"Listen," the super says, "I'll hand you a pink slip sure as hell! Now, I'm telling you for the last time to get out of that hole! What the hell do you think you're doing anyhow?"

George stops digging and leans on his shovel. He looks up at the super and the foremen.

"Maybe," George says calmly, "maybe I'm digging your grave if you don't watch out. See this pick? I'll bury it clean in your head if you don't go away and stop bothering me. I ain't got long to live, and I don't mind taking you along for company when I go. I won't bother you if you don't bother me. Just leave me be, mister, and go on about your business."

The super's face flushes, but he figures George means what he says. He tells the foremen not to bother George, and he tells the other workers to stay away. The super goes to attend to something else, and George goes back to digging his private hole.

The four-thirty whistle blows, and we knock off. One of the men notices that George did not come out of the hole, so he looks in to see what is the matter. Excitedly he calls the foreman over. The foreman calls the super. The super takes a good look into the hole and yells for someone to call an ambulance. There is a big crowd around the hole, and I have to force my way through to get a look. George is lying flat on his back, his hands resting on his chest. Blood is coming from his nose and mouth. He is staring up at the crowd with glassy, angry eyes. Madden starts down in the hole to help him, but George tells him to get the hell back out of his grave. Madden backs out of there fast and scared. An old colored man kneels beside the hole and tells George to pray with him.

"Niggers are always praying," George says. "The harder niggers pray, the more the white man gets. The harder they pray, the more the white man stomps them. God is just tired of all that praying and carrying on and no *doing*. So don't pray for me, brother colored fellow. I want to go to heaven, and you'll just *pray* me out of there. Just get away from my grave and let me die in peace."

We all slowly move away from the hole.

It is a long time before the ambulance arrives, and it has come too late. They put George on a stretcher and carry him away.

"Now, ain't that one for you?!" a man says to me. "We all thought the guy was nuts, but he knew what he was doing all the time—digging his own grave!"

"Yeah," I say, and I wonder if those guys up in the office George hated so much will try to give him a pink slip for digging his grave on the job site. What a crazy, funny thought.

At home, I tell Ma what happened.

She says, "They are never satisfied. Even when he dies, he has to make trouble. I'll say this for them, though—I've never heard of one of them ever hurting his mother. They appreciate a mother more than most whites do. Yes, I will give them credit for that much. I've never heard of one of them being smitten by a mother's curse."

"A mother's curse? What is that?"

"There is no greater love in the world than a mother's love for her child. But if a child mistreats his mother, abuses her, a mother can curse a child so that he will never have any luck or happiness in this world. Her curse can even make him shrivel and die. Oh, yes, I know it sounds like a superstition, but it's true. I've seen it happen. And my mother has told me stories of it happening in the old country—in the South of France. God has given all mothers this power, this supernormal power to punish an abusive child. It is all right there in the Bible—one of the commandments. Honor thy father and mother. Oh yes, a mother can put a curse on an offensive child so that he'll wish he was never born."

It gives me the willies. But I have nothing to fear from this. I would rather cut off both arms than to offend Ma even a little.

## 10

At last there is a window in my dark room. The bird flies in and sits on the sill like an old friend. It cocks its head and looks at me. It begins to sing to me. Oh, I must have this beautiful singing bird! Slowly I get out of bed and try to sneak up on it. I talk softly so as not to frighten it. I move closer, slowly closer. . . .

"Pretty bird . . . here, pretty bird . . ."

I make a sudden leap for it. The bird is gone, and I am falling, falling, falling headlong out of the window, down, down, down. . . .

I wake up screaming!

**I**T IS MONDAY of the week I do not have to work because I have put in my fifteen days of the month. I am restless. There is nothing to do around the house but read. I am tired of that because I read myself to sleep every night anyway, working or not. I would like to see a movie, but I have no money. Although we have food in the house because we have credit at the grocer, there is not even a dime to spare, and my check does not come until the end of the week.

Ma is sitting at the kitchen table, sewing an old dress and humming a tune. She does not like me to go out nights, but I am tired of sitting around with her. I have been in nights for two weeks straight. I feel entitled to go out for a while now if I want to. Quickly I put on my jacket and hat.

"Ma, I'm going out for a while."

She surprises me. She looks up and smiles.

"All right. You've been a good boy. Run along if you must."

Suddenly I feel a little guilty about leaving her all alone. I turn at the door.

"I'm just going for a little walk, Ma. I'll be back before you know it."

"All right, my sweet. But you take as long as you want to. I'll be here alone waiting for you. Ma will always be here waiting for her darling son."

"But, Ma, I told you I won't be long."

"Yes, and I believe you. I do. Now run along and don't worry about me."

A little thing like going out! You would think she would let me do that much without making me feel so bad about it. Now I know that I will have to rush back and not enjoy my walk. It would have been better all around if I had not decided to go out.

I have not seen any of the old gang in a long time so I take a walk around Hudson Avenue, hoping I will see Arnie or Charlie Ding Dong. It is early evening and the weather is nice for December. Christmas is only three weeks away, and everybody seems to be hustling for some extra change. The big stores are open later than usual. A lot of peddlers are around with pushcarts full of Christmas-y junk. Even the whores are hustling much earlier in the evening than usual, sitting at their windows, tapping on the panes whenever a likely John passes. I would like to get Ma something nice for Christmas, but I know damn well I cannot get it digging holes on W.P.A. Stealing is no good because there is nothing around big enough to take the risk for. I won't go after petty thieving like Arnie or Ding Dong and run the risk of getting caught for something so small just when Ma needs me most. I will not cause her heartache and agony for that. Something in the hundreds—well, that is a horse of another color.

I start for Nucky Johnson's poolroom. I get there just as Arnie and Charlie Ding Dong are coming out of the door. Arnie sees me and greets me with a big smile.

"Hello, Harry, keed! Where the hell you been hiding?"

"Not hiding—working."

"No kidding!" Arnie says. He tries to look very sad. He pats me on the shoulder. "That's a dirty shame. Too bad, kid. How'd a nice guy like you get trapped into a job? Wise me up. I don't never want to fall into a trap like that."

Ding Dong laughs. "Me nudder," he says.

"Cut out the kidding, you guys," I say. "I have to look out for my mother. I'm on W.P. A."

"The W.P.A.? Oh, well, that's different. I thought you said you was working."

The three of us laugh.

"Well, what are you doing for a living?" I ask Arnie.

"Hustling, naturally."

"How're you doing? Your clothes don't look as if you're doing any better than I am."

Arnie winks slyly and says, "Look across the street."

I look. There is the same three-storied house that has always been there, but it has now been painted a battleship-gray color. There are Venetian blinds on the windows above where there once were curtains. On the ground floor, where the grocery used to be, there is a barbershop with a bright pole in front. I look back at Arnie.

"I guess that's your new piece of property." I kid him.

"That's the new headquarters of Mr. Louis (the Owner) Varga," he says proudly. "The whole house and the barbershop, too."

"What are you so proud about? I'll bet they won't even let you in to get a haircut."

"Don't be so sure. I got an in over there like I told you I wanted to get."

I look at him. He is dead serious. I start getting curious.

"You're not kidding?" I ask.

"Ask Ding Dong."

I look at Ding Dong. He grins.

"That's right, Harry. I'm in on it a little bit myself."

"Who you got an in with—Louis the Owner?" I ask.

"Not yet, but I will before long." Suddenly he turns to Ding Dong. "Say, what time is it?"

Ding Dong leans back and looks through the window at the poolroom clock. "Eight thirty," he says.

"All right. We got a little time." Arnie takes my arm. "Come on, Harry, take a little walk with us. I'll tell you all about it."

We start walking in the direction I have just come from. I am anxious to hear all about it, but Arnie takes his time. He acts very mysterious about it before he starts talking.

"Remember me telling you about Abie the Bug, don't you?"

"Yeah . . ."

"Well, it's him I got the in with."

I whistle!

"Nothing palsy-walsy or big—*yet*. But I'm just beginning to let him know I'm around and I'm on the ball. I been running a few errands, wiping off his car—just flunkying around, see? Nothing important yet. But the *real* thing is that I know he's got his good eye on me. Last month I delivered a bag full of dough for him to a guy over in South Brooklyn. That shows he trusts me, see? And now another real big thing is coming up next week. He wants me to steal a car for him."

"Whose car?"

"Anybody's car. He don't want it to keep for himself. He's probably gonna do a job or something in it, then ditch it."

"Man!" I say. "You're sure traveling in good and fast company."

"You're telling me!" he says proudly.

We come to a tavern.

"Come on, let's stop for a beer," Arnie says.

"I'm broke," I tell him.

"It's on me."

We step into the tavern. It is deserted except for an old man at the far end of the bar. Arnie orders beer. Ding Dong starts for the men's room.

"Got to get the lead out," he says.

Arnie turns to me in a confidential way. "Listen, are you above making yourself a piece of change tonight?"

"Doing what?"

"Putting a mug on a guy."

"No, thanks. I'm not looking to go to jail for a couple of quarters."

"No quarters. This guy is noted for carrying a nice roll."

I am interested a little. "Who is it—a lush?"

"No. It's a guy who use to live around here, but he lives up on the Heights now. Maybe you remember him. They called him Old Remus."

"Old Remus . . . an old guy?"

"Not so old. He carried a sporty metal cane all the time."

"No, I don't remember him."

"He's a real faggot. he likes to be pushed around by strong boys, so we won't have much trouble with him on that score."

"You mean he likes to get robbed?"

"No—but he likes to be treated rough. He won't put up much of a fight."

"How do you know?"

"Because I mugged him once before. I sneaked up behind him on a dark street. I did it alone, too. It was the funniest thing I ever seen. When I put the mug on him and started feeling around for his wallet, he started cooing to me like a woman." He puts his glass down and laughs. "That son of a bitch! He thought I was feeling him up instead of robbing him! I got the wallet and shoved him on the ground."

"How much money you get?"

"About fifty or sixty dollars was in that wallet, I think."

It all sound like good money but little risk to me.

"You think he'll be carrying that much tonight?"

"Could be more, Harry. What do you say? Want to come in? Me and Ding Dong was gonna pull it alone, but with you, too, it'll be that much easier. Whatever we get, we split three ways."

I think on it, but not for long. Christmas is right around the corner.

"Okay. What'll we do?"

Arnie says the fag works in a tailor shop, a few blocks from his house. We wait for the guy in his hallway, which is a good place for a mugging. Ding Dong waits near the tailor shop. When he sees the guy come out of the shop at nine o'clock, he starts walking in front of him and passes the house. When we see Ding Dong go by from the hallway, we know the fag is coming right behind. When he comes into the hallway, we jump him. Ding Dong doubles back and stands in front of the door to lookout.

It is a good plan. It is very near nine o'clock. We finish our beer quick, pull Ding Dong off the john and hurry out.

Me and Arnie wait anxiously in the hall behind the foyer door. It is a large hall with a white tile floor. It is dimly lit by a small yellow bulb in the ceiling. There are no apartments on the first floor. A wide stairway leads up to a dark landing on the second floor.

"Who is going to grab him first?" I ask in a whisper.

"I'll put the mug on him because I got the know-how. You just frisk for the wallet. Once you got the wallet, go through every pocket and take everything that feels like money. Then feel his wrists and take the watch if he's wearing one. When you think you got everything, just holler okay and run out the door with Ding Dong. Don't worry about me. I'll knock him out and follow you."

I am nervous, but I am also excited and look forward eagerly to the mugging.

"Nervous?" Arnie asks.

"No. Why should I be?"

He smiles and pats my arm. Suddenly he says, "Get back!"

"Him?"

"No."

We stiffen, our backs close to the wall. An old woman with a bundle comes in, walks by us without noticing and goes up the stairs. We relax. Arnie moves out again where he can see Ding Dong as he passes the front door. I begin to feel very uneasy and impatient.

"What if somebody comes in the hall just as we jump him?" I ask.

"Forget it. That's Ding Dong's job." Suddenly he jumps back again. "There goes Ding Dong!"

We stiffen against the wall again. We wait, quiet.

A heavy man, wearing a funny little hat and carrying a cane, walks in. He goes right by us and starts for the stairs. Like a cat, Arnie quickly sneaks up behind him and throws an arm around his neck, pulling his head back. I come out right behind Arnie and start going through the guy's pockets. I can see Ding Dong standing calm in the doorway, facing the street. I keep my head down so the fag cannot see my face as I search. I know that Arnie must have one hell of a mug around his neck because the guy does not struggle or make any sound at all. I find the wallet and some other stuff that feels like money. I push it all in my pockets. I am ready to go. Suddenly something comes over me. I want to go, but I stand confused, trying to make up my mind about I do not know what.

"Beat it," Arnie says. "Hurry up!"

But I am angry with this man. I want to hurt him. I ball up my fist. With all my might I punch it into his belly. I hear kind of a grunt, and the guy lets go of his walking cane for the first time. It falls to the tile floor and makes a funny sound that I hear as I run out of the door.

We meet at the poolroom. Me and Arnie go to the toilet in the back to count up the money. We leave Ding Dong in the front because it would look suspicious for the three of us to go to the tiny toilet together. We stand over the john and hurriedly count the money. There is a hundred and twenty-six dollars and sixty cents in change. I whistle. It is a good haul. Arnie gets a greedy look in his eyes.

"Let's split the hundred between us and give Ding Dong the twenty-six."

"No. We got to level with him," I say.

"He won't know the difference. We'll tell him we got only— what is it?—twenty-six apiece. Around seventy-some dollars."

I look at Arnie. I do not like it.

"Why do you want to cross him, Arnie?"

"It's not crossing him."

"You said it was going to be a three-way split."

"Sure, but we did all the work by mugging the guy. All he did was stand there and lay chicky."

"He took the same chances we did. I don't like to cross a friend, Arnie. And this has started me to think . . . suppose you and Ding Dong were in here counting up the money and I was outside . . . would you give *me* the short end, too, Arnie?"

His face reddens. He looks a little scared. Suddenly he laughs nervously.

"Aw, forget about it, Harry. I was only kidding. You take everything so serious. Forget about it, will you? Okay, a hundred twenty-six sixty. Break it down. What do we get apiece?"

It is forty-two dollars and twenty cents apiece. I give Arnie Ding Dong's cut and stuff mine in my pocket. Arnie keeps the wallet to destroy later.

"Gee, why'd you hit him so hard, Harry?"

I do not look at him. I am embarrassed. "I don't know. What's the difference? You were going to knock him out. Did you?"

"I didn't have to. Soon as I took the mug off, he groaned and sank right to the floor."

"I hope I killed him."

Arnie stares at me, bug-eyed. I am shocked myself at what I have said. I quickly change it to what I really meant. "I mean, I hope I *didn't* kill him."

Arnie says, "I hope you didn't, either. I don't want to sit in the hot-seat for a forty-buck haul. Come on, let's get out of here."

We meet Ding Dong up front and go out of the poolroom. Arnie gives Ding Dong his cut.

"How much was it?" he asks.

"A hundred twenty-six bucks and sixty cents," Arnie tells him. "Forty-two twenty apiece."

"Woweee!" Ding Dong shouts, kissing the bills. "And I thought we're lucky if we wind up with just ten apiece!"

Arnie gives me a look that seems to say, "See, you chump, we could've got away with it."

I shrug. I tell them I'd better be getting back home.

"If I get another mark I'll let you in on it, Harry," Arnie says as I leave. "You're good luck to us."

"Okay."

I leave them and go on down Hudson Avenue. I do not regret what I have done. I have forty-two dollars in my pocket—more money than I have ever had in my life! Besides, it was exciting.

The only bother—the sound of the cane hitting the floor as I ran. It is a nagging memory that I reach for but cannot grab.

I give Ma thirty dollars and keep the rest for myself. I tell her I found the money in an old pocketbook laying in the gutter. She is overjoyed. She takes the money and kisses my cheek.

She asks only one question.

"I wonder what your father is doing tonight?"

I am in a place I have never been before. It is like a forest, and there are tall, gray trees shooting straight up to the sky. I am alone, and all is hazy like it is going to rain. The clouds in the sky are dark and fat and move slowly along. I am sad and afraid because it is so lonely. Suddenly I hear a bird singing. It comes very soft. It sounds beautiful, and I know it must be beautiful, too, but I cannot see it. I must see it because it is so beautiful. I look up in the tree near me, but it is not there. The singing comes louder. I rush back and forth looking into and behind every tree, but I do not find it, and the singing becomes louder and louder. I stand there desperately wanting that bird, and it is singing, calling to me, and I do not know what to do. Suddenly it comes shooting down out of the sky to me. Oh, how beautiful and delicate it is! It flies to me, but as I reach it flies away again. It turns, flutters its wings in the air and sings to me. I go for it again. It escapes me again. Oh, I must have this bird! I chase after it around a winding path. It does not fly very fast, for it is always just beyond my fingertips. It turns and flies backwards, looking at me with twinkling eyes. It is teasing me. All of a sudden, it is gone. It has disappeared completely. I want to cry. I do not know what I will do now. I rush about everywhere looking for it. I look behind a tree—and there it is sitting on a bush! Slowly I reach for it. Just as my hand touches its feathery back, a wonderful feeling comes over me. But the bird flies quickly away before I can close my hand. I must touch it again. It is such a wonderful thing to touch that I know I must stroke it again or die. It flies up and around, escaping my eager fingers everywhere. It darts off and away and disappears over a hill. I rush up the hill, praying that I will find it on the other side. I reach the top of the hill, and I am surprised to find it there—waiting for me on a nest of moss. I go to it, begging it not to fly away, begging for just one little stroke of its back. It looks at me. It pities me and does not fly away. I reach. . . . I stroke its back and a wonderful, heavenly feeling goes through my whole body as the clouds explode and rain rushes down on me.

Suddenly I sit up in bed. What is it? It was all a dream. That bird dream. But I *am* wet. I turn on the lamp and throw the covers back. It has happened! I am filled with wonder and happiness, but I feel sticky and uncomfortable. I go to the bathroom and wash. I get back in bed. I know sleep will come back to me quick because I feel peaceful and content. I have waited so long for it, and now it has come. Now, I am truly a man.

**I** CANNOT UNDERSTAND IT. Only a couple of weeks ago it happened. Now, no matter what I do, it does not happen again. I stroke it gently, slowly, very fast, pull, shake. I think hard of the girls, even the bird again, but everything is useless. I am puzzled and worried over it. Once it begins to happen, it should happen all the time. It is supposed to be just like shaving. Once the beard comes, even though you shave it off, it comes back again. What is wrong with me? How can I find out what to do about it? I cannot ask Arnie or any of the fellows and let them know I am not grown up yet. I am all of eighteen years old. I am ashamed to ask anybody a thing like this. Tonight I will go to the library. Maybe there is a book about these things somewhere.

I find just the book I need! It is more than I had hoped for. I am surprised to find such a dirty book in the library. I am embarrassed when I take it up to the lady librarian. But she says nothing and checks me out with it.

I sneak into the house with the book under my jacket.

I get in bed and read. The book is called *Miracle of Human Reproduction*. There are pictures of male and female sex organs. I do not like to look at the male parts, but the female organs are very interesting and do not make me uncomfortable to look at them. There are so many different parts with names—labia majora, labia minora, clitoris. I am surprised there are so many different parts. I had an idea there was just a plain opening like the behind. And there are even more different parts on the inside! It is all so fascinating, but I leave the pictures, for the time being, and go to a chapter called "The Mechanics of Intercourse." I read where the penis goes into the vagina—and right away it comes to me what is wrong. It comes to me like a flash. It is so simple that I laugh at myself for being such a dope and not thinking of it sooner. *You must have a girl to do it with*! There is nothing wrong with me. When I put it into a girl, it will happen. What a scared fool I have been. But I must try it with a girl to make sure. Only I am not attracted to girls yet. I do not like the idea of being too close to them. But I will force myself because I must make sure it will happen. I do not know how to go about it—how to find a girl and ask her. I puzzle a minute . . . I have it! The whores around the block. I will go to one of the whores on Hudson Avenue, and I will pay her to do it to me.

I hide the book beneath the mattress.

I go over to Hudson Avenue. It is almost eight o'clock in the evening. The girl's name is Lola. She is pretty and plump.

It does not go. The whore looks at me and says, "What's the matter with you?"

"Nothing," I say.

"Well?"

I try again.

"That's not the way to do it," she says impatiently. "First, you got to get some lead in your pencil." She uses her hands on me. Nothing happens. She looks at me suspiciously. "Look, I got no time to waste, sonny. Do you want a woman or not?"

I begin to get frightened. "Yes," I mumble.

"Well, what's the matter with you?"

I blush with shame. "I don't know."

"You ever have a girl before?"

"No."

She sits up on the bed and throws her dress down. "Well, this ain't no free weaning house. Ten minutes a trick. Fork over another two bucks or your time is up."

"Never mind, I'm going," I tell her.

I dress quickly. I can feel her eyes on my back. I am too ashamed to look at her. I start out.

"You don't want a girl. I think maybe it's a *man* you need, sonny-boy," she says. She laughs loudly and mockingly as I go through the door.

I am angry and miserable and frightened.

## 2

I stand across the street from the doctor's house. The one unboarded window is dark. I see no light, movement, nothing. I get up my nerve. I cross the street, go up on the porch and knock. I wait. No answer. I knock again, harder. Wait.

The door opens slightly. A man's bearded face comes out of the darkness.

"Yes?"

"Are you a doctor?" I ask.

"Yes."

"I want to get a physical examination."

"Why do you want a physical examination?"

"I want to find out if I am—all right."

"Aha, still uncertain. Very well. Come in."

I step into the dark house and the doctor closes the door. He has a large lamp in his hand. He leads me through what I believe is a dark hall into a dark room. He puts the lamp up on a mantel or shelf and takes another smaller, unlit lamp down and lights it.

He says to me, "You can undress here while I go for my instruments."

He goes out with the small lamp. I look around me. I am standing beside an easy chair and a desk. I can see nothing beyond the circle of orange light that the lamp above me makes. The rest of the room is buried in pitch blackness.

It is very strange. A feeling has come over me that I have never felt before. I feel calm and restful as if I belonged here. It is a feeling of being at home. I feel more at home here than I have ever felt in my own house. And the strangest part of all is that I have a feeling that I have been here before, or that I am not here now but will be standing here like this in the future. It is queer and gives me a little giddy feeling like the pictures on the Moreland's Tonic bottles.

I undress slowly.

"All right, you can put your clothes back on now," the doctor says.

He sits down at the desk and lights a long cigarette. He inhales deep and long and lets the smoke float out of his mouth into the air. The room becomes filled with the smell of burnt tea. I am anxious to know what he has found and also afraid to know. The doctor says nothing. He just sits there smiling at me and smoking his cigarette.

"How am I, Doctor?" I ask finally.

"Fine," he says. "You were built to last."

"But what's wrong with me?"

The smile goes. "What do you mean, what's wrong with you? You asked for a physical examination. I found nothing unusual. Do you have a complaint?"

"Am I normal, I mean, for my age, am I normal? I'm eighteen."

He really squints at me now. He looks at me a long while in silence.

"In what way?" he asks quietly.

"Sex." It comes out before I realize it.

The doctor motions to an empty chair beside the desk. "Come sit down, young man, and tell me what is on your mind."

I sit down. I rub my hands together nervously. I do not know how to begin. The doctor looks at me with sympathy and begins for me.

"You appear to be a normal boy physically. However, pull your pants down again."

I drop my pants and underwear. He examines my organs carefully.

"Your genitals are normal." He sits up, looks at me as if he already knows what is on my mind. "Why do you ask if you are normal sexually?"

I know I must tell him now. This is the time to find out once and for all.

"I don't go for girls," I say quickly.

"What do you mean go for girls? You mean you don't chase them?"

"Yes."

He smiles, shakes his head. "This is nothing. You are just a boy still. There is plenty of time for the chase."

"I want to know—am I queer? A fag?"

"Well, let me ask you something . . . Do you go for men?"

"Hell, no."

"So. You've answered your own question. If you were a homosexual, you would go for men with a vengeance and not with your 'Hell, no.' There is not the slightest doubt about this. You like girls, I presume?"

"Not in a sex way. That's what is worrying me. Other fellows my age do but not me."

"Have you ever had intercourse with a girl?"

"I tried but, my thing, it wouldn't get—hard."

"Have you masturbated? Have you tried to make it get hard by yourself?"

"Yes—but it wouldn't."

The doctor looks up at the ceiling and thinks a moment. "Tell me, have you ever had an ejaculation?"

"What's that?"

He looks at me. "It is a way that nature rewards us for reproducing ourselves. There is this most wonderfully thrilling sensation in the world that comes over our entire bodies when semen—"

"Oh, yes. I know what you mean. Yes, that's happened to me . . . but not with a girl."

"In your sleep?"

I am surprised. "Yes! How did you know?"

He smiles and shakes his head. "Because it is normal. This happens to almost all boys. What is your name?"

"Harold."

"Very well, Harold, listen and I will give you good advice. You are a normal young man. What your friends can do at your age, and you cannot, means nothing. The sex urge varies with people. Some have a very strong appetite, others have almost none. Some are in-between. Do you see? Now, you may be among those who have very little for this. But I doubt it because you are so young. You have not reached manhood yet. So! Why should a boy like you have a man's sex urge?"

"But I have no urge at all."

"Then why did you try it with the girl? Why did you try to masturbate?"

"I—I don't know."

"So! I will tell you why. You are in such a big hurry to be a man. You want to prove to yourself that you are as much man as your friends. Ah, yes, I know they boast to you about what powerful men they are with the girls. They are all lying, just cockcrowing. But you believe them. You want to be a big Casanova, too, and deflower every virgin in town. But you can't. Sex can't be forced. This is the way of nature. The sexual urge is a thing deep inside you. When your body is ready for it, it comes to you in a natural and easy way. When your penis would not get hard for you the first time, you started to worry about it. And the more you worried about your manhood, the less chances you had of having an erection. So you see, that is your whole trouble. Like most things, it is all in your mind. You are worrying so much in your mind about not being a man, that you are not giving your body a chance to become one. Now, as soon as you put all of those worries out of your mind, forget them completely, the sex urge will come to you in normal and easy fashion. Is that all clear to you now, Harold?"

It is wonderful and clear. There is nothing wrong with me that way! I feel like shouting to the roof. I feel like hugging the doctor. He is the smartest, greatest man in the whole world. I laugh. I grab his hand and shake it hard.

"Thank you, Doctor, thank you! You saved my life."

"Nonsense." The doctor laughs and slaps me on the back. "But please don't run out of here now and get any girls pregnant. It would be all my fault."

We laugh. I thank him again. I want to give him all the money I have, but he refuses it.

"It is enough fee for me to see that you are at last certain of something. You are a splendid young man and I enjoy your company. Please come and see me again—just to talk."

I promise him I will come visit. We shake hands again. He leads me back through the long, dark hall and I go out.

I go down the street, whistling. What a relief! I think on it—nature and the mind. They work in funny ways.

## 3

"What is the meaning of this, Harold? How dare you?!"

She has found it. Ma is standing over me in the kitchen, holding the book up in the air. I sit in the kitchen chair and keep my eyes on my feet. I am so full of shame and embarrassment I want to drop right through the floor.

"How *dare* you? How dare you to bring a filthy book like this into the house? Why did you read this—this filth?"

I feel terrible. I want to make myself as small as I can.

*"Answer me!"* Ma shouts.

"What, Ma?" I say meekly without looking up.

"Why did you bring this into the house?"

I don't know how to answer her. I am too ashamed.

"I don't know," I say.

*"You don't know,* is it? Well, I will teach you to know!"

Ma beats me on my back, head and ears with the book. It is a hardback book and hurts, but not as much as the shame and disgrace

I feel inside me. I bend over, putting my head in my lap, and she beats and beats me on the back until she is tired and stops. I cry in my hands, but it is not from the pain in my burning back. Ma shoves the book in the coal stove, burning it up. She turns and rushes to her room, slamming the door behind her. I hear words, "disgusting," "filthy," "his father." Now she is crying. Every now and then she wails long and loud. With every wail there is a hurt in me. I want to go to her, but I am too ashamed and too sorry for hurting her this way. I go to my room and lay across the bed in the dark. I shut up my ears.

It is all quiet now. It has been a long time since Ma has stopped crying. I switch on the lamp next to my bed. I hear Ma's room door suddenly open. I try to hurry and turn off the light again, but before I can, Ma is standing in my doorway. She has changed. Her face is no longer angry or sad. Her hair is combed and there is lipstick on her mouth. She has taken off her dress and is wearing a thin housecoat.

She stands there watching me and not saying anything a moment. Now she comes slowly into the room. She sits down in a chair near the bed and crosses her legs.

"So you want to know about such things, do you?"

I try not to look at her. I do not answer.

"Did you read all of that book?"

"No, only a tiny little bit, Ma. I swear."

"The pictures?"

"I didn't look at any of them—not one."

Ma is quiet a moment. Now she sighs and says, "Well, I can tell you about things like that. I suppose it is my duty, since you have no father to tell you. I can tell you all you want to know, but I will not have you learning it from filthy, disgusting books and your friends in the streets. No, sit up, Harold, and look at me. Don't be ashamed. Tell Ma what you want to know about those things."

I sit up. I look at her, pleading. "I'm sorry, Ma, I swear to you! Please forgive me."

She shakes her head, yes. "I know you are sorry, Harold. You are sorry because you are a very good boy. I know you will not do such a thing again and you will listen to your mother. Now, what do you want to know about the things that were in that book?"

"Nothing," I say.

"Nothing at all?"

"Nothing."

I hope she will not go on about it because already I am black with shame.

"Well, I can tell you all about it, all right, about girls and things. A young boy like you has to watch his step. The girls today are not what they use to be when I was coming up. There is altogether too much looseness. And I don't believe a decent boy can find one decent girl out of a hundred today. These girls today are forever conniving and scheming at every chance to get their claws into a good boy like you . . . to get him to woo her and marry her, one way or another . . . to get him to slave for the rest of his life to support her, and her at home loafing and fooling with other men behind his back while he sweats for her. Oh, I know all about these young sluts running around today and I wouldn't be a woman if I didn't. I know all about them the way they run around today, tempting a young boy like you with that *sex* thing. That's what they use, the *sex* thing. All right, they have that thing between their legs, and I don't suppose I have to tell you what it looks like because you know. Boys always do, somehow or other. It must be born into them because they seem to know what to go for the first time they are with one of these sluts. The devil gets into a boy when these girls show themselves off, and a boy loses his head and has no control. They get together, yes, they do, him on top of her and— Well, what he has—this thing—he puts between her legs where the hair is and it goes up into her belly and she wiggles and he huffs and puffs like an old goat and they do one thing and another and ah—hmm—Well, yes—they go on and on like that until something happens. It is supposed to be a pleasure, but let me tell you it is a disgusting, filthy thing altogether. Oh, I don't mean when you are married to a nice girl (God knows where you will find one today!) and want to have children. Of course, if you want to have children you must do that to have them. But it is good for nothing else.

Otherwise, it is all filthy sex, sex, sex, and a boy who is good will stay away from it. Then there is disease. Most of these girls have terrible diseases between their legs, a pox that they give to a boy doing that. Festering sores break out all over his organs. And there is another disease that makes him go crazy, so that he has to be shut up in an asylum for the rest of his life. Oh, I could go on and on and warn you about these terrible things, these terrible women, but I know it will do no good. I know talking never did your father any good. I know deep in my heart, in spite of all I tell you, the minute a girl tempts you with sex, you will forget about me and go right off with her."

"No, Ma!"

"Oh, yes. The minute she shows you what is between her legs (as if she is the only woman in the world who has this!) you will go running off and marry her. You will betray me for a disgusting thing like sex and leave me old and alone in the world. That is the way you will repay me for struggling to bring you up without a husband's help. You will betray me just the way Hap has betrayed me."

What she says hurts and makes me feel like a guilty dog. I know even she does not believe what she is saying, but says it only because she knows it hurts me. It is a way of punishing me. I deserve it, but I plead and plead with her to stop. Finally she does. She looks at me a long time without speaking.

"Very well," she says. "Are you sure you will not betray me, Harold?"

"Never, Ma. I could never do anything to hurt you."

"But if you read filthy books like that, you might be tempted—"

"No, Ma. I'll never read another book like that again in my life. I swear that to you, Ma."

She smiles. She comes over to me and kisses my cheek.

"As long as we have each other, we have everything," she says. She goes.

**VIII**

IT IS CHRISTMAS EVE. I have decided I will buy Ma a new housecoat with the few dollars I have left from the mugging.

Ma has bought a little Christmas tree. She is struggling there on the living-room floor with hammer and nails, trying to make that old stand hold the tree straight. While she is so occupied I think I will take this chance to sneak out and buy her Christmas present. I get my hat and jacket, but she spots me just as I go by the living room.

"Where are you going?" she asks, kneeling there on the floor with her hair all mussed up.

"Oh, just for a walk," I say. But I cannot help smiling. I know I have given my secret away because she smiles, too, and seems to understand what it is all about, but pretends not to.

"All right," she says, "but don't take too long. I want you to help me decorate the tree."

"I'll hurry."

It is seven o'clock in the evening and Fulton Street is crowded with shoppers, mostly women. It is hard to walk without bumping into them with their arms full of bundles, darting in and out everywhere. There is a gay, surprise-like feeling in the air and on the faces of people. All the big department-store fronts and clothing stores are lit up bright with cheerful, colorful things in the windows. Namn's window is decorated with a gay Christmas scene. A huge dummy Santa Claus that moves his head and eyes sits in a sleigh full of toys. The sleigh rocks back and forth, back and forth on a snowy country road. Music comes from inside the stores. A Salvation Army band is playing Christmas carols.

I start into Namn's store and surprise! Arnie Devivo bumps into me as he rushes out. Ding Dong is right behind him.

I laugh. "Hey, Merry Christmas, you bums!"

They look at me with startled, scared faces but do not say a word. They rush right on by me, disappearing in the crowd. I pause a moment, but the people pushing in and out do not give me time to puzzle over it. Before I know it, I have been pushed into the store by the rushing crowd.

I find my way to the ladies department. A nice, elderly saleslady helps me pick out a beautiful green-and-red-trimmed housecoat. It costs five bucks! I will not have any money at all left, but I know it will be worth it just to see the surprised, happy look on Ma's face when she opens the box. The saleslady wraps it up in a beautiful Christmas box and I start pushing my way to the street again.

I get back to the house. Ma has begun to decorate the tree. She looks at the package in my hand.

"What have you got there?" she asks, teasing-like.

I smile and put the package under the tree. "You are not suppose to notice it," I tell her.

"All right. Hurry and get out of your jacket and help me with the tree."

It is a lot of fun dressing the tree with Ma. We sing Christmas carols as we go along. Ma goes to get the tree lights from her bedroom closet. I notice a fancy box beneath the tree next to my package. It has not been wrapped yet. I think it is my present. I cannot resist to take one little peek. I open the box slightly. Three beautiful neckties of different colors! And they have my initials stitched into them with fancy letters—"H. O." I hear Ma coming and close the box back quick. I fool with the snowflakes on the tree. Ma comes in with the lights.

"What are you smiling about?" she asks.

"Because it's Christmas," I tell her.

We finish with the tree. It is real pretty.

"Come," Ma says.

I follow her into the kitchen. "What is it?" I ask.

She opens the top and bottom doors of the icebox. "Look!"

"Wow!"

It is crammed with food—a big turkey with all the trimmings, and there are all kinds of fruits and vegetables and nuts. I figure Ma must have saved the money I gave her from the mugging for this day.

"Gee, Ma, we're going to have a bang-up Christmas this year. I don't ever remember us having one as good as this before."

"Once before—when your father was home. But we don't need him this year—or ever. We've done it all ourselves and we'll enjoy it all to ourselves. Where he is he can stay." She takes a bottle and two glasses down from the closet. "Christmas cheer, too! And now a little nightcap for mother and son." She pours two drinks of red wine and gives me one.

I toast her. "Merry Christmas, Ma."

"Merry Christmas, my dear."

I go to bed. I try to read but I cannot concentrate. I keep thinking of the big feast tomorrow and my present and the look on Ma's face when she sees the housecoat. I toss the magazine away and turn out the light. But sleep does not come easy. I twist and turn, twist and turn. Christmas Eve is always the longest of nights.

I awake with a start. Noise shaking the house. I hear Ma screaming somewhere. I jump out of bed, anxious and fearful. I rush out into the kitchen and stop dead. I am startled and struck dumb. The house is in a crazy uproar. The radio is blaring and Christmas packages are everywhere. A man is laughing hoarsely. Ma is crying and laughing. When the sleep clears from my head and eyes, I realize what is happening. Hap has come home again.

He jumps up from the table where he has been eating. He hugs and kisses me. I smell the whisky on his breath.

"Harold, my boy! My boy!"

I am embarrassed and confused. I do not know what to think or say.

"Gee, Hap, hello, ah, hello."

"Is that all you're going to say—after two years?! Aren't you glad to see me?"

"Sure, Hap."

"You'd better be or I'll knock your block off," he says jokingly. "Say, stand away—let me have a good look at you."

I stand back. Hap looks me up and down. I feel silly.

"My God, how you've grown! Look at him, Kate. . . . Why, he's as tall as I am!"

Ma stands there smiling, a glass of wine in her hand. "He's been such a good boy, too, Hap."

"Look how handsome he is!"

"Why not? Look at his father," Kate tells him.

I feel more foolish by the minute. "How are you feeling, Hap?" I ask to change the subject.

He mimics me. "How you feeling, he says to me. Look at him— just like a man!"

Ma laughs. "But he has been man of the house while you were away—and a good one, too. He's working now."

"No!" Hap says in surprise. "Where?"

"Well, it's only W.P.A. but—"

Hap frowns and shakes his head. "No good—but we'll talk about that later. Come on in the living room and see the presents I brought."

We go to the living room. There are open boxes all over the floor. Hap brings me a good-looking topcoat.

"I see now it's too small," he says. "I never realized you had grown so much."

"You mean that's for *me?*" I ask, surprised.

"Sure. Do you like it?"

"I love it!" I rub my hand over the beautiful, soft cloth. I have never had a Sunday topcoat in my whole life.

"Well, don't worry about the size. We'll take it back next week and get your right size."

"Thanks, Hap. Thanks a million."

There are a couple of kid games on the floor. There is also an Erector set and an electric-train set. I look at them but do not say anything. Hap looks at the toys, then looks at me sheepishly out of the corners of his eyes. He scratches his chin.

"Well, I guess I didn't figure on you being quite so big, Harold," he says a little sadly.

Ma hugs him. "He appreciates them just the same. Besides, he's not too big to play with electric trains." Ma gives me a meaningful look to agree with her. "Isn't that right, Harold?"

"Sure, Hap. I appreciate them very much."

"Of course, he does!" Ma says.

Hap is not sure. "Naw. This stuff is not for a big boy like I have. Next week when we go to change the coat, we'll pick out something more for his age. It's funny—I've been gone two years, but all the time I was away I thought of you as being the same size as the day I left. I'm sorry, son."

"Don't be sorry, Hap. This is great. I never expected anything at all."

Hap looks at me in silence a moment. Now his eyes get bleary and suddenly he is crying and sobbing. He flops down on the sofa with his head in his hands. Me and Ma try to console him.

"I'm no good," he says. "I've been no good! I've been a real stinker. Look what a wonderful wife and son I have, and I've been a stinker to them. For two whole years I've been neglecting you—running around throwing my money away on a bunch of stinkers just like me . . . a bunch of dirty stinkers. But thank God—" He breaks down sobbing again.

"Please, Hap," Ma says. "You know we forgive you."

But Hap waves her off. "Let me finish. I thank God for letting me see what a stinker I've been before it was too late. You know what happened to me the day before yesterday? I'm out eat the track and I win a bundle—a thousand bucks. I'm on my way home. I have a little place down in the Village where a bunch of freeloaders hang out because they know I'm a good-time Charlie. I know there is going to be a bunch of them waiting for me, there's always a bunch. I'm walking down the street, almost home, when something stops me. It was Christmas spirit that did it. Really, the Christmas spirit. I heard that Christmas song coming from a record shop—"Silent Night." It was so soft and beautiful. It made me think—A man belongs with his family on Christmas, not only Christmas, but all year round—but especially Christmas. So here I was taking a thousand-dollar bundle to throw away on a bunch of freeloaders when maybe my own family didn't even have a Christmas tree! I said to hell with that. I turned right around and got me a hotel room. All day yesterday I spent riding around in a cab, picking up presents for you—and here I am. Not just for Christmas, but to stay! I'm making more money now than I ever made in my life, and it's going to take care of my wife and son. I tell you, I've changed and I'll be a good husband to you, Kate, and a good father to you, Harold, if only—if only you'll forgive and give me another chance."

He takes Ma's hand and kisses and cries into it. She hugs him and cries along with him.

"Of course, we forgive you, Hap," Ma says. "We love you. And now you're home again, so let's all be happy this Christmas day."

"Thank you, Katie." He wipes his eyes and stands up. His jaw is firm, and he clinches his fists. "And by God, I'll show you what a real *man* I can be!" Suddenly he looks quickly around the room. "Katie, where's the bottle at?"

Ma gets Hap a drink. She turns to me and begins to show me her presents. There is an electric mixer, a silver service set, and best of all a fur coat. Ma tries it on for me.

"How do you like it?" she asks, turning around.

"It's beautiful. What kind of fur is it?"

"Mouton lamb."

"It sure is nice. You really needed a nice winter coat, Ma."

"Your father thinks of everything. He's so wonderful!"

Hap snorts. "Aw! I got a lot to make up for."

It comes to me that Ma has not seen the housecoat yet.

I say, "Ma, there's something for you under the tree from me."

She looks under the tree and finds the package. "Oh, I wonder what it can be?"

Me and Hap smile and watch her open the present.

"Oh, how beautiful—a new housecoat!" She gives me a great big kiss. She throws her arms around me and Hap. "I'm so proud and happy. I'm the luckiest woman in the world to have such a thoughtful husband and son. And now I am going to show my appreciation by cooking you a wonderful Christmas dinner."

She goes off into the kitchen, wearing the fur coat and carrying the housecoat over her arm. Somehow, I am embarrassed alone in the room with Hap. I start to follow Ma out but Hap stops me.

"Wait a minute. I want to have a talk with you, son."

"Okay."

"Not here. Do you drink yet?"

"A little."

"All right. Get your coat and hat. We'll stroll down to the bar for a few while your mother is cooking."

We go down to the bar and order drinks. Hap tells me to quit the W.P.A. job now that he is home. I jump at the chance. I tell him how much I hate it.

"Well, forget about it. You can quit now and go back to school."

"I don't want to go to school, either. I want to work—but not in a ditch."

Hap shakes his head. "Jobs are hard to find now. I guess I'm pretty lucky. I'm in the garment industry. I'm foreman of shipping. Maybe I can get you on—*maybe*. We'll see. Come on, drink up and let's take in a movie."

We finish our drinks and stroll along Myrtle Avenue. We turn up Hudson Avenue and pass by Louis Varga's place. I look across the street at the poolroom, expecting to see Arnie or Ding Dong, but no one is there and the place is closed.

Hap says, "The old neighborhood's getting famous. I read in the papers the other day that Louis Varga and Abie the Bug were questioned by the police about that Russ Gooney murder last week. Did you read it?"

"Yes. Do you think they did it?"

"Who knows? The police let them go, anyway. One thing I *do* know—That Abie the Bug is one mean customer."

"You know him?" I ask, surprised.

"No, but I've seen him operate just once—and that was enough. Last year our company had some trouble with the Drivers' Union. They're all racketeers run by Bill Miller. Abie the Bug must've been in his mob then. One day him and three other hoods came into the shop and spilled acid all over the merchandise. One of my men protested and this Bug fellow made the other hoods hold this worker. Do you know what he did? He took a crowbar and, just as cool as a cucumber, broke both the man's legs. The Bug never even frowned or cursed or anything when he did it. He was so impersonal about it—as if he was breaking a toothpick instead of a man's legs."

"They got away with that?" I ask.

"Sure, they did. They were arrested, all right, but they walked right back out again. Who is going to be a witness against them? Not anybody in his right mind. The poor fellow who got worked over finally told the cops he just couldn't remember how he got both legs broken." He shudders. "I never want to see another thing like that as long as I live!"

We go to the Brooklyn Paramount on DeKalb and Flatbush avenues. It is the first time I have ever been in this theater and it is a big surprise. It is the most beautiful place I have ever seen. They have beautiful statues and rugs, and artistic paintings hang on the walls. The men's room is built like a rich man lived in it. There are big soft chairs and fancy decorations everywhere. Why, they even have ice in the urinals for you to pee on. It is a wonderful and marvelous place.

We buy candy and sit in the back row. Hap puts his arm around the back of my seat. I do not like it. I know that he is only trying to be a "pal" with me and I want to let him, but it embarrasses me. It makes me very uncomfortable. But it is Christmas Day and he has been very nice to Ma and me, so I endure it. Also, I take the trouble to agree with him when he makes remarks about the picture. For this reason, I do not enjoy the movie or even know what half of it is about.

We walk in the house. Ma has the table all set for dinner and she is standing in the kitchen with her hands on her hips, glaring at us as we enter. She is not really angry but pretends. I wonder, what is there about her?

"Where in the world have you two been? I was beginning to worry."

Hap kisses her. "We took in a movie. Mmm that smells good!"

"Why couldn't you take me to the movies, too?" She pouts.

"Because we'd have no dinner if I did," he tells her, plucking her under the chin. "Besides, I wanted to have a talk with Harold."

Ma looks apprehensive. "What about?"

"Nothing in particular—just man talk. How's the dinner coming? Is it ready?"

"In a little while. Chase yourselves into the living room until I call you."

Now I realize what there is about Ma. She looks dressed up and pretty. She is cooking in the brand-new housecoat. I do not like it.

"Ma, you're wearing your new housecoat!"

"Yes, certainly I am. Doesn't it look grand on me?"

"But you're *cooking* in it!"

"What's wrong with that? Can't a woman look pretty when she cooks?"

"But you'll grease it all up—you'll ruin it!"

Ma laughs and looks at Hap. "That's all right—your father will buy me another one."

This hurts me. Hap looks embarrassed. He says, "But Kate, it's the boy's present to you. His Christmas present to his mother, Katie—*you know*."

"Well, if he doesn't want me to wear it when I want to, he can have it back."

She glares at me and I know that she is angry.

I say, "I'm sorry, Ma."

I go quickly into the living room. I sit down on the sofa. I do not know what is wrong or what is happening to me, but I am miserable. I look at the Christmas tree with all the trimmings. It might as well be an old johnny-pump for all the cheer it gives me. I hear Hap speaking in low tones to Ma in the kitchen. He comes into the living room and sits down beside me. He is quiet a moment. He pats me on the hand.

"She doesn't mean anything by it. I guess Kate just doesn't understand these things."

I look at him. I would be surprised if Hap understood them too.

Ma calls us to dinner. There is turkey, dressing, mashed potatoes, cranberries, green peas, turnips and sprouts. Hap has a half gallon of red wine close at hand. For all this I have no appetite. I nibble at the food on my plate. Ma and Hap are talking and joking and drinking, paying no attention to me at all. They are like two love-birds billing and cooing, with Hap teasing and pinching her, and Ma acting very kittenish and cute. It is disgusting—especially Ma, at her age, talking that baby talk and popping raw onions into Hap's big mouth.

I finish eating and move from the table. I want to be alone by myself away from them. It is a little early for bed, but I will get a book and read in my room until I am tired.

I go to my room. The lamp is not on the table beside my cot. I look along the wall for the cord leading into Ma's room. It has been taken up. What has happened? I rush back into the kitchen. They never even noticed that I was out of the room. Ma is now sitting in Hap's lap singing a song to him:

*"You're the Sheik of Araby,*
*Your love belongs to me."*

"Ma," I say, "where is the lamp?"

She is annoyed. "What lamp? Oh. I took it out. It's in my room."

"But I want to read."

"Read in the living room."

"But I want to read in bed the way I always do."

Ma gives me a stern look now. "If you really want to read, you can read in the living room just as well. Besides, I'll be needing the lamp in my room now."

"But you have the overhead light," I protest.

She smiles at Hap lovey-dovey. "A woman my age needs a softer light in her bedroom to help her look attractive to her husband."

Hap laughs and pinches her nose. "Why, there isn't a wrinkle on your pretty face, Katydid!"

"Then it's not going to be in my room any more?" I ask.

"No."

"Oh—" I start to curse but catch myself in time.

I am disgusted. I rush off to my dark room and slam the door behind me. I get in bed. To hell with the reading. I do not have to read. And I do not need that stinking lamp of hers. Putting it in my room was all her idea in the first place. To hell with it.

No, I do not care about the lamp or anything else. It is not going to worry me. But the housecoat—cooking in it, wiping her greasy hands on it. Now, that is one thing she should not have done, that is all.

My eyes burn until they are moist.

**IX**

**H**AP HAS REALLY CHANGED. He only takes a drink once in a while. His face looks fresh and young. His eyes are bright—not the way they were before with that mean, drunk look in them. And he is smiling all the time now. In all my life I have never seen him smile so much as in the past few days since he has been home. Maybe his cheerfulness has been better for Ma's stomach than the Moreland's Tonic because she is not vomiting in the toilet every morning now.

But why does Ma always take him back when he is going to do the same thing over again the minute he takes a notion? Oh, yes, he will look around and find some excuse to leave her high and dry again, you can bet on it. I know this deep in my heart. But she makes me sick, believing every word he says about how things are going to be different. She forgets all about me and throws me out in the cold again. Yet, the minute he takes off, she will come sucking around me again. Well, the next time he takes off I won't be so much "take-care-of-Mama-little-man" for her. I won't play Hap's second fiddle again, you can be sure. And I will not let her put that lamp back in my room just for her to take it out again in case he comes back! I will show her that I mean what I say and I am not like Hap. I will show her that a real man is not weak. Then I will be appreciated for myself and loved for myself, and not just because I happen to be the only one around.

**2**

It is payday for Hap.

After supper he calls me into the living room. He shoves a couple of dollars in my pocket.

He says, "I'm taking your mother to the movies tonight. Why don't you find yourself a nice chick and step out, too, once in a while?"

"Maybe I will," I say. "Thanks."

"What's that you're reading all the time?"

I show him the magazine. *"Weird Tales."*

He takes the magazine, thumbs through it. He frowns. "Why do you read trash like this?"

"That's not trash. Those are good spooky stories in there."

Hap reads, " 'Corpse in the Cradle,' 'The Headless Wonder,' 'Bloodbath for Benjamin.' Why, this book is full of nothing but mayhem and murder!"

I shrug. "I like plenty of action."

*"Action,* yes. I do, too. But there is good action and bad. This stuff is definitely trash. Have you ever read anything by Jack London?"

"No."

He studies my face. "Have you ever *heard* of him?"

"Sure."

"What books did he write? Name me one."

I am annoyed and embarrassed. "Gee whiz, Hap, I don't know. I told you I never read anything by him. But almost everybody has heard of Jack London."

"All right, all right. I'll get you some good books to read and you can throw that penny trash away. Now, about you stepping out once in a while. When you make a date with a girl, Harold, you don't have to worry about pocket money. I'll give you spending money. Whatever you need."

"That's very nice of you, Hap, but I don't get around very much."

"Your mother was telling me. She's worried about you. She says you hang around the house too much. You should get out more with your friends. She's right, you know. A boy your age should be burning up energy instead of storing it. Reading is fine in its place, but try to get out with your friends more. Play ball, go to dances and stuff."

"Working on W.P.A. never gave me much time or money to do those things, I guess."

"Well, now you have both. I'll give you what you need." He slaps me playfully on the shoulder. "Enjoy your youth, son. It only comes to you once. See you later."

"Okay, Hap."

Ma stops on her way out and says to me, "Harold, if you decide to go out, turn out all the lights and make sure the front door is locked."

"All right."

I sit down on the sofa. I try to read my magazine but I am too restless. I throw it aside. Trash, he called it. What difference does it make to him what I read? Trash—at least, it is not full of sex. And where does he get off complaining when Ma never did?

I wander through the house aimlessly. I switch on the Atwater-Kent. I switch it off again. I do not know what to do with myself. I pet Bozo sleeping by the kitchen stove. He opens his eyes and wags a lazy tail. I think of Arnie and the fellows. I decide to take a walk.

I leash the dog, lock up the house and we go out.

The sky is clear and the weather is nice and mild. We have had a pretty good winter so far.

I find Arnie, Charlie Ding Dong and another kid I do not know standing in front of the poolroom. Arnie gives me the glad-hand greeting.

"Harry! H'ya, keed?"

I say hello to Arnie and Ding Dong. I give the new kid a curious look. He returns it.

Arnie says, "Harry meet Sid. He's new around. He just moved into the neighborhood a couple of weeks ago."

"Hey," I say, "what happened with you guys when I saw you running out of Namn's Christmas Eve?"

Arnie laughs. "The bulls was on our ass."

"Catch you?"

"Hell no, man! Friggin' bulls . . ."

Ding Dong laughs. "All them creeps in that store to steal from, Arnie's got to pick out a lady bull to clip!"

"Aw, knock it off or I'll dump you!" Arnie angrily tells him.

"What else you been up to besides petty thievery?" I ask.

He winks at me. "I'm starting to get that little mob together I was telling you about. What's doing with you?"

"My father's home again," I say. "He came back."

"No kiddin'? Well, what d'you know, what d'you know. To stay?"

"Yeah. I quit the W.P.A. He doesn't want me to work on it."

"Good for you. Your old man wasn't such a bad guy—except for leaving your old lady, off and on, I mean."

"Yeah, I guess he's okay. He treats me pretty swell since he came back."

This new kid, Sidney, acts restless, as if he has got to go to the toilet in a very bad way.

"What the hell is taking Big Nasty so long?!" he asks.

"Take it easy," Arnie tells him. "Maybe he run into trouble."

"What trouble is stealing a gun off his old man when his old man ain't even home? Come on, let's go to the show or something and come back later."

Arnie does not even look at him. "We wait," he says and spits.

"What's coming off?" I ask.

"We gonna pull something if we can get hold of a gun. Big Nasty's old man has one stashed somewhere in his house. He went to look. Wanna come in with us, Harry? You got real balls. I sure would like to have you with us, keed."

"You mean a holdup?"

"Yeah."

I whistle. "I don't know . . . I don't know. That's pretty hot stuff to fool around with."

"Sure, it is. But if you hit the right place you get the big money."

Sidney cuts in. "You got the joint cased?"

"I didn't even pick out a joint yet," Arnie tells him.

"Then what the hell we waitin' around for? Let's get going."

Arnie lets out a heavy sigh and looks bored.

"Look, Sidney, you been around here a couple weeks and you ain't learned nothing yet. I don't know what kind of a mob you come from over in Ocean Hill, but with me everything's got to be figured out one thing at a time. Now, the first thing is to get a gun—"

"But jeez, we don't even got a joint to take!" Sidney complains.

"Can you pull a hold-up without a gun?"

"Some guys do."

Arnie spits, disgusted. "Some *jerks* do! What if the mark calls your bluff and all you got is a cap pistol? What you gonna do then?"

"Run outa there."

"And if the mark's got a gun you get it right in the back—bang! You stupid jerk, ya! That musta been some bunch of knuckleheads you was running with over in Ocean Hill!"

Sidney looks hurt. "We did all right," he says with pride.

"How many times you been out on a holdup?" Arnie challenges him.

"Twice."

"How many times you get caught?"

"Well—twice."

Arnie turns away from Sidney in disgust. He has a look of smugness. He closes his eyes, leans back against the poolroom window and spits through his teeth. "You see, Sidney, it's just like I been telling you—the first thing is to get the piece."

Ding Dong bends over to pet Bozo.

"H'ya, little pup. Say, ain't this a new mutt you got here, Harry?"

"Yeah."

Arnie says, "You know what kind of dog that is? That's a pure-blooded 'justa soon.'" He says this and waits.

I look at him. I wonder where he has heard it.

Ding Dong bites. "A *'justa soon'*?"

"Yeah—he'd justa soon eat as to shit!"

They all laugh.

"That's an old joke," I tell them because I am peeved.

Ding Dong asks, "What happens to your other dog, Harry?"

"Somebody stole him," I say.

"Who?"

"I don't know. I came home one day and found him gone."

"How do you know somebody lifts him? Maybe he run off."

"No. When a dog likes you, he sticks with you. He won't run off. Next to your mother, a dog is your best friend."

Arnie grins. "Harry sure likes dogs. Ever since I can remember, Harry's got a dog."

"They're loyal," I say. "That's why I like them. They never go back on you for nothing or nobody."

"I go for dogs, but I ain't a nut on 'em. You're a nut on 'em, Harry, keed."

"Some people go for cats, I go for dogs, that's all."

Sidney says, "I go for broads. Give me a nice fat-ass broad any day, and you can have all the dogs and cats in the world. I don't go for nothing I can't eat or screw."

They all laugh.

Arnie says, "I don't like cats at all."

"Me, nudder," Ding Dong says. "But I respect them. A cat shows me respect, I got to respect him, too."

"I don't trust them," Arnie goes on. "A cat is a sharp operator. You ever notice the way they sneak along alleys and streets? They're always on the make, ready for any kind of action. He just slinks along, shooting the angles. A cat comes and goes, and you don't even know he's been he's so quick and quiet. He has you made before you can make him. Anytime you spot a cat, you can bet money on it that the cat made you first. I'm telling you, a cat is a real cool operator."

"A cat is a very clean animal," I put in.

"A cat's got a lot of respect for hisself, too," Ding Dong says. "Anybody ud ever seen a cat get his hump?"

Nobody has.

"That's what I mean," he continues. "Everybody's seen a dog do it. A dog takes his hump where he finds it—anywheres. Even in Macy's window if he gets a chance. But a cat—he's got more self-respect. He cons the broad cat into a pad to get his hump."

Sidney says, "Balls! I wouldn't give you a nickel for a cat, no matter where he takes his hump. Come on, Arnie, let's do something. Big Nasty got himself lost."

Arnie is not listening. A big, beautiful convertible pulls up to the curb and stops. He is watching it intently. A tall man in a tan camel's-hair coat gets out of the car. He is sharp from the top of his brown fedora to the tips of his patent-leather shoes. Arnie moves away from us and goes over to the car. He stands there staring in awe as the man locks the door of the car.

**113**

"Gee—" he finally says. "Gee, hello, Mr. Pinkwise."

The man turns slowly, just glances at Arnie and looks across the street at Louis the Owner's barbershop.

"Hello, kid," he says.

"Gee, I'm sure glad to see you back, Mr. Pinkwise. You look great, real great. It's been almost a month, ain't it? Well, it sure is good to see you again, anyway."

"Sure, kid." The man just stands there fingering his car keys and staring across the street. "You know if the Owner's over there?"

"Mr. Varga? Yes sir, he's in there. I saw him myself go in only a couple hours ago. Gee, it sure is good to see—"

The man moves away, running his hand playfully through Arnie's hair as he goes. He disappears into the barbershop. Arnie just stands there staring. The three of us go over to him.

"What's the matter?" Sid asks. "Who was that?"

Arnie seems not to hear him. He looks at the car with gleaming eyes.

"Look at that, boy, look at that Caddy!"

"Yeah, it's a beaut, all right," Sid agrees. "Who is that guy?"

Arnie moves his hand along the fender of the car lovingly. He looks at the dirt on his fingers.

"It could stand a good wiping," he says. He turns to Ding Dong. "Run inside the poolroom and see if Nucky's got an old rag. I'm gonna give the car a good wiping."

Ding Dong goes into the poolroom. Sid looks at Arnie in confusion.

"What the hell you wanna fool around here for?" he asks.

Arnie rubs his hand along the car as if he is petting a dog. "What a baby! What a terrific baby!"

"Balls!" Sid curses. "It seems to me if we're looking to pull something, we ought to be out casing a joint instead of fartin' around some guy's car!"

"I told you before, Sidney, you got to do one thing at a time and the first thing is to get the piece."

"Okay, we get the gun first! Jeez, you sound like a guy who's pulled forty, fifty good holdups!" Suddenly Sid looks at Arnie with suspicion. "Say, how many stick-ups you really pulled, Arnie?"

**114**

"I ain't never pulled no stick-up before."

Sid blows up. "Well, where the hell you get off shootin' off how to do it?! If you ain't never pulled no stick-up, how the hell you know your way is better than mine?!"

"Because I know that my way is the way *he'd* do it."

"Who? The guy belongs to this car? And who the hell is he?"

Arnie looks at Sid as if he is the dumbest guy in the world. "Just Abie Pinkwise—the Bug."

Sid's eyes get big as saucers. His mouth pops open. "Abie the Bug?" he whispers.

"Abie the Bug, Sidney. That's all who this here guy is—just Abie (the Bug) Pinkwise!"

"Jeez!"

Sid backs quickly away from the car, as if it has suddenly become alive and deadly.

**H**AP HAS BROUGHT MA A SECOND-HAND PIANO. The moving men had to hoist it through the window because the halls were too narrow to bring it up the stairs. It cost Hap ten bucks just to have it moved in!

Ma is delirious over the piano. She polishes it every five minutes and treats it just like a baby. She sits there in the living room and sings and plays it all day long. Ma plays the piano pretty good, much better than I expected, but she does not sing as good as she thinks she can. There seems to be only two things on her mind these days, and they are the piano and Hap. She does not pay any attention to me or anything else. I go and come now as I please. She does not ask where, why, or what of me any more. It is just as well and I guess it is all in my favor. Right now she is playing and singing "Because," which must be her favorite, because she has been yelling it all week long and I am damn sick and tired of ". . . you speak to me in accents sweet." So I get the hell out of there in a hurry.

I go around to the poolroom. Arnie is there. He is just finishing up a game with Big Nasty.

"Hey, Harry, keed. Stick around. I want you to go somewhere with me."

I sit down on the bench and wait until the game is over. Arnie pulls me aside.

"I'm gonna clip a car for the Bug. Want to come along?"

"What the hell—I got nothing else to do."

He slaps me on the back. "Come on."

We take a ride on the Myrtle Avenue el. On the way, Arnie tells me what it is all about.

"The Bug wants a car for a getaway or something. They always use a stolen car for a job so the cops can't trace it. Then we put different plates on the hot car."

"Why do we have to go so far to steal a car?"

Arnie sneers at me like I am awful dumb. "Never outa the same neighborhood you might use it in. Maybe the real owner spots it. But this here particular car I'm going after has been cased already. I been casing it over a week."

"I didn't know you had to case a car."

"You don't have to, but I do it—when I can. If the Bug ain't in a hurry for the car, that gives me time to look around. It's better that way. Then you can pick out a car that the owner only uses it once in a while. That way he won't miss it right away, and the bulls won't be on the make for it. But we always take out double insurance, anyway, by putting stolen plates from another car on it."

"Man, you're pretty sharp," I say. "You're really moving up in the world!"

"Sure. Why don't you come on up with me, Harry?"

"What do you mean?"

"I mean there's room for a couple of smart, young guys like you and me in the Varga mob. The Bug told me himself. He said,

'Get yourself a couple of good Joes, guys you can trust and know how to keep their mouths shut, and I'll throw a couple of good things your way.' That's what he told me. He don't want dopes. He wants young guys who know the score. Sid, Big Nasty, Ding Dong—they're okay. They're tough enough and all that shit, but they're short in the brains department. Now, take you, Harry, you got almost everything. You're big and husky, you got balls, you know how to keep your mouth shut and you're smart. You even got a little high-school education. Why, the Bug and Louis Varga himself never even finished grammar school. So what do you say, Harry? Why don't me and you team up together and work our way in. I got to have a partner and I rather have you than anybody else."

I think about it a minute. "What are the couple of good things the Bug will throw our way?"

"Things like this—taking a car, getting rid of a hot one—odd jobs. But if we do enough of them and do them good, we're in for a promotion. The Bug told me all this in person. They might give us a concession here and there."

"What kind of concession?"

"There's all kinds of angles," he says, a little impatient with me. "Shylocking, slot machines, maybe some whores—" Suddenly he looks out the window as the train stops. "Come on, we get off here."

I follow Arnie down the el steps to the street. Quickly we walk a few blocks and Arnie stops in front of a drugstore.

"Wait right here for me," he says. "Make like you're looking in the window. I'll bring the car around and pick you up."

I make a show of looking in the window and Arnie disappears around the corner. I do not have to wait long. I hear my name called. I turn to see Arnie beckoning to me from a Ford with the door open and the motor running. I get in quick and we drive off.

"Where to now?" I ask.

"The drop," he says.

"The *what*?"

Arnie looks at me and shakes his head. "Harry, keed, I see right now I got a lot to teach you. But you'll catch on quick because you're smart. The drop is where we stash the hot car until it's needed, or where you work it over, or change the plates. In this case the drop is Louis Varga's garage over on Third Avenue."

"Maybe I won't make such a good partner, after all. I'm pretty dumb about these things."

"You ain't dumb. You just didn't know. You think I was borned knowing what a drop is or how to take a car? I learned from being in jail and from my old man and from the Bug. You'll learn, too, and quick because you're gonna have an ace teacher—me."

Arnie pulls into the garage on Third Avenue. The attendant, in greasy coveralls, comes up to us.

"This is for the Bug," Arnie says. "He wants it on ice."

"I know, I know," the attendant says as if he is offended. "Take it on in the back and park near the Chevy."

Arnie does so. We get out. The attendant comes over with a couple of license plates.

"You gonna put 'em on," he asks Arnie, "or do I gotta?"

Arnie thinks a moment, then he says, "No, I better do it myself and be sure. I don't want no slip-ups with the Bug."

"Who does?" the attendant says and walks away.

Arnie changes the plates on the car. He gives the original ones to the attendant and tells him to break them up.

As we leave Arnie says hopefully, "Maybe I get to drive it in the getaway . . . *could be.*"

We pause a moment in front of the barbershop.

Arnie says, "Come on in with me. I want the Bug to get a look at you. But keep your mouth shut."

I follow him in. Two barbers in white jackets are standing around talking. There are several customers, some sitting and reading, others just talking. No one is getting a shave or haircut. Everyone quickly looks us over as we enter, then just as quickly ignores us. I wait by the door as Arnie goes all the way in the back to a sharply dressed guy I recognize as the Bug. Arnie whispers something to him. He shakes his head and gives something to Arnie. Arnie smiles and whispers something again and, at the same time, motions his head toward me. The Bug looks over at me with a stone face. He looks me over from head to foot. No expression. I might just as well be the hands on a clock and he is not early or late. Finally he shakes his head slowly up and down and says something to Arnie that looks like okay, and Arnie comes back and we go out. Arnie is smiling.

"I told him you're my partner now. Is that okay?"

"I don't know," I say.

"This make a difference?" he asks, putting something in my hand. "That's your cut."

I look at what is in my hand. It is a ten-dollar bill. It makes a difference.

We laugh and go into Nucky Johnson's for a game of pool.

## 2

Arnie teaches me how to drive a car and I get my license.

He teaches me how to get into a locked car and how to start the motor without a key. He was right. He is an ace teacher.

It is after supper and me, Hap and Ma are in the living room. Ma is at the piano, banging and yelling away at "Love's Old Sweet Song." Hap is sitting beside me on the sofa with a sour face, puffing hard on a cigarette. I am trying real hard to concentrate on a Jack London book Hap has given me. All of a sudden, I cannot stand the noise any more and decide to go over to the poolroom. As soon as I stand up Hap stops me.

"Say, Harold, there's a good fight over at the Arena tonight. What do you say you and me go over?"

"Sure!" I say, jumping at the chance.

The piano playing suddenly stops. Ma turns around slowly on the stool. She looks offended.

"The prize fights?" she asks. "Why, I thought you were enjoying my music."

"Sure, we enjoy your music, Kate, but have a heart! We hear your singing every night, but a fight like this comes along only once in a blue moon."

"Listen to it on the radio," she says.

"But we want to *see* the fight." He goes over to the piano and pinches her chin. "Besides, if we just wanted to *listen* to something, we'd much rather listen to your lovely voice than an old fight."

This crap makes Ma feel better. Hap sure knows how to put her on. But it disgusts me the way she melts all over the floor when he turns on the juice.

"Well then, take me, too," Ma says with a pout.

"But Katie, dear, this is *our* night out—father and son. You remember your promise—at least two nights a month for me and Harold."

"Oh, go on, then!" she says testily, turning back to the keyboard.

Hap takes her up on it quickly.

As we put on our coats in the kitchen we hear her mumbling in the living room: "Two grown men and I have to be left all alone in the house. Suppose something happens? The only time I get a little pleasure and they want to go running—"

"Come on," Hap says.

We hurry out and down the stairs. On the street, Hap sighs heavily.

"I never knew anybody could murder a song the way your mother can," he says with a shudder.

It is funny. I feel the same way he does about Ma's singing. I do not like it one bit, either, but I resent his criticizing her. Suddenly I want to defend her.

"I've heard worse singing," I say.

Hap looks at me with astonishment. "You *have?*" he asks. "Where?"

"Places. Even on the radio," I lie.

He shrugs. "Maybe so, maybe so. I guess it's all a matter of taste. Come on, let's take a cab."

We hail a cab at the corner and Hap says, "Broadway Arena."

We have good seats and it is a hell of a fight from the first bell. Mickey Bello, a good, fast-moving boxer and counter-puncher, against Joey Rolf, a wade-in slugger with knockouts in both hands.

It is the third round and the house is in an uproar. Rolf has Bello down for an eight count and bleeding over the eye. Bello gets up and onto his bicycle to stall until his head clears, but Rolf will not give him a chance. He is crowding right after him, swinging wildly, sometimes missing, sometimes connecting, even stumbling, but every second right on top of Bello. Blood is being splattered all over the ring and the fighter's trunks. Bello is bleeding now so badly they will stop the fight if Rolf does not knock him out quickly or the bell does not ring. I am on my feet with the rest of the crowd, screaming for the kill. I am unaware of Hap until I feel a tugging at my leg. I look around and Hap is still seated, bent over as if he is in pain. There is fear and distress on his face.

"Harold, quick! Get me out of here—please!"

"But the fight—"

"*Please!*"

I do not understand. "What's the matter?" I ask, taking him by the arm.

"Just get me out, Harold!"

Quickly I help him up and lead him down the aisle through the screaming and shouting mob. As we go through the Arena door, I take a quick look back and glimpse Bello still eluding Rolf.

We reach the hall outside and Hap suddenly vomits on the floor. I jump back quickly so that it does not get on my pants. Hap's pants are full of it. A guard stationed in the hall rushes over.

"What's the matter? What's the matter?"

"I'll—be—all right in a minute," Hap says between retching. "Just—where is the toilet?"

"Take him in there," the guard tells me, pointing to a door across the hall.

I take Hap in. He vomits again into the john. He stays there, bent over until finally he is through.

"I'm all right now," he says panting. "You go back in and watch the fight."

"No," I tell him. "I came with you, I stick with you."

He looks at me kind of surprised. He smiles and pats my shoulder. He goes to the sink and begins to rinse out his mouth and wash his face. I get some tissue for him and he dries his face and hands. We get some more tissue, wet it and clean the mess off his trousers.

Hap says, "I need some air. You go watch the rest of the fight. I'll wait outside for you."

But as we come out of the toilet we know the fight is over because the noisy crowd is filing out of the Arena, laughing and talking about the fight. I am disappointed as hell and angry with Hap. I feel that he has given me something and stolen it back again.

The guard comes up to us. "How is he now?"

"Okay," I say. "Who won the fight?"

"Bello by a knockout in the fourth. It was a dinger of a fight. What a comeback the kid made in the fourth round."

This makes me angrier, but I smother it quickly. Oh, well, what is a fight to get upset about? Besides, it is not Hap's fault getting sick. We go out.

We do not talk. Hap looks ashamed and now I feel embarrassed for him.

He says, "Let's have a drink."

We go into a bar near the Arena. We drink. Nothing is said. Finally Hap says, "I'm sorry I made you miss the fight, Harold, I swear to God. But I'll make it up to you, you'll see. It was that damn beefsteak we had for supper. It was too rare. Rare beefsteak always upsets my stomach. I'm sorry."

I notice that he fidgets and tries to avoid my eyes as he talks.

"That's all right, Hap. It wasn't your fault."

Now he looks me right in the eyes. There is pain on his face.

"Harold, that's a lie. It wasn't the beefsteak. I guess if we're going to get along like we want to, we've got to be truthful to each other. It was the blood that made me sick. I don't know why, but I can't stand the sight of blood, Harold. I'm sorry."

He looks so miserable about it. I feel sorry for him.

"That's nothing, Hap. Lots of guys faint at the sight of blood."

His face beams suddenly. "Then you know about it—that there are people like this?"

"Sure."

"And you don't mind? I mean, because I can't stand the sight of blood, you don't mind?"

"No. Why should I mind?"

He smiles and puts his arm around me. "I'm glad, Harold. Damn glad! I was afraid you might get the idea that—Hell, I'm just as much man as the next guy, but it's just that little . . ." He takes his arm from my shoulder and turns to his drink. He looks at me out of the corner of his eye. "I guess I'd better tell you I hate prize fights, too."

"Then why did you come, Hap?"

He looks at me full-faced. "For you, Harold."

"For *me?*"

"For you."

"But I could've come by myself. . . ."

He opens his mouth to say something but it does not come out. He frowns and shakes his head.

"You don't understand, you don't understand."

Somewhere in the back of the bar, a woman laughs mockingly and I want to find that mouth and put my fist into it.

**I** HANG AROUND THE POOLROOM most of the time lately. I like it more and more. The fellows all like me. I feel more at home here than I do in my own house. Some of the guys have done time in jail, and all of them are hustlers of one kind or another. Everybody is on the make for a quick dollar. They all look up to Arnie and me because of Arnie's connection with Abie the Bug. They make room for us when we strut in, and whenever Arnie speaks, everyone else shuts up. I do not talk much. I would rather listen. I just like to sit around and listen to the fat, lazy pool balls blob one another as they roll around the table. I like to hear the stories the guys tell, too, about jail life, and the jobs they have pulled, and how to do this and that. I am learning a lot from Arnie, but I also learn a lot more just sitting around listening to these guys.

Because of the headline fight last night, I feel I have something special to say because I am the only one among them who was at the Arena. Everybody is interested and quiets down to listen. I tell them about the fight. (Not about Hap, though!) I tell them how it starts off fast with Rolf coming out at the bell, swinging for a quick knockout. And Bello, counter-punching and dancing in and out, in and out. I tell them how Bello is cut over both eyes and how the blood is splashing around. Then gradually I notice that no one is listening to me any more. All eyes are turned on the door behind me. All is quiet. I look around. It is Abie the Bug. He has just got the door of the poolroom cracked open a little bit while he searches the faces in the room. He spots who he is looking for.

"Arnie," he says. "Come here, kid." He turns to go away again.

Arnie takes his jacket off the hook and starts out. The Bug turns back to the doorway again.

The Bug says, "Bring your partner with you."

Arnie grins and beckons me with a move of his head. I get my coat, too. We strut out together. All the guys are watching, bug-eyed, with their mouths open. Damn, I feel important!

The Bug is standing in the doorway of the house next to the poolroom. He has on a dark, gray coat with the collar pulled up. We go over to him, Arnie first. I notice that I am as tall as the Bug, which also makes me feel good.

"Listen, kid," the Bug says, "do me a favor."

"You name it and it's done, Mr. Pinkwise," Arnie says.

The Bug looks at me. This time his eyes are friendly and he has a little smile on his face. "What's your name, kid?"

"Harry."

"Okay," he says. "Pleased to meet you, Harry. Arnie tells me you got plenty of moxie. . . ."

"I'm not scared of anything if that's what you mean."

He laughs. "That's what I mean!"

"He's got balls and he's got a head on his shoulders, too," Arnie says proudly.

"Glad to hear," the Bug tells him. "Listen, you guys know how to do a shlumping?"

"Sure," Arnie says quickly.

"Well, there's a guy I want you to take care of for me. He's in deep with my bank and he's slow paying up. Don't hurt him serious.

Just shlump him enough to make him want to get it up in a hurry. Make sure he understands he'll get worse if he don't. Okay?"

"Okay," Arnie says eagerly. "Who is the bum?"

"You know the candy store next to the coal man on Johnson Street near Prince?"

"I think so—but what's the number?"

"I don't know the number. What am I—a mailman? He's a big, fat, bald-headed guy. His name is Fischetti but they call him Fish."

"Oh, Fish! Yeah, I know that guy—yeah!"

"Okay. Wait till nobody's around you shouldn't get made. Shove him into his back room there. I want you to go over there right now. And, remember, not too much, but just enough."

Arnie hesitates a little. "But—ah—suppose he squawks to the bulls. He knows me and—"

"He won't squawk if he knows what's good for him. But even if he does—don't worry. The Bug will look out for you two guys. The bulls won't lay a glove on you. Go on, scram now. And, remember, this is your big chance to show me how good you can operate on a deal like this."

"Don't worry," Arnie assures him. "You want us to come right back and tell you how we make out?"

The Bug frowns. "I won't be in Brooklyn until tonight. See me in the barbershop around nine tonight."

The Bug gets in his Caddy and drives off. Arnie and me put our heads together. I am eager and excited.

"We watch until the store is empty," Arnie begins. "Then I'll take him in the back while you lock the store door."

"No," I say. "I'll take him in the back. I'm bigger and stronger than you. He might give you trouble alone."

He thinks about it. "Okay, you take him while I lock the door. But don't start shlumping him until I get back there with you. I got to tell him why he's getting it while his head is still clear."

"I think we ought to get Ding Dong to go in the store first and make sure nobody is lurking around. Then Ding Dong can stand outside, just in case."

"Good idea," Arnie agrees. "Come on."

I call Ding Dong out of the poolroom and the three of us head for Johnson Street.

"What is happening?" Ding Dong asks.

"Just do like we tell you and keep your mouth shut," Arnie says.

"Sure, Arnie, you know me, you know me."

We reach the candy store. We walk past first to see who is inside. There are two kids buying candy. We cannot see Fischetti. We wait in front of the coal man's place. The kids run out of the store with their candy.

Arnie says to Ding Dong, "Go inside the store and buy a nickel's-worth of gumdrops. Case the joint, then come out and tell us." Ding Dong hesitates.

"What's the matter?" Arnie asks.

"I don't got no nickel," Ding Dong says.

Arnie hands him a dime. Ding Dong goes into the store. In a little while he comes out chewing on some candy.

"I can't see nobody in there but a fat guy with a cue ball for a head," he says.

"Okay," Arnie says. "When me and Harry get inside and close the door, you stand outside in front. Anybody wants to come in the store, you tell them the guy went out to eat or something."

"Okay."

We walk in. The fat guy is sitting on a stool behind the counter with a big cigar in his mouth. He jumps up as Arnie begins to close the door.

"Hey, what're you do? What's goin' on?"

I reach across the counter, grab him by the collar and pull him toward the back of the store. He is confused. He does not know what is happening.

"Wait a minute—wait a minute. . . ."

"Your name Fischetti?" I ask quietly.

"Yeah, I'm Fischetti but—"

I pull him into a darkened room in the back. He struggles hard against me but I handle him easy. I hear the lock on the front door click and Arnie comes quickly toward us. All of a sudden, the guy gets the idea. Terror whitens his face and the cigar pops out of his mouth.

"The Bug! Oh, please! Now, wait a minute, boys. I pay! Tell the Bug—"

Arnie comes into the room and slams Fischetti across the face.

"Shut up, you bum!" he says. "We're gonna teach you to keep up with the bank."

All at once I do not know what is happening to me. Fischetti's face seems to be changing, and I am frantic to throw fists into it before it does. I push Arnie back. I throw punches, punches, punches, so fast, so furious I cannot see. Everything spins. I am in a whirl of excitement, punching, punching. Moans. Grunts. Screams. A body moves, falls, only nothing must keep me from punching, punching. I kick, claw and punch.

Suddenly it is over.

I am kneeling over the man who is on the floor, moaning and bleeding. Arnie is pulling me off him.

"Harry, for Christ's sake, that's enough!"

I get up. Arnie quickly pulls me along through the store. I am groggy. My face feels hot and flushed. Outside. The fresh air hits me like a welcome splash of cool water. Arnie hurries me along the street, Ding Dong tagging behind.

"Jesus, Harry," Arnie says, "you could've killed him!"

I stop. I look at Arnie. I am confused and frightened.

"What is it, Arnie?"

He looks at me as if he is afraid of me—as if he has never seen me before. He shakes his head.

"You're a *tiger*, Harry. Goddamn it, I never seen such a tiger!"

"Is he all right?"

"Who? Fish? I guess so. He was still moaning when we left."

I get such a racing, eager feeling in me. I want to do something, do something! I do not know what.

"Do we go back to the poolroom?" I ask.

"No. We better make ourself scarce around the neighborhood until tonight. Come on, let's go to a movie. Maybe we can pick up a couple of broads."

Broads!

\* \* \*

We go to the New United Theater on Myrtle and Hudson. We get three seats together in the balcony. We smoke. My eyes wander from the screen. I go to the toilet. It stinks and guys are standing around in there watching each other. I come out of there. I go back to the balcony, but Arnie has already picked up a girl and she is sitting in my seat.

"Get up, Ding Dong, and let Harry sit down," Arnie says.

"And where I sit?!" Ding Dong wants to know.

Arnie slaps him. "There's a seat behind me. Get going."

Ding Dong comes out and goes in the row behind. I move in and take the seat. Arnie gets busy right away with his hand up the girl's dress. She jumps up suddenly. She slaps at Arnie, misses, then runs out of the balcony. Arnie looks at me surprised.

He shrugs. "What the hell got into her?"

Ding Dong leans over with a grin and says, "Your hand."

We watch the picture. It is about horse racing and I hate race-track movies. They are all the same. How can they be different? You know whose horse will win the big one. Restless, restless, restless.

"Let's go," I say. "This stinks."

"But we just come in," Arnie protests.

"Okay, okay," I tell him and settle down to stick it out.

I close my eyes. I doze. . . .

The bird comes fluttering before my gaze. I reach out greedily and grasp it in my hands. . . .

I wake with a violent tremor! I am startled.

"What's the matter?"

I look. It is Arnie. Oh, yes, we are in the movies.

"Are you okay, Harry?" he asks.

"Sure, I'm okay."

I feel terrible. I must go to the toilet again and clean.

"Mind my seat," I tell Arnie.

I go to the toilet. The guys are still standing around in there. To hell with them. Let them watch.

We come out of the movie. It is seven thirty. We still have time to kill before we see the Bug. I tell Arnie and Ding Dong I will meet them at the poolroom in an hour. I go home for supper.

Hap and Ma are already eating when I come in.

I sit down. Ma makes a face and gets up to fix my plate.

"Late again for supper," she says. "Every single day this week!"

"I'm sorry, Ma."

"I haven't seen you since this morning. Where have you been all day?"

Hap stops eating, looks at her. "Katie, leave the boy alone. First, you said he hung around the house too much, now you're complaining because he's gone all day. What do you want him to do?"

Ma puts the food in front of me. "I don't care if he goes and comes—but, at least, I'd like to know where he is half the time."

"What is he supposed to do—run in every fifteen minutes and report to you?"

Uh-huh. They are not so lovey-dovey anymore. It is the bickering again. That is always the way it begins. I eat in silence and do not look at either one of them.

"Is it wrong for me to want to know where my son has been all day, I'd like to know?!"

"No, Kate, no. But—"

"I wouldn't be surprised if he is hanging around with those hoodlums on Hudson Avenue again."

"Hoodlums? *Harold*? No, no, Kate. Harold is too smart for that. He knows crime doesn't pay."

*Crime doesn't pay*! I think. Who says so? I got ten bucks just for riding with Arnie in a stolen car. Abie the Bug rides around in a great big Cadillac, and I hear he owns more than twenty suits of clothes. *Crime doesn't pay*! It is a dream world they are living in. But I keep quiet and finish my supper.

I ask, "Anything you want me to do, Ma, before I go out again?"

"Out *again*? I should think you've had enough of the streets for one day!"

"I'm sorry, Ma, but I have to meet somebody."

"A girl?" she asks, fixing her eyes on me.

"Sure," Hap says. "Why not a girl? Can't he meet a girl if he wants to?!"

"Of course, he can. I didn't mean that. I just wanted to know. All right, Harold, wash up the dishes and you can go."

"No," Hap says. "You run along, Harold. I'll wash the dishes."

Ma does not like this arrangement. I can tell by the way she looks, but I get out of the house quick before she can think of something else to spite me with.

It is after nine o'clock when I reach the poolroom. Only Arnie is there. Ding Dong is not around. We start across the street to the barbershop. The Bug's car is parked at the curb.

"He's back now," Arnie says.

I stop at the door of the barbershop. "I'll wait for you out here," I tell him.

He shrugs and says okay. He goes in. I watch through the plateglass window. The Bug is standing all the way in the back. Besides the three barbers, there are four others guys in the shop. The Bug suddenly sees Arnie and lets out a big laugh. He puts his arm around Arnie and asks him something. Arnie starts talking excitedly. The Bug lets out with another big laugh and pats Arnie on the shoulder. All the other men in the shop crowd around Arnie and the Bug, inquisitive-like. The Bug explains something to them. Now, everyone in the shop is laughing. One of the guys asks Arnie something. Arnie grins and points to the window. It comes to me he is pointing at me. All eyes turn. Suddenly I am embarrassed. I do not know what is going on, but now I know it concerns me because several of the men saunter over to the window and look out at me, look me over. They are smiling . One of them winks at me and they move away again.

Arnie comes out of the shop, smiling. He has some keys in his hand.

"Come on," he says, starting across the street.

"Where to?"

"The Bug is taking us for a little ride in his Caddy. He says wait for him in the car. He wants to talk to us."

Arnie opens the door and we climb in the back.

"What was going on in there?" I ask.

"I don't know for sure myself. The Bug is gonna tell us about it. All I know is what we did sure went over big with the people who count. Especially you, Harry. All those guys in there wanted to know who the big, curly-haired guy was and where was he. That's when I pointed to you at the window."

I am surprised—and pleased. "No kidding!"

"No kidding. The Bug will give us the knockdown. Here, he gave me forty bucks. Here's your twenty."

I pocket the nice, juicy twenty. *Crime doesn't pay*, says Hap! Twenty bucks for a five-minute job. On W.P.A. I worked hard a whole week for less. Why do parents tell their kids such Goddamn lies?

The Bug comes across the street and climbs in the car. He is still smiling. He takes the keys from Arnie and starts the car up. We pull out.

He glances back at me. "What's your name again, kid?"

"Harry."

"Harry, huh? Well, Harry, that was some shlumping job you did today."

*"This is a tiger!"* Arnie says.

"Why, you're the talk of the town, Harry. What did you do to him?"

I shrug.

Arnie quickly speaks up. "You shoulda seen him, Mr. Pinkwise. He's a tiger. He was all over the bum just like a tiger!"

"A big cat, huh? Well, after the shlumping, Fish comes running around to my bagman with his face all swollen and his eyes black and blue. He's so scared he's shivering in his shoes. He comes with a box full of money—every cent he owes—and more yet! He begs us not to send Harry after him no more. He says the big guy with the curls. He gives you a name, Harry. What did he call you? Yeah— a gorilla with a saint's face. That's what he calls you." He laughs and shakes his head. "My bagman says he never saw a guy so scared. Even though he's all clean with us now, he gives us an extra hundred bucks. This is insurance money, he says, against us sending you after him in case he gets another loan and falls behind. He says if he ever sees you coming after him again, he'll jump off a roof."

We laugh. I have a strong feeling of pride.

"That ain't the half of it," the Bug continues. "The news gets around fast. Guys who are behind with the bank come running in left and right to get squared, or if they ain't got it they beg for more time and please don't send nobody around—meaning the big, curly-haired boy. What do you think of that?"

"I think we done a good job," Arnie says.

"What do you think, Harry?"

I shrug. I try to sound tough and indifferent. "You told us what to do—make him want to pay up. We went out and did it, that's all."

The Bug gives me a curious look. He pulls the car over to the curb and stops. He rests an arm on the back of the seat and looks at Arnie.

"Arnie, hop out of the car and go get me a pack of Old Jack cigars."

"Okay," Arnie says, getting out. "Say, where's a candy store around here?"

"Find one. Around the corner somewheres. Take your time."

Arnie goes off. The Bug takes a midget cigar out of his pocket, lights it and smiles back at me.

"Arnie split the forty with you?" he asks.

"Sure," I tell him.

He goes in his pocket and hands me a ten-dollar bill.

"Here," he says. "This is just for you."

I try to be calm taking it. "Thanks. I'll split it with Arnie."

"But it's just for you alone. You don't have to split. It's a bonus. What Arnie don't know won't hurt him."

"Thanks, but I'll split just the same. We made a deal. We're partners. We split everything down the middle. Whether he knows about it or not, I stick to it. I don't go back on my word."

The Bug studies me a moment with a kind of half-smile on his lips. I can see that he is impressed. Now he shrugs. "Well, it's your bonus. Do what you want with it." He flicks an ash off his cigar into the built-in ash tray. He takes a look at me again. "You know, for all your balls, you're a loyal son of a bitch, too, ain't you?"

"Mr. Pinkwise, I'm this way. I will not call a guy a bastard behind his back if I haven't got balls enough to call him one to his face. If I give my word I keep my word. And another thing—I would rather cross myself than betray a friend who trusts me."

The Bug grins and offers me his hand. "Then that includes me, Harry, because something tells me we're gonna be good friends."

I take his hand eagerly. I say, "That would be the greatest honor in the world to me, Mr. Pinkwise."

"You," the Bug says, "*you* can call me Abie."

We smile at each other. We understand. I feel like I am in the company of royalty.

Arnie comes back. He leans against the window of the car with a worried look on his face.

"Gee, Mr. Pinkwise, the candy stores I went in never even heard of them Old Jack cigars."

The Bug snorts. "Forget it, kid. I had some in my pocket all the time and didn't know it." He starts the motor up. "Get in."

Arnie climbs into the back seat with me. The Bug turns the car around and we shoot on back to the neighborhood.

**I**T IS A WARM, SPRING AFTERNOON. The house is quiet. After lunch, I lie across my bed, puffing a cigarette, wondering what the day will bring. Arnie wants me to go out on a holdup with him. I do not know about this. Though he knows all the ropes, Arnie is not my idea of a very bright customer. And there is something about him I do not trust. Ding Dong is a complete jerk, but I would trust him in a minute quicker than I would Arnie. I will look him up today. I want to find out exactly what he has in mind before I go sticking my neck out with him.

I crush out the cigarette and come out of my room. Before I

leave the house, I had better ask Ma if she wants me to run any errands or anything.

I go to the door of her room. She is lying on her back with her legs spread, taking a nap. I had better not wake her. Sweat rolls down her forehead. No wonder! It is stifling hot in her room with both windows closed. I tiptoe in the room and open both windows a little for her. Yes, that is much better. I toetip out again and go into the kitchen.

Omaha. Where is Omaha? Is it a state or a city? I know so little about the country. It is a wonder I ever got promoted in school at all. Omaha. Hell, I'll bet any little kid knows where it is on the map. I will look it up.

I go to my room and get an old geography book. I put it on the kitchen table and turn to a map of the United States.

Nebraska! There it is, Omaha, right in the middle of the country. I slam the book shut. Any fool should have known that without having to look it up. I am angry with myself for being so stupid.

I wonder if Ma is still asleep? I go back to her room and look in. Yes, she is still asleep. She has turned over onto her side now. The room is much cooler.

I get my jacket and go downstairs. I stand in the doorway, watching the people go by, wondering what I will do. I light a cigarette. I see a guy coming toward me with hands in his pockets, hat cocked to one side on his head. He looks about my age, but thinner. His suit is wrinkled and baggy, and his tieless white shirt is dirty. He is smiling at me. Do I know him? He looks very familiar. He comes straight up to me and holds out an unlit cigarette.

"Say, give's a light, will you?"

I hold my cigarette up and he presses his against it. I study his face as he puffs. Where have I seen him before?

"Thanks," he says. He stands beside me, grinning and puffing. Why doesn't he move on?

"How's tricks?" he asks.

"Can't complain," I tell him. "Haven't I seen you somewhere before?"

"Sure. You're Harry Odum."

"That's right. And you?"

**134**

"Madden. Name's Madden."

"Madden," I repeat, trying to recall. "I know that name. I once had a monitor named Madden."

"A *monitor?*"

"No, I mean a *foreman*. When I was on the W.P.A. I had a foreman with the name of Madden."

He laughs. "That wasn't me!"

"I know—but your face is so damn familiar."

"Don't you remember where we met?"

"No. Where?"

"It was a long, long time ago. We were both little kids. It was upstairs."

"Upstairs where? My house?"

"Yeah. You chased me out."

I think on it. *I have it!* "Say, were you that little fresh kid who had a message for my mother—and she was taking a bath?"

"That's me, kiddo!"

I laugh. "Well, what d'you know! You haven't changed much—still got that silly grin."

"You're the same, too."

"Say, what was that message you had for my mother? We never did find out."

"I didn't really have no message. I just said that. I was just a little crook out looking for angles. I wanted to get in some place. The door was open and nobody was around, so I just walked in. When you caught me, I had to give some excuse."

"But you tried to go in the bathroom where she was."

"Sure."

"What a fresh kid. Man, if I had caught you that day, you would have got one hell of an ass-whipping!"

"That's what I can't understand. Why did you want to do that?"

"You know *why*!"

"Just for wanting to look at a naked broad?"

I am shocked to anger. "Hey, now wait a minute, you bastard. Don't you talk that way about my mother. In the first place, she's no broad."

"Sure, she's a broad. Ain't she got a—"

I swing out, hitting him flush on the jaw. He goes sprawling onto the sidewalk. I stand over him with clenched fists. He holds his jaw and looks up at me.

"I'm sorry," he says. "I want to be your friend."

"If you want to be my friend don't talk that way about my mother!"

"Okay, Harry. I swear, I won't do it no more."

My anger goes. I step back and let him get up. He rubs his chin.

"Gee, you hit like Joe Louis!"

"Remember that the next time you want to get nasty with me."

"Sure, Harry. Well, I guess I'd better see you later. My jaw hurts too much to stand here."

Suddenly he takes off running down the street as if for dear life! I am surprised.

## 2

We eat our supper in silence. Ma and Hap are angry again and have not spoken to each other in two days.

Supper over, Ma begins to clear the dishes. I linger over a second cup of coffee. Hap picks his teeth. He looks as if he is worried about something. Ma leaves the room. Hap get up. He comes over to my chair and leans over my shoulder.

"Harry, when you finish, meet me downstairs in Prince Bar and Grill. I want to have a talk with you. Don't let on to your mother."

He takes his hat and goes. Now what is up? Has he found out about me flunkying for the Bug? So what? He cannot tell me what to do any more. But I am curious. Ma comes back into the kitchen.

"Where's your father?"

"Gone out."

"That man!"

She goes to wash the dishes in the sink. I finish my coffee. I take my jacket off the hook and pull it on. Ma looks around at me.

"Where are you going?"

"Just out."

"You, too? Eat and run, eat and run—that's all the both of you seem to know these days. You throw me away like an old rag. I'm nothing more than a drudge to the both of you."

"I won't be gone long, Ma. I promise you I'll—"

"Go! Go, then! This is the bed of nails I've made for myself."

I walk in and see Hap standing at the bar of the saloon with a drink in front of him. He sees me and beckons with a smile. I go over to him.

"Have something to drink. What'll you have?"

I hesitate. "All right, give me a beer. I'll have a beer."

He orders a beer and another double whisky for himself. I look around. There are only a few quiet people in the bar. The juke box plays softly.

"What do you want to see me about, Hap?"

His fingers tap the bar nervously. He looks at me sadly. "Harold, I'm going to leave your mother—this time for good. She doesn't know it yet."

He looks at me as if he expects me to say something. I am not surprised. Why is he telling me? What does he expect me to do—beg him to stay? He is not breaking my heart by going.

"I guess I can't expect you to be sorry about it, but there is just some things I want to say to you."

"Go ahead. I'm listening."

"Well, now, you know, your mother and I—we never could get along. We're just not suited for each other any way you look at it. I know this but I'm afraid Kate doesn't."

"Then why did you come back in the first place, Hap?"

"I'm glad you asked me that." He orders another whisky. "I came back for two reasons. Number one: I thought I could make a go of it. Number two: Because a man needs a son." He swallows the drink and stares at the empty glass. He plays with it on the bar, making small, empty circles with it. "It won't work, Kate and me. It never will, no matter what—because Kate is what she is and I am what I am, and neither of us can or will change. But Kate doesn't see it this way. She thinks everything is hunkydory, the fights and all. She thinks all this fighting and bickering is all a part of a good marriage. But to me, it is a living hell. And all her impossible superstitions! Years ago I used to laugh them off, but I've come to see that she really believes in them. She used to tell me about a curse a mother could put on a child. Now she's invented one for me—a curse to put on me if I leave her. It's called the 'distressed wife's curse.' It involves shrinking my genitals so I never can have another relationship. Oh, I tell you, Harold, it's become intolerable. I cannot and will not live with this woman another day!"

I am annoyed by this. "What are you telling me for?"

"Because, to my mind, you are the tragedy of all this, Harold. It is always the offspring who suffers most in a home like ours. You are old enough to understand now, and that is what I want to try to ease for you, to try to explain to you what this thing is about. Why it is.

"Your mother—your mother loves me too much. She wants possession of me completely. She wants my thoughts, feelings, everything I am she wants exclusively. She is jealous of every thought or action that excludes her. And you—your mother loves you, Harold, but—and please don't be upset by what I say—your mother loves you, but—Well, it is just *unnatural* for a mother to love her husband more than her child to the exclusion of that child. I'm sorry, son, but that is the way it is shaped up with Kate."

Fury is churning inside me. If he were someone else for a moment I would tear into his guts. But he is my father, and I cannot strike my father.

"Harold, I'm leaving Kate because you will get her real affection if I'm not around. I don't want her to know where I am, but I want to keep in touch with you. I want to be a father to you without her knowing I'm even alive. Will you enter in a secret pledge with me—not to tell her where I am? This way, you'll get from your mother the feelings you deserve, and you will have a father, too. Clandestinely, but a father just the same."

I cannot keep quiet any longer. "You don't care about me," I tell him. "That's not the reason you're going. You just want to ball it up with your friends, that's all. Why don't you say what you mean? Stop alibiing."

"Harold, please believe me."

"What do you mean, believe you? Why should I? This isn't the first time you've run out on us. Ever since I can remember you've

**138**

been running out on us. Well, you can run out all you want, I don't care. But don't give me that stuff about doing it for my good."

"You're right. I have gone off before, and not for you. You're right, Harold, you're right. It was just to get away from your mother. And I realize I never gave you a father's love. I know I should have and I wanted to, I guess, but—I'm not making excuses when I say— it was your mother, she prevented me. Not physically, but she fooled me. And I'm just as much to blame because I didn't take the trouble to find out. But you're wrong when you say I don't care about you. I've always cared, Harold."

"You cared! Is that why you let us go hungry? Is that why I had to walk over twenty blocks to high school because of no carfare? Is that the way you cared?!"

"But I supported you all the time I was away!"

"The hell, you did! Ma didn't even know where you were."

His eyes get big. "She *did* know where I was! Why, every Friday she came down to my job to pick up money I gave her for your support. Each time I left I sent money home to take care of you. Didn't Kate ever tell you?"

"Stop lying, Hap! And why did you have to disappear on the day I graduated?"

"I explained. Didn't you get the note I left for you?"

"What note?"

"The note with the wrist watch, of course. The watch I left as a graduation present? You got it, didn't you?"

"Hap, are you drunk or are you crazy? You know good and well you left nothing for me."

He is silent a moment. "And, I suppose, you never got the letters I wrote to you after the last time I left? I used to write you once or twice a month." He studies my face a long time. "No. No, I guess you never did. I guess you never did."

"Is that all you have to say to me?"

"Yes, I've finished."

"Well, I guess I'll run on back home. You coming or are you staying here?" "Yes, you run along, Harold, run along. I will be in here for some time this evening."

**139**

## 3

I get up in the morning to find that Hap has gone for good. Ma will not talk to me. She locks herself in her room and cries and cries and cries. I get the hell out of this stinking house!

I start for the poolroom but change my mind a half block from the house. I do not want to be too far away from Ma when she is upset like this. I am afraid something might happen to her. I go back to the house and stand downstairs in front of the door.

"Hey, Harry!"

I turn to see Ding Dong running down the street to me, waving his arms excitedly.

"What's up, Ding Dong?"

"Harry, I been looking all over for you. You hear what happens to Arnie?"

"No."

"He got busted in a stick-up. Him and Big Nasty and Sidney."

"Who told you?"

"I heard his old man talking on it. Then I up and down sees it in the papers! Boy, they'll throw the book on him with his record."

"What happened?"

"Nothing happens. They got caught, that's all. They tried to stick up a liquor store in broad daylight time. Imagine that? Broad daylight time! I thought Arnie was smart. What ud do you thunk of that, Harry?"

I shake my head in disgust. "No wonder they got caught. That Arnie must have rocks in his head. He was talking to me about a stick-up. Glad I turned it down."

Ding Dong laughs. "You're too smart for that, huh, Harry? You're too smart for that!"

"Sure, Ding Dong."

"Harry, you gonna need a new partner when you do jobs for the Bug. Want to will you cut me in? I could use some change. I would ud do anything you tell me, Harry."

"I'll think about it, Ding Dong."

"Okay. Say, you coming around the poolroom now?"

"No. I won't be able to get around to the block for a while. My father ran out on my mother again last night, and she's upstairs throwing all kinds of fits. I have to stick around and see that nothing happens to her."

"Gee, I'm sorry to hear it, Harry."

"It's nothing. I know how to handle it. It's happened before. In a couple of weeks she'll be over it, and I'll see you then around the poolroom."

"Okay, Harry. I'll be waiting. So long."

"So long, Ding Dong."

**I** AM STANDING in front of the poolroom, throwing the bull with Ding Dong, hoping I will get a nod from the Bug. Suddenly Abie pops out of the barbership across the street and sees me.

"Hey, kid!" He waves for me to come over.

I cross the street quickly, hoping he has a job for me.

"Where the hell you been?" he asks. "I been looking for you a couple of weeks now."

"I wasn't able to get around."

"I want to talk to you. Come on, let's get some coffee by the Greek's."

We go down to the corner and into the Greek's sea-food restaurant. We order coffee and take a table in the rear.

The Bug talks, he seldom looks at you. His eyes are always turning around the room, taking in everything, watching whoever comes and goes.

"What do you think of your partner?" he asks.

"Arnie? That was a bonehead play."

"Yeah. I figured he had more brains than to try a thing like that. It rattled me when I first heard—I thought you got busted with him."

"He wanted me to come in on it, but I refused. We broke up our partnership right then and there."

"Wise! Don't get yourself tangled up with a shmuck. I knew I had you pegged right from the start. A guy like you can score big time. It's all a matter of using your head."

I laugh. "That's what Arnie used to say."

"Talking wise and being wise are two different things. You got to keep thinking all the time. The main consideration in this business is not to get caught. That's the first law. And the second one is, if you *do* get caught—don't talk."

"That's not news to me. But thanks for telling me, just the same."

The waiter brings the coffee. We stop talking until he goes away again.

The Bug says, "I got a little job if you're interested."

"I'm interested."

"I want you to clip a car for me and leave it over the drop where you and Arnie left the last one."

"Okay. When do you want it?"

"Drink your coffee," he says.

I put sugar in my coffee, stir and sip.

The Bug continues. "There ain't no hurry for it. Take your time. By next Saturday I need a car. Nothing flashy. Pick one you couldn't tell from a dozen others—and take it from out of the neighborhood."

"All right."

The Bug pulls out a fat roll of bills and gives me a ten. We finish our coffee and get up to go. He looks me over.

"Say, you're about my size, ain't you?"

"I think so."

"What size shirt you wear?"

"Large."

"I got a suit for you and a lot of nice shirts I don't want no more. Next time I think of it, I'll load 'em in the car and bring 'em over."

"Thanks, Abie."

Suddenly he turns on me angrily. "What did you call me?"

"Abie. You said I could call you Abie."

He stares at me. His face softens. He smiles a little.

"Oh, yeah—I forgot. Okay, kid, see you around."

## 2

I have been casing this black Ford on Pineapple Street over on the Heights for almost a week. It looks like a Sunday driver to me, so I steal it and take it over to the garage on Third Avenue. I ask Jerry, the attendant, for the stolen license plates to put on the car.

He says, "I ain't got none. Nobody told me nothing about no plates."

I figure maybe something is wrong, so I take the bus back across town and go looking for the Bug. I find him in the barbershop.

"I got the car over at the garage but there are no plates to go on it," I tell him.

"Never mind about the plates," he says. "Listen, tomorrow night I want you to be standing on the corner across the street by the poolroom at ten o'clock, get that?"

"Yeah."

"A car will pick you up. You go with them. Don't ask no questions. You'll be told what you're supposed to do, understand?"

"I got it."

"Wait here a minute," the Bug says in a new tone of voice. He goes through the door in the back of the shop. He comes out again with a bundle in his hands. He gives it to me. "Here are the clothes I told you about."

"Thanks, Abie."

"Forget it. Now scram and be on time tomorrow night."

I tell him positively and start out. When I reach the door, I hear the Bug call my name.

"Yeah?"

"Wear gloves tomorrow night, Harry," he says. "Make sure to wear gloves."

"Okay."

I go out wondering. I know he does not want me to wear gloves on account of the weather. I am going out on something big. I know the Bug is too much of a big shot to stoop to holdups or burglary. But I also know you do not put gloves on to steal pennies off a newsstand.

I am excited.

##  3

I look up from my magazine to the poolroom clock on the wall. It is three minutes to ten. I roll up the magazine, stick it in my back pocket and go outside on the corner. It is a chilly and windy night, and I am glad I thought of putting on a sweater beneath my leather jacket. I put my gloves on as I look up and down the lonely streets. There is no sign of the car yet. I step into the doorway next to the poolroom to get out of the wind. I keep my eyes open. It suddenly occurs to me that whoever is coming for me might not be able to see me in the darkened doorway. I come out again and stand on the corner.

A black Cadillac pulls up to the corner and stops with the motor running. The driver leans out the window and calls.

"You Harry?"

"Yeah," I say as I go over to the car.

"Get in."

I climb into the back seat and the car pulls out. I notice for the first time there is somebody else in the back with me. He is a big, stout man, bundled up in an overcoat and scarf, his hat pulled low over his eyes. He puffs steadily on a big cigar. I say hello to him. He just nods and looks out the window. Somehow, I feel I should be excited now but I am not. I am only curious. I settle down and wait to see what will happen.

The car pulls up to the curb and parks on a dark, deserted street. The man beside me asks the driver, "What time is it?"

The driver looks at his wrist watch. "Ten thirty."

"Okay. Keep your eyes peeled and the motor running."

We wait in silence.

We wait a long time. I am bored. I take out my magazine and try to read by the dim light.

"Put that away," the man beside me says. "You'll roont your eyes."

I stop trying to read. Suddenly we hear a car coming. The man next to me and the driver look alive.

"Get out," the man says to me.

I am confused but I step out onto the street. Another car pulls up alongside. It is the hot Ford. Two men quickly jump out. One of them is the Bug. As the other guy climbs into the Cadillac the Bug turns to me.

"Okay, kid. Take it out of the borough somewhere and ditch it."

A voice in the Cadillac asks, "How'd it go?"

"N.G. Somebody made us," I hear the Bug answer as he climbs into the Caddy.

I jump in the hot car and take off.

I am over the bridge in Chinatown. I drive around slowly, looking things over. I pull the car over into an alley off Mott Street and park. A Chinaman comes out of a side door in the alley to throw some garbage in a can. He sees me and comes running over to the car, yelling and waving his hands in the air. I cannot understand what he says, but I get the idea he does not want me to park in the alley. To hell with him. I jump out of the car and run out of the alley. I start looking around for the nearest subway station.

I sit in the subway train. The car is empty. I wish I had something to read. My magazine! I do not have it. I do not remember what happened to it, but I must get back and make sure I did not leave it in the hot car because it is a subscription magazine, and my name and address are on it.

The train stops. I get off, cross to the Manhattan-bound platform and take a train back.

I come out of the subway and hurry up the street toward the

alley. I turn into the alley and stop dead in my tracks. There is a police car parked behind the hot car! The back door of the hot car is open, and the Chinaman is talking to two cops. He sees me and excitedly points me out to them.

I turn around quickly and walk out of the alley. I hear a shout. I keep walking fast.

"Hey, you—stop!"

Should I run or stop? My heart begins to beat fast. I keep walking but I look back. The cop behind me has a gun in his hand. My mind is made up. I stop quick. I try to act calm.

"You calling me, Officer?"

"Yeah, *you*, wise guy!" He comes up to me. "Turn around and get over there against the wall with your hands up. Lean there."

I do so. The other cop comes running up. They frisk me. They find nothing but my wallet.

"All right, turn around and put your hands down." He searches my wallet. He finds my driver's license.

"Harold Odum, 170 Myrtle Avenue?" he asks.

"That's right. What's the matter?"

"That your car, huh?"

I figure they found the magazine and saw my name. "No, it belongs to a friend of mine. I borrowed it from him."

"What's your friend's name?"

"Joey," I pull out of the air.

"Where is he now?"

"I don't know."

"Okay, fella, let's see your hands."

I hold out my hands. Handcuffs are snapped onto them!

"Say, what's the idea? What's going on?"

"You're under arrest, kid."

"What for? What's the charge?"

"That's for the people over in Brooklyn to decide. Your car was used in a murder tonight, and very probably the gun we found on the back seat, too. So offhand, I'd say the charge will be murder."

I get ice cold all over. I look him straight in the eye. "I never saw that car before in my life!"

The cop smiles. "Said he, as they placed him in the hot-seat."

# 4

I sit worrying in the dark cell in the back of the station house. I do not know anything about the murder or the gun, but I know I am in deep trouble now. I figure the best thing for me to do is to keep my mouth shut and deny everything. Even though the Chinaman saw me park the car, I will deny it. After all, it is only his word against mine. I am not sure whether they found my magazine in the car or not. If they did I am a dead duck. There is no way I can get around that except to deny everything and clam up. I keep telling myself not to be afraid, but I feel miserable. I hate to think of what Ma will do when she finds out.

I lie down on the cot. What will happen to me? What will happen? I console myself that the Bug will get me out of it somehow. I doze. . . .

"Wake up, Odum!"

The clanging of steel against steel. I sit up on the cot. The cell door opens. A uniformed cop and a detective stand there.

The detective says, "Come on, kid, get the lead out."

I walk out of the cell. I ask, "You turning me loose?"

"No sirree, not in a million years! We like you too much."

He takes me by the arm and leads me past two other cells. We turn down a corridor, and he pushes me into a small room with a desk and a chair. Another bull is sitting on the desk. He has red hair and is in his shirt sleeves. He smiles at me.

"Sit down, Harry."

I sit.

The detective who brought me in says, "Let me bounce this son of a bitch around first, Chief. I know how to soften these young punks up."

The redhead waves his hand. "None of that. Wait outside a while, Benedict."

Benedict goes out. The redhead gives me a cigarette and lights it.

"My name is Taft. Relax, kid. You're not in trouble unless you want to be."

I keep my guard up but relax a little. Maybe things are not as bad as I figured.

"What's this all about?" I ask. "I didn't do anything."

He smiles. "Well, maybe *you* didn't do anything bad. I know how it is. Some dirty hoodlum makes you steal a car for him and then leaves you holding the bag."

I think, oh, oh, he has something. I tense but try to look ignorant.

"What car?" I ask.

"The car you parked in the alley—the stolen car."

"I didn't park any car in no alley."

"The Chinaman says he saw you park it."

"He must be nuts. It wasn't me."

"Didn't you tell the arresting officers that the car belonged to a friend of yours? Didn't you tell them you borrowed it from a person known as Joey?"

"Sure, but I was scared. They had a gun on me. They made me say it. I never saw that car or gun before in my life."

"Oh, come off it, Harry! We know you drove the getaway car last night."

"What getaway? What are you talking about?"

"Where were you about ten thirty last night?"

"Out for a walk."

"Alone?"

"Yes, alone."

"Do you go out walking alone every night?"

"No, but last night I did."

"Anybody see you that could prove it?"

"Maybe. I don't know."

"Where were you walking?"

"Oh, just around—different streets. One place was where they picked me up."

"Do you know Abie Pinkwise—the Bug?"

"No sir."

"Don't give me that! You live in the Navy Yard district and don't know Abie the Bug?!"

"Oh, I've heard of him, but I don't know him personal. I never even laid eyes on him."

"You know Louis Varga—the one they call the Owner?"

"No, sir."

"How about Georgie Whistle?"

"No, sir."

He frowns. "Harry, we can get very tough around here. I told you when you first walked in that you weren't in trouble unless you wanted to be. It looks like you want to be."

"What do you mean?"

"I mean you've lied about everything I've asked you. Now you're in trouble. And I'm gonna tell you what we know and how deep you're in. We've got Abie Pinkwise under arrest for murder. We have an eyewitness. He shot and killed a man last night."

I get a sinking feeling. "What's that got to do with me?"

"Nothing. Only that car you were driving was the getaway car. That's all you got to do with it, Harry. And when the report comes in from ballistics on the gun we found in the car, I'm betting you'll be looking right dead at the chair along with Pinkwise."

"I don't know what you're talking about. And I don't know anything about a gun."

"Okay, Harry," he says angrily. "I tried to give you a break. You won't co-operate. All right. I'll see what Benedict can get out of you." He calls, "Benedict!"

Benedict comes into the room with a grin on his face. "What's the matter? He won't open up?"

Taft says, "Sure, but he don't like me. Maybe he'll like you better. Talk to him."

Taft leaves the room. Benedict puts both hands on his hips and grins down at me.

"Now, we're gonna get real chummy, ain't we, sonny? You're gonna talk to me and talk fast, or I'll smash in the pretty-boy face of yours so your own mother wouldn't know you."

I stare back at him, straight in the eyes. A fierce anger grows in me. I think, if he takes a punch at me he is going to get a surprise.

"Now, I'm gonna ask you some questions. And every time you don't answer with the truth, I'm gonna give you a good taste of my fat fist. Now, question number one: Did you drive the getaway car for Pinkwise last night?"

I brace myself. "What getaway car?"

The punch comes, right to my stomach, but I partly block the blow with my arm. The pain does not matter. A sheet of fire springs up before me. I am up and punching at him wildly. My fists collide with sinking flesh. Through the angry haze I see him sprawled on his back on the floor, bleeding. I dive onto him. He screams in terror as I bring my fingers tight around his throat. I want to kill, kill, kill!

Screams . . . people rush in . . . hands grab me . . . fists strike, feet kick . . . I hold onto him . . . something strikes my head, again and again . . . blackness.

Head aches, aches.

I open my eyes to blackness.

"The cominaround thesonofabitch . . . throw sommore water onasonofabitch . . . thelousy . . ."

Shock! Air! Air!

Coolness on my head . . . water. Blackness goes. Hazy faces around me.

"Boys, we got ourselves a Goddamn cop-fighter!"

The faces clear. Benedict, his nose bleeding! I leap at him. Hands grab me, fists hit me. I feel nothing, see only Benedict.

"Hold him wide open. I want to show this prick what we do to cop-fighters."

Fists crash on my jaw, stomach, arms, shoulders. I curse them.

I am lifted high, high in the air. I am hung up in the air, in the clouds, my feet cannot touch the ground. I swing my arms helplessly. Fists explode against my body. I scream with pain. Everything spins around and around to blackness.

My head throbs. I ache all over. Where am I? Open my eyes. Light blinds me. Shut eyes tight again. Open slowly. Ceiling spins round, stops. Want to vomit. I am lying down, something cold on my head, someone near me. I look. Taft, holding something on my head. I am in cell on cot.

"How do you feel?"

Want to punch him, but too weak. "You dirty bastards."

"Take it easy, kid. But what the hell do you expect when you try to fight a room full of cops."

"You dirty bastards. Dirty bastards, bastards, bastards, bas—"

Blackness.

Voices . . .

". . . what the hell is this, Taft?"

". . . resisted arrest."

". . . hell, he did . . . don't . . . me that."

". . . jumped Benedict . . . almost killed . . . took four . . . us . . ."

". . . overdo it . . . hell, just a kid."

". . . more like . . . couple gorillas . . ."

"Well . . . get anything, anyway?"

"Nothing."

"Holy cow! Well, let me tell . . . fouled-up investigation . . . D.A.'s office . . . need a doctor?"

"Hell, no . . . tough as nails . . . wind is . . . knocked out . . . be all right, sir."

". . . clean . . . up . . . and . . . him down the line-up . . . the Chink and the other waiting."

"Yes sir."

Blackness.

Light, Hands, hundreds and hundreds of hands reach out for me, touch me, grab, me, fondle me. I want to sleep. Hands won't let me. Water splashes my face. I choke. Hands come again, push me along through smoky nothingness. Leave me alone. I want to sleep. Hands prop me up on a shelf like a doll and leave me standing there with other dolls. Light glares in my face. I cannot see into the darkness before me.

"What's the matter, you deef? You in the leather jacket there. Wake up! What's your name?"

The voice comes from the darkness. Is it talking to me?

"*You!* What's your name?"

**151**

Somebody nudges me.

"Harry Odum," I say.

"Where do you live?"

Cops! To hell with them. I do not have to answer these bastards.

"Where do you *live*?"

Hands take me off the shelf, move me along. Down hallways, around corners. Cuffs bind my wrists. I am pulled along out on the street. Fresh air cools my hot face. Pulled into a closed truck. Paddy wagon? I look around me. Others sit in the dim place with me. Stern, quiet faces. I am so tired! I want to sleep. My body aches, my mouth stings.

Truck stops. Hands pull me into a building. Inside I am separated from the others. I am pulled along into a room. Cuffs are taken off. Pushed down in a chair. I am tired and sick. I look up. A smiling, bald man stands before me, offers me a cigarette.

Didn't this happen before? Am I dreaming about it now? I guess I will have to go through the whole thing again, beating and all. Okay, I am ready. Throw the first punch.

"Smoke, son? Come on, take it. You'll feel better."

Frig him and his cigarette. If they are going to start punching again, let them get going and get it over with. I am ready for you bastards. Bring on the punching. Screw the preliminaries. Let's get to the heart of the matter.

"I'm Myron Gold, the district attorney."

Good for you. What can I do for you? When are we going to start the punching, you bastard? Come on.

"Were you beaten, Harold? Did anyone hit you? You can tell that to the district attorney, son, and I'll have them taken care of."

"Nobody beat me."

"But I thought—Oh. Very well, then. Now, Harold, I want you to relax. I want to ask you a few questions about last night—about the car you were driving."

I am tired. "What car?"

"Why, the murder car, of course. The one you drove for Abie Pinkwise."

To hell with this bastard. I am going to sleep.

"I'll refresh your memory. Last night, Abie Pinkwise and . . ."

"Odum! Wake up! Wake up!"

I am startled. "What? What?"

"Are you going to co-operate?"

"What?"

"I said, are you going to co-operate or will we have to throw the book at you?"

Oh. Cops again. "Kiss my ass."

*"Get this psycho out of my office!!"*

Hands cuffed. Pulled, rushed out, along. Pushed into . . .

I look around. Bars. A cell. Bench against a wall. I sit down. Oh, so *damn* tired, aching! lay down. Sleep . . .

"Wake up, Odum!"

"What?"

Hands, hands, hands again.

"Leave me alone!"

Slap! "Shut up, you young punk!"

Pushed, pulled down a narrow way. Around a corner into a large room with seats.

What? A courtroom? Yes. I stand before a judge. He looks down at me. I look up at him. He is in with them, too, the bastard. A man is reading something aloud. What is it?

"Grand larceny, resisting arrest, felonious assault." He looks at me. "Guilty or not guilty?"

Somebody says, "No record, your Honor. Make it Tuesday."

"Tuesday?" your Honor asks.

"Yes."

"All right, Tuesday," your Honor says.

I do not care what day it is. Please, let me get some *sleep*.

Rushed along, pulled, shoved. Hands, hands, hands! Leave me alone!

Jail. Into a cell. A cot! Rush to it, fall on it and sleeeeeep. . . .

## 5

I open my eyes. I roll them around. A smiling, freckle-faced kid stands in the doorway of the cell, chewing gum and watching me. I rise and sit up on the cot. My head aches."H'ya," the kid says with a bright smile. "Have a nice sleep?"

"I guess so."

He laughs. "You been sleeping all day. Ain't you hungry? I came to call because we're gonna have chow in a little while."

"What jail is this?"

"Raymond Street Jail."

"I didn't know they kept teen-agers in Raymond Street."

"Only in this part of it. We're separated from the big-timers. Say, what they bust you for?"

"I don't know. Stolen car, I think."

"You steal it?"

"No."

He smiles. "Ain't nobody in this place guilty. I'm innocent, too."

"Innocent of what?"

"Breaking and entering and attempted rape. The way it was, I'm burglarizing this joint, see? I hit a good place. I got me a pocketful of rings, bracelets, stuff like that there, and a portable radio under my arm. I swing the flashlight over to the bed, and there is this blond broad laying there with no clothes on, fast asleep! Jeez, what is a guy gonna do? I don't know which to take—her or the joolry. I said to hell with the loot and took off my pants. I know I shouldn't a done a stupid thing like that, but I guess I figured she wouldn't wake up. Shows you the trouble a broad can get you into."

"And you're innocent of that?"

"Yeah," he says with a straight face. "I'm innocent of that and lots more they ain't never found out about. Say, what's your name?"

"Harry."

"I'm Sal. Glad to meet you, Harry. Say, why don't you come on outside? There's a room where they let us kids play games."

"No, I don't feel like it. I got a headache. They keep these cell doors open all the time?"

"No, only certain hours. They treat us innocent kids better than the innocent big-timers. We almost got the run of the joint."

A guard comes up. "Hey, Sal, get out of there! You know you're not supposed to be in there."

"Okay. See you later, Harry." He runs away from the cell.

The guard comes up to the cell door. He looks up and down the corridor in a secret way, then he steps into my cell. He comes over to the cot and looks down at me. He pats my shoulder.

"How do you feel, kid?"

"Okay," I lie. I stare at the floor. I do not want to look in his face in fear I will start punching again.

"I got a message for you, kid. You got good friends outside. Listen good to what I'm gonna say. The message goes like this: The boys in the barbershop are proud of you. Just keep on being dumb. Don't worry about anything. Everything is being taken care of. A lawyer will be in to see you tomorrow and your mother is being taken good care of. Anything special you want, just ask me and I'll get it for you. Okay?"

I look up in his face. He smiles at me.

"Is this message from Abie?" I ask.

"All I can tell you is it's from the barbershop."

I am a little relieved but puzzled. I am right in the middle of this thing, but I do not know what is going on. And who knows? Even this message is a sneaky cop trick. I decide to say no more about it.

"Okay," I tell the guard. "Thanks."

"Anything special you want?"

"No."

"Nothing at all?"

"Well, cigarettes. You can bring me a couple packs of cigarettes."

"Okay." He starts out. He stops at the cell door and looks around at me curiously. "What's with your mother, kid?"

Suddenly I am frightened. I jump to my feet. "What happened to her? What happened?"

"Oh, nothing's wrong, but—Well, she was in to see you, but she raised so much hell they wouldn't let her up. She screamed and hollered and fainted. She woke up and started screaming and hollering all over again. They say she tried to tear the jailhouse down to get to you. Oh, well, what are you gonna do? That's mother love for you."

I am surprised and puzzled. Ma has never carried on like that over me before. But then, too, I have never been in jail before, either.

## 6

Tuesday.

I am taken to court. My lawyer, Mr. Sax, is there to greet me. He gets into a huddle at the bar with the D.A. and the judge. I give them little attention, I am so busy searching among the faces in the courtroom for Ma's. I do not see her and I am worried.

The charges are reduced and I am freed on bail!

Outside the courtroom, Mr. Sax takes me aside to a corner of the hall.

"All right, Harold, you have nothing to worry about now. When your case comes up in a few weeks, the charges will be dropped altogether for lack of evidence. Feel better?"

"Sure. Who put up my bail?"

"The same people who hired me—your friends."

"Why isn't my mother here?"

"She's all right. She's at home. You know, your mother is a very emotional woman and—ah—we thought it best that she remain at home. We like to handle these things quietly without the risk of—ah—publicity. Anything else you want to know?"

"Yes. Where do they get off charging me with resisting arrest and assault?"

"They hit you, didn't they?"

"Yes."

"A cover-up. All right now, I have some instructions for you—from your friends. You are to go home, stay in the house. Don't even go out for a walk—until someone contacts you. Is that clear?"

"Yes. But how long will it be before I'm contacted?"

"Okay a few days, I suppose. But make certain you don't go out until you get word."

"Okay. Are you sure those charges against me will be dropped?"

He smiles and pats my shoulder. "Don't worry about it, I tell you! It's all settled right now. We just have to go through the motions when the case is called. Now, you go right home from here. Good luck, and I'll see you soon."

"Goodbye, Mr. Sax."

He goes back in the courtroom. I head for the sweet freedom of the streets.

I climb up the squeaky stairs. It seems as if I have been away from home months instead of days. I wonder what Ma will say and think?

I knock on the door. It opens. Ma stands there in a torn and dirty housecoat. Her hair is mussed up, and her face pale and drawn. She looks at me uncertainly with large, tear-filled red eyes.

"Harold?" she asks hoarsely.

"Yes, Ma, it's me. I'm okay. I've—"

Suddenly she falls into my arms in a fit of wild weeping.

"Don't cry, Ma. Everything's going to be all right now. Everything will be all right."

"Oh, my baby! My baby!"

I look around the house. At once I am startled! The place is in shambles—furniture pulled out of place, drawers pulled out and their contents spilled all over the floor, closets emptied, curtains pulled down, a stuffed chair overturned. It looks like the outcome of a barroom brawl!

"Ma! Ma, what happened? What's happened to the house?"

"I couldn't find it," she says through her tears. "I searched *everywhere*, but I couldn't find it for days on end."

"Find what, Ma?"

"The doll . . . but it does not matter now. It does not matter at all."

# XIV

**I**T IS MY THIRD DAY HOME, but I have not heard from the Bug or anyone. I am very curious as to what really happened, but I must follow instructions and sit tight. It is pretty lonesome here in the house with Ma out on a part-time job. There is nothing to do, and I have read all the magazines in the house. I have even managed to bull my way through the two Jack London books Hap gave me. I go to the living room and look out the front window. I pull a chair up and sit. It is a cold day outside, but the sun is shining bright.

I keep worrying and wondering. A million questions confront me. Whatever happened to that magazine? Did I really leave it in the hot car? The cops never mentioned it. And if they did find it, how could I have gotten out so easy? Is Abie still under arrest or is he out, too? And who are my "friends"? Did they bail me out to kill me and make sure I never talk? This makes me nervous as hell. I wonder if—

A car pulls up in front of the house and stops. A tall man gets out. I jump, flipping over the chair. It is Abie! My heart pounds with fear, and I cannot make up my mind what to do. He enters the house. I want to see the Bug to find out what happened, but I am also leery in case he thinks I talked.

I jump at a knock on the door. Should I open it? Will there be a gun pointing at me if I do? Suddenly it dawns on me that the Bug cannot possibly think I ratted on him because he would be in jail now if I did. My fear subsides but I am still leery. The knock comes again. I take Ma's paring knife from the kitchen table, stick it in my belt and pull my sweater down over it. If I have to go, I will go out fighting. I open the door. The Bug is standing there smiling.

"Hello, kid," he says.

"I didn't talk," I say quickly.

He laughs. "We know all about it, kid. Get your coat—somebody wants to see you."

I take my coat from behind the door and we go out. I feel to make sure the knife is still in my belt.

And I let the Bug go downstairs *ahead* of me.

The Bug leads me through the barbershop to a door in the rear. We go in and I am surprised. The room is busy with people. There are tables with adding machines and papers and telephones. It is either a horse room or a numbers bank or both. I cross the room behind the Bug to another door. This one has a lock on it. The Bug takes out a key, unlocks it and I follow him through. We go up a narrow flight of stairs to still another locked door with a peephole in it. The Bug pushes the button. The peephole flips open, eyes look out and the door opens up. We go in and I am again surprised. We are in a beautiful living room with fine furniture and paintings on the walls. The room is very large with a private bar on one side and bookshelves on the other. On the sofa there is a big guy sitting in his shirt sleeves, smoking a cigar. On the little table in front of him there is a shiny coffeepot with cups and saucers. The man who opened the door for us goes over to the bar and pours a drink. The Bug takes me by the arm and leads me over to the sofa. Suddenly I recognize the man sitting there. It is the same guy who sat beside me in the car the night of the murder.

"Louis," the Bug says, "this is Harry."

He smiles and offers his hand to me. "Hello, Harry. I'm Louis Varga. We made a meet once before, but not formal."

Holy smoke! I say to myself. *The Owner, himself*!

"Hello," I say. I see a *Horror Tales* magazine on the sofa beside him. I stare at it wonderingly. He sees my look.

"It's yours," he says, throwing the book to me. "You left it in my car that night."

"Thanks."

I sit down in a chair facing him. The Bug sits beside the Owner. They are both smiling at me. Louis Varga leans back.

"Well, tell us about it," he says.

"About what?" I ask.

"We hear the bulls really gave it to you."

I shrug. "It didn't bother me much. I can take all they got."

They laugh.

"Looka him!" the Bug says. "Man, has he got balls. They sweated the hell out of him. They even hung him up on the door by his coat collar and slugged him—and he still wouldn't give them the time of day!"

I am puzzled. "How did you know?"

The Bug winks at me. "Kid, we got our pipeline, not only in the back rooms of police headquarters, but straight into City Hall, too. We know everything. We know everything they asked and everything you said—which wasn't much."

Louis Varga confirms this by shaking his head. He looks at me with sympathy. "We're sorry you had to take such a beating, kid."

"I told you right along the kid wouldn't talk on us," the Bug says.

"How did you get out of it?" I ask the Bug.

He smiles. "The D.A. ain't got no more eyewitness."

"What happened?"

"We buried him," he says."Is that how I got out, too?"

"No. Hey, Louis, tell him the funny story about the Chink who fingered him."

Varga laughs. "We send a couple guys over to take care of this Chink witness. They go to this temple or meeting room in China-town where this guy is supposed to be. The room is full of Chinks! They wait outside until the meeting's over. The Chinks start coming out, two at a time, three at a time, like that. The boys look at each Chinaman careful, then they look at each other. They come running back to me. They say, 'Them Chinks all look alike. We can't tell one from another. The only thing we can do is hit every Chink bastard down there to be sure we get the right one.'" He laughs. "They really mean it, these dumb bastards. They figure they can clean up the whole of Chinatown and get away with it! Well, lucky for us and Chinatown, it turns out we don't have to do this. The Chink who fingered you decides to dummy up automatical. They're like that. You know that motto they got—see nothing, say nothing, hear nothing. But the real funny part was—this Chink tells the D.A. he can't identify you, Harry, because all white people look alike to him. He can't tell one from another!"

We all get a big laugh out of this.

Louis flips a cigar ask into a saucer. "But joking aside, things coulda been pretty hot for us but for you, Harry. My people, we appreciate little things like that. You got a job?"

"No."

"I been interested in you some time now. The Bug has been giving me the knockdown. He tells me you're a wise kid with balls. You proved it on me. I'm convinced." He crushes his cigar out in a saucer. "How would you like to work for me?"

"I'd give my right arm," I say quickly.

"Okay. I start you with fifty bucks a week. Later on, if you're a good boy, I'll cut you in on something besides."

I almost fall out of the chair, I am so happy. "Thank you, Mr. Varga. What do I do?"

"What I tell you. Right now, I want you to buy some clothes. Good clothes." He throws me a roll of bills. "There's a hundred fifty bucks there. Not pay—that's a bonus—in appreciation. You go now and do what I say. Tonight at seven o'clock I want you back here. You gonna have supper with me and my missus. Afterwards you and me are gonna make a nice talk-talk. You got all that?"

"Sure. Thanks, Mr. Varga."

"You can call me Louis. You're one of the boys now."

"Okay, Louis." I try to control the excitement in my voice.

I walk out giddy with elation, squeezing the fat roll of bills in my pocket. I am *in*, I say to myself over and over again. I am *in*, I am *in*. I am big league!

## 2

Ma gives me a big argument about working for Louis Varga. I am firm. I tell her this is one time I will not listen. There is no danger of any trouble. She keeps staring at the new suit, shirts and shoes on my bed. "But it's not right working for him," she says.

"Why not, Ma?"

"Why, everybody knows what that crowd does!"

"And what is that? Just a little numbers, Ma, and bets on the horses. What's so bad about that? Everybody plays a little numbers and bets on the horses once in a while. You've played numbers yourself a couple of times."

"Yes, but—" She strokes the suit on the bed. "It's just that I don't want you to get in any trouble, Harold."

"I tell you there won't be any trouble, Ma."

"You got into trouble before with them."

"But the cops were trying to frame Abie Pinkwise, Ma. They tried to make me lie on him so they could frame him. Besides, they got me out of it, didn't they? They came around to see you while I was locked up, didn't they?"

"Yes. Mr. Varga was very nice."

"Sure! And because I wouldn't help the cops frame him, they gave me a fifty-dollar-a-week job and a bonus. Now, is that so terrible? Here, Ma, here's half the bonus I got—seventy-five dollars. You take it for yourself and the house."

She takes the seventy-five dollars quick. "Well, as long as you say you won't get in any trouble."

"I promise you, Ma."

"Always remember, you're all I have in the world now that your father's gone."

"I know, Ma, and I'm going to take better care of you than he ever did."

She smiles and pats my cheek. "You are a good boy. You always were a *good* child." She looks at the suit, strokes it gently again. "It is a beautiful suit," she says and goes out of the room.

I am relieved that she has gone. I start to dress hurriedly to be on time for supper with Louis Varga.

Nobody has to tell me how sharp I am dressed, but I feel self-conscious, as if everybody is staring at me, and I suppose they are. I have a few minutes to kill before seven o'clock so I drop over at the poolroom to let the guys once me over. I walk in. All of the fellows are there, and they are bug-eyed. They greet me and crowd around.

"H'ya, Harry!"

"Man, get a load of that suit!"

"What a knockout!"

They ask me how I feel, where I bought the suit, and how much I paid for it. I tell them.

"Man, you musta made some *haul*!"

I wink at them. "I did all right."

A guy says, "What happened with you and them bulls? Gee, was I surprised as hell to read in the papers they busted you. I couldn't believe it!"

"Me, nudder," Ding Dong says. "I couldn't believe what ud I'm reading. But there it was in front of my face. My old pal, Harry, busted in the Shylock murder!"

I feel proud and important with everybody flocking around and treating me like a big shot. It is true, I am one of the wheels now. It is a thrilling feeling. I am so pleased that everyone recognizes this that I want to do something wonderful for them all, but I cannot think of anything at the moment.

"What was it all about, Harry?"

I shrug. "They tried to pin the murder on me and the Bug," I say to impress them more. It does.

"What'd they have on you?" somebody asks.

"Nothing," I say. "We were clean." I smile with this to let them know we were not *very* clean.

"Wow!"

Somebody whistles. "Harry's sure gone up in the world!"

"One thing about Harry—he sure ain't no high-hat with a swelled-up head!"

"You know me, fellows, I never change," I say.

"A nice guy!"

"The same old Harry!"

I would like to stay with them longer but I see by the clock on the wall it is seven o'clock.

"Well, fellows, I have to go now. I just dropped in to say hello again. Anything I can do, just look me up."

"Where you going, Harry, to a party?"

"No." I am glad someone has given me this chance to say, "I am having supper with Louis the Owner."

All is quiet. I know all eyes are on my back as I start out. I go out feeling *real good*.

Ding Dong runs out on the street behind me. A freckle-faced kid comes out with him.

"Say, Harry, can I see you a minute?"

I stop. "Sure, what is it?"

"Well, now that you're in—I mean, maybe there'll be something you want me to do. You know what I mean. Maybe you could throw a couple things my way. I mean, if anything comes up I can handle?"

"Sure, Ding Dong." I look at the grinning kid beside him. "Who are you?"

"Leo," he says.

"Yeah, Harry. Leo is a new kid. We getting teamed up, looking for a hustle. You know how it is."

Leo is a bright-eyed, husky kid with freckles all over his face. His clothes are full of patches. He is looking at me as if he wants to brush my shoes but he is afraid I will explode any minute.

"Hello, kid," I say.

He grins wide. "Pleased to meet you, Mr. Harry."

I am startled and flattered. It is the first time in my whole life that anybody has ever called me mister!

I try not to show my surprise and pleasure. I turn to Ding Dong. "You broke?"

"Not a nickel," he says.

I pull out my roll and give two dollars to Ding Dong and a buck to the kid.

"Gee, thanks!"

"Thank you, Mr. Harry!"

"Forget it," I say. "Just keep your mouth shut. Anything comes up, I'll let you know."

I cross the street for Louis' house feeling like Abie the Bug and Edward G. Robinson all rolled into one. Goddamn it, *nobody* can touch me!

I go to the front of the house this time—not through the barber-shop. I ring the bell, and a maid answers.

I say, "I'm Harry Odum. Louis Varga is expecting me."

She says yes and I step in and she closes the door. I follow her up a long flight of stairs. I notice that one of her legs is skinny and shorter than the other. She leads me into the living room. Louis Varga is standing in the middle of the room, puffing on a cigar. Abie the Bug leans against the bar, smiling. A woman is sitting on the sofa with her legs crossed. She has red hair streaked with gray, but she is a very pretty woman. The three of them look at me in silence as the maid goes out. I smile and try to look pleasant.

"Well, here I am," I say.

Varga looks me over from head to toe. I sense something wrong. I begin to wonder.

"Where'd you buy that suit?" Varga asks.

"Buddy Lee's over on Fulton Street," I say.

"How much you pay?"

"Twenty-one bucks."

"Turn around."

I turn.

Varga snorts. "You coulda done better. A belt in the back is going outa style."

I face him uneasily. "I didn't know."

"You don't know a lot of things!" He growls at me. "You don't know how to buy clothes. You don't know how to dress. Look at you—like you just got off the banana boat! You got on a tan suit and you're wearing black shoes. No good. You got to match 'em up."

I am embarrassed. My face feels hot and I know that it is turning red.

"Oh," I say weakly. "I never bought a suit before. This is my first time."

"I know it's your first time!" he shouts. "A blind man could see it! Who tells you this? Louis the Owner tells you. You never bought a shirt before, neither. That's a plaid sports shirt you're wearing. You're wearing a business suit with a plaid sports shirt and a blue tie. You don't wear a tie with a sports shirt, neither. I never seen a combination like you before. I swear to my mother, you come right outa the funny papers!"

I squirm. I do not know what to do with my hands.

"I'm sorry," I say. "I guess I have to learn."

"Sure, you got to learn. There are a lot of things you got to learn. You also got to learn not to go shootin' off your mouth, acting like a big shot in front of your old friends."

I do not understand. He reads it on my face.

"I'm talking about a little while ago when you was across the street in the poolroom strutting your stuff."

I am struck dumb! I feel small and naked before all the eyes in the room. I want desperately to crawl somewhere and hide but I cannot. I begin to wonder how he found out.

"I got eyes everywhere!" He seems to answer my thoughts. "The minute you walked in that poolroom, somebody was on the phone giving me a word-by-word knockdown."

"I didn't let out anything."

"No, I know you didn't. But you was showing off. You want the kids to know what a big man you are now so you start throwing my name around and the Bug's—and you mentioned about the murder."

"I didn't say anything that wasn't in the papers."

"That ain't the point!" Varga shouts. "The point is—you're outa that class now. You ain't no kid punk no more. You're working for me now, Louis the Owner! And when you work for me, you're big-league. We don't play for marbles and pennies up here."

"I'm sorry," I say. "I guess I was showing off. It was a dumb thing."

"A *kid* thing! Okay, you want your old friends to know you're a big shot now? You don't walk in the poolroom and say, 'Okay, fellers, here I am. Look on me, I am a big shot.' No! You ignore them punk bastards. You snub them. Let them run errands for you and throw them a couple of quarters. The difference between us and them is that we're the rulers and they are the ruled. Do you understand?"

166

"Yes."

"You know," Varga says very slowly, "a show-off is only a few steps away from being a canary."

This makes me a little sore, but at the same time I begin to feel fingers of fear creeping up my spine.

"I think I proved I'm no canary," I say.

"I wish I was as sure as you," Varga says thoughtfully.

"Well, all I can tell you is that what happened tonight will never happen again."

He studies me a moment, then suddenly spurts out, "Okay! Let's all go eat."

He turns and quickly goes out of the room, followed by the woman. I am frightened now. Shakily I start to follow them as the Bug comes over to me from the bar. He smiles at me and pats me on the shoulder.

"Don't worry, Harry. Do like he says, but don't worry about it. He really likes you a lot."

"But he's sore as hell at me."

"No, he's not as sore as he sounded."

"How can you tell?" I ask.

"Because if he was as sore as he sounded, he wouldn't chew you out like that. He wouldn't even mention it."

"What would he do?"

He shrugs. "Nothing. But somebody might find you out in Canarsie."

"Canarsie?!"

"With a hole in you," he says. "Come on, let's eat."

I follow him into the kitchen not feeling very hungry.


After supper, the Bug goes downstairs to the barbershop and Varga takes me back into the living room to talk.

"Sit down, sit down," he says, picking his teeth.

I sit uncomfortably in an armchair. Varga goes over to the bar.

"You drink?" he asks.

"Sometimes."

He picks up a bottle, hesitates a moment. He looks around at me. "You like to drink?"

"No."

"Good—good," he says. "In this business people who like to drink and get drunk are no good to us. They are a very bad risk. Now and then to take a drink is not bad. Sometimes it's even necessary. But to get drunk—never! What do you want—wine or whisky?"

"Well, I'll take a wine—to be sociable."

He pours a glass of wine and hands it to me. He sits on the sofa opposite me with a glass for himself. I sip my wine and wait for him to begin talking. He studies me a moment, then starts in.

"First off, you take orders from only me, the Bug or Georgie Whistle. And keep in mind that the Bug and Georgie Whistle take orders from me, so that you always know who your real top man is. We run a little business group here. And I hope I don't have to tell you we ain't exactly legal—but we're making money. Now *you'll* be making money—more money than you ever saw before *if*. Now let me explain my *if*. We're bringing you in because we need a boy like you—a good, tough strong-arm. There are a lot of muscle guys hanging around and hustling for us, but not one of 'em's got all the things you got in you. You're tough, you got balls. The bulls can't make you talk and another thing that I especially go for—you got loyalty. I ain't shittin' you. I'm leveling it to you straight, so you'll know I ain't bringing you in just from the goodness of my heart. I expect these things out of you. You do what you're told. No questions asked! If you have personal trouble or you get pinched for anything, we get you out of it. I don't care what you get pinched for, it's our duty to spring you. And we got the connections and the backing of a national organization. Now, we're gonna break you in, show you the whys and wherefors. If you're a bright boy and catch on neat we'll cut you in on a piece of the business. Meantime, you're gonna work along with the Bug out of a Shylock bank on Willoughby Street. You know anything about six-for-five and the numbers?"

"A little," I say.

"Never mind. There ain't much you need to know about that now anyhow. The Bug will show you all you need. Well, what do you say? Have I got the right boy?"

"You've got the right *man*," I say.

He likes that and laughs.

"Good—good. Go downstairs to the barbershop now and get acquainted with the boys. The Bug is there."

We get up. Varga puts his arm around my shoulder as we walk to the door.

"How is your mama, Harry?"

I am surprised that he asks. I look at him. "She's pretty good."

"I went to see her when the bulls had you. She's a very nice lady. She told me you are a very good son to her."

"I try to be. I want to do a lot for her. She's had a very hard life."

"Your papa dead?"

"Might as well be. He deserted her."

"He don't send no money?"

"He doesn't even send a post card. She doesn't know where he is. To hell with him, though. I can take care of her now."

He pats my shoulder. "That's the boy! Always take care of the mama. I wouldn't give five cents for a guy he don't treat his mama good. Besides," Varga winks, "it's lucky!"

He slaps me on the back and I go downstairs.

## 3

Two weeks with the Bug and I learn a lot. I go everywhere he goes. I am like his shadow but he treats me like a kid brother. We hang around the big floating crap games that Georgie Whistle runs every Saturday. Most of the gamblers are respectable big business-men. There are also a few cops rolling the bones like everybody else. When a gambler goes broke and wants to get even, the Bug makes himself very handy and loose with the dough.

I begin to get the idea how our mob sizes up. Varga, Abie the Bug and Georgie Whistle are the partners. They are in everything—

numbers, horse bets, protection, crap games, Shylocking, shaking down the big money-making pimps and I do not know what all. They have all the Navy Yard section sewed up. Georgie Whistle handles the crap games and bookies; Abie the Bug, the Shylocking and shakedowns; and Varga handles the numbers and supervises everything else. Though nobody has said so, I get the idea that the Bug is also the muscle department. When he walks into a room people look alive and try not to get in his way. Even within the gang itself he is feared. I can tell by the looks on their faces and the way they try to keep in his good graces. Only Varga and Georgie Whistle do not fear him. Ever since I can remember I have been hearing about how tough and mean the Bug is. They nicknamed him "Buggy" because of his recklessness and guts. Now it is a little hard for me to believe all those stories because he treats me fine, almost gentle. He is always giving me advice and encouraging me as to how far I can go in this set-up if I am wise.

I listen close and make sure I stay on the ball. I am eager to learn, and I begin to like the Bug more and more each day.

## 4

I am on my way to pick up a collection for the Bug and I see Ding Dong coming out of a grocery store. I want to duck him but he sees me before I can get around the corner. I know I must cut the old ties like Varga says, but it is hard and embarrassing to do it to Ding Dong. The others I do not mind. But I have always been friendly with Ding Dong and I like him a lot, even though he is a little jerky.

"H'ya," Harry!" he says with a big grin.

"Hello, Ding Dong." I do not smile. I do not look at him. I pretend to have more important things on my mind.

"How's things?" he asks.

I shrug. "Can't kick."

"Say, you hear about Arnie Devivo?"

"No."

"You remember Slapsie McMan, the guy used to fight in the Golden Gloves?"

"No." I remember but I do not want to encourage conversation.

"Well, he just come outa jail—where Arnie is. He says Arnie is a broad up there. They made a regular broad out of Arnie."

"Yeah?" I say indifferently but I am surprised and shocked.

Ding Dong laughs. "Yeah, now ain't that something? Who ever thinks Arnie can be bunked?"

"Yeah."

"That's something now, ain't it, though?"

"Yep."

"Boy, oh, boy!" Ding Dong chuckles.

"Yep. Well, I got to be running along."

"Oh, sure, Harry, Say, Harry, there ain't nothing wrong is it?"

"No."

"You ain't sore at me for something, are you?"

"No, I'm not mad at you, Ding Dong. It's just that I'm in a hurry."

He looks a little disappointed and sad. "Oh, sure, Harry, sure. I understand. Don't forget to let me know if I can do any little thing for you."

"I won't."

I rush off. I feel like a skunk for giving Ding Dong the brush-off. He is really a good kid and I like him a lot. To hell with the other guys, but Ding Dong is just *different*. I decide to ask Varga if I can make an exception in Ding Dong's case.

I find Varga and the Bug in the back room of the barbershop where they are watching the girls count up the numbers take. I call them aside and tell them about Ding Dong. Varga chews on his cigar a moment, squinting at the floor. Now he looks at me.

"This kid ain't no friend of yours no more," he says. "The only friends you got now is me, Georgie Whistle and the Bug. And don't you ever forget that!"

"Oh, sure, Louis."

The way he said that I figure it is better to let the whole thing drop. But Varga smiles a little and puts his hand on my shoulder.

"But I'll tell you what you can do—since you like the punk so much. I like to keep our family happy, so you can keep this guy around as your special flunky. I'll put him on the payroll—in the barbershop. I'll kick out one of the old barbers and put your boy in."

"Thanks, Louis, but—but, you see, Ding Dong can't cut hair or shave. He's no barber."

Varga looks at me astonished. Now he smiles and puts an arm around my shoulders. He says, confidential-like, "Harry, my boy, none of the barbers in my barbership is barbers."

It hits me right in the face. Now I know why I have never seen anyone getting a haircut or shave in there. The three of us get a laugh out of how stupid I was not to be wise to it long ago.

"What a jerk!" I say of myself.

The Bug winks his eye at me. "That's the kind of stuff you got to watch, Harry."

I HAVE BEEN WITH THE VARGA OUTFIT over a year now, and it has been easy riding all the way except for the cops picking us up every once in a while for questioning. The Bug calls these pick-ups "token grabs" or "the nuisance pinch." "Forget it," he says. "Don't pay attention. We got to look for these things and take them in stride. It's all part of the game."

It is all okay with me as long as I can keep getting out.

But sometimes I wish I was far, far away from home. . . .

I have money in the bank, Ma and me have nice clothes to wear and plenty to eat, but Ma is still not satisfied. She broods and picks on every little thing to nag and harp about. Even though I spend every single evening at home with her, she still complains about how unhappy and lonely she is. I know it is Hap. Ever since he left it has been this way. And I know she will agonize me with this until doomsday if something is not done about it.

I have an idea. It is a new apartment. Maybe if I got a new apartment in another neighborhood and put new furniture in, the change would make her forget. Everything around here reminds her too much of Hap. And there are things here that I do not like to think of, either. Anyway, it will be a change and sometimes a change is all for the better. It is a good idea and I will look for an apartment tomorrow.

I find a vacancy in an apartment house on Adelphi Street. It is not far from the old neighborhood and it is a little better-class district, too. It is on the third floor. The super takes me up and lets me look it over. We enter a long, narrow hall with two bedrooms along the side, a neat little bathroom, and next a kitchen with a gas range and refrigerator. Finally the hall ends at the entrance to a large living room. I like it very much. I especially like the bedrooms because they both have electric outlets, so I will not have to run an extension in from Ma's room like at the old house. The rent is ten dollars more than at the old place but it is well worth it. I give the super a deposit and tell him we will move in as soon as my mother looks it over.

I have a hard time selling Ma on the idea.

"But I don't *want* to move!" she cries.

"Why, Ma? You're always complaining about this dump."

"I know, but—but we've been here so *long*. Why, you were raised out of here! It's just that no place else would seem like home."

"You'll get used to the new place, Ma. Look, it's even got a refrigerator and a gas range. Isn't that better than this old icebox and the coal stove?! I'll buy new furniture and you can fix it up real nice. You won't be ashamed to invite your friends in."

"I haven't any friends, you know that. You're all I have in the world."

"You can *make* friends, Ma. Didn't you say you didn't want any friends because you'd be ashamed to have them visit?"

"Well, I didn't mean it like that. I meant—well—Now, see here,

**173**

Harold, I won't have you talking to me in this way. Remember, I am still your mother. I will not stand for this disrespectful talk from you."

"Disrespectful? How am I being disrespectful?"

"Yes, you are. I know. You are trying to be forceful. You are trying to be forceful just like your father, yes, you are. But it will not get you far with me."

I sit down in a chair, exasperated. "All I'm trying to do is *move*."

"Yes, and you are trying to do it in that way. In that same way your father used to make me weaken to him. You think that if you are forceful enough—"

"Ma, I don't even know what you're talking about!"

"Oh, yes, you do, my fine young man. And get it into your head right here and now that none of your father's tricks can get me to give up the only home I've known for the past twenty years and go packing off to God knows where. You get that straight, my boy. You are bringing the money in but I am still your mother, don't you ever forget that, and I make all of the decisions around here."

"Ma, just give me one good reason why you don't want to move?"

"Why, Harold, I don't have to give you a reason. I don't have to give you not even one little reason at all. I don't want to move and that settles it. That is the finish of it all, right here and now, period."

I sigh. What is the use? I cannot understand why she is so upset about it, but I give up on it.

"Okay, Ma. You stay here—but I'm going to get myself a room elsewhere."

Her mouth pops open and she looks at me as though she has been shocked.

*"What did you say?"* she asks slowly.

"I said I'm going to get a room. I'll still give you money for rent and whatever else you need, but I want to move."

"You want to leave me *alone*? You want to leave me like your father did—after all we've been *through*?"

"Ma, I am not leaving you alone. I told you I'll still take care of you, but—"

"This is the first step—a room away from the house."

"If you want me to, I'll come and have supper here every night and sit and talk like always."

"But it is not the same."

"I know, Ma, but—"

"It is not the same thing as living at home with your mother. You know that, don't you, Harold? You know that? It is not the same as giving her companionship and devotion."

"I know all of that, Ma, but I asked you if we couldn't get another apartment together and you—"

"Why do you want to get a room by yourself, Harold?"

She eyes me suspiciously. What is the use? I am tired of arguing, tired of it all.

"I just want to get a room."

"But, surely, you must have a reason?"

She waits. In vain. I do not answer.

"Have you got a girl? Do you want to get a room because you have a girl you want to—"

"Don't say that! It's not a girl. I haven't got a girl."

"If it's a girl, Harold, and you are ashamed to bring her here, why, I can fix the place up and if you want to—"

"I told you it's not a girl."

"Then why do you want a room to yourself?"

"I don't want a room to myself. I just want to move. You won't move with me so I'll move alone."

"But why, Harold?"

I have taken all I can. I stand up, shouting. "Because it stinks here! I hate this house, I hate it! I hate that stinking room I sleep in with no lights. I hate that lousy bed with the bedbugs crawling over me all night. I hate the smell of vomit every morning in that leaky toilet. I hate the roaches crawling up and down the walls and the rats under the floors. I hate every stinking inch of this stinking house!"

I do not know what has come over me. I sit back down, spent from my outburst, and I find I am close to tears. I cover my eyes with my hand. All is quiet a moment. I sense Ma moving close to me. I feel her hand gently on my bowed head.

"Harold, I didn't realize," she says quietly.

"Well," I assure her.

"I didn't know you were so unhappy here."

"Well, I am," I mumble. My eyes are stinging and I rub them with my hand.

She strokes my head slowly. "Well, if you hate it here so much—Why, I suppose we'll just have to move if that is the way you feel about it."

"That's the way I feel, Ma."

Her tone of voice changes at once to cheerfulness.

"Then that settles it. We'll move! Say and think no more about it. I'll go over and take a look at the apartment and we'll move right in as soon as we can pack up."

All that fuss and, bingo! it is settled just like that. Sometimes Ma confuses and frightens me.

## 2

I get the day off from Varga to help Ma get ready for the moving men tomorrow morning. It is a hell of a job packing all the dishes and stuff in barrels and moving the heavy old-fashioned furniture around. We could have saved all this trouble just by putting all new stuff in the house like I wanted to, but Ma clings to this old beat-up furniture like it is made of one hundred per cent gold. She will throw nothing else away, either. Old hats, clothes, magazines, picture frames, clothespins, hangers, flatirons, a big, broken lamp-shade—everything goes into the barrels.

I argue with her to throw out the big living-room chair.

"Are you *crazy*?!" she asks. "Why I've had that chair ever since I first started housekeeping!"

As if that makes up for the fact that whenever you sit in it a little hard the springs make a loud noise and the left leg falls off. Every stick of this furniture is precious to her except the stuff in my room. Probably because my bed and chest were not part of her wedding furniture. I get no argument out of her when I say I am going to buy a new bedroom set for myself.

Things that have been missing for years turn up in this moving business!

It takes us all day, but we finally get the furniture and everything conveniently arranged for the moving men. Ma scrambles some eggs for supper, but we remember that all the dishes and silverware have been packed in the bottom of one of the barrels beneath all the clothing. We eat from the frying pan with our fingers and make a big joke about it.

I am dog-tired. I go to the bathroom, wash and start for bed. As I pass Ma's room I look in. She is sitting on the bed, crying. She has an old, wrinkled baby shoe in her hand, and as I walk in she tries to hide it.

"What's the matter?" I ask.

"Nothing," she snaps. "Go away."

I leave her alone. Ma is very sentimental and I guess a lot of her memories are hurting ones.

### 3

Varga has made a killing on some kind of a deal. He invites me, the Bug and Georgie Whistle out to celebrate. He closes up the shop. I send Ding Dong over to the new apartment to tell Ma I will be late and to give her a hand moving the furniture around.

We go to an opera!

Varga is crazy about this kind of stuff. He has records by Caruso and other opera stars.

Abie and me sit together. Varga and Georgie Whistle have two seats directly behind us. We watch and listen for a while. The Bug looks at me, I look at him.

"You like this crap?" he whispers.

"No," I crooked-mouth back.

I never did go for this kind of music. It did not make much sense when Miss Greer tried to shove it down our throats back at P.S. 5 and it makes even less sense watching it.

"If I knew he was coming here, I wouldn't come," the Bug whispers.

"Shh!" Varga says.

"Want to dog it?" the Bug asks.

"Sure, if it's okay with Louis."

He turns to Varga. "Say, Louis, me and Harry want to duck out a sec to have a smoke. Okay?"

"No," Varga says. "Stay. Stay and watch. This is a good one."

We settle in our seats. We look at all the people on the stage, the scenery, the costumes, the fake wigs and beards. We listen to the women screaming and the guys hollering and hamming it up until the Bug can stand no more of it. He curses, gets up and walks out.

Varga leans over and whispers to me. "The Bug got no appreciation and he's too old to learn. But you stay, Harry, and learn appreciation. A young dog will learn new tricks."

I will stick it out. What else can I do? The boss has spoken. I cannot even go to sleep because of the noise. I *have* to stick it out.

We come out of the opera house. The Bug is waiting for us in the lobby.

"What happened to you?" Varga asks.

"I'm dying in there! It don't bang me to sit around listening to a lot of guys trying to out-holler each other."

"What do you mean, *hollering*? That's real fine singing."

The Bug shrugs. "By me, it's just a convention of guys hollering."

Varga turns to Georgie Whistle. "What d'you make of this guy?! Them singers spend half their lives sometimes learning to sing like that and *he* calls it *hollering*!"

Georgie Whistle shrugs. "Everybody to his opinion."

"It's a big racket," the Bug says. "Like everything else, it's a racket. Them opera singers got Louis and all the rest of the opera bugs suckered in."

"Don't knock it, though, Georgie says. "It really is artistic."

"I'm not knocking it. I give them singers credit for thinking up a sweet racket like that. I give them credit. I wish I had opera going for me. I wish I could holler like them guys and take in the money. And it's legal yet!"

"Come on," Georgie says, "let's get outa here. People are giving us dirty looks."

We go to the car. Abie gets behind the wheel. Me and Georgie Whistle sit in the back with Varga between us. The car pulls out.

"Abie," Varga says, "you ain't got no kinda culture at all." He starts to light a cigar. A thought seems to suddenly occur to him. He looks at Georgie Whistle. "How did you like the opera, Georgie?"

Georgie Whistle sighs heavily. "Louis, I can stand a lot of things," he says.

Varga turns to me. "What about you? You didn't like it, either, huh?"

"Well, it wasn't so bad, Louis."

He shakes his head. "Sonamagun! I was sure you guys would like Wagner opera. I always had it figured that if a hard guy is gonna get to like opera he'll go for Wagner every time. Wagner's music is bang-bang with plenty of guts to it. Wagner's really got *balls*." He shakes his head again. "Sonamagun!" he repeats.

The car pulls up in front of a brownstone house in the East Sixties. We pile out. Me and the Bug pair off and follow Varga and Georgie Whistle up the steps. Varga rings the bell. A little colored maid opens the door.

"Good evening, Mr. Louis. Miss Royce is expecting you."

We go into a foyer. Varga, Georgie Whistle and the Bug start taking their hats and coats off. I do not know where we are but I follow suit. The maid takes our hats and coats just as a tall, thin woman in an evening gown enters the foyer.

"Hello, Louis—all of you gentlemen. Come into the living room and make yourselves at home."

We follow her into the living room and I am stunned by the beautiful furnishings of the room. I have never seen anything as fancy as this, outside of the men's room in the Brooklyn Paramount. Everything is colorful and clean. There are large paintings, fancy vases and drapes on the windows. The rug on the floor seems to be six inches thick. I figure this must be the house of B.M., the big wheel I have heard them mention once in a while.

Varga and Georgie Whistle are talking to the tall woman. I turn to the Bug beside me. "Is this B.M.'s place?" I whisper.

"No, this is a whorehouse," he whispers back.

"A *whorehouse?!*" I shout in surprise.

Everybody turns to stare at me. I am so embarrassed I want to drop through the floor. But they all start to smile at me.

The woman says, "Yes, son, it's a whorehouse—but *what a whorehouse!*"

Everybody laughs loudly at that. The Bug slaps me playfully on the back. I muster up a smile.

The woman says, "I suppose you gentlemen would like something to drink first. The girls will be in shortly."

"Sure," Louis says. "Bring us some scotch or whatever else you got. But no cocktails—nothing mixed. You got men here now."

She laughs and goes. We take seats. Varga and Georgie Whistle take armchairs. Me and Abie sit on the sofa. Varga lights up a cigar and looks over at me, smiling.

"You never seen a whorehouse like this before, eh, Harry?"

"It sure surprised me," I say.

"This is nothing. You should see the whorehouse they got across the street. Over there, if you want to use a rubber, they give you one made out of silk-and-gold threads."

"Yeah?"

"I'm telling you! It's the snazziest grind joint you ever heard of. And if you happen to catch clap from one of the broads over there, you don't have to worry because it's a higher class of clap. It's what they call royal clap. The germs have been brought over by the crowned heads of Europe."

Now I know that he is kidding me. We all laugh and I wave him away. The maid comes in with a tray of drinks and passes them around.

As Georgie Whistle takes his drink he says casually to Varga, "B.M. wants that little matter over in Philly taken care of."

"Later," Varga says.

"B.M. wants it as soon as possible. You give the Bug the knock-down yet?"

"Not all of it."

The Bug perks up. "What is it, Louis?"

Varga waves him aside. "The Philly thing. But later, not now, please. No business at a time like this."

"Okay, but remember it's got to be cute."

"Don't worry. When the Bug handles them they're always cute."

Miss Royce comes in with four girls. They are beautiful girls—like movie stars. They are young and fresh-looking.

Miss Royce says, "Well, gentlemen, here are my wares. My selection is small, but I'm sure you'll find the quality superior."

Everyone laughs. The girls spread about the room, making themselves friendly to everyone. Two girls are blonde and one is brunette and the other a redhead. They are so pretty it is hard to believe they are whores. The only whores I have ever seen have been either flabby, sloppy, ugly, old, skinny or all those things at once. But these girls have everything. Beautiful faces, beautiful hair, nice shapes and fine clothes. The brunette and redhead sit between me and the Bug on the couch. Suddenly it dawns on me that I am supposed to take part, too. In the beginning I thought only Varga and Georgie Whistle came for a girl, but now it turns out there are four girls and four of us. I begin to worry. I do not know if I can go through with it.

Varga smiles at me. "Go ahead, Harry, take your pick. It's my treat. Don't be bashful."

The brunette smiles at me and takes my hand. "Oh now, don't tell me you're going to be shy with *me*!"

I am embarrassed and confused. I pull my hand away. "I—I don't feel like anything now."

"Well, there's no hurry," the girl says sweetly.

Varga laughs. "When I was your age I was always in a hurry for it."

Everyone laughs. The Bug jumps up, pulling the redhead with him.

"Well, I ain't bashful," he says. "Come on, baby, let's take a walk. Which way?"

"Right this way," she says.

He follows her out of the room.

Varga stops smiling. "Go ahead, Harry. Have some fun."

He is watching me with a curious expression on his face. I do not want him to get any funny ideas about my manhood. I take the girl's hand and get up quickly. I put on a big front.

**181**

"I was only kidding," I say. "Come on, girlie. I'm gonna give you a humping you'll never forget!"

I feel terrible saying this, but Varga and Georgie Whistle laugh. I am surprised to find the girl giggling also at my remark. Now she seems more like a whore to me and I am no longer embarrassed. But I have the fear I might not be able to carry out my threat.

She leads the way. We go out of the living room, down a long hall and into a bedroom. The bed has only a clean white sheet on it and two pillows. She goes to the bureau and gets a towel and spreads it across the bed center. She looks up at me still standing by the closed door.

"You really *are* bashful, aren't you?"

"Well, not exactly," I say.

"Well, you don't have to be with me. I'm all yours for the taking so just relax." She looks at me silently a moment with a smile on her lips. "You know, you're very handsome, too."

I have nothing to answer that. I do not know what to do. I just stand by the door, telling myself to take her, take her, but I do nothing because I do not know what to do.

She stands by the bed and kicks her shoes off. She puts her hands behind her neck and fusses with something on her dress. She looks at me with pleading eyes.

"O-o-oh, please, Harry, help me get out of this thing."

I cannot stall any longer. What the hell. I will make a try. Maybe it will come out all right. I go to her. She smells sweet and clean. I pull the zipper in the back of her dress down to her waist.

"Thank you, darling," she says. She slips out of her dress and she is all pink and lace frills in step-ins and bra. She looks up at me. "Aren't you going to undress, honey?"

I am miserable and ashamed, but I keep telling myself maybe it will be okay, maybe everything will be all right, after all. I take off my pants and shorts and put them on a chair. I sit on the edge of the bed. She has taken off her step-ins and lies still on the bed, her legs parted. I look at her body there but nothing happens to me.

She coos softly. "Come on, baby, do it to me. Do it to me while I'm hot!"

I take my hand and stoke the patch of kinky hair between her thighs. She whimpers and wiggles her body around and around slowly against my hand. She closes her eyes and sucks her tongue, making a hissing noise.

"Please, Harry, *now*. I'm ready now. Please do it to me now!"

Nothing happens. It is no use. Desire does not come. I only feel the filth and disgust of it all. I am hot with shame for what we are up to. I curse myself for going this far. I turn away from her.

"Please, Harry."

"No," I say. "Let's talk."

She jumps up on the bed, startled. *"Talk?!"*

I go for my clothes. "Yes. I'm not in the mood for this."

"Then why'd you waste time like this?"

"Put your clothes on and I'll tell you."

We dress quickly. She looks at me with wonder and suspicion on her face. We sit on the edge of the bed. I give her a cigarette and I light one.

I say, "Those fellows out there—my friends—if I didn't come in with you, they would kid me about it afterward. They'd tease me about not being much of a man. To avoid all that I just came back here with you. Can you understand that?"

She kind of pouts. "Sure—but my time was *wasted*."

I see what is on her mind. "Oh, you'll get paid. We'll just make believe we did it and Varga will pay you just the same. This is our secret—just between the two of us. Okay?"

Her face brightens with a smile. "Sure, I understand. That's fine with me."

"Here." I take a ten-dollar bill from my wallet and give it to her. "That's a little something for being a good sport. Come on, let's go back."

"No, wait a minute," she stops me. "Not yet."

"What's the matter?"

"It's too soon. We haven't been in here long enough to turn a good trick. Sit down and wait a little while longer."

We sit and wait, puffing on our cigarettes.

She says, "Sure, I understand how you feel. I guess if you're not in the mood for sex, you're just not in the mood, that's all."

"I'm sorry I couldn't help you out," I tell her.

"Help me out? How?"

"By doing it to you. You were pretty hot."

"Me?!" She laughs. "I wasn't hot. I was trying to make *you* hot!"

I look at her. I am astonished. "You mean all of that twisting and moaning on the bed was phony?"

She looks at me slyly out of the corners of her eyes a moment. Now she smiles full-faced at me. "Well, let's put it this way—a good prostitute also has to be a pretty good actress in bed."

We finished our cigarettes and decide we have waited long enough. She primps in front of the mirror a moment and we go back into the living room.

The Bug is already back with his girl; Georgie Whistle is missing; and Varga is seated in the armchair, talking and drinking with a blonde. Everyone looks our way as we enter.

"Well, how'd it go, Harry, my boy?" Varga asks.

I smile and try to look devilish and shake my head.

My brunette screams with delight. "What a *man*!" she shouts, holding up four fingers to Varga and the Bug. This is supposed to mean I have used her four times straight. Everyone laughs.

I see where my little prostitute is a pretty good actress *out* of bed also.

The party is over. Varga and Georgie Whistle have stayed in Manhattan on business. The Bug is driving me home in his Cadillac. We are crossing the Manhattan Bridge. A light, misty rain has begun to fall.

"Harry," the Bug starts out, "pack a few clothes in a bag—not much—a few shirts and socks, enough to last about a week. We're leaving town in a couple of days."

"Okay. What's up?"

"We're doing a favor for B.M. There's a guy over in Philly needs to get hit in the head. You're coming with me. I'll need about a week over there to get things lined up."

I get leery. I do not know about this. Shlumping a man is one thing, killing is another.

"I don't know. I don't know about that, Abie. Let me think on it a while. I never killed anybody before."

"There's a first time for everything," says the Bug.

"Sure, but killing—" I shake my head. "A thing like that, I just have to think on it a while."

"Okay, you got five minutes to make up your mind."

"A couple of minutes?! I can't make up my mind about murder in a couple of minutes!"

The Bug is silent. He keeps his eyes straight ahead.

"Harry," he begins, "I'm gonna give you some advice because I like you. I once told you you could go far. Well, you can, but you're getting ready to make a bad mistake on your first big test. Louis wants you on this job and so do I. Now suppose I tell Louis tomorrow morning you don't know about going on this job because you got to think it over. Well, now, he ain't gonna like that about you thinking it over. Suppose after you think it over you decide not to go on the job. Well, a thing like that is going to be very bad because you already know we're going to hit somebody over there. If things happen to go wrong in Philly, why, in no time at all you could become a corroborating witness. Now, Louis is a real sharp operator. He thinks years ahead. He considers it very bad business to have corroborating witnesses standing around loose, no matter how deaf and dumb they are. He likes them nailed down tight— underground. Now, either you're in the mob with us or you're out. It's your mind, so make it up. You got a couple of minutes left."

I do not need a couple of minutes. "Okay, I'll be packed and ready when you are," I say.

"Good boy! You're smart, Harry. That's why I know you won't make a bad mistake like that again. I won't mention this to the Owner."

"I think I would've made up my mind to go along anyway after I'd thought it over."

"Sure, you would've, but stalling around like that would only start people wondering about you. But don't worry, kid, you won't have to do anything over in Philly but lend a hand. I'm handling the whole thing. Now you'll see how I really operate. We want you along because you got to start learning the business. I got to break you in sometime, sooner or later."

"The business? What business?"

"The murder business. That's our branch of the organization. I'm top pro." He looks at me in a curious way. "Didn't you know, Harry?"

I did not. I do now and I am not so sure I am happy about it.

I enter the hall. The house is dark except for the light in Ma's room.

She calls, "Harold, is that you?"

"Yes," I say. I go down the hall to her room and stand in the doorway. She is sitting up in bed with a hair net over her hair and a newspaper in front of her. She is knitting.

"Where have you been?" she asks.

"Out with Varga and the boys. We saw an opera."

"Really, now? Wasn't that nice! What opera did you see?"

"I think they called it Wagner."

"Well, which one by Wagner? Wagner is a composer."

"Oh. I don't know. I didn't care for it very much. Louis likes that stuff, though."

"Oh? He must be a very cultured man. I thought there was something special about him. What else did you do?"

"We went—we went and we took in a movie."

"What picture did you see?"

"Some crazy picture."

"What theater did you go to?"

"Some movie house in Manhattan. I don't remember the name. Did Ding Dong come over?"

"Yes. He helped me a lot, that boy. We got every stick of furniture in place. What a fine gentleman he is! Why do you call him Ding Dong when his real name is Charles?"

"Yeah, Charlie Trolley. It's because a trolley goes ding dong. We made it up. It's a kid thing."

"Well, you're grown men now. It seems so silly to call a grown man Ding Dong."

"I guess so. Well, good night, Ma. I'm tired. I want to get some sleep."

"Yes. I'm going to sleep, too, now that you're home. I worry so much when you're out late nights."

"That's silly. I know how to take care of myself."

"I know you do. I know you are very capable. It's just that—Oh, well, a mother always worries. Come, then, and kiss me good night."

I go over to the bed, bend over. She takes the lapels of my coat and I kiss her on the cheek. I start to straighten up again but she holds on to the lapels. She gives me a queer look.

"Kiss me again," she says.

I kiss her again. She still does not release the lapels.

"What's that smell?" she asks.

"What smell?" I pull away, straighten up.

"Perfume!" she says triumphantly.

"Perfume? Where?"

"It's somewhere in your clothes."

I get uneasy. I sniff at my shoulders and chest. A faint smell of the whore is there. "I don't smell anything," I say.

She begins to knit again. "Oh, it's perfume there, all right. And a very nice perfume it is, too."

"Yeah? I wonder how the smell got there?"

"Did you have girls with you in your party tonight?"

"No. Maybe it came from Margie, Louis' wife. She wears perfume."

"Was she in the party tonight?"

"No, but I was in his apartment today. Maybe I brushed against her or something."

Ma looks at me very sternly. "Harold, I hope you don't feel you have to explain a thing like this to me."

"No, Ma, it's just that—"

"You're a grown man now and you're entitled to your own private life out of the home. If you have a girl outside—"

I feel ashamed. "Ma, I *haven't* got a girl outside!"

"I know you haven't. But I was just saying *if* you have a girl outside, why, it's certainly good and proper if you *want* to. The only reason I remarked about the perfume was that you had said you were out with Mr. Varga and the boys. You didn't mention about a girl, and then when I smelled the perfume on you, why, I just naturally—"

A feeling of filth arises in me so suddenly and sharply that I must spit it out quickly and be rid of it. I sigh and flop down on the edge of the bed.

"Ma, we were at a place—a house."

"Oh?" She does not look at me, only knits. "What kind of a house, Harold?"

"There were girls there. These girls were there—"

Ma begins to knit faster and faster. "*Nice* girls?"

"No, Ma. They were like the girls in the places on Hudson Avenue."

"Oh!" She knits, knits, knits!

I talk fast. "Varga and the others wanted to be with these girls. I didn't, Ma. I didn't even know what kind of place it was until we were inside, and they told me. Louis and the others were with these girls, but I wasn't. I only talked to one of them. I swear to you, Ma, I wasn't. It all disgusted me. Please believe that, Ma."

She stops knitting. She looks up at me and smiles. "Of course, I believe you. And why shouldn't I? I'm sure you would never betray the trust I have in you. Do they—those other men—do they go places like that often?"

"No. This is the first time that I know of."

"If they ever go again I'm sure you won't—"

"Never, Ma. I told you I wouldn't have gone the first time if I had known."

"You are a good, sweet boy, Harold. I'm very proud of you. Do you want me to fix you a snack before you go to bed?"

"No, I'm not hungry." I kiss her and get up from the bed. "Good night, Ma."

"Good night, Harold. Turn my light out. I'm going to sleep now."

I press the button as I go out. I go to my room. I feel along the wall for the light switch. I press it but no light comes on. Maybe there is no bulb. The room is pitch dark. I strike a match. I see the lamp on the bed table and switch it on. The room brightens. Ma has fixed the room up very nice, and everything is neat and clean. I look at the ceiling light. I am surprised to find it is not there. I look closer and find that the electric cord has been cut off close to the ceiling. I wonder what has happened. I go quickly down the hall to Ma's room.

"Ma, what happened to the ceiling light in my room?"

There is no answer. I switch on the light. She is curled up on her side with the covers over her head. I call again. She does not answer. She must be asleep. I decide to leave it until morning. I go back to my room.

I sit on the edge of my bed and take my shoes off. I notice that the cord to the lamp on my bed table runs along the wall and out of the room. What the?! I am bothered by what I suspect. I get up and follow the cord out into the hall. It is true. The cord runs along the hall and into Ma's room! Now, why did she have to do that in this house when there is no need for it? There are two outlets in my room. This stupidness angers me. I remember the missing ceiling light. Is there something wrong with the outlets also? I go back into my room. Where are they? I search along the baseboard. I recall one outlet was near the window where a lounge chair is now pushed against the wall. I push the chair back. I am astonished! The metal sockets have been torn from the baseboard. I find the other outlet near the bed. It is the same way, with only the naked, torn wires showing. I am confused and upset. I do not know what to make of this crazy thing. Goddamn it, I could cry! This is exactly what I tried to get away from in the other house. Now it is the same room all over again. It is like sleeping in a vacuum.

# XVI

IT IS A FRIDAY MORNING. Me and the Bug arrive at the bus terminal early. We meet a man called Blinky near a magazine stand. The Bug takes him aside and they talk. I am not in on it.The Bug says, "Okay, Harry, let's go."

We buy tickets and magazines and the three of us board the bus for Philadelphia. Me and the Bug sit together in the back, the one called Blinky sits up front. The bus pulls out.

I am very curious. I know it is not good to be too curious about these things, but since I am going to be in on it there are things I feel entitled to know.

I ask, "Who's the guy in front? Is he in on it?"

"He's just going along to finger the bum. The guy we're going to get I wouldn't know from Adam."

He shuts up and begins to read a magazine. I do not like the way he has cut me off and I get a little peeved. If a guy is going to be killed I will be just as guilty as the Bug. The electric chair can burn my ass just as easy as it can his.

"Listen, Abie, we're going to pull something. I'm going to be in it just like you, but you don't tell me anything. You think I'm getting a fair shake? I don't even know what I'm supposed to do or how."

He looks at me blankly a moment. He smiles. "You're supposed to do *what* I tell you, *when* I tell you and *how* I tell you. But relax—you're just going along for the workout, anyway. There's not much you need to know. I don't know much myself. All I know is its a grudge job, not over business. It's a personal matter with B.M. so it's got to be cute."

"What do you mean by cute?"

"You make a murder look like an accident or a suicide or anything that it ain't. It seems this guy and B.M. has had a long personal feud over the years. This guy has got a lot of brothers, real rough guys. Now, if we pop this guy in the ordinary way, all them hard-guy brothers are gonna be looking to pop B.M. And the one thing he don't want at this time is a lot of guns going off, especially at him, so we got to point suspicion away, away from B.M., and that's my specialty—making it look like what it *ain't.*"

"What's the plan?"

"I ain't got one yet, but I'm working on an idea that's real cute. So why don't you relax, Harry? Read a magazine while I figure things out. Hell, you already know more about it than I do."

I laugh and take a magazine from him.

"You're the boss," I say.

"Atta boy!"

The Bug slumps down in his seat and pulls his hat down over his eyes.

## 2

We spend three days in Philly.

Four hours after the man is dead we are back in the bus terminal in New York.

I feel strange. All during the trip back I have had a feeling of anxiousness as if something terrible is going to happen to me.

We take a cab back to Brooklyn. We go up to the Owner's apartment through the barbershop. We go into the living room. The little maid is there dusting.

"Oh, hello, Mr. Pinkwise," she says.

"Where is Louis?"

"They went out, him and Mrs. Varga. I think they went to a party."

"Georgie Whistle around?"

"I think he went with them."

The Bug curses. "Hell, a party. They coulda waited for us. He didn't mention nothing when I phoned in yesterday. Did they say where the party is?"

"No, sir, but it's in Manhattan somewhere."

The Bug snaps his finger and turns to me. "Hey! I'll bet it's B.M. throwing an alibi party! Want to go over?"

"No," I say and flop down on the sofa. "I'm too tired."

The Bug goes to the bar. "You want a drink?"

"Yes."

Maybe the drink will calm this churning feeling inside me. He pours two drinks and hands me one. He downs his quickly.

"I'm going over. What are you gonna do?"

"Sit here a while, then beat it on home and get some sleep."

"Okay. See you bright and early tomorrow."

He goes out. I down the drink and stare into the empty glass. I sit there feeling this thing inside, wondering what is happening to me. It is a great restlessness. I am aware of Iris, the maid, without looking up. I just *feel* her presence. I am beginning to get a headache. I look up. Iris is dusting the bookcase and her back is toward me. Her back is in an orange dress. Her back is very pretty, curving down to her plump buttocks. The headache gets worse. Madden comes into the room. He sees me watching Iris.

"H'ya, Harry. Who's the broad?"

"Louis' maid. What are you doing here? Go away, I got a headache."

"Take a drink, it might help. It'll give you courage."

"No, it might get worse. Listen, Madden, you'd better beat it. You got no business being up here in the Owner's apartment."

He keeps staring at Iris. "Louis won't mind," he says.

"You know Louis?"

"Sure. He likes me."

"That doesn't mean he wants you up here," I tell him.

"Man, lookit the nice, fat, round ass on her!"

"Why don't you get lost. What are you doing up here, anyway?"

"I came up for *her*," he says. "I'd like to try her out. But just for size, though, mind you—just for size. Just to keep in practice, so to speak, for the big date."

"I ought to kill you," I say. "If I didn't have such a headache, I'd beat your filthy brains out."

He laughs. "I'm going to rape her and you can't stop me." He goes over to the maid and taps her on the shoulder. "Iris . . ."

She turns and looks at him with innocent eyes. "Yes?"

"Come—come into the bedroom," he says.

She is surprised. "What for?"

"I want to—You know what for. Come on."

"No!"

He grabs her firmly by the arm. "Please, now. What's that to you? You don't lose nothing. Be nice."

"No! No!"

Iris is terrified. She struggles hard, but she is like a doll in Madden's strong grip. He looks at her angrily. He takes a knife from his pocket and shows it to her.

He says, "You see this? I once killed a man and I can kill you just as easy if you don't behave. I don't want to hurt you, but I will if you don't be nice."

"Oh!"

Iris goes limp. I think she is going to faint, the way she is looking at Madden. He puts the knife back in his pocket. He strokes her hair the way I used to stroke my dog when he was frightened.

"Please don't be afraid," he says to her quietly. "I won't harm you. I just want you for a little while."

Madden partly carries her into the bedroom because she is shaking so much she can hardly walk. I follow them into the bedroom. Madden pushes her across the bed on her back. She begins to cry.

"But I can't," she says. "I don't know how. I never did this before."

As Madden's eager hands go searching beneath her clothes, I hear myself repeating her words: "I don't know how. I never did this before."

Madden goes.

Curled up on the bed, her face buried in her hands, Iris whimpers. Suddenly I have such a great feeling of pity for her. I want to soothe her hurt.

"I'm sorry," I say. "I know I should have stopped him, but I just couldn't. I had such a headache. I'm sorry, Iris."

She looks up at me a moment in silence, and suddenly she is screaming again.

I guess I had better go. I do not want to get involved.

# 3

I am down in the barbershop shooting the breeze with Ding Dong."Hey, Harry," he says, "trot upstairs. The Owner wants to see you."

I go through the bank and upstairs to the living room. Varga is sitting on the sofa with an ugly face on. The Bug smiles as I enter and hides his face behind a newspaper. I ask what is it.

"Harry," Varga says, "what did you do to Iris, the maid, last week?"

Goddamn it, I knew it! Now I must take the blame for that Madden bastard.

"What did she say I did to her?" I ask.

"She didn't say what you did to her. She's just scared as hell of you. But ten-to-one you laid her!"

"No, that was a friend of mine, not me."

"Don't give me that bull! She said your name. She said the one called 'Harold.'"

Might as well. "Well, yes—Okay, I did it."

"Sonamagun!"

"I'm sorry, Louis. I didn't figure you'd mind."

"*Mind*? I don't *mind*. I don't give a damn if you lay every girl in Brooklyn. But it's my *wife* who minds. She's left me. She left me on account of you had to go and screw her maid!"

"What do you mean?"

Varga curses, turns to the Bug. "Tell him, Abie. I'm too God-damn disgusted with this lover-boy!"

The Bug wipes the grin off his face. "You see, Harry, Margie had this maid a long time. She thinks the world of Iris. But now Iris has quit and won't come back to work because she's scared of you. Now Margie has left Louis and says she won't come back until Louis gets Iris to come back." The Bug shakes his head sadly. "It's one hell of a big family mix-up you caused, lover-boy."

I am relieved when the idea comes to me that Varga is not seriously angry over it, but is only annoyed.

He says, "I went over to her house personal and offered her more money to come back, but she wouldn't. I tell you, you got the kid scared to death. I thought that whore over Fanny Royce's was kinda kidding when she said four times, but now I believe it. You must be one hell of a nasty son of a bitch in bed!"

The Bug laughs. "Look at that babyface! To look on him, butter wouldn't melt."

"I didn't harm her. What's she so scared about?"

"Did she give it to you or did you took it?"

"Took what?"

"The trim, the grind, the scratch—in plain, everyday English—the pussy!"

"Oh. Well, I guess it was took."

Varga throws up his hands. "Sonamagun! You don't call that harming her? Don't you know that's rape? You think you can take a broad when she don't want it, and she's gonna like you for it? Don't you know nothing about broads? Why didn't you con her out of it?"

I shrug. "I don't know."

"He don't know, he says! Well, I'll tell you what you're gonna do. You gonna go over to her house and apologize for what you done. Then you're gonna date her. You're gonna take her out and sweet-talk and treat her swell. You're gonna make her like you so much that she'll be dying to come back to work."

"I don't think I can do that."

"What do you mean? Broads go quick for a good-looking boy like you. You can do it. I'm ordering you."

"I mean, I won't like to do it."

"I don't give a damn what you like. All I want is my wife back. I ain't letting you break up my Goddamn happy home!"

"But I don't know *how* to woo a broad," I protest.

"*Woo* a broad? What the hell kind of talking is that—you don't know how to *woo* a broad?"

"It means—"

"I know what the word means. But it just sounds kinda funny. I never heard a guy use that word talking before. How come you said it?"

"I don't know."

"Well, don't use it no more around me. It makes me nervous."

The Bug laughs. "I thought at first he said he didn't know how to *screw* a broad."

"Oh, he knows all about that, all right. He knows too damn much about that. What he don't know is how to get it without stealing it or paying for it. He don't know nothing about romance. And that's where you and me come in, Abie. We're gonna show him. We gonna be the cupids. Get my hat and coat. We're gonna take him over her house right now."

The Bug brings the car to a stop in front of a two-storied wooden building on Johnson Street. Varga gets out of the car, closes the door and talks to me through the window.

"Now, I'm going upstairs and bring her down. I'll do all the talking to her, at first. You just agree with everything I say. When I give you the nod, you start apologizing to her. Tell her how you lost your head over how pretty she is. Tell her you'll always be a perfect gentleman from now on. After that, you invite her to a movie, get it?"

What is it to me? It is no skin off my nose to tell her these things. I shrug. "Okay."

Varga goes into the house. I think hard. I try to remember some of the things I have heard actors say in the movies when they are wooing a girl. I remember, too, some of the love conversations I have read in books. I think some are pretty good.

The Bug helps me out: "You can't tell a broad how pretty she is too much. Keep saying it in different ways. Broads go for that everytime—especially ugly ones like Iris."

"I'll remember that."

Varga comes back out of the house with Iris. He leads her by the arm over to the car and opens the door. Now she will tell them. They will find out it was Madden and not me.

"Get in," Varga tells her.

Iris climbs into the car beside me. She looks at me, now looks quickly away. She stares shyly at the floor of the car, her face getting the redder and redder. She really believes I did it! Now I realize what it is all about. The poor kid was so scared she has me confused with Madden! Oh, well, I will go along with it. I have come this far.

Varga climbs into the car on the other side of Iris. "Drive around somewhere," he tells the Bug.

The car pulls out. It rolls along at a leisurely pace.

Varga begins: "Like I was telling you upstairs, Iris, the boy don't know what got into him to do a thing like that. He's so ashamed of himself right now for what he done, he can't even talk. But I'm gonna tell you something I been knowing for a long time. He wouldn't tell you because he's too bashful. This boy has been crazy about you for months now! You do things to him—straight at the heart. Why, he used to make up excuses to come up to the apartment just to get a look at you. He's been frantic for you all these months. But he don't know nothing about girls. He ain't even ever been out with one before. That's why, when you two was alone in the apartment there, the poor kid had all he could take. He lost all control of himself, and before he knew what he'd done—he'd already done it. Now, he's so ashamed and sorry about it, he's nearly going crazy. He wants you to be his girl friend but now, after what happened, he figures you'll never give him another chance to screw—to *woo* you."

There is a sudden snicker of a laugh from the Bug up front, who quickly smothers it. I almost laugh myself. There is a long silence in which I know Varga is trying to collect his wits again.

"Ah, now, ah, let's see, now, where was I? Oh, yeah. I was saying that Harry is really suffering about it all, and—ah—he wants to apologize. Tell her, Harry."

I brace myself. Suddenly the things I had planned to say, the words I have heard and read in the movies and the magazines are gone. The shame and remorse and pity I feel now are very real as if there had been no Madden at all, and I am alone to blame.

"I'm sorry, Iris. I'm very sorry for what happened. I wouldn't really want to hurt you for anything in the world. You've just got to believe me."

"It's all right," she says. "It's over and done with, Mr. Harold."

"No, no, please don't call me mister anything. I'm not worth any kind of respect. Would you be good enough to forgive me?"

"Yes, I forgive you. It's just that—you scared me so!"

"I didn't mean to. I hope I die if I ever try a rotten thing like that again. It's a thing that only a filthy dog would do. I wouldn't blame you if you hated me the rest of your life for it."

Varga stares at me with a surprised but pleased expression on his face. The Bug turns around to make sure it is me he hears talking.

"Oh, I don't hate you," Iris says. "I couldn't hate anybody."

"That's very sweet of you. But you've got to let me make it up to you in some way. I feel like such a dog."

"There's nothing to make up. What's done is done. You apologized. What else can you do? I understand."

"Could I take you out sometime—maybe to a show and supper or something?"

"Well—I don't know. I really can't say."

Varga cuts in. "Sure, you can! Go ahead, Iris, give the poor guy a break. You'll have a nice time."

She looks at me uncertainly. I say, "I'd appreciate any kind of a little chance to make things up to you."

She says, "Well—When do you want to go?"

"Anytime you say. How about tomorrow night? We could have supper together and take in a show."

"All right then—tomorrow night."

"What time shall I call for you?"

"About seven. Is that all right?"

"Sure."

Varga says, "Okay, Abie, take us back to Johnston Street." He turns to Iris with a big laugh. "Now, you see, Iris, everything's made up. He ain't such a brute like you thought, eh? Yes, sir, I guarantee you, my Harry is a perfect gentleman!"

"Butter wouldn't melt," the Bug adds.

I call for Iris at seven o'clock. I do not go upstairs. I ring the bell. She looks out the window, smiles and waves to me. She comes downstairs. She is dressed nice and neat and her face is made up pretty. Her cloth coat is a little frayed.

She smiles at me. "Why didn't you come upstairs?"

I shrug. "I don't know your people. They might object."

"My mother and father are dead. I live with my grandmother and my kid brother."

"Oh."

We walk along slowly.

I say, "Well, um, shall we go to a movie?"

"All right. Which one?"

"I don't know exactly. Er, is there a particular picture you'd like to see?"

"No, not any particular one."

We pause a moment on the corner to think. I do not know what direction to take. "Well, I guess there are a lot of movie houses around."

"Yes."

"I don't want to take you to—I mean, we don't want to go to just any dumpy old show."

"I don't care. Any place you want to go is all right with me."

"You ever been in the Paramount Theater?"

"No."

"Then let's go there."

"Okay."

We go toward Flatbush Extension. I shove my hands in my coat pockets, and before I know it, she hooks her arm through mine. I feel ashamed. I do not like her holding on to me like this at all, but I do not want to hurt her feelings so I try to ignore it. I keep my head down as we go up the Extension toward the Paramount.

We sit and watch the picture. It is a musical. I cannot concentrate on it. Sitting here with Iris is like trying to steal something with everybody watching. I got this real uneasy feeling inside. Her leg and elbow are slightly touching mine as we sit together. I inch my leg away and fold my arms across my chest. I am glad when the show is over.

We come out onto the street. The weather has turned colder. Iris puts her arm through mine and snuggles up close to me.

"Freezing!" she says.

We walk along. I do not like this business of her holding on to me, but what the hell can I do about it. I suppose it is the custom when a guy walks with a girl, so I guess I will have to go along with it.

"That was a good picture, wasn't it?" she asks.

"Yeah, Bing Crosby. Yeah, yeah."

"Do you like him?"

"Yeah."

"How did you like that song they did with the voice orchestra? What was it called? Oh, yes—'The Moon Got in My Eyes.'"

"Yeah, that's it."

"Remember when they were singing it and *she* walked into the room? Wasn't it cute the way Bing Crosby changed the words to fit the situation? He sang, 'Well, if it isn't little Vicky! You know, I can't believe my eyes.'"

"Yeah, that was pretty cute, all right."

Goddamn it, how do you talk to a girl? I do not know what to say. I do not want to talk anyway. Why does she make it necessary by talking so much?

"Is there something wrong, Harold?"

I do not like her calling me Harold. Where the hell does she come off?

"No, no, nothing's wrong."

"Oh."

We walk along. She is very quiet. Maybe I have hurt her feelings by not talking much. I do not want to do this. I try to think of something to say.

"Cold," I say.

"Yes."

What else is there? Oh! "Say, is it nice and swell in the Paramount's ladies' room?"

"Yes, it is."

"I thought so. While you were down there you should have taken a peek into the men's room. It—"

"Harold!" She smiles, blushes.

"I didn't mean that. I—"

Foot in the big mouth! I had better shut up. I am better off. We come to her house and pause in front of the door.

"Would you like to come up for coffee, Harold?"

"No, I have to go. Yep, I have to be getting along. Thanks just the same."

"Are you sure you won't come up for just a *little* while?"

"Sure, I'm sure. Yep, I'm sure of that, Iris."

"Well."

"Okay, good night, Iris. I'll be seeing you."

"Good night, Harold. And thanks for a wonderful evening."

"Forget it. Just keep your mouth shut." She looks at me with surprise. I am surprised myself. "I mean, I'll see you around, Iris. I'll see you around."

I move away from her fast. Now, why did I say a crazy, stupid thing like that? I cannot understand it. Girls—they just mix me up altogether.

I FINISH SUPPER and put my plate in the sink. The garbage can is overflowing. I put it on the dumb-waiter. I notice a queer-shaped bag in the can. I look inside the bag. There is an empty wine bottle. It is the third empty wine bottle I have found around the house this week.

I go into the living room, where Ma is knitting and listening to the radio.

"Ma, did you have company this week?"

"No. How did you enjoy your supper?"

"Fine." I pick up the newspaper and sit down. "Say, Ma, you haven't been drinking, have you?"

"Drinking? Certainly not, Harold! What makes you ask?"

"Nothing."

No company, no drinking, and three empty wine bottles. It is another mystery I have to cope with.

# 2

I am on my way to the barbershop. A familiar voice calls me from across the street. I turn. It is Arnie Devivo in front of the poolroom with a couple of fellows. I grin and start to greet him warmly, but I remember my standing and how things are different now. Arnie comes rushing across the street to me with a big smile on his face and his hand outstretched. "Harry! My old pal, Harry, keed!"

But I cannot cut him cold altogether. I take his hand and smile a little.

"Hello, Arnie. When did you get out?"

"Just yesterday. I'm on parole. And boy, am I glad to see you. You look great—just great!"

"Well—thanks, Arnie. You look okay, too. You got fat, didn't you?"

"Yeah, I put on a little weight. Say, I heard all about you in the can. I couldn't believe it—my pal, Harry, keed, one of the wheels in the neighborhood!"

"I'm doing pretty good," I admit.

Arnie quickly looks over his shoulder and speaks to me in a crooked-mouth whisper. "Say, I hear you're strong-arming for the Owner. That true?"

"Well—I work around."

"I get it. Deaf and dumb. But why dummy up on me? I'm Arnie, your old pal—remember?"

"Sure, sure, Arnie. But I can't talk to you out here like this. Some other time—okay?"

"We don't have to talk out here. Let's go get a couple of beers."

"What about your parole? You can't go in a bar."

"Balls! Frig the parole. We can drink the beer up my house, anyway."

"I'm sorry, Arnie, but I got something else to do."

"Okay, then I'll just tag along with you. You can fill me in on what been happening."

"No, it's business. You need any bread? I can let you have a couple of bucks if you want."

"Oh, sure. I could sure use a couple of bucks. I ain't got a thing going for me."

I give him a five-dollar bill. "Okay?"

"Sure, thanks, Harry, but—but it ain't so much the money, it's—Well, I just come out and I sure would like to get my hand in something. I figured maybe you could put the good word in for me with the Owner—you know, for old times' sake."

"I'll try, Arnie, but I can't promise anything. You know, after all, I'm only taking orders myself."

"Oh, sure, I realize that. But say, how about you and me getting together tonight over some beer and talk over old times?"

"No, some other time."

Suddenly he looks hurt. At last it has come to him just what is happening.

"Oh, Oh, sure, Harry. Whatever you say. Sure, some other time."

I leave him standing there at the curb. He is still standing there bewildered as I enter the barbershop. What the hell. I do not feel too bad about giving Arnie the brush-off. I have an altogether different feeling about him now since I found out he is a fag.

I ask the Bug about it. I cannot understand how Arnie was okay before he went up the river, then suddenly turns into a fag. I have even heard him knock fags.

The Bug says: "A stir broad and a faggot are two different things, Harry. Guys up there are doing long stretches without women. You can't take a guy's lay away from him. He'll do it to a hole in the wall if he ain't got nothing else. A new fish goes up there, especially a young ass like Arnie, the old cons feel him out. Then they start to pressing him, grabbing at his dinky. Pretty soon, if the kid is a little weak he gives in. He becomes some con's old lady. The old con looks out for him, gives him things and protects him from the other wolves. The kid even gets to like being a broad. But that same kid, the day he gets out, he's all man again. He wants a real broad just like any other guy. A real faggot is always a faggot, but a stir broad is only a faggot in jail. But don't knock him. If you been in and out of jail as much as I have, you'd see there's need for them kind of guys. The cons need them. Don't hate him for it. It's all part of the life. Arnie is okay."

I think on it.

I still do not get it. I do not hate Arnie or feel disgusted with him for being a broad up there. It is just that I cannot have the respect I used to have for him any more. I still do not see the difference between him and a full-time faggot.

## 3

We sit on the sofa in Varga's living room, me and the Bug. Varga paces the floor, chewing at me."Goddamn it, she ain't back yet! Trouble is, you ain't doing nothing to her. What's sitting in a show and talking?! You got to love her up."

"But I told you, I don't know how," I say.

"You got arms to hold her, ain't you? You got a mouth to kiss her, don't you? What else do you need to know?"

"Aw—"

The Bug says, "Listen, Harry, you take her to a nice dark place, like in the movies—"

"I'm tired of taking her to the movies," I interrupt.

"It don't have to be the movies," Varga says. "Any romantical spot will do. What's a romantical place this time of year, Abie?"

"Wait a minute, let me finish telling him. Now, Harry, you take her to a nice lonely place. You start telling her how much you love her. You put your arms around her and pull her to you. You kiss her hard on the mouth. While you're doing that you take one hand and sneak it slow up her dress—"

"No, no," Varga protests. "None of that, none of that. I want this nice, nice."

"Okay, so you don't put your hand up her dress. You just keep kissing her and telling her how much you love her."

"But I don't feel that way about her."

"*Make believe! Make believe!*" Varga shouts angrily.

I am frightened. Quickly I say, "Oh, sure, I can do that. Sure, I know how to do that."

"Okay," Varga says, cooling off. "Now, the main thing I want you to tell her is to come back to work. Tell her you want her to come back so you can see more of her."

"Okay."

Varga scratches his chin. "Now. Where is a romantical place he can take her, outside the movies?"

"It's hard to find them kind of places in the winter," the Bug says.

"I got it!" Varga says to him. "You'll drive them around in your car. Drive them up around Prospect Park. Park the car around some bushes and you cut out. Leave them alone for an hour or so."

"Aw, nuts, Louis," the Bug says. "I don't feel like riding around some—"

"I'm gonna have trouble outa you, too?"

The Bug gets up. "Okay, okay." He turns to me. "Come on, lover-boy, let's go courting."

The Bug brings the car to a halt in front of Iris' house.

"Balls!" he says, turning to me in the back of the car. "To hell with Louis' parking in the bushes way out in Prospect Park. Why waste all that time? And you probably won't open your mouth twice the whole time. Tell you what. You go up and get the broad and I'll tell her all that crap for you."

I am relieved. It sounds like a good idea to me. I get out of the car and go upstairs. I knock. Iris opens the door. She is surprised. She smiles.

"Oh, hello, Harold. Come on in."

"No. I just wanted to see you about something, Iris. I mean, a friend of mine has something to tell you."

"Who?"

"Abie Pinkwise. He's downstairs in the car. Can you come down for a minute?"

"I guess so. Wait, let me slip something on."

"Sure."

I wait.

Iris comes out of the house, pulling a coat on.

"What does he want to see me about?" she asks.

"Me."

"*You?*"

"Yes. Come on."

We come downstairs and get into the rear of the car. Abie looks around at Iris.

"Iris, what are we gonna do with this Harry here?"

"What do you mean?"

"This boy is very much in love with you."

Iris looks at me, then back at the Bug. I keep my eyes straight ahead.

Iris says, "You and Mr. Varga tell me this, but I never hear him say it."

"He's too bashful. Okay, do you want to hear him say it now?"

"Not particularly. Not if he doesn't want to say it. But what if he is in love with me? What do you want me to do about it?"

"You're not afraid of Harry any more, are you?"

"Of course not."

"Then why don't you come back to work for Margie? Harry wants you back around there so he can see more of you."

"Why, I didn't know Mrs. Varga still wanted me back!"

"Sure, she does."

"And if Harold feels this way—Why, yes, I'll be glad to come back to work. It will have to be part time, though. I have another job now."

"I guess that will be all right."

"When shall I start?"

"I'll tell Louis you're ready to come back and he'll let you know." The Bug turns to me. "Well, Harry, your troubles are over. She's coming back."

I feel I should say something. "Yeah-ah—Thanks, Iris, thanks."

She looks at me curiously. "I don't know, but it's so hard to believe that you—Oh, well. Harold, would you like to come upstairs and meet my grandmother?"

"No, Iris," I say quickly. "Me—ah—Me and the Bug here, we got something to do. Yep, I guess you've got things upstairs you have to do, too, so we don't want to hold you up. Well, so long, Iris. We have to be running along in a hurry. I'll see you around."

Iris gets out of the car. She stands there on the curb, staring at me. The car pulls out. The Bug is laughing.

"What's the matter, Abie?" I ask. He says nothing, just keeps on laughing. "What is it? What's so funny, Abie?"

"Nothing, Harry, it's nothing," he says. "I just thought of something funny, that's all."

He keeps right on laughing to beat the band. I guess this is one of the reasons they call him the Bug.

## 4

Varga has gone to Chicago for a big meet with wheels from the organization all over the country. There is going to be a national crime investigation by the politicians.

I am in the barbershop, shooting the breeze with Ding Dong. The Bug sticks his head out the back door.

"Hey, Harry, run upstairs a minute. Margie wants to see you."

"What does she want?"

"I don't know."

I am leery. I figure maybe she is still sore about Iris and is taking this chance to chew into me while Varga is out of town. I look up at the clock.

"It's after eight o'clock," I say. "I was just going home."

Abie shrugs. "Better run up and see what she wants. It won't take a minute."

I cannot get out of it. I go through the back room and upstairs to the living room. Margie is standing at the bar with a drink in her hand. She is wearing a silky negligee with white-fur trimmings. I clear my throat. She turns.

"You want to see me, Mrs. Varga?"

She smiles. I am relieved.

"Hello, Harry. Sit down, make yourself comfortable."

"Thanks."

I sit on the sofa. She looks at me in a funny way, smiling. Her face is all made-up and she looks very pretty even though her red hair is streaked with gray.

"Want a drink?" she asks.

"No, thanks, Mrs. Varga."

"Please don't call me Mrs. Varga. Call me Margie."

"Okay."

"Relax," she says. "There's no one here but you and me." She turns back to the bar. "I'll pour you a drink, anyway. It'll make you feel more comfortable."

She pours a drink and brings it to me. I think she is high because she walks a little wavy. She has on a lot of nice-smelling perfume. She sits down in the armchair across from me and smiles.

"I been wanting to talk to you alone for a long time, Harry, but I never got the chance. You know, I've always liked you very much."

I get uneasy. I do not like the way she is looking at me. I do not like anything about anything that is happening. Suddenly she crosses her leg like a man, an ankle resting on the knee. Her negligee parts and slides away, and I see that she is naked underneath. I am stunned and embarrassed. I am scared, too, because she knows that I can see, yet she does not cover up but just sits there smiling and staring at me. I swallow my drink in one gulp. I cough. She gets up quickly and reaches for my glass.

"Let me get you another."

I do not want another, but anything to get her out of that sitting position across from me. She brings the drink back and sits down beside me this time. I think that maybe this will be much worse. I smell a lot of alcohol on her breath, and now I am sure her head is tight. I am desperate to find a way out of this situation. I do not look at her. She moves closer and breathes hot on my neck. It gives me a terrible, nasty feeling. She runs her fingers through my hair and I feel ice down my back.

"Don't you like me, Harry?"

"Sure," I say, not knowing what else to say. I begin to sweat.

"And I like you. I've always wondered what it would be like."

"What?" I squirm away a little. She squirms closer.

"Do you know what they call you, Louis and Abie? They call you the Cat. Harry the Cat. Louis tells me you're a tiger in bed with a woman."

"That's not true," I say.

"Oh, yes it is! What about Iris? The little fool—it was all wasted on her. It wouldn't be on me. Why don't you do it, Harry?"

"Do what?"

"Do it to me like you did Iris."

I try to look shocked. I am more scared and miserable than shocked, but I try to look shocked. "But Mrs. Varga—!"

Her face angers. "Don't call me *Mrs. Varga!*" Her face quickly softens again. She coos. "Come on, Harry. I'll make it good. Do me like you did Iris."

"But I *can't.*" I say desperately.

Her smile goes. She gives me a fierce look. "Why can't you?"

"Because I just can't. You're the boss's *wife.* I can't do a thing like that!"

"You're afraid of him. You're just like the rest. Afraid to touch me, afraid to even look. Why are you all so afraid of him?!"

Madden stands in the doorway of the living room, watching us, grinning.

"He's the boss, I tell you."

"He won't know anything unless I tell him—and do you think I'm a fool? I can handle Louis, don't worry about that. We could have lots of good times together. There'll be extra money in it for you."

Madden is gone. Suddenly I am filled with such a powerful feeling of grief that I cannot contain it. I burst into tears.

"What's the matter? Why are you crying?"

"Leave me alone! Please leave me alone!"

"Why, you're just a boy—just a little boy! This is even better. Now I know I must have you, tears and all. Come on, Harry, I've got to have you now. If I made you hot enough you'd do it, wouldn't you? You'd say to hell with Louis, then, wouldn't you?"

"Leave me alone!"

She drops to her knees before me and reaches for my fly. I can take this agony no more. I jump up quickly, accidentally hitting her on the jaw with my knee. She goes sprawling over on her back. I am more frightened than ever now. She raises herself up on one elbow and glares murderously at me, her face turning a purplish red.

"I'm sorry!" I say quickly. I go to help her up. Her palm goes up and comes stinging across my face before I can duck.

"You dirty, lousy son of a bitch—I'll teach you to kick me!"

I hold my face. "I'm sorry. I didn't mean it."

"You son of a bitch. You went for that crippled little wop bitch, but *me*—you kick me in the face even when I throw myself at you! Well, I'll fix your Goddamn britches. When Louis comes back you'll find yourself at the bottom of the river. I'll tell him you raped me like you did Iris. You'll see how I'll fix your britches for making a fool out of me like this!"

I am almost terrified now. I know that Varga will believe her.

"Please don't do that—"

"Get out," she screams. "Get out, get out, get out! I'll have your guts for this, you pussy-particular son of a bitch!"

She breaks down crying as I take off from there like a bat out of hell.

## 5

For a couple of days I brood over what has happened between me and Margie. It really has me worried. Varga is due back soon, and I know he will believe Margie if she tells him I have raped her. I begin to see pictures of myself shot-up and dead out in the sticks somewhere. I figure I had better get somebody on my side, so I tell Georgie Whistle and the Bug what happened. To my surprise, they laugh.

"Forget about it," Georgie Whistle says. "She won't tell Louis that."

"But suppose she *does*?" I ask.

"Even if she does," the Bug begins, "Louis won't believe her. The Owner is no fool. He knows Margie's got hot pants. She pulled the same thing off on me once. On Georgie Whistle, too."

"She did?" I ask, surprised.

"Sure, Margie is famous for that. You got nothing to worry about. Forget it."

I am relieved. I begin to smile along with them.

"Man, she had me in a hell of a spot," I say. "What did you do when she pulled it on you, Abie?"

"I got the hell outa there—*fast!*"

"Not faster than me," I say.

"Boys," Georgie Whistle begins, "you're looking at the world's champeen of running from Margie's pussy!"

We laugh.

The Bug turns to me seriously. "Watch her. She might try you again. She's got ways of tricking guys into laying her. It's just like my uncle Max used to say, you always got to be looking for the curve ball! Make sure you never find yourself alone in a room with Margie—especially if her head is tight. Give Margie plenty of elbowroom and you're safe."

I think on it. That is good advice he will not have to give me a second time.

##

I have a pain in the little toe of my right foot. Ma says it is an ingrown toenail.

After supper, she takes my foot in her lap and picks at it with a little knife.

"These things can be very serious if you let them go too far," she says.

"What do they come from, Ma?"

"Yours comes from those tight, dressy shoes you're wearing. You shouldn't wear narrow shoes like this. It would be different if you had no choice and had to wear hand-me-downs. But you've got a choice. Shoes! That reminds me when I was a child. There were so many of us, and almost every single payday Papa had, somebody needed a new pair of shoes. Shoes were the big thing in our house, next to food."

"How many brothers and sisters you had, Ma?"

"Ten of us, all told, but only six of us are alive now. Four girls, two boys. There is Helen, the oldest, Colette, Denise and myself. The boys are Frank and Willie. We have French blood in our veins— from Mama's family. Oh, we were some bunch as children—playing, fighting, bickering. Papa was easygoing, but not Mama! She would get in and fight right along with us, yes, she would. She would nag and bicker and play one child against the other and things like that, you know."

"She was a good mother, though, wasn't she? She was a good mother?"

"Oh, yes, there is no question about that. She had a lot to contend with, with all those children. I remember toys were another thing hard to come by in our house. And if you got a toy, watch out! or the others would get it from you. Yes, that's the one big thing I remember about my growing-up years—holding on to things, struggling to keep what belonged to me so the others wouldn't get it. I was the youngest and the weakest, you know, so you see I had a very hard time of it. The thing I remember—I remember most, I mean—it was a big hurt—was the time, one time—oh, I must have been ever so tiny then—I had this little baby doll I was so crazy about. It wore a knitted blue bonnet and something like a clown's suit, with big, brass buttons running down the front. It had big, blue eyes and blond hair, and it was more than a doll to me. Oh, I just adored it. I wouldn't let it out of my sight for a moment. Not for a moment! I carried it around with me during the day. I ate with it in my arms, I went to the bathroom with it, and at night I carried it to bed with me and we rocked to sleep together. Yes, I held it tight in my arms and we rocked to sleep just like that. Well, now, one day I was playing on the floor, and I happened to crawl beneath the cupboard. I discovered a hole in the wall behind the cupboard. It was like a little niche about the size of a shoe box. I guess Mama had pushed the cupboard over there to hide it. Well, that little secret place came in very handy for me when I started going to kindergarten. Yes, it did. You see, they wouldn't let me take my doll to school, and so I hid it back there until I came home again. Well, that worked out fine for a while. Just for a while. And one day—oh, it was horrible—one day I came home from school and they had taken—someone had found my secret place, took my doll and cut it up into a million miserable little pieces! Indeed they did. Whoever did it, Mama never could find out who, one of the children, took those tiny little pieces of my beloved and scattered them all over the back yard. Oh, how I cried and cried for days. No other doll, nothing anyone could do would paci—"

"Ouch!"

"Oh!"

"You stuck me."

"It slipped, darling. I couldn't see so good." She rubs her eyes hard.

"What's the matter?"

"Eyestrain. When I look at anything too long my eyes blur. I guess I'm getting old. I'll be needing glasses soon. Put your foot back over here again." I put my foot back in her lap. She goes to work on the nail again. "Now, what was I saying?"

"About the doll."

"Oh, yes. Well, that was that. Oh, I got over it all right. But it is just one of the mean things children will do. Children can be very mean."

"Where are your brothers and sisters now, Ma?"

"God knows! Scattered all over. We don't keep in touch. The family, they didn't want me to marry your father, and we sort of drifted apart because of that. And when Mama died, they blamed that on me, too. Said I had broken her heart. No such thing! But I suppose they were forgiving, too. When Hap first left me and I was having such a hard struggle alone with you, they invited me to come back home. But I wouldn't."

"Why, Ma? It would've been easier for you."

Ma sighs deeply. "Harold, if you could know what it means—means to go against the whole of your family, mother, brothers, sisters—people you've loved for so long and deep—to go against them, away from them for someone you love just as much, but in another way, and with them telling you not to because the person is no good and—Well, you just can't help yourself and you do.

**213**

You marry him and go away. Then it turns out they were right about the man you married. Of course, it happened gradually, of course. I didn't realize what Hap was until you—until it was too late, and then it was too late. Well, you can't ever realize what a heartache and a humiliation it is to face them who told you so. I mean, you try to hide it. You don't want them to say that to you, that you were so wrong.

"All right, that nail is about out of there now. How does it feel?"

I take my foot down. I wiggle the toes.

"Much better," I say. "Thanks, Ma."

"You buy yourself another broader-type shoe, young man, or it will grow right back in again."

"Okay." I kiss her cheek. "I'm going to bed. Anything you want me to do first?"

"Yes. Go in the bathroom and get my bottle of tonic."

"Stomach bothering you again?"

"A little."

I go in the bathroom and get the bottle down from the medicine cabinet. I look at the label with the little girl holding the bottle with the same picture on another bottle—and another bottle and another picture and another bottle and the same picture and the same picture—and this damn thing drives me crazy. Why does this thing *annoy* me so much? It is a nuisance to see. The label is half off the bottle. I finish the job and pull it all the way off, flushing it down the toilet. I give Ma the bottle and start for bed.

"Pleasant dreams, Harold."

"Sure, Ma."


I am walking along the street in a crowd of men. Big overcoated men with hats pulled low over their eyes. They are all dressed alike. What a crowd! They bump into me, push, jostle me from side to side. I cannot see their faces. I want to see their faces and see what they are about and what is going on here. There are men behind me, men walking before me and men coming toward me. I look for the faces of the men coming toward me and suddenly they are walking backwards. I turn one of them around, but it is the back of his head again. I am annoyed because I must see their faces and find out what is happening. I go from one to another, turning them around only to face the back of their heads again and again. I am angered at this frustration. I am in a crowd of faceless men, jostling and pushing me along. Now I am frightened. I wonder. Why am I here among them? Slowly I bring my hand up to feel my face. I have none! I feel only the back of my head where my face should be. I am terrified. Two hands from the crowd behind me take me by the shoulders and shake, shake, shake. . . .

"Harold?"

I wake. Ma is shaking me. I roll over, look up into her face.

"Wake up, Harold. Mr. Pinkwise is here to see you."

"Abie?" I ask with surprise.

"Yes."

I sit up, rub my eyes. The Bug is standing in the bedroom doorway.

"Sorry to wake you up so early," he says, "but we got business."

"What time is it?" I ask.

"Six o'clock."

"What's up?"

The Bug glances at Ma, then back at me. "Nothing to get upset about—just business. You get dressed and I'll wait for you downstairs in the car." He turns to Ma and pats her gently on the shoulder. "You go on back to bed, Missus Odum. I'll drive Harry back in an hour or two so he can finish his beauty nap."

The Bug goes out and Ma goes back to her room. I dress quick, turn out the light and start. Ma is standing in the hall waiting for me. She has a worried, frightened look on her face.

"Harold, you're not going to get in any trouble, are you?"

"Trouble? Ma, you know me better than that." I kiss her cheek. "Go back to sleep. I'll be back for breakfast in a couple of hours."

I run downstairs, get in the car and we pull out.

"I'm not due in the shop until ten o'clock, Abie. It'd better be one hell of a reason for getting me up at six o'clock in the morning."

"The Owner's back from Chi."

"That ain't good enough."

"He's pretty upset. He phoned me he wants to make a meet with us right away. I think it's got something to do with that crime commission that's looking to move in all over."

"You scared hell out of Ma. I don't like her getting frightened like that."

"I'm sorry, but there was no other way. You ought to get a phone in. I coulda phoned and she wouldn't know from nothing."

"Yeah. I guess I'd better do that first thing."

Louis is in the living room with Georgie Whistle. He is in his undershirt, puffing on a big black cigar and walking back and forth.

"How do you like this?" he asks as we walk in. "I have to go all the way to Chicago to find out what's happening right here in my own territory!"

"What's up?" the Bug asks as we sit down.

"Man, have we got a smooth-working organization. It gives me a feeling of pride to belong. But them Goddamn bulls and politicians are tumbling to us. They got people all over the country, digging information to use when they start moving in on us. But we got some aces up our sleeves, too! You know what I find out in Chicago? Benny Blake is talking to an investigator from the commission."

The Bug's mouth pops open in surprise. "Benny 'Brownfingers' Blake?!"

"*Brownfingers* Blake! The son of a bitch is talking on me and Georgie about the Fabian Line shakedowns back in thirty-three."

"Man! I never figured Benny Blake would talk on *anything*!"

"That's the way it goes. Shows you how right your uncle Max was about the curve."

"Sure—but Benny Blake!" The Bug shakes his head.

"You know where he lives?" Varga asks.

"Sure. He's got two rooms over the fish store on Myrtle."

"Go over there now—you and the Cat."

"You want us to take him? Now?"

"Why wait for him to do more talking?"

The Bug gets up. "Come on, Harry."

I start to follow the Bug out. Varga stops us.

"Be sure you make the bum dead. But remember, I want you to make it nice. Leave everything nice, nice."

"Okay."

"And meet me over B.M.'s afterward. I'll be in New York."

"I got you."


Benny Blake is not home yet. The Bug says he hustles during the night, sleeps all day. We kill a couple of hours riding around in the car until we figure he is home. We park the car a few blocks away and start for Benny's place.

"Benny Blake," I wonder aloud. "Do I know this guy?"

"Maybe you seen him around. Been around for years. Skinny guy with nicotine stains on his fingers from clipping butts. Some people call him Brownfingers. He's not in with us now, but he used to be."

"Oh yeah, I think I heard of him."

"He's a hustler—this and that, now and then. Right now he's pushing horse for Joe Diddy and we take twenty per cent in the district by arrangement with Diddy. Harry, you got your knife with you?"

"Yeah. Why?"

"We'll use that on him. We'll cut his throat."

"Why don't we just shoot him?"

The Bug frowns. "A gun is like a fingerprint. If I can get out of it I don't use one. You shoot a guy and you have to get rid of the piece because the bullet in the guy matches it. Guns cost money. It's cheaper to cut his throat."


We leave Benny Blake sprawled across an overturned chair.

We climb into the car. The Bug starts the motor up.

He says, "We go over to B.M.'s now and meet Louis."

I have a giddy lightheaded feeling. "No," I say. "You go. I don't feel like making the trip."

He looks at me. "What's the matter?"

"I'm still sleepy," I lie.

"Okay, I'll ride you back home."

"No! No, I have something to do first. I'll walk."

I climb out of the car.

The Bug says, "Okay. See you later."

The car pulls away. I stand there on the corner, shaking all over with mounting wild excitement. The world seems gray, misty and unreal. Am I having another dream? This is impossible. My head aches and there is a throbbing at my temples. I need a drink. Maybe a drink will quiet me down. There is a bar up the street. I hurry there. The faces I pass on the street look at me. Can they see? Do they know me?

I order a double in the bar. I take it in one swallow. It is mild going down—fire feeding fire. Memories and thoughts race through my mind in furious confusion. It is a kind of confession. Thoughts whirl. The memory of Margie's naked thighs comes out of the whirl, and the heat inside me becomes white-hot. I am stunned and overwhelmed by the memory of her hungry body, the smell of her, the idea of her. . . .

"H'ya, Harry! How's my pal?"

I turn to see Madden standing next to me at the bar, his black hat cocked on his head, grinning stupidly.

"Where did *you* come from?" I ask.

"I spotted you through the window. I said to myself, 'There's my old pal, Harry!' So here I am. Say, what are you doing in a bar so early in the morning?"

"Can't you see what I'm doing?"

"Oh, sure, sure."

"You want a drink? It's on me."

"No, thanks, Harry."

"Well, what do you want? What are you hanging around for if you don't want a drink. Beat it."

"Aw, can't a pal just spend the time of day, Harry, old pal?"

"You're no pal of mine. You got me in trouble with Louis the Owner. You raped Iris and I got the blame for it. Even Iris thinks it was me."

"Aw, gee, Harry. I'm sorry about that. Honest to God, I really am."

**218**

"I had to apologize to the broad and everything. Why don't you get me off the hook?"

"Why, sure! What do you want me to do?"

"Tell Louis what really happened. Tell him it was you, not me."

"Well, why don't *you* tell him?"

"I did but he wouldn't believe me. Besides, I'm no rat. I never named you."

"Okay, Harry, I'll tell you what I'll do. The first chance I get, I'll go up to Louis and tell him it was me. Okay?"

"Okay." I order another double whisky.

"Say, Harry, I been thinking of something."

I look at him. "Oh, oh, you've got that gleam in your eyes!"

Madden laughs. "I saw you that time in the living room with Margie."

"I saw you, too, you lousy Peeping Tom."

"Did you give her what she wanted?"

"No. You know I don't go for that stuff. Why didn't you come in and rescue me?"

"I sure wanted to. But I had an idea you two wanted to be alone. I was just coming upstairs for a drink when I saw. I tiptoed back down."

"You should have come in. She had me up a tree. If you had come in, she would've stopped, or grabbed you. And I know you would have loved that, Madden, my boy!"

"You're telling me! I could use her right now. I'm in a real bad way for a broad."

"You filthy dog, you always are!"

"You think I ought to try her? I hear she's always in the mood for it. I hear she's really got hot pants."

"No, leave her alone. Louis will kill you."

"I hear Louis doesn't mind if she gives it up."

"Maybe Margie will mind. No, come to think of it, you and her are two of a kind."

"I saw Louis leave the apartment a couple of hours ago. I'm going over there now. Want to come along?"

"Sure, I'll go along, just to see her chase you out of there."

Madden chuckles. "I'll show you how it's *really* done."

"You dog," I say. "You filthy bastard!"

We hurry along. We go into the barbershop. Ding Dong is there. He says something I do not hear.

"What?"

"I said, you got some bleed on your tie, Harry."

I take it off, hand it to Ding Dong. "Burn it," I say.

Madden is standing by the back door. He beckons impatiently to me. We go into the back room. Georgie Whistle is there talking to some runners.

Madden whispers to me, "I'd forgotten all about Georgie. I'll have to get upstairs to the apartment without getting him suspicious."

Georgie Whistle looks over at me. "How'd it go, Harry?"

"Okay," I say. "All over."

"Nice?"

"Nice."

"Where's Abie? New York?"

"Yeah."

He resumes talking with the runners. Madden tries to sneak over by the door leading upstairs, but Georgie Whistle is standing in such a way he will see if he tries to go up.

"What the hell," Madden whispers to me. "To hell with him! I got to get upstairs." He reaches for the door.

"Where you going?" comes Georgie's voice.

Madden turns slowly. "What the hell," he says to me in a crooked-mouthed whisper, "I'll kill him if I have to." He turns to Georgie Whistle. "I'm going upstairs."

"Louis ain't here. He's in New York."

"I know—but I need a drink. You think he'll mind?"

"No, go ahead."

We go through the door and quickly upstairs to the apartment. The living room is empty.

"She's not here!" I say happily.

"But she *is* here," Madden insists. "I can smell her. She's somewhere in the house. I know it. Listen, I hear a noise in the kitchen. She must be in there." He calls softly, "Margie, Margie!"

We hear footsteps down the hall. Someone is coming into the doorway.

Madden says, "Margie, I—"

He stops. It is not Margie. It is Iris. She stands there with a dish in her hand, drying it with a towel. She smiles brightly.

"Hello, Harold."

"Where is—Margie?" Madden asks.

"Gone out," she tells him. "There's nobody here but me."

She smiles very sweetly at Madden.

"Iris," he begins.

"What is it? Is something wrong?"

"Yes. No, but—gee, Iris!"

She seems to understand. But it is not like the last time. There is no fear. There is only pity in her eyes. Pity and softness and understanding.

"Just one thing," she says a little bashfully. "I suppose you know by now how I feel about you. Couldn't we—not like this all the time—but couldn't we go steady?"

I am amazed!

"Yes," Madden says, "I want to go steady." Madden will say anything just to have her!

Iris smiles. She reaches out and takes him by the hand.

"Come," she says quietly.

She leads him into the bedroom.

Madden goes. I weep.

I go into the bathroom and wash and scrub and scrub my hands.

# XVIII

*A*NOTHER SUMMER AGAIN!

It is a nice sunny day as I turn up Hudson Avenue. The street is crowded. People are everywhere, sunning themselves on porches, talking in little groups, and leaning out of windows just watching. These people are like ants. During the cold winter months, they hole up in their anthill tenements, so that the street is practically deserted. But as soon as a warm day comes along, they flow out in droves, and you are surprised at the number of people in the neighborhood. Windows fly up and heads pop out. These are the watchers. There are certain people whose only pleasure in this world seems to be watching other people. We keep a very sharp eye on these watchers, too.

As I walk along I see many faces I have not seen in almost a year. Some people smile and speak to me, many others avoid my eyes and give me plenty of room. The Bug says this is the way it should be with a good enforcer. *Fear*—nobody runs to the police. *Fear*—less resistance, less trouble. *Fear*—everybody wants to stay in your good graces. Fear is a more powerful weapon than a gun itself.

I go in the barbershop. Ding Dong and a few runners are shooting the breeze. I go in the back room. Varga and Georgie Whistle are seated at the table, going over a book of accounts with the bookkeeper. A big pitcher of lemonade is on the table. They are all in their shirt sleeves and sweating because it is hot and there are no windows to let the air in. An electric fan buzzes on a shelf.

Varga looks up. "Have some lemonade," he says to me.

I pour myself a glass. "Where is the Bug?" I ask.

"Jersey. Should be back some time today."

"Jersey?" I say. "What's he doing over in Jersey?"

"You know."

"Business?"

Varga nods.

"How come I didn't go with him?"

"This time, two is a crowd."

I feel peeved and irritated that I have been left out of it. I slump down in a chair. "What the hell—I thought we're supposed to work together!"

Varga studies my face a moment, smiles. "I'm a sonamagun! He's sore because he didn't get in on it."

Georgie Whistle looks over at me. "Harry's a good boy. He likes his work."

Varga looks at me keenly, curiosity in his eyes. "You really like it, Harry, to take somebody?"

I am stirred by a feeling of guilt and resentment. "It's not a question of like or dislike. It's my job, that's all."

"See?" Georgie Whistle says to Varga. "I told you, Harry's a good boy. Leave him alone!"

"Don't I know that?" Varga says. "Whose idea was it to bring him along? Mine!" He comes over to me, puts a hand on my shoulder. "Take the day off, Harry. There's nothing for you to do around here now. It's a hot day. Why don't you take your mama or Iris down Coney Island for a swim?"

"Is Iris upstairs?"

"Yeah. Run up and tell her I said to take the day off. Margie ain't here, anyway."

I go upstairs to the living room. Iris is running a vacuum cleaner over the rug. She sees me and smiles. She shuts off the motor.

"Hello, Harry."

"Hello, Iris."

I flop on the sofa and look at her. She is not a pretty girl at all. She has a rag tied around her hair, and a dirty apron covers a loose-fitting house dress. She flutters nervously and pulls up her falling stockings.

"Gee, you shouldn't always pop in like this while I'm working. I know I look terrible!"

"You look okay. Want to go down the beach with me?"

"Beach?" she asks with a surprised look. "What beach?"

"The Island."

She smiles happily, fusses with the rag on her hair. "Well, gee, I'd love to, Harry. Only—I have to work."

"Louis says you can have the day off if you want to go."

"He did? Oh, then I'd love to go, Harry. But I'll have to go home and change first. I'll have to put on something nice."

I get up. "All right. I'll be waiting for you down in the barber-shop. Will you take long?"

"No, I'll hurry. Shall I fix a lunch?"

"No. There are places to eat down there. See you downstairs." I start out.

"Harry."

"What?"

"Thank you."

"What for?"

"For wanting to take me out once in a while."

A thought occurs to me. I think on it a moment, "Iris, do you want to be my girl?"

"Very much," she says slowly and deliberately.

"Okay, you're my girl, so you don't have to thank me now when I take you out. I'll see you downstairs."

I go downstairs. I feel good about it. This way, maybe I can save her from Madden and at the same time make Louis happy. She is just too nice a girl for Madden and his tricks. Iris is really cute, too, in a way. I am surprised to discover that I am beginning to like her very much. I must be careful not to get in love. I have seen too much of it with Ma and Hap. That kind of thing is not for me.

I stretch out on the sand in the warm sunshine to dry off. Iris kneels down beside me and pulls her bathing cap off.

"That water's cold," I say, "but it feels nice here."

"Can I cover you up?"

"If you want to."

She begins packing sand around my feet and legs.

"Harry."

"Hmm?"

"Did you really mean it—about me being your girl friend?"

"Yeah . . . yes, I meant it."

"I mean, do you really like me that much? I don't mean love. I never believed what Mr. Varga and Mr. Pinkwise said about you being in love with me. I knew they were only doing that to get me to come back to work. But do you really like me enough to be my boy friend, or are you just being nice to me?"

I close my eyes. "I wouldn't take you out if I didn't like you, Iris."

She is quiet a long while. I feel that my answer does not satisfy her.

"Harry, I want to tell you something. I must tell you something."

"What?"

"It's not easy for a *girl*—to say what I'm going to say—to a *boy*."

"What is it, Iris?"

"I love you, Harry. I love you above everything else I've ever known."

I open my eyes and look at her. She does not look at me. She plays with the sand, her face flushed darkly. I am embarrassed. I do not know what to say. I close my eyes and remain silent, hoping the moment will end at that.

"I never knew how to cope with boys—the grabbing kind. But, somehow, I always managed to escape—until you came along. I was terrified at first, but, Harry, I believe you put up a tough front, but underneath I know you're gentle and tender and kind."

I lie there quiet with my eyes closed. If she only knew, if she only knew!

"Harry, why do you like me enough to want me to be your girl?"

This is a question I have asked myself a thousand times. I think I know the answer, but I do not think I should tell her.

"Oh, I don't know, Iris. I just like you, that's all."

"But there must be some little reason. I mean, if you thought about it real hard. What in the world could have attracted you to me in the first place?"

"Well, if I tell you, will you promise not to feel bad about it?"

"Okay."

"I think—your affliction."

Her feelings are not hurt at all. She smiles at me and says, "Well, isn't that surprising! The same thing first attracted me to you."

"What?"

"*Your* affliction."

Surprised, I look at her. "But I have none!"

I look questioningly at her. She does not say anything. She looks at the sand, plays with it. She is probably confusing me with Madden again. He has a deformed right hand. I close my eyes and relax in the sand again.

I think about love. What is love? Just two years ago Iris and me were complete strangers, and now today she has this feeling for me. I am curious to know what it is like.

"Iris, what is love?"

"It's what I feel for you."

"That's no kind of answer. Tell me what it is."

"Harry, are you kidding me?"

I look at her. "Kidding you? About what?"

"About love."

"No, I'm serious. Why would I kid you about it?"

"I don't know."

She looks at me, bewildered. But I am damn serious about this love business. "Will you tell me about it?" I ask.

"About love? Oh, but, Harry, you *can't* be serious!"

"Why not?"

"Because all boys know about it and—"

"I don't. I've never been in love."

"You must have read about it."

"Reading it and feeling it are different things."

"But why ask me? You're so much smarter."

"Look, you say you're in love with me. Okay. Well, all I want to know is what it is about. Can't you tell me that?"

"Well, if you really mean it—"

"I really mean it."

"I don't know if I can but I'll try, Harry."

"How does it make you feel?"

"It makes me feel—Well, it's a lot of things together. You feel full of joy and happiness all the time, and there's a sadness in it, too. Have you ever been so happy in your life that you wanted to cry?"

"Maybe."

"Well, it's something like that—and more. Much more. Whenever you're close to me, like right now, I get weak in the knees if I'm standing up. And do you know what? When I'm hungry and I sit down to eat, if I happen to think of you, suddenly I'm full right up to my neck and I can't eat!"

"You feel all of those things? It sounds like a sickness."

"It *is* a sickness in a way."

"And you like the feeling?"

"It's the most wonderful feeling in the world when you can have the one you love, like I have you."

"Suppose you can't have the one you love?"

"That's when it becomes a sickness. It would be terrible. Some people kill themselves to escape the agony of it."

Strangely I recognize this agony. Why is this? It is like a memory woven from nothing. I reach for it, it goes. Yet, it is a feeling that I have known. Where does this memory come from? How can I know what it is to love and not be loved when I have never been in love at all? It is another mystery for me.

I wake from my nap. The sun has gone down and the beach is nearly deserted. Iris' head rests on my shoulder.

She sits up as I stir.

"Have a nice nap?" she asks.

I sit up. A chill breeze makes me shiver. "Yes. It's getting cold. Let's get dressed and go get something to eat."

"All right."

We start getting our things together and putting them in the beach bag. I pick up the blanket and begin to shake the sand out of it.

"Harry, do you know all about love now?"

I laugh. "No. I'm dumber than when I came in."

"There's another part of it I didn't explain," she says shyly. "It's something special between you and me."

I kneel down to stuff the blanket in the bag.

"What is it?" I ask.

"Remember that first time—the time at Mr. Varga's when you forced me to—in the bedroom?"

Here I go again, taking the blame for Madden.

"Well, I didn't love you then," she continues, "and I think I almost hated you for forcing me. But now that I'm in love with you—Well, it's a different thing altogether now. I want—I mean, I feel I belong to you now. Before, it was fear that made me surrender my body to you, now it will be love."

I am disturbed. "That's not love, that's sex."

"Sex is a part of love, Harry."

"It isn't!"

"It is."

Suddenly I am furious with her for saying it. I have the urge to slap her across the face. "You crippled little bitch, I ought to—"

Terror on her face. "What's the matter, Harry?!"

I turn quickly away from her. "Nothing," I say. "Come on, let's get the friggin' hell out of here!"

I snatch up the beach bag and start for the boardwalk. Iris trails sheepishly behind me like a dog with its tail beneath its belly.

## 2

I twist and turn in the bed. Thoughts and strange feelings keep me awake.

Sex and love. Iris just does not know very much. Sex is sex. Love is love. Sex is a sneaky, dirty kind of pleasure you can get from any whore. Love is a feeling you have for a person that has nothing to do with sex. They are two different things altogether. Forget about it.

And what is this strange thing that comes over me when we take somebody? It is like a wild drunkenness. Does the Bug feel this way? I must ask him.

What did Georgie Whistle mean when he said: "Harry is a good boy. He likes his work."

Do I really like it? No. But even if I did, what is the shame of it? There are much worse crimes in this world than murder. Besides, do not think about it. I will never get to sleep.

But I must think about it soon. I feel like there is something closing in on me. There are too many things I do not have answers for. I think the back of my head is becoming like our old house, full of cobwebs and junk. I do not like this feeling. I must get around to deciding what should be kept, and what should be thrown out. Then again, on the other hand, it is like going in a circle. The more I think about things, the more mysteries I find. Some people say it is not good to think too much. Maybe I would be much better off in this world, doing the kind of job I do, without a brain that keeps on bothering me when I do not want to think. Yes, this is my problem deep down; because I do what I do for the mob, I should not think so much.

Why do I feel peeved because I did not get to go with the Bug to Jersey?

It seems like Madden's face is grinning at me in the dark. He knows. That Madden, he knows too damn much!

**T**EN O'CLOCK IN THE MORNING I go in the barbershop. Ding Dong stops me at the door.

He whispers, "What's happened with the Bug?"

"What do you mean?" I say. "He get back yet?"

"He come in yesterday. In the afternoon. Where was you?"

"Down the Island. What happened?"

"I don't know. But you shoulda seen him. He come in the shop yesterday like a crazy man—crying and mumbling to hisself. It scared me. I never seen the Bug like that before. He acts like he is drunk, but he wasn't. Georgie Whistle and the Owner hustles him outa here upstairs. He's still up there. He didn't go home all night."

I leave Ding Dong and hurry into the back room. Georgie Whistle is sitting there talking to some guys. He turns as I come in.

"Hey, Harry, hurry upstairs. The Owner wants to see you right away."

I go through the back door and up the stairs two at a time. In the living room I see the Bug with his shirt off, slumped down in a chair, staring at the floor. Louis is standing over him talking softly and offering him a drink. I walk in slowly, quietly, wondering what in hell has happened. Louis looks around at me, then turns back to the Bug.

"Ah!" he says. "Here comes Harry. Here comes your boy."

The Bug looks up at me. Suddenly he yells out, "Harry!" and bursts into tears, his face in his hands.

"What's the matter?" I ask.

Varga whispers to me. "Later." He bends over the Bug. "Come on, Abie. It don't do no good to act like this. What's done is done. Come on, take another little shot."

We watch silently as the Bug's crying subsides to a whimpering and then goes away altogether. He sniffs, wipes his nose and eyes and looks up sheepishly.

"I'm okay now," he says.

"Sure, you are!" Varga says. "Here, now, take this drink."

The Bug takes the drink. He downs it in one gulp.

"That's better," Varga tells him. "Now, here's what I want you to do. Harry will take you home. He'll stay with you while you get some sleep."

"No—I can't sleep."

"I got some pills." He turns to me. "Harry, I want you to take a few days off—you and Abie. You stick with him everywhere he goes, day and night. Cheer him up. Keep him company until he feels better. Abie's had a bad experience."

The Bug pats my knee affectionately. "Harry, my pal, Harry," he says.

I look inquiringly ar Varga. He winks secretly at me. "Come on in the back. I want to give you them pills for him."

I follow him through the hall into the kitchen. He takes a box down from a closet shelf. He pulls me close and whispers.

"The poor guy! He didn't know it. Nobody knew it."

"What happened?"

"You know that business he went out on in Jersey? Him and a local boy took care of it. The guy they hit turned out to be his Uncle Max. He didn't realize it until he started shooting."

"Damn! Who ordered that?"

"It come from inside. They just send the Bug to Jersey to work with a local boy who knew the uncle. Nobody knew it was a relative. Abie has hit maybe twenty, thirty people all over the country he never saw before. All of a sudden, a relative pops up. It can happen in this business. But who ever figures it? He ain't seen this uncle in years, but he liked him a lot. I think it's the only relative Abie had. You see how low he is. Stick with him and try to cheer him up. Try to make him feel that it wasn't his fault."

"Sure."

Varga hands me the little box. "Sleeping pills. Take him home and put him to bed. He didn't sleep all night. Give him three pills—no more. Return the rest to me. If three pills don't make him sleep, forget about it. Them things is very dangerous. Just hang around with him for a few days until the shock wears off. One drink is okay for now, but make sure you don't let him get glued on a bottle. Whisky and the Bug don't go together. We might catch hell getting him off again, once he gets glued on a bottle. Go to the movies and the ball games with him. Just wean him along—without the bottle—until the shock wears off. Okay?"

"I got you."

"Phone me once in a while. Let me know how you're doing."

We go back into the living room. The Bug is still slumped over in his chair, staring at the floor. I feel sorry for him. It takes something out of me to see a hard guy like Abie sitting there in pieces like this. We get him into his shirt, and I take him by the arm.

"Come on, Abie. Let's go and try to get a little rest."

He stands up uncertainly. He smiles weakly at me. "Sure, Harry. Anything for my boy, Harry."

I put an arm around his shoulder, and he responds by putting his arm around mine. We start out.

Louis is pleased. "Don't forget, keep me posted," he says.

The Bug has a nice three-room apartment with a little kitchenette, where he does his own cooking and everything.

He takes the three pills and lies on top of the covers on the bed in his pajamas. I pull a chair up by the window, a few feet from the bed, and open up my *Weird Tales* magazine.

I say, "Now, just relax and go to sleep. Anything you want, just call. I'll be right here."

He lies still on his back, staring at the ceiling, his eyes watery.

"It was the Goddamnedest thing that ever happened to me in my whole life!" he says suddenly.

"Forget it. Don't talk about it."

He turns his face to me. "But I want to talk about it. I got to talk about it."

"Okay," I say, pulling my chair closer to the bed. "Okay, tell me about it."

"It was the Goddamnedest thing, Harry. You know my Uncle Max. You heard me talk about him?"

"Sure, lots of times."

"Always watch out for the curve, he'd say. Ieee! My sweet Uncle Max! I grew up in the orphan's. But my Uncle Max always remembers me. My dead mother's brother. He comes to see me, brings presents—money. Always laughing, always kidding. He said he liked me special because I look like him. 'A *ponim vie a ferd's tuchas*,' he'd say. Means I got a face like a horse's ass. That's what he'd call me—'Tuchas face' or 'My face.' Oh, poor Uncle Max, always laughing, always free with a buck. When I first come outa the homes, he gives me good advice, helps me get started on a job. Legit, not like I'm doing now. This was my own idea. He helps me out so many times I can't remember. Then one day he's gone—but not forgotten. He travels all over the country. But wherever he is, he sends me a card—California, Nevada, Chicago—even Canada once. Always he writes, 'Hello Tuchas face! Doing fine. Watch out for them curve balls!' What a guy! Till yesterday, I ain't seen him in six or seven years."

"What was he—a salesman?"

"Naw! He didn't work. He was sharp. Sharp, but not balls hard. What the hell, he made a little book once in a while. Sometimes he'd con some sweet old lady out of her dough. I remember one time him and a pal used to work a little three-card monte. You know, shooting little corny angles like that. Nothing real big. He was as honest as a crook can get and still be a crook."

The Bug laughs a little at this, and I with him. He is feeling better.

"He must have had a connection with the organization you didn't know about," I say.

The Bug shakes his head. "I don't know, I don't know. And it's something I'll never know. But in all the years I been moving around, I never once ever heard his name come up on the inside. What the hell, he just coulda been a witness to something, or got too heavy on some Shylock bank. Who the hell knows?"

"Who sent you?"

"B.M. But it ain't him. It's mob business. You don't ask questions on mob business, you know that. B.M. sends for me. He says he heard there's a guy over in Jersey has got to be hit in the head. He tells me to make a meet with a guy name of Bobby Evans at the Sadler Hotel. That's all I know. Routine. The way I went out plenty of times before."

"What happened?"

"I make the meet. I don't know where they got this guy from. A sloppy-looking, fresh kid. Knows everything, this kid. Right away he's going to take over the whole operation. I wait in the lobby of the hotel around eight in the evening while he makes a phone call. He comes over to me and says, 'Okay, we got the bum where we want him. He's in a drugstore a few blocks away.' We get in a car and pull out. But I'm leery about whether this shmuck knows his business or not. I ask him, 'Whose car is this?' 'Mine,' he says. I say, what the hell are you looking to do? No dice, I tell him. We got to have a hot car. The jerk tells me, don't worry. He's taking care of everything. He's doing it his way. I'm a son of a bitch, I shoulda walked off the job right then and there. Them outside guns don't do business like we do it in Brooklyn. We use technique. Them sons of bitches are all farmers. Pop, pop and run. That's all they know. You know what he says when I ask him what about a crash car? He says, 'What's a crash car?' Right then, I know what I'm in for working with this stiff. There might be trouble if I walk out on the job, so I make up my mind to stick it out, but keep my good eye on this stupid jerk.

"Well, we drive up and park across the street from the drugstore. He gets out, leaving the motor running. 'Wait here,' he says. I say, 'Wait a minute—you going to shoot him, now?' No, he says he's just going to make sure it's the right guy. He goes in the store, and in a little while he comes out again and climbs back behind the wheel. 'That's him, all right,' he says. 'He's making a phone call.' 'That's perfect,' I tell him. 'Let's go in and get him.' 'No,' he says. 'Too many people in there.' I tell him, that's good. There'll be a lot of confusion, screaming and running, and we'll be screaming and running along with everybody else. I tell him it's like a camouflage. He looks at me down his nose. He says, 'You Brooklyn guys think you know it all. I hearda *you*. That's why they call you the Bug—for taking crazy chances like that with all them witnesses. I don't take chances,' he says. 'We'll wait here and pop him when he comes out.'

"I lean back in the car and say what the hell. I start to get my gun ready. Then I notice this guy is also pulling out a piece. I tell him, what are you going to do—shoot or drive? 'Both,' he says. That's the finish. I can't take no more of this cowboy. I tell him nothing doing. Either one guy does the shooting and the other drives, or I'm pulling out of the deal, consequences or no. He thinks it over. He's scared to do the job alone so he says, 'Okay, what do you want to do?' I say, 'You just sit tight and keep the motor running. I'll go in and take him.'

"I leave the car and go in the drugstore. There are three or four women customers at the counter. I look around for the phone booths. They are in a lonely little corner of the store. I go over there quick with the gun ready in my pocket. There are two booths, one is empty. As I get there, a short, fat guy is just opening the door to come out of the other one. I point the gun, and the guy looks up at me. It's Uncle Max, but it's too late—I'm already shooting. He hollers, 'Abie!' But I can't stop shooting, I swear to God. I keep banging away at him, trying to stop that voice from saying my name. Goddamn, I tell you, Harry, it was awful. Everything took only a couple of seconds. But I felt like I was going crazy when I saw his face. It was like the whole world was all crazy. The next thing I know people are screaming and running all over the place, and I am beating it the hell out of there. I tell you, Harry, it was the damnedest thing!"

I say, "How can you be so sure it was your Uncle? You only saw him for a couple of seconds."

"It was him, all right. Didn't he say my name? Jeez, as long as I live, I'll never forget the look on his face. He's looking at me like a big question mark. I killed him. I killed my old, sweet Uncle Max!"

"What's done is done, Abie. Try to look at it this way; it wasn't your fault. You didn't know it was him."

"I done it just the same."

I have no answer for that. I say, "Okay, why don't you try to get some sleep now. Do you feel the pills working yet?"

"A little."

"Then go to sleep."

"Don't let me die here, Harry!"

"Don't worry, you won't die. Go to sleep."

I move my chair back to the window and pick up my magazine again. I cannot concentrate on the story. I think of what has happened to Abie. This business becomes more complicated for me all the time. It is like we are at war with an unknown enemy. The only time we know our enemy is when we are about to kill him. And the enemy can suddenly turn out to be a friend or a relative. Who knows but that one day I might find myself pointing a gun into the face of a relative? It happened to the Bug, it could happen to me. It is crazy and disorderly, yet I seem to sense a planning, a keen design to it. Whose design? I do not know. I only sense a direction in me that what I do is right for me to do. I do what I must do like a lion who kills because it is his very nature and right to kill. I feel like a robot. Sometimes I am surprised to find myself a part of it all. Sometimes I wonder if I really know what I am doing or who I really am.

A paralyzing sadness overcomes me. I can feel the very hand of death itself taking the pulse beat of my heart, and only the Bug's loud snoring on the bed reassures reality and keeps the panic in me still.

**L**OUIS IS GETTING THE JITTERS. He is chewing everybody out. The crime commission will be moving into town soon, and the new district attorney, Myron Gold, is frantically looking around for something big to beat them to the punch with. We hear they are going over a lot of old, unsolved murders and asking questions about Louis and Georgie Whistle. The D.A. seems to be particularly interested in one particular murder the Bug calls, "the Gooney Package." This thing was before my time with the mob, so I do not know anything about it. We are all in Louis' living room discussing it. They are trying to recall all the details of the hit to see if there were any slip-ups anywhere, and whether or not the alibis are all tight. I cannot put two cents into the conversation or understand much of it, so I get very bored with all the talk. I go downstairs to see what is doing in the barbershop.

I walk in the shop and see Ding Dong talking happily with two fellows who look vaguely familiar to me. They turn and smile at me, then it comes to me who they are. Big Nasty and Sidney Bock, who were in jail with Arnie Devivo.

"Hello, Harry," they greet me.

I do not smile. I remember my position. I just nod to them and flop down in one of the barber chairs. Ding Dong looks embarrassed for them.

He says, "You remember Big Nasty and Sidney, don't you, Harry? They just got outa the can."

"Sure, I remember them. How you doing, fellows?"

"Pretty good," Sidney says. "We heard all about you up there, Harry. We sure got the good news. You look great, too!"

I look over at them. "You guys look okay, too. Jail must have been good for you. Did it teach you not to go pulling stick-ups in broad daylight behind that shmuck Arnie?"

"Aw—that Arnie!" Sidney says, as if there is a nasty taste in his mouth.

Ding Dong grins. "Hey, Sidney, is it true what we hear—that Arnie was a famous queen up there?"

"He was that—and worse!" Sidney answers.

"What do you mean by that?" I ask.

"He's a friggin' canary. He ratted on us in that holdup. The bulls caught him first. They shove him around a little and right away he starts to sing. Wasn't for him, we wouldn't got busted."

Another surprise about Arnie! A broad and a rat, too. I was right to give him plenty of my cold shoulder.

"Jeez, I never figured him for a canary," Ding Dong says.

"Who ever figured him for a broad?" I ask, "the way he used to knock fags."

"We can't touch him now," Big Nasty says. "On accounta the parole, we can't touch him. But the day we get our chance, we're gonna bust him up good."

"Give him a couple of licks for me, too," I say. "For luck."

"Sure, Harry."

"You fellows better beat it now. The Owner doesn't like the poolroom guys hanging around the barbershop."

"Oh, sure thing, Harry," Sidney says. "We just stepped in a

minute to say hello to Ding Dong. So long. Nice to see you again, Harry."

"So long."

They go out. Ding Dong turns to me with a puzzled and amused look on his face. "What ud you make of that Arnie?!"

I shrug. "I guess you never can tell about some guys."

I know now that this is the reason Louis is so careful about the people close around him. Georgie Whistle, the Bug and myself. Our loyalty has been tried and true. It is only the outsiders he has to worry about.

Ding Dong settles down with a newspaper. The Bug comes into the shop.

"Hey, Ding Dong," he calls. "Who won the ball game?"

"Brooklyn wins it in a romp, fourteen to three."

"Yeah? Great. Who pitched for Brooklyn?"

"How-d'ya-call-it? I forget his name. How-d'ya-call-it."

"Oh, Howdoyacallit pitched! He's a good pitcher, that Howdo-yacallit. Last year he's MVP."

"Aw—" Ding Dong says.

"Man, this is Brooklyn's year to win the pennant," the Bug tells him.

"Hell with a pennant," Ding Dong says. "This is the year they got to win a World Series."

"Ding Dong," the Bug begins with patience and humor, "they got to win the pennant before they can play for the World Series."

Ding Dong looks at Abie, startled. "Say, that's right! Jeez, I didn't thunk on that at all."

The Bug slaps him on the head. "Well, *thunk* on it, then!" He saunters over to the chair I am slumped down in and sits on the arm. "Paper says another heat wave's coming in."

"How'd it go upstairs? You guys got it all figured out yet?" I ask.

Abie grimaces. "Louis is too jittery. We're clean on that."

Something in the back of my mind is trying to push through. It keeps bothering me, but I do not know just what it is.

"Who was in on it?" I ask.

"The Gooney thing? Me and Georgie Whistle and a guy up the river name of Red Murphy. That's all. Nobody else."

It is coming through. "You use a getaway car?"

"Sure."

"Who drove?"

"I did. No, wait a minute. It was your old friend. What's his name? Arnie—he drove it."

It has come through. I say, "Come into the back room. I want to talk to you."

The Bug gives me a puzzled look. He follows me in the back. I close the door.

"What did Arnie know?"

"He don't know nothing. All he knows, he is told to wait in front of a certain building at a certain time with the motor running. Me, Georgie Whistle and Red Murphy go in the building. In a few minutes we come out, get in the car and tell him to take off. Five blocks away, we get out and get into my car. We send him off to ditch the hot car. That's all. What does he know? He don't know from nothing."

"Remember what you told me about the law of corroboration?" I ask.

Abie frowns. "Corroboration, balls! Where the hell's there gonna be corroboration? You mean, me or Georgie or Louis is gonna sing us all into the hot-seat? You mean one of us is gonna turn out to be a canary?!"

"I didn't mean that. I mean what you told me once about Louis not taking any kind of chances."

"Forget about it. We come out clean on this deal."

"I don't know about that," I tell him. "I just saw the guys who were sent up with Arnie on that holdup. They say Arnie squealed on them."

The Bug looks at me as if he did not hear me right. "What do you mean? They said that? They said he talked on them?"

"That's what they said. And they ought to know."

He thinks on it a moment, now brushes it off. "Aw, that's

nothing. All right, so he's a canary. We remember that for the future. But the Gooney Package—what the hell! He don't know nothing to sing about."

I do not like the way the Bug is brushing it all off and the way he tries to avoid looking me in the eye.

"I always thought you were a very careful guy," I say.

"I *am* careful, but there's nothing here to be careful about."

"Maybe we ought to ask Louis," I say.

He turns on me angrily. "Ask Louis?! What the hell is there to ask Louis about?!"

I keep calm. I know I am master of the situation because I am not trying to cover up anything. I suspect Abie is.

I say, "Louis likes to be careful, too."

"What the hell are you looking to do—get Arnie killed? I thought he was a friend of yours? Just because the kid was a jail broad, you act like you want to get him hit in the head all of a sudden. All of a sudden, you're looking to do him something!"

"It doesn't bother me one way or the other. I don't decide who is to get it. All I say is maybe we ought to tell Louis about it."

"Tell me what?"

It is Louis. He is coming into the room from upstairs, followed by Georgie Whistle. I look at the Bug. His eyes shift about.

Louis looks from me to Abie. "Well, tell me *what?*" he repeats.

The Bug fidgets, his eyes still shifting. "Aw, it's about Arnie. You remember—the kid who used to take cars for me before he got sent up."

"The kid used to be Harry's partner? So? What about him?"

"I forgot to mention. He drove the getaway for us that night."

"What did he know?" Louis asks.

"Nothing!" the Bug snaps. "All he knows, he's driving a getaway car, that's all. He don't know getaway from what."

A gleam comes in Louis' eyes as they narrow into slits. "*Still—*" he begins slowly, "maybe somebody can put dates and places together for him and he can put two and two together." Suddenly he looks over at me. "What gives? You and him was partners, Harry. What do you think?"

I know the Bug is giving me a desperate look, but I avoid his eyes. I do not know what is on Abie's mind, but I am loyal to Louis. I must say what I think.

"Arnie stooled on the fellows who were with him in the holdup."

"Uh-uh," Louis says, shaking his head. "That's bad. Come on, let's go back upstairs and make some more talk-talk."

We all follow Louis upstairs to the living room and sit down. The Bug goes over to the bar.

"This guy still around?" Louis asks me.

"Yeah, he still hangs around the poolroom."

Louis gets up, paces the floor a while. I can see that his brain is going a mile a minute. He stops pacing, turns to the Bug at the bar.

"What do you think, Abie?"

The Bug keeps his back to us. "He don't know nothing. He can't talk on what he don't know."

"But I got to be sure!" Louis says. "I don't want nothing laying around loose. If it was something nobody was interested in, I'd say we could maybe take a chance. But Gold is really poking around this Gooney Package. I don't want no holes showing. Georgie, you got any ideas?"

Georgie shrugs. "I don't know, Louis. But one thing, we sure don't want no holes showing. And after all, if the kid is a canary . . ."

"That settles it. We'll have to take him out. Abie, you want to handle it—you and Harry?"

The Bug's back is still turned to us. "Sure," he says. He pours a drink and swallows it.

"Okay," Louis says. "But don't take him from the poolroom. Don't heat up the block. Take him from somewheres else. And make everything nice, nice. Will the kid go with you, Harry?"

"I don't know. I've been giving him the cold-shoulder treatment since he got out of jail. He might get suspicious if I suddenly turn friendly."

Georgie Whistle says, "He will go with Abie. Abie can trick him into the car, and they can take him out in Jersey somewhere."

"How about it, Abie?" Louis asks.

His back to us, taking another drink, the Bug says, "I'll handle it. Don't I always handle it?"

No one disputes this.

# 2

I have not seen Arnie for a week. We are riding along Myrtle Avenue in Abie's car. Suddenly I spot Arnie standing in front of the United Theater.

I say to the Bug, "There he is!"

"Who?"

"Arnie . . . standing by the movie. Pull over!"

The Bug drives right on by the movie house and cuts around the corner on Hudson Avenue.

"What are you doing?" I say. "Why didn't you pick him up?"

"Wait a second," he says. "I'm trying to think of something. I'm circling the block."

"He might be gone when we get back!"

"He won't get far," the Bug says.

I look at him wonderingly. "What's on your mind?"

"I'm trying to figure what to use on him. I got nothing in the car but my gun. I don't want to use my gun on him."

"What the hell—we'll think of something once we get him somewhere. That's the important thing."

"Yeah, I guess you're right."

We circle the block and get back on Myrtle Avenue again. By luck, Arnie is still standing in front of the show, looking at the pictures outside. The Bug slows down. He brings the car to a stop near the curb. Quickly I get out of the front seat with the Bug and climb into the back. The Bug leans over to the window and calls.

"Hey, Arnie!"

Arnie turns, recognizes the Bug and breaks out into a big grin. He hurries over to the car.

"Hello there, Mr. Pinkwise. Good to see you. How's every little thing?"

"Get in," the Bug says, pushing open the door.

Arnie climbs in. He sees me for the first time as the car pulls out again.

"Oh, hello, Harry. I didn't see you there. How are you?"

"Okay," I say. "And you?"

"I feel okay but I'm beat to my socks. I ain't made a score since I don't know when. Say, about that five bucks I owe you—"

"Forget it."

"No, I'm going to pay you back, I swear. It's just that I can't seem to score. But as soon as I get my hands on something—"

"Okay," I tell him, "but I'm in no hurry for it."

"You're a swell guy, Harry." He turns to Abie. "How do you like my old buddy, Mr. Pinkwise, ain't he something?"

"He's blowed in the glass, kid."

"You wanted to see me about something special, Mr. Pinkwise? I sure could use a couple of bucks."

"Yeah," the Bug says. "You can make yourself an easy ten bucks. We want you to go with us somewhere."

"Baby!" Arnie shouts with joy. "What a break! I was looking to go in the show. Lucky for me I didn't."

The Bug drives the car over the bridge into Manhattan.

"Where we going?" Arnie asks.

"Jersey."

"Oh."

We bounce along in silence. I try to think of a way we can take him without using a gun or knife.

Suddenly the Bug says, "I got to take a leak bad."

"Pull up at the next gas station," I tell him. "Can we use some gas, too?"

"No," he says. "I can't wait. I'll find a bar someplace."

He pulls the car over to the curb and stops. He climbs out.

"Hurry it up," I say.

"I won't be long."

The street is full of people. I watch him disappear in the crowd. I lean back and light a cigarette. I offer Arnie one. He takes it. "Thanks."

I watch him puffing there in the front seat, holding the cigarette between stubby, dirty fingers. I am still curious about his sex switching. What the hell—maybe it is just a lot of jail gossip, after all.

"Mind if I ask you something, Arnie?"

He turns to me with a smile on his face. "No. Anything, Harry."

"It's something I heard about you up in stir. . . ."

The smile leaves his face. His eyes shift. He turns the back of his head to me again.

"What?" he asks.

"I heard you were a queen up there. Is it true?"

I watch the back of his neck. It slowly turns a dirty red. He sits still as a stick. He does not move a muscle.

"Who told you?" he asks in a low tone.

I shrug. "I heard it here and there—around. Is it true?"

His neck gets darker.

"It's a Goddamn lie!" he finally says.

"That's what I figured," I say, thinking, you son of a bitch, you're going to get it good!

We do not speak. We sit and wait. Me, in silent contempt; Arnie, in silent shame.

An hour passes. The Bug is not back yet!

"Jeez, he must have fell through!"

Arnie laughs a kind of sickly little laugh.

Two hours pass. No Bug. I get out of the car to go look for him.

"Sit tight," I tell Arnie. "Something must have happened."

I go up the street looking for a bar. There is none on the block. I turn the corner. I see a big bar-and-grill sign halfway down the block. I hurry down. I go in. It looks empty. I see one little guy in overalls, standing at the bar over a glass of beer. The radio is blaring out the ball game from Ebbets Field. I go up to the bar, about to ask the bartender if he saw anyone like Abie, when I spot the Bug at a table in a dark corner. I rush over to him.

"Abie!"

He looks up at me with bleary eyes. He is stewed.

"Harry, my boy! Have a drink."

"What the hell's the matter with you?!" I say in a whisper. "We got *business*!"

"It'll keep. Sit down and have a drink."

I am angry. I sit down. I am so full of disgust it is hard for me to look at him or talk to him without blowing up.

The crowd cheers, the radio blares: "Strike three! And he struck him out with the curve!"

The Bug mumbles. "My Uncle Max told you. The curve will get you every time. You know what happened to my Uncle Max, Harry?" He starts to cry.

"Oh, for Christ's sake!"

"I threw the curve at him actual. I did it. Poor, funny little Uncle Max!"

"Listen," I say, "we had a job to do. You said you were just coming in to take a leak. You wind up drunk. This isn't what you taught me."

"Take it easy," he slurs. "We can still take him."

"You're drunk!" I say in disgust.

"Then you take him alone. Drive 'im out in Jersey and pick me up on the way back."

"I don't know nothing about Jersey. Besides, I can't leave you here like this. You're drunk now. You'll be stiff when I get back."

The radio blares: "High and inside!"

"Sometimes that's as bad as the curve," the Bug says.

"Come on, let's get the hell out of here."

"One more drink. You take one, too."

What the hell, I might as well. I take his empty glass back to the bar and order two doubles. I down mine quick at the bar and carry the other back to the table.

"Here's to Uncle Max," the Bug declares, lifting the glass.

The radio blares: "—a little dribbler down the third-base line. Bogess charges in—"

The Bug downs the drink.

The radio: "He's out!"

"He's out!" the Bug shouts crazily. "My Uncle Max, I took him out!"

"*Shut up!*" I help him up from the chair. "Let's get out of here."

The bartender and the little man in overalls stare at us. I maneuver the Bug on his wobbly legs toward the door.

"You know what I am? I'm a killer," the Bug shouts. "I'm a killer-diller-killer from a-way back!"

I rush him out of there fast.

I open the door of the car and get Abie inside. He sprawls drunkenly across the back seat. Arnie is staring bug-eyed at us.

"What happened?"

I curse. "He got drunk," I say, climbing in behind the wheel.

"Jeez! I never knew he lushed."

"Well, you know it now."

The Bug kicks the back of the front seat where Arnie sits. He slurs, "Let's take this son of a bitch like I took my Uncle Max."

Arnie looks at me with leery eyes. "What's he talking about?"

"How should I know? He's drunk. He said that to the bartender, too. Listen, Arnie, the job is off for now because he's loaded. Here's a couple of bucks for your troubles. Get out and take the subway home, will you? I got to drive him somewhere else."

"Sure. Thanks, Harry." He climbs out of the car and closes the door. He leans his head a little into the window. "Maybe tomorrow? I can do the job then, I mean?"

"We'll let you know when," I say. "Just make yourself available around the neighborhood."

"You bet, Harry, and thanks again."

I pull out and head back for Brooklyn.

I get Abie to his place and into bed. He is not hard to handle. He is like a little baby and does everything I tell him. As I pull the covers over him he is crying again.

"Jeez, I messed it up, didn't I, Harry? I messed it all up."

"Forget it. We'll get another chance."

"What a knucklehead play! I didn't mean to get drunk. I swear, I didn't, Harry. I don't know what got into me. I only meant to take one drink. But the ball game was on, and the pitcher kept throwing curve balls, and all I could think about was Uncle Max."

"Okay," I say. "You just sleep it off now. I'll see you later at the shop."

I start out. He calls me back.

"Harry, don't—Please don't tell Louis about this. He might think—"

"Don't worry. I won't mention it."

"We'll get that canary, don't worry. Next time I won't mess it up on you, Harry. You wait and see."

"Okay. Get some sleep."

"Thanks, Harry. You're a real good partner."

I go out. I sense something bad is building up between me and the Bug. Yet it is almost impossible to believe he is trying to dog anything. I push it from my mind.

I feel annoyed and frustrated. I go to the back of the barbershop. Louis is alone here, going over the books. He looks up with a frown.

"Where you been?" he asks grouchily. "I pay you to be around when I need you!"

"We were out looking for the canary."

"Find him?"

"No."

"Where's Abie?"

"I don't know. I think he went to eat."

He curses. "I want you to go over to Feltman's shoe store. Get the protection money. He's overdue three weeks."

I am eager to go. I start out quickly.

"Harry!" Louis calls.

I turn. "Yeah?"

"Don't shlump him. Even if he ain't got the money, don't hit him. We don't want no unnecessary trouble these days. Give him another week and a warning."

"Okay."

I go into the shoe store. Feltman and a clerk are there. I grab Feltman and pull him into the stock room in the back of the store. I grab him tight by the collar.

"You got the money?" I ask.

"Sure, I got the money," he says, going into his pocket. "Don't get excited, I got the money." He hands me forty dollars. "I would've had it sooner, but I was having a little home troubles."

I put the money in my pocket. I ball up my fist and punch it hard into his belly. He groans and doubles over. I hit him on the side of the head and he crumbles to the floor. I hurry out of there, past the trembling clerk who stares at me, terrified.

I feel teased and feverish.

I look eagerly up and down the street, but Madden is nowhere in sight. The shlumping did no good. There is only dying, disgusting desire. It has got to be a hit and nothing else will do.

A man who is going insane must feel something like what I do.

# 3

Before going to bed, I put the garbage can on the dumb-waiter. I notice another odd-shaped bag. I look in. Another empty wine bottle. She cannot kid me any more, and I do not like it one bit. I go into the living room where she is knitting.

"Ma, you've started to drink, haven't you?"

She looks outraged. "*Me? Drinking?* Why, what ever gave you such an idea, Harold?!"

"Either that or you're having company who drinks. I'm finding wine bottles in the garbage. I found the fourth one tonight."

"Oh, *that.* Well, yes, I have been taking little sips once in a while. I have this nagging little pain in my chest, and a little wine seems to soothe it."

"I don't want you drinking, Ma. I don't want you to become another Hap."

"But this is for medical purposes, darling. Surely, you wouldn't call what I do *drinking!* Why, it's only once in a great while that I take a sip or two."

"Well, if it's only once in a while, okay. I don't mind it once in a while, but—"

"I'm sure you must realize that Mama is well aware of the evils of drink. Wasn't it me who was hurt so much by your father's drinking? Well, never you fear, my pet, that Ma will take after that. No, indeed. And I'll tell you what I'll do—just to show you how much I love you. I'll cut out the sips altogether."

"Well, I wouldn't mind if it's only once in a while."

"No, indeed. Altogether! I can manage very well without sipping wine, thank you. There will be no more talk of wine in this house. I don't want to do anything that will make my baby the least bit unhappy."

"Okay, Ma."

I kiss her good night and go off to bed.

I wake up suddenly! What is it? I am nervous and frightened. I turn over and try to get back to sleep. It is no use. Sleep only comes halfway. Strange things are churning up inside me. It is a terrible feeling of aloneness and doom. It frightens me because I cannot understand this thing. It has come before like this in the night, always with the half-sleep. It is a sneaky thing. It creeps up on me. It is like something intends to strangle me, but I am helpless because I cannot see it or hear it or fight back. I can only wait for it to strike. But, somehow, it never seems to strike, yet it is always coming, always slowly coming. Is it real or just my imagination? At any moment, it seems, I am about to die. It is just like something right out of *Horror Tales*.

I toss and toss the whole night through.

**M**E AND THE BUG are walking up Hudson Avenue, returning from a collection. It is afternoon and many people are on the street. We spot Arnie standing by the Greek's restaurant on the corner. He sees us, too, at the same time and waves. I wave back.

"Okay," I tell the Bug. "You take the money on down to the shop and come back with your car. I'll stall him on the corner until you get back."

The Bug thinks a moment. "Naw," he says. "We can't take him

from the corner. There's too many people around. Tell you what. Make him steal a car for us tonight and bring it to the drop. Down there we'll have him all to ourselves. We can use the hot car to dump him in, too."

Smart! I think. The Bug is using his cute head again. He continues on up the street to the barbershop with the collection. I cross the street to where Arnie is standing.

"Hi, Harry. You guys ready for me yet?"

"Yeah, we're ready," I say. I stand close to him. I do not look at him, but keep my eyes peeled for anybody who might be watching us. I speak to him crooked-mouth. "Look Arnie, we want you to take a car for us and bring it around the drop for us around eight o'clock tonight."

"Can do!" he says with a sly wink. "Any special kind?"

"No—regular plain kind. You know."

His eyes light up. "Say, I got just the job. I been casing it, you know, just to keep my hand in. It's been parked over a certain place quite a while now."

"Take it and bring it to the drop. Work alone and don't talk to nobody. And remember, eight o'clock."

"Will do!" He winks again.

I go to the barbershop. I tell Ding Dong, "Be in the garage office about seven o'clock tonight. I got a job for you."

"Down the drop? Sure, what's up?"

"You just be there, that's all. And don't be late."

"Sure, Harry. Whatever you say. Whatever my boss, Harry, tells me, I do."

It is about seven o'clock. We pull up to the garage in the Bug's Caddy and drive in. There is plenty of parking space. Only two other cars are there, Varga's roadster and a big Chevy with one hind wheel jacked up. We get out of the car and go in the office. It is a dim little cubbyhole with a grease-stained roll-top desk. Used auto parts, oil cans, tires, inner tubes are scattered about the dirty room. Ding Dong has arrived ahead of us and is talking to Red, the mechanic, as we walk in.

The Bug says to Red, "Wanna make yourself scarce a couple of hours?"

"Sure," Red says, wiping his hands on a greasy, black rag. "What time you want me to come back?"

The Bug thinks a moment, then shrugs. "What the hell, take the rest of the night off. We'll lock up. Come back in the morning."

"Suits me," Red says and goes outside to wash up.

I say to Abie, "You want to have coffee?"

"Sure."

I give Ding Dong a quarter. "Go around the corner and get two containers." He goes. I turn to the Bug. "He'll be here at eight. How will we take him?"

The Bug thinks a moment. He starts poking around in all the inner tubes and auto parts on the floor along the wall. He picks up a monkey wrench from a toolbox, considers it, then throws it down quickly as he spots a length of clothes-line rope on the desk. It is about three feet long. He wraps the two ends around his big hands and stretches it.

"This will do it," he says. "When he comes, you bring him into the office from the garage. I'll stand here behind the door. You walk in first. When he gets in, I'll jump him from behind and choke him."

"Let me do it," I say.

"No, I'm bigger than you. Let me get the jump on him first, then you can pitch in."

Red comes back into the office, dressed for the street. He says good night and goes out of the office front door, which faces the street the same way as the big garage doors.

Ding Dong comes in with the coffee and puts the containers on the desk.

"Nickel change," he says.

"Keep it," I say. "What time is it?"

"About seven thirty or quarter eight."

"Now go have yourself some coffee," I tell him. "Stay in the diner until I call you. Don't come back until I call you."

"Okay," he says and goes out.

The Bug surprises me by taking out a pint of whiskey. He breaks the seal, spills half the coffee from the container onto the floor and makes up the difference with whisky. I watch him disapprovingly.

"Don't get high," I warn him. "Remember the last time."

"Don't worry. I know what I'm doing now. Want a shot?"

"No."

We sit on the desk and wait in silence.

We hear the sound of a car pulling into the garage. I bound off the desk with excitement.

"That's him!" I say. "Get ready."

The Bug takes the rope and steps behind the door. I go out into the garage just as an old Ford is pulling to a stop. Arnie is behind the wheel.

He smiles and winks at me. "Here she is, old pal. Where'll I put her?"

"Park it over by the wall back there near the Chevy."

He drives over. I go and slide the big garage doors shut and lock them. I turn as Arnie is climbing out of the car.

"Nice going," I tell him.

"Thanks," he says. "But it was a real cinch. I didn't even have to cross the ignition. The bum had the keys hid up in back of the rear-view mirror."

*"Inside?"* I say, trying to sound surprised. "No kidding?!" I start walking casually toward the office.

"They're really asking for it when they hide the key in the car. Some guys make it a real pleasure for you to clip a car on them. Not that an expert like me needs a key."

I get to the office door, turn. He is not following me. He still stands by the hot car.

"Okay, Arnie," I say. "Come into the office and I'll pay you off."

"Sure," he says. "You alone here, Harry? Where's the—Where's Mr. Pinkwise?"

"He didn't come," I tell him as I go into the office. Arnie follows me in.

"Say, I sure would like to call him Abie the Bug like you do. Do you think he'd get sore if I did?"

"No, he wouldn't mind."

I reach the desk and turn, facing Arnie as he comes toward me. There is no movement from the Bug.

"I think I'll take a chance, then, and call him Abie. I always feel like such a punk kid saying 'Mr. Pinkwise' alla time."

Nothing happens. My eyes move over Arnie's shoulder, looking toward the door. Suddenly everything seems to be happening at once. The Bug is moving slowly toward us, his face white and twisted as if he is in pain. The rope dangles loosely from one hand. Arnie catches my look behind him. He turns and is suddenly frightened stiff to see the Bug behind him. He jumps, knocking me into the desk.

"I can't do it, Harry," the Bug is mumbling. "I can't go through with it!"

Arnie looks at me, wild-eyed. At once he tumbles to it. Suddenly he screams. I try to grab him but he ducks and runs past the Bug back into the garage. I curse and snatch the rope from Bug's hand. I race into the garage after him.

He is yelling with all his might and frantically trying to get the garage doors open. I pounce on him from behind. I put my hand over his mouth to stop his screaming. I start to bring the rope around with my right hand. Suddenly I scream with pain and let go of him. He has bitten my hand. I curse and spit. He starts running for the office door again.

I yell, "Get him, Abie!"

He changes his mind, veers away from the office, but there is no other exit for him. He stops a second and looks desperately around the garage. I start for him again with the rope. He lets out another yell and runs behind the jacked-up Chevy. I start after him around the car, but he begins to circle, keeping the Chevy between us.

"What's the matter, Harry? You gone crazy, Harry? What's the matter with you?"

He keeps circling. I try to figure how I can get to him.

"What did I do, Harry?" he whimpers. "I didn't do nothing. For God's sake, Harry, don't do nothing to me. Please, don't. Is it the money I owe you? I'll pay you every cent. Every nickel I'll ever make I'll give it to you, Harry. I swear to God, Harry, please."

I stop circling after him. He stops circling. We are on opposite sides of the car, watching each other through the windows. He is on the side near the garage wall, near a little corner. I study the situation. He sees my determination. Tears are streaming down his face.

"Please, why don't somebody help me?" he pleads. He yells feebly, "Mr. Pinkwise!"

I decide to go quickly on top of the car and pounce on him any way he runs. I go up quickly. Arnie jumps back, stumbles and falls backward into the corner. I stand there poised on top of the car. I can jump him either way he goes now, but he does not attempt to get up. He just sits there with his knees buckled up under his chin, looking up at me with a whimpering plea. Slowly I climb down off the car, keeping my eyes on him. He still does not move, just watches me. Silently, fearfully.

He seems hypnotized by fear. He has surrendered himself to me. He is my pigeon now. My insides come alive. He is mine! He is all I have denied myself. He is anger and hate, pleasure and pain, fulfillment and death. He sits there waiting resignedly for me. I feel like a beast of prey. I tighten the rope in my hands. Arrogantly I move in to cut him down, as though it is my natural right to take him. I do not rush. He will wait.

Even as I put the rope around his neck, he does not fight or protest. There is no trouble. I manipulate him around as I wish. I throw him onto his stomach. I take hold of the two ends of the rope and make a loop. I prop my knee into his back and bring the loop tight around his neck. I pull as tight as I can. There is a gasping, gurgling sound from him. I hold the cord tight for a long, long time. . . .

The erection comes.

I drag him over to the hot Ford. I lift and shove him into the back of the car on the floor. One leg sticks out, so that I cannot close the door tight. I bend the leg back and hook it under the rim of the seat. I shut the door tight. I open up the garage door and look out on the street to see if there is anyone who might have heard Arnie yell. There is no one. I go into the garage office. The Bug is sitting on a little stool, his head bowed in his hands.

"What happened to you?" I ask, annoyed. "How come you had to dog it like that?"

He shakes his head. "I don't know, Harry. I don't know what got into me—but I just *couldn't*, Harry. I just couldn't stand to touch him."

I am too eager and feverish to bother with him now. "All right," I tell him, "go get in your car and wait for me. I'll do the driving."

I go out and get Ding Dong from the diner around the corner. We come back into the garage. The Bug is sprawled out on the back seat of his Cadillac, sucking on the bottle. I tell Ding Dong to drive the hot car around over on Bergen Street and dump it. I tell him I will trail him in the Bug's car and pick him up. He climbs into the Ford, and I open up the garage doors.

"Drive slow," I caution him. "Take it easy. We don't want to draw any attention."

He pulls out. I pull out behind him and stop. I get out of the car, lock up the garage, and get back in the Caddy. I begin to trail slowly behind the Ford along Third Avenue. I look keenly at the dark streets ahead expecting Madden to pop up any minute. But he must not come before I finish this business! He must not come yet. Ding Dong comes to Bergen Street. He turns and disappears around the corner. I pull up at the curb and park with the motor running.

Ding Dong comes from around the corner, walking very fast. I push the door open for him, and he climbs in quickly beside me. He looks a little shaken. I pull out.

"What were you walking so fast for?" I say. "I told you to take it easy!"

"Harry, I didn't know there was a package in the car. You shoulda told me. I like to wet myself when I tumbled."

"You keep your mouth shut."

"You don't have to tell me. I'm sorry I seen it the first place."

We do not talk any more. I look along the street for Madden. I pull up in front of the barbershop. Ding Dong gets out first.

"Anything else, Harry? I wanna shoot a couple games of pool before I go in."

"No." I hand him five dollars. "Remember what I told you."

"Don't worry!"

"See you tomorrow," I say.

"Sure, Harry. So long."

He goes across the street into the poolroom. My head begins to ache. I look back at the Bug as he takes another pull on the bottle.

I say, "You go up and tell Louis we got him. I got somewhere else to go."

I climb out of the car. I look anxiously up and down the street for Madden. I begin to fear that he will not show up. I break out into a cold sweat. There is a war inside me. I fear there will be horror if he does not come. Abie leans over to the car window.

"Harry, I'm sorry about what happened. Jeez, I don't know what it was come over me. The next time I'll—"

*This headache is killing me!*

"Harry, please don't tell Lou—"

I have no time for him. Relief comes to me like a downpour in a heat wave. Hat cocked jauntily on head, cigarette dangling from smiling lips, Madden comes briskly down the street.

I lie on my back in the bed. The bedroom is dark except for the orange glow of the street light coming in through the lone window. Iris snuggles up to me, laying her head on my chest and wrapping her warm, moist arm around my waist. This revolts me, and I pull away from her, pretending to get a cigarette from my pants' pocket on the bedpost. I find one, light up and keep the distance I have gained. I lie with my back to her, puffing on the cigarette.

It is a warm night. The light breeze flowing in through the window makes the curtains dance and cools my hot face. We lie here in silence. What are her thoughts? What must she make of all this? I can hear her breathing softly. The smell of her body, a mixture of sweat and perfume, offends me. I wonder how it affected Madden? No doubt, in some obscene way! I curse to myself.

"Harry," Iris calls softly.

"What?"

"Harry, why does it always have to be this way?"

"What way?"

"Like it was tonight. Well, I don't see you for a long time and then—then all of a sudden you show up like a wild man."

"That was Madden. I'm sorry about him."

"I don't mean whether you are sorry or not. I mean—Well, don't you like me a little in other ways? I mean, is that all you want me for?"

"I want you because—I like you in a lot of ways, Iris. You're my girl, aren't you?"

"But you don't treat me like your girl."

"What do you mean? I took you down the Island, didn't I? I took you to movies."

"Yes, a few times. But people who go steady, they see each other all the time. They go to dances and do things together—and often. You seem to only want to see me once in a blue moon. And then it's only just for this business like tonight."

"Aw, there's not much to do. My job keeps me pretty busy."

"You don't work all the time. What do you do when you're not working?"

"Well, I spend a lot of time with my mother. She's very lonely. I'm all she has left in the world."

"Oh." She is silent a moment. "I'd like to meet your mother. Would you let me meet her sometime?"

"Naw. No, you wouldn't like to meet my mother."

"Why not?"

"Well, my mother is—She's—ah—Well, no, no, you wouldn't like to meet her. Forget about it."

"All right. Harry, will you take me to Mass next Sunday?"

"Mass? I don't go to any Mass."

"Aren't you Catholic?"

"Nothing."

"Don't you believe in God?"

"Sure, but not in religion. It's a big racket. We don't believe in it."

"We?"

"Me and my mother. What my mother believes in, I believe in. Don't you believe what your mother believed?"

"Yes."

"Well, same thing here." I sit up. I flip the cigarette out the window into the alley. I take my pants off the bedpost. "I'm going."

She sits up in the bed. The springs squeak. "When will I see you again? The next time you want to—?"

"Don't say that, Iris!"

"Well, it's true, isn't it? Those are the only times I see you except for the trip down the Island and the couple of movies."

"But I really don't mean it to be that way. That's how it just happens."

"Will you take me out on another date? Without this part of it, I mean?"

"Sure. When do you want to go?"

"Whenever you want to take me, Harry."

I think a moment. "All right, in a couple of days we'll go out somewhere." I feel along the floor for my shoes. "Why aren't there any lights here?"

"Edison cut them off. We couldn't pay the bill."

"Why don't you put a jumper in the box?"

"There's no man around the house now. And I don't know how."

"Where's your brother?"

"He hitchhiked his way all the way out to California. He's living and working out there now."

"Yeah? Smart kid." I lace up my shoes. "Who is that old lady in the front?"

"My grandmother. You shouldn't have frightened her like that."

"*I* didn't frighten anybody." I get up, put on my coat. "Well, Iris, I guess I'll be going."

Softly she asks, "Will you kiss me good night?"

I grin. "I can hardly see you." I bend toward her form on the bed. Her arms come up and embrace me tight around the neck. Her mouth finds mine and presses hard. A while. I pull away from her. I feel I should do something for her. I pull five dollars from my pocket and hand it to her.

"What's that?" she asks.

"Money."

"I don't want it."

"Take it."

"No."

"Why not? It's good American money."

"Harry, I just don't want *money* from you."

I cannot make it out. I put the money back in my pocket. "Okay, Iris, I'll see you around."

I go quickly out of the bedroom. Iris begins to cry. The old woman is sitting at the kitchen table sewing by the kerosene lamp. She looks at me and shudders. She makes a sign of the cross as I pass her for the front door.

Before I put the key in the lock, I can hear Ma all the way in the living room, singing and playing the piano.

> *"You're the Sheik of Araby,*
> *Your love belongs to me.*
> *At night when I'm asleep*
> *Into my tent you'll creep."*

I come in, walk through the long hall to the living room and sit down. She looks around and smiles.

"Hello, Harold. You're late. I'll fix your supper."

"No, Ma, keep on playing. I ate out."

"Oh."

She plays softly but does not sing. I listen a while. I study her back, as she sits there playing. She looks so tired, and the red of her hair seems to be getting grayer every day. Poor Ma, she has had such a rotten life ever since she was a kid, with all those mean, grabbing brothers and sisters and a selfish mother. And after that, she had to get stuck with Hap! Hap, the lover-boy. Oh, the dirty lies he must have told her when they were wooing! But in spite of everything, Ma is not mean. She is good and kind and sweet. Everybody Ma loved, including me, has been rotten to her, but Ma remains kind and sweet. What a great feeling of pity I feel for her now! I have the urge to rush up to the piano and throw my arms protectively about her. I am more determined than ever to make the rest of her days as good as possible for her.

"Ma, is there anything you want or need?"

"Like what, Harold?"

"You know, clothes or something special for the house or you—you know, things like that."

"No, I don't believe I need anything."

"Do you want more money for the house?"

"No. You're a good provider, Harold. Yes, I might say that you're exceptional when it comes to that. Why do you ask?"

I shrug. "I just thought there might be something. I want you to know all you have to do is ask."

She looks around at me, smiles. "My, what a generous dear I have for a son!"

I go over to the piano and put my hand on her shoulder. "I'm real tired, Ma. I'm going right to bed." I kiss her cheek as she plays. "Good night," I say.

"Good night, Harold, my dear."

I am really exhausted. I am even too tired to bathe. I undress and get into bed. I stretch out between the clean, crisp sheets. The bed feels so, so, good. Drowsiness comes quickly. I doze off.

Suddenly I am awakened before sleep comes fully. What is it? Nothing—only Ma at the piano. It is loud as if she is pounding the keys angrily. She is now shouting the words of the song:

*"The stars that shine above*
*Will light our way to love . . ."*

But I am too tired for the noise to bother me. I doze off again with the words almost a soothing monotone in my ear.

**XXII**

RIS AND ME, we go on a picnic to Prospect Park.

We visit the zoo. We feed the elephants popcorn and laugh at the playful chimps in the cages.

We leave the zoo and look for a place to picnic. We find a nice, grassy spot high on a hill, near a narrow, running brook. Iris spreads a blanket and we sit down. We eat. It is a hot day, but we are cool here beneath the shade of a tree. I feel drowsy and stretch out for a short nap. Iris starts reading a book.

I wake with a start. I turn over. Iris is smiling down at me, the book opened in her lap.

"What's the matter?" she asks.

"I don't know."

"You must have had a bad dream."

I sit up, stretch. "How long did I sleep?"

"About an hour. Go back to sleep if you're tired. I don't mind. I'll sit here and keep the bridge."

"Keep the bridge?"

She laughs. "Oh, that's just a turn of speech."

I brush a green bug off my arm. I look around. The scenery is really beautiful and green. It is so much like the country that it is hard to believe we are really surrounded by a city. It is so peaceful. If only it was this way within me!

"Is this the biggest park in the city?" I ask.

"No, Central Park is. This might be the next biggest."

"It's so big I'm lost. If you left me now I wouldn't know how to get out of the place."

"Is this your first time here?"

"Once before—when I was a kid. I got lost then, too."

"You couldn't lose me here! I know this park like a book. My father used to bring the family here on a picnic almost every Sunday during the warm months. He loved to play and roll on the grass with me and my brother. This park has a special place in my heart."

"You had a good father, huh?"

"Yes—my mother, too. They were very much in love, my parents. My father was what you call a Socialist. Not an atheist, as some people seem to think of a Socialist. He was very, very religious. But he was what they call a fighting Socialist. I guess it's because we were always so poor. He used to write pamphlets about improving the conditions of the poor. He would even make speeches on street corners."

"Oh, yeah, a Communist."

"No, not a Communist—*Socialist*. There's a difference. You ever hear of Sacco and Vanzetti?"

"No."

"Well, they were my father's idols. They were two Socialists who—Oh, I don't think you're interested in that!"

"My father had two idols, too—women and whisky."

"Harold! Don't talk that way about your father!"

"Well, it's true."

"Maybe he wasn't very nice to you, but after all, he is your father."

"Yes. I admit he had his good points. I'm hungry. Got any more sandwiches left in the basket?"

She feels around in the basket. "Yes. There's a ham and cheese . . . salami . . . hard-boiled . . . what do you want?"

"Hand me anything. What's that—a bottle of wine?"

"Yes. What it?"

"Sure. Why didn't you tell me?"

"I didn't know if you'd like it. It's Italian wine."

I uncork the bottle and take a big drink from it. "Good. It's a little warm, but it's okay." I munch on the sandwich. "Come on, tell me some more about your father. I like to hear you talk."

"There's not much more—that you'd want to hear, anyway. He was a bricklayer—when he could find work."

"Did he beat you much?"

"Not at all. I suppose your father did?"

"No. I can remember only one time . . . and I deserved it."

"My father didn't believe in forcing children. He believed in guiding us so that—so we could develop our own personalities naturally. He used to say too many parents force their own individuality on their children. And if the parents are twisted, they twist the children, too. He said he was satisfied if he could just teach us compassion for all living things. To him, compassion was the finest of all human emotions—even finer than love. He said compassion was what Christ felt for humanity."

"Go ahead. Keep on talking."

She smiles and looks at me in an embarrassed way. "Why?"

"I like to hear you talk. You talk so nice, Dark Eyes."

"And you don't talk at all, Gray Eyes!"

"Aw, what have I to talk about?"

"Plenty! Everyone has. My goodness! Whenever we're together, Harold Odum, you act as if you're afraid something will slip out if you talk to me. It's the strangest impression I get!"

I put my arm around her shoulder and playfully pull her down on the blanket with me.

"Okay, I'll talk about something," I say. "What do you want me to talk about?"

"Well, how about *your* father? Tell me about him."

"Oh, I don't know much about him. He was never around long enough for me to get a good look at him. Him and my mother didn't get along. Fights, fights. He was always walking out on her."

"Whose fault was it?"

"He was to blame."

"Maybe both of them were. It takes two to make an argument. They should have compromised for your sake."

I smile at her. "You're a wise little broad, you know that? I used to think you were just a mousy little dope. How come you put up such a shy front when we first met?"

"Well, considering the circumstances of our first meeting, you couldn't expect me to behave any other way. Harold, you had me absolutely terrified!"

I think on it. I cannot remember exactly the way it was.

"Well, I wouldn't frighten you now for anything in the world."

"You couldn't—because I love you." She laughs with glee. "O-o-oh, I'm so shameless!"

It occurs to me. Should I say it? What the hell, it can do no harm to tell her.

"Iris, I want to tell you something."

"Yes? Go ahead."

"It has to do with—something." I am embarrassed. "I don't know exactly how to tell you. I don't know how to say it."

"You think you're in love with me—or you're falling in love?"

I am astonished. "How did you know?!"

She laughs and pulls my arm tighter around her shoulders. "Oh, a girl can tell!" She plays with the fingers of my hand. "I hope you fall very deeply because I want you so much."

Quickly I say, "But I'm not too sure about it, remember. I'm not making any promises."

"You don't have to."

"It's just that I get this feeling about you. I think about you too much. Lately, I want to be around you more and more. It feels good to be with you like I am now . . . just hearing you talk, and being close. Is this the way it comes, Iris?"

"Yes."

"Well, what do you know?! I never thought it could happen to me."

"You know, I'm all of twenty-eight. I hope that's not too old for you."

"You're not too old for me, no matter how old you are."

"How old are you, Harold? You can't be much more than twenty-one or twenty-two."

"Let's put it this way; you're young enough for me and I'm old enough for you."

"Fair enough."

Twilight begins to fall. Iris becomes very still. She seems to have something heavy on her mind.

"What's the matter?"

"There's something I want to ask you, Harry."

"What is it?"

**264**

"Well, will you try not to get upset? I mean, will you try to look at it intelligently?"

"Sure."

"Well, the question is this: Why is sex such a horror to you that you have to steal it from us by pretending to be someone else?"

"What do you mean?"

"Madden."

"Oh, well, he does that."

"There is no Madden. You pretend."

"I can't face this."

"You can't face sex? But you've had relations with me."

"No, Madden does that."

"But you realize you are Madden—you are one and the same, don't you?"

"I don't know. I just don't remember."

"Don't you remember having intercourse with me?"

"No, I never did."

"Do you remember lying naked beside me in bed?"

"Yes."

"Well, what do you suppose you were doing there like that?"

"Yes, I guess something had happened. I figure that I—that Madden has had relations. But I don't recall. It's so confusing, Iris. It's such a wildness those times. He's there and he isn't there."

"Can't you have a relationship without making him up?"

"No."

"This is terrible, Harold. You have to get it from your mind."

"Don't you think I want to? I hate Madden. I know you think I'm crazy."

"I did at first. But now I know it's an affliction—like my leg."

"If anyone else knew they'd call me crazy. I'm not sure myself whether I'm crazy or not."

"Maybe there's a way to get the illusion from your mind."

"To hell with it. Leave it as it is."

"And what about me? It's terrible for me when you take me like that. It's a real horror for me when you pretend to be this clawing thing. And it's also a sin for me to do what we do. You always force me, but it's still a sin for me because I do nothing about it. I don't complain or go to the police. I don't do this because I love you, Harry. It would be bearable for me if you could only take me in a normal way. I mean, I would want it if it could be a thing of giving instead of you just taking. You give to me and I give to you."

"I'm sorry, Iris. I swear I am. I don't want—this. But—I—Well, damn it, I just have to have Madden!"

"Why?"

"I don't know. There's something there."

"Sex is too painful?"

"Yes, and something else there. I don't know. Iris, I hate sex. I hate it! But there are times when I'm crazy to have it."

"Whenever I do something."

"When?"

"Whenever I do something."

"What?"

"I can't tell you."

"Tell me one thing. Are you really in love with me?"

"Yes, I think so."

"Sex out of marriage is a sin for me, but—"

"All sex is a sin for me!"

"Then look at it this way. Maybe it would help—if we sinned for each other."

"What do you mean?"

"All right. I will commit a sin, Harold. I will give myself to you willingly. Could you try to forget your sin that sex is nasty and be with me without pretending that you're really someone else?"

"It wouldn't work. I'm not in the mood for it until something happens."

"If you really love me you can desire me without anything outside of our love."

"Do you think so, Iris?"

"Yes."

"But I've tried it before with girls. It didn't work."

"Maybe because you weren't in love."

"I don't know. Yes, maybe that will make the big difference.

Maybe that's the whole thing. All right, Iris, let's try. Where will we go?"

"There's no one around here. How about those bushes right down there?"

"Okay. But we'll wait until it gets a little darker."

"It's dark enough now."

"*Real* dark. It must be secret, Iris—secret."

We lie in the inky blackness of the bushes. Crickets chirp, Iris' breathing becomes hot and heavy. Her lips wet my throat.

"Oh, Harold!"

"I can't find it."

"Let me. Now."

"But see—I'm soft. It won't work."

"Let's wait a little. Maybe you're too excited."

"I'm not excited at all!"

"Try a little harder, Harold."

"Okay."

"Squeeze me tighter, closer."

"One thing, you are nice and warm."

"Touch me here."

"Yes."

"Give your lips to mine."

"Yes."

"Do you love me?"

"I love you."

"I want you now, Harold."

"I know, I know, Iris, but—" Abruptly I turn away from her and sit up. "It's just no use, Iris. You're not *sorry*. If only you were *sorrowful!*"

I stand up and adjust my clothes. Iris does the same thing.

"Harold, I'll do anything you want me to."

"No, it just won't work—not this way."

"You give up too easily."

"I haven't given up. I have an idea. Tomorrow we'll go to a hotel . . . and we'll try it again."

# 2

I pick Iris up after work and take her to a small hotel on Bridge Street. The elderly clerk looks up from his newspaper on the desk.

"What can I do for you?"

"I want a room."

"For the night?"

"Yes."

He looks over at Iris standing at the other side of the desk. He looks back at me. "The two of you?"

"Yeah," I tell him. "The two of us." What the hell is the matter with him?

He seems to be studying the situation. He scratches his chin, squints at me over his glasses. "I suppose she's your wife. I couldn't rent you a room if she wasn't."

I get it. "Sure, sure, she's my wife."

"Sign here. That'll be four dollars and fifty cents."

I put the paper bag under my arm and sign the register. I pay the fee. The old man gives me my change and a key with a number on it.

"One flight up," he says, "and turn to your right."

We go upstairs to the room. There is a bed, a dressing table with a mirror, a chair, and a sink.

Iris sits down carefully on the bed. "I hope there are no bedbugs here," she says.

"I hope we won't be here long enough to find out."

"Yes. Well, I guess I'd better undress."

She takes her clothes off and gets into bed naked. I make sure the door is locked, and I pull the shade all the way down on the lone window. I take off all my clothes and reach for the paper bag.

"What have you got in the bag?" she asks.

I take it out, hand it to her. "Put it on," I say.

"What is it?"

"Weeds, I think they call it."

"Why, it's a mourning veil!"

"Wear it."

"In the bed?!"

"Yes!"

I climb in bed with her. She puts on the veil. . . .

I have an erection!

**I** SIT DOWN to a plate of eggs for breakfast. They are scrambled and well done, just the way I like them. I feel refreshed and my appetite is good. Ma comes over to the table with the coffeepot and pours into my cup.

"Have a good night's sleep?"

"Fine!" I say.

"Those chocolates you brought me last night were delicious, Harold! I went through half the box last night. They must have been expensive."

"Well, I wanted something special for you."

"Indeed? Why?"

I look up at her, surprised. "*Why?*! Because you're my mother, that's *why*!"

She smiles, pats my cheek. "Of course. You're such a good son, Harold, and I realize what a perfect gem I have in you, oh, yes, I do. There aren't many sons your age who are as good to their mothers as you are to me. Even when you were a little tot. Whenever your father went away, I knew I could always depend on you. And it is the same way now. I know I could never doubt it even for one little moment."

"You'll never want for anything as long as I can help it, Ma."

"I know—I know. That's what makes me so proud. You are growing up to be such a man."

"What do you mean—growing up? *I am* a man!"

"Not yet!" she says crisply as she turns away from me to the closet.

I am irked by this. I am as much man now as I ever will be. If she only knew how I am feared by other men and the things I have done! But I think on it. Maybe, to a mother, her child never really grows up. I let it pass.

Ma goes to the refrigerator. "Harold, who is that girl?"

"Huh? What girl?"

She takes the milk out, closes the door. She leans back against the refrigerator with a sigh. She smiles at me and her eyes twinkle.

"Harold, my sweet, now, you're *not* going to tell me you haven't got a girl friend!"

I shift uneasily in my chair. "No, I haven't."

"But you *must* have. Surely, you *must* have!"

I am annoyed. "I tell you no."

She thinks a moment, now snaps her fingers. "Ah! Now I know. Then it's only some girl chasing after you."

"No."

She places the milk on the table and shakes her head with a puzzled look. "How curious. Oh, I know you wouldn't lie to me about it if you had a girl. There's no possible reason for you to lie, so you must be telling the hundred per cent truth. Yes, and I know that you are. I know there is no question about that. But—it's just so *curious.*"

"What, Ma?"

"The hairs."

"The *what?*"

"Wait."

Ma goes to her bedroom, comes back into the kitchen with an envelope. She holds it open for me to look inside. "See?"

"What is it?"

"Hairs! Long, golden-brown hairs." She pulls out the strands, holding them between her fingers. "A girl's, and pretty. At different times I've found them—on your coat collar, your shirt, your hat— and last night, one bundled up in your underwear."

Iris! It suddenly comes to me. Ma is too clever. I decide to tell her. What is there to it, anyway?

"Oh, that must be from Iris," I say casual.

Ma smiles triumphantly and sits down opposite me at the table.

"Who is Iris?" she asks pleasantly.

"She's not my girl," I say quickly. "Don't get the wrong idea. She's not my girl."

"Who is she, then?"

"She's Mrs. Varga's maid. She's a little, homely kid. She has one leg bigger than the other."

"Homely? She has very beautiful hair."

"Yes, she has."

"And she's not your girl?"

"No."

"How does her hair get all over you so much, Harold?"

"I don't know." I hedge.

"You'd have to be very close to her a lot."

"Well, to tell you the truth, Ma, she's not my girl, but she likes me. She says she's in love with me. She wants to be my girl."

"Oh?"

"It's nothing serious. But I *have* fooled around with her a couple of times."

"What do you mean, 'fooled around'?"

"Took her to the show, to the beach—Stuff like that."

"Well, this is certainly a surprise to me! Are you in love with her?"

"Of course not, Ma!"

"Well, do you *like* her?"

"I don't—Well, yes, I like her. She's nice kid. I feel sorry for her. She's crippled and she's not very pretty. Nobody ever took her out before."

"I see. Are you going to have more dates with her?"

"I guess so. I like her—I told you that, Ma. But it's not serious."

Ma studies me gravely as she drums her fingers on the table. Suddenly she gets up.

"Do you want more coffee?"

"No, I've had enough."

"Well, Harold, I'm glad you've found yourself a nice girl to date. It's a good sign."

"A good sign?"

"Yes. I was beginning to worry about you. All boys your age should be interested in girls. I was worried that you weren't—or, at least, you pretended not to be. It only hurts me now because you kept it hidden from me."

"I'm not interested in *other* girls. Only Iris is—"

"Yes, she's special. There's always a special one. I never gave men a tumble until your father came along. He was special for me."

"Well, I don't think Iris is special for me—"

"She's the only one you like, isn't she?"

"Yes, but—"

"Then that's enough for me. If you like her, I like her.

I look at her close. "Do you really feel that way, Ma?"

"I most certainly do! I'm glad you've found someone young that you enjoy being alone with. I'm growing old. I can't expect you to sit around evenings, growing old with me. You're young. I want you to have fun while you're young. God knows, you deserve it. You've been such a devoted son to me."

I am delighted with her. I kiss her cheek. "A good mother deserves a good son."

"When are you going to see Iris again?"

"I don't know. Whenever I want to, I guess."

"Why don't you bring her to the house for dinner one Sunday. I'd like very much to meet her."

I am surprised. "You *would?*"

"Of course, I would. Let me know in advance when you're bringing her. I want to make a special dinner. After all, she could be my future daughter-in-law."

"No, no, nothing like that. But I'll bring her. She'd like to meet you, too."

"Wonderful! Then it's all settled."

"Okay." I get up to go. I kiss her cheek again. "Goodbye, Ma. See you tonight."

"Yes. And give my regards to Iris."

"If I see her."

I take my hat and go.

There is a bright, snazzy car parked in front of the barbershop as I come up the street. Entering the shop, I wonder who it belongs to.

"Morning, Harry!" Ding Dong cries.

"Yeah. The Bug get in yet?"

"I ain't seen hud of him."

I go in the back room. Varga and Georgie Whistle are talking. Louis' eyes light up, and he grins as I walk in.

"Hello, Harry! Notice anything outside?"

"Like what?"

"Come on," he says, clamping his teeth down on his cigar. I follow him outside to the street. He points to the snazzy car parked in front. "How do you like it?"

"It's a beaut," I tell him.

"Then it's yours. Take it."

He slaps a ring with two keys on it in my hand. I look at the keys. I look at him. "I don't understand."

"It's yours—the car. It's a present from me."

I stare at him, surprised out of my wits. I am overwhelmed.

"What's the matter?" he asks. "Don't you want it?"

"Sure, I want it! But it's such a surprise. I don't know what to say."

"You don't have to say anything. The car is for being a good boy. It dawned on me—me, Georgie Whistle and the Bug all got cars. So how come our favorite boy has to walk? So me and Georgie Whistle chipped in. It's a present from me and him."

I see Georgie Whistle standing in the doorway with Ding Dong, grinning at me. I wave thanks to him, he waves back okay.

"It sure is a beauty," I say. "It's better-looking than the Bug's."

"It ain't new," Louis says, "but you'd never notice it. Come on, get in and try her out for size. Also, I want to make a little talk-talk with you."

I climb in behind the wheel. Louis gets in beside me.

"Where to?" I ask.

"Anywheres. Drive us up Flatbush Extension and up to the big clock and back."

I head the car down Hudson, onto Myrtle, and over toward the Extension. She rides smooth as grease.

"Nice going!" I say. "Goddamn, I'm going to love this baby. Wait'll my mother sees it."

"Hot nights you can take her out for rides. Take her out in the country once in a while. It's pleasant. She'll love it."

"So will I!"

"I'll give you the paper on it later."

I turn up Flatbush Extension and head for the big clock. It gives me a feeling of real pride to know that I am behind the wheel of my own car.

Louis knocks dead ashes off his cigar and lights it up again. "Harry, you been doing real well since you been in the club. I want you to know we appreciate you."

"I appreciate you guys. Look at this car!"

"Remember what I told you when you first come in with us— that you could go far?"

"Yeah."

"Well, the time has come. From now on, you're off salary. You don't work for no salary no more. I'm turning over the Shylock bank to you. All we want is a certain percentage each week to the club. The rest is all gravy for you. You'll pull in an easy two hundred, three hundred bucks a week for yourself."

"That won't make me sore!"

"I didn't figure it would. We'll work out the details when we get back to the shop."

Something dawns on me. "But wait a minute—I thought the Shylock bank was going for the Bug."

"No more! I'm taking it away. To hell with him. He's getting to be a regular pea-head now. He won't come off that bottle."

"That thing about the uncle is bugging him."

"To hell with that! He shoulda got over that long ago. It ain't only that. He always was a little screwy. He's just starting to really blow his top now."

"You really think so?"

"Sure. Where do you think he got that nickname—the Bug?

Any guy who'll walk alone into a room full of rival guns blazing away *has* to be bughouse."

"That takes guts, too," I remind him.

"Sure—but tell the trut'—ain't it a little crazy when you can hide outside and wait for the guy you want to come out and then pop him?"

"It seems so."

"He's a worry and a pain in the ass! At a time like this, with trouble stirring up for us, we should all stick together close—like stink and fish. But the Bug picks a time like this to become a lush. Suppose somebody is listening when he's drunk, and he blabbers something about the Gooney Package?"

"What's this Gooney Package?"

"I'll tell you. A guy name of Russell Gooney. It was before you come in with us. He clipped me for five hundred. The Bug, Georgie Whistle and a guy up in Sing Sing now called Red Murphy, they hit this Gooney in a house over on Lawrence Street. This Murphy guy, he don't know why Gooney is getting it, and he don't do no shooting. He just goes along because Gooney's a friend of his and will open the door to him. Later on, this Murphy is busted on another rap and gets sent up for a long stretch. But for some reason, he figures it's all our fault. He figures we could've bribed the D.A. or somebody to get him off, but didn't. All this time he's been laying up in jail, brooding over it. Now the new D.A. comes poking at all the meat laying around Brooklyn and gets interested in the Gooney one. Red Murphy sees his revenge. We hear he's making a deal to start talking."

"He'll put the finger on Georgie and the Bug."

"What else?"

"Uh-uh, that's real bad. We can't get him in jail. What'll we do?"

Louis shakes his head. "I don't know, but we got to do something soon or the roof will fall. I sent one of Murphy's relatives in to see him with a message he'll get a bundle of money if he dummies up. I ain't heard nothing yet."

"Does the Bug know about it?" I ask.

"Sure, he knows about it."

"What does he say?"

"What does he say?! He takes another pull on the bottle, that's what he says! That's how much he's worried about it."

I whistle. "Looks like we got a real problem."

"Here's what I'm thinking, Harry. This Murphy guy—maybe he can't hurt us so much. After all, that kid, Arnie, is outa the way, so now it's only Murphy's word against Georgie's and the Bug's, and they both got good alibis. But if the D.A. ever got his hands on the Bug while he's drunk—who's to say he won't blabber something out? If the Bug talks, too, then we're all looking at the chair. That includes you, too, if he starts talking about other things."

I am doubtful. "Naw," I say, "the Bug won't talk."

"Maybe not. But you can't tell about a guy who lushes, and I just don't like no holes showing, Harry."

Louis throws his cigar stump out of the window. He sighs heavily and leans back, relaxed, in the car. He lights a fresh cigar and puffs thoughtfully on it.

I ask, "What's on your mind?"

"Well—maybe you don't go for it."

"You're the boss," I say.

"Even so—"

"Talk to me."

"Okay. Me and Georgie figure the Bug is too dangerous to us this way. What do you think?"

"I don't think he'll talk—but you're the boss."

"All right, I want you to take him. Can you handle it?"

"I guess so, but—"

Louis cuts me off, talking eager and fast. "It ought to be a cinch for you. It'll be a cinch. He'll go with you anywheres. Just trick him into the car and ride him out the Rockaways one night."

"No," I say, "I will not trick him."

"What do you mean?" Louis asks, surprised. "I can't understand what you mean."

I explain it. I tell him I will not betray the Bug like that. I will not trick him into any car. Someone else will have to do that. I will hit him because he is dangerous to us all with his drunken blabbing.

But I will not be his Judas goat because me and the Bug have been tight.

Louis stares at me as if he cannot believe his eyes and ears. He blinks. Now shrugs. "Okay, you do it any way you want. You handle it. But make it nice. Leave everything nice, nice."

I turn the car around, and we head back to the shop.

## 2

For a week I have been running the bank alone. The Bug has been absolutely no help to me. These days he hangs around the barbershop all day with a bottle in his pocket, sucking on it and making a nuisance out of himself. Louis and Georgie are getting impatient. They are giving me questioning looks, but I keep putting it off because I have not yet figured out the best way to do the job.

Standing in the back room, I watch Louis, Georgie and the girls count up the day's numbers take. The Bug is sitting over in a corner of the room by himself, nipping on his bottle every now and then, not paying much attention to anybody else in the room. Slowly he gets up and weaves over to me. He smiles sickly. His eyes are bloodshot.

"Hello, Harry. I didn't notice you in the room."

"Hello, Abie."

"I ain't seen you in a couple of weeks."

"You saw me yesterday."

"I did?" His brow wrinkles. He scratches his unshaven chin. "Jeez, I'm getting to be a real lush. I don't know what's happening to me."

"Why don't you lay off the booze? You can straighten yourself around."

He shakes his head. "Naw, naw. I see too many things when I'm sober. They scare me. I see my little old Uncle Max. I see him coming around corners, looking through windows, waving at me. I see him everywhere. That little old guy sure gets around. I see him when I'm drunk, too, but it don't scare me then. That's because I can blame it on the booze. He comes up to my room, too, once in a while. We sit and talk."

I smile and try to kid him out of it. "You got a bad case, Abie."

"Sure, sure," he shakes his head. "That's what my Uncle Max keeps telling me. I try to plead my case with him. I try to explain I didn't know it was him in the booth. No dice. All he does is sit there, chewing on his fat cigar, and says I got a very bad case." He looks around at Louis and Georgie at the table. He turns back to me confidentially. "You're my friend, Harry. Will you tell me something?"

"What?"

"What's going on around here?"

"What do you mean?"

"I don't know. There's something funny going on. I'm being ignored around here. Nobody likes me no more except you. Louis won't even talk to me. And Georgie just grunts when I go to talk to him. He ducks me. Everybody's ducking the ol' Bug. You'd think I done something. I didn't do nobody nothing but my Uncle Max. What's happening, Harry?"

"You got your head bad all the time. Why don't you lay off the drink? Nobody wants to talk to you when your head is tight all the time."

"You're right," he says. "I'm getting to be a regular peahead. I'm falling down on the job. Who's looking out for the bank?"

"Me."

He pats me on the shoulder. "Good old Harry! You been standing in for me. Tell you what I'm gonna do—just for you. After tonight I ain't gonna drink another drop. I swear it." He takes out a pint bottle, takes a long drink from it and hands it to me. "Here, throw the rest of that away for me. I'm finished for good. I'm going home now and get a nice night's rest. Tomorrow morning when you see me I'll be one hundred per cent different man. Okay, Harry?"

"That's it, Abie, and everything will be fine."

"Good night, Pal. See you in the morning."

"Good night, Abie."

He staggers out of the room. I look at the pint bottle in my hand. It is half full. Louis rushes over to me.

"When-er-yuh-gonna-take-him. When-er-yuh-gonna-take-him?" he asks in a hurried whisper.

I show him the bottle. "He gave me this. He says he's gonna shake the stuff."

"To hell with what he *says*. He's always saying that. Listen, you got to take him and take him quick—tonight!"

"What's up?"

"Red Murphy sent back word to us to go to hell. He's gonna talk. Georgie Whistle is gonna get out of town. Where'd the Bug go to?"

"Said he's going home to sleep."

"Get him in the apartment. He'll open the door for you."

I look at the bottle in my hand and get an idea. "You got any more of those sleeping pills you had that time?"

"Come on upstairs."

I follow him upstairs to the living room. Margie is sitting on the couch, reading the newspaper and eating chocolates. Louis goes in the back. I wait in the living room. Margie looks up from her newspaper, sticks her tongue out at me and goes back to reading her paper. Louis comes back in the room with a little box in his hand. He hesitates, looks at Margie.

"Beat it, Margie, I want to make talk."

"I'm comfortable where I am," she snaps back.

Louis gives her a menacing look. "You looking to get bruised-up?"

Margie takes the hint. She jumps up, throwing the paper down. She gives me an angry look. "Some nerve! I got to get out of my own living room for Louis and his girl friend."

"Now, take it easy," I say.

"*You* take it easy, you son of a bitch!"

She rushes out of the room.

Louis says, "These are the pills. How many do you want?"

"How many is dangerous?"

"Four is very dangerous."

"Give me eight."

He counts them out in my hand. "What are you gonna do?"

I put the eight pills into the bottle and watch them dissolve in the whisky.

"This will take care of him," I say, putting the bottle in my pocket.

"Listen, what's with you and Margie?" Louis asks.

"What do you mean?"

"She hates your guts. Why?"

I get uneasy, "Oh, I don't know."

He looks at me keenly. "Did she try to lay you, Harry?"

"Well—"

"You don't have to tell me. I know Margie. Sonamagun! So that's why she's always knocking you. You turned her down."

"Sure!"

"Harry, I admire your loyalty, but you're a fool. You just can't do a thing like that to a beautiful broad and get away with it. Now Margie will hate you the rest of her life for that. Every chance she gets to do you harm, she'll do it. A vengeful woman is like a tiger on your back. You shoulda laid her. You woulda had a nice time, I wouldn't know from nothing, and Margie would be going out of her way to do you favors. Now, she's looking to get your throat cut. You shoulda laid her, and everybody would be happy all around."

I look at him with amazement. "But she's your wife!" I say.

"I have my fun, I let her have hers. Doing that is like a hobby with Margie. She just can't help herself. You shoulda laid her. He thinks I don't know about it, but Georgie Whistle tears himself off a piece every once in a while."

"And you don't mind?!"

He is annoyed. "Why should I mind? Can he break it? He can't break it."

I tiptoe quietly up the stairs and knock on the door. I wait. There is no answer. I knock a bit harder, hoping he has not fallen asleep already. I hear a noise inside.

Abie's voice says, "Who is it?"

"Harry," I say.

"Get lost!"

"Come on, Abie, open up. It's me—Harry."

The door cracks open, and Abie peers out suspiciously. His drunken eyes light up as he recognizes me.

"Oh, it is *you*, Harry!"

"Sure. Who'd you think it was?"

"My Uncle Max," he says, closing the door behind me.

I smile. "Quit kidding."

"I ain't kidding. He does that all the time. He fools me. I think it's somebody else at the door. When I open it, there he is, standing there grinning, with a cigar in his mouth and his big, fat belly."

I sit down on a chair near the bed. The Bug stumbles over in his stocking feet and flops across the bed. The springs yelp.

"I was just going to bed. You want some coffee?" he asks, pointing to the pot on the gas stove in the kitchenette.

"No." I take the bottle of whisky out and offer it to him. "I thought you might want to finish your little nightcap once you got home."

He sits up, throws his feet on the floor and wiggles his toes. He looks at the bottle, licks his dry lips.

"I told you I was through with it—and I mean it, Harry."

"Sure, you mean it. But one more can't hurt. You're going to bed right away, anyhow."

He looks at the bottle, hesitates, then reaches for it. "That's right. Sure, Harry. Thanks. It'll help me to sleep."

Slowly he screws the top off the bottle. I try to appear unconcerned. I look around the room. "How much rent you pay for this place, Abie?"

He does not answer. I look at him. He is staring at me in a curious way. He holds the bottle poised in the air as if he had been just about to drink but suddenly stopped.

"What's the matter?" I ask.

A faint smile is on his lips. "You come up here just to give me *this?*" he asks, waving the bottle.

I tense. I think fast. I know Abie is no fool, even though he is drunk.

"No," I say. "To tell you the truth, Abie, Louis asked me to come up and talk to you."

"About what?"

"Your drinking. He says nobody can talk to you. He figures maybe I can talk you out of it because we're partners. I sure hope I can, Abie."

He smiles, shakes his head. I relax. He empties the bottle in two long swallows. He coughs, frowns. He wipes his mouth with the back of his hand and puts the bottle on the floor. He looks at his hands.

"You ever notice about hands, Harry? We do everything with the hands. They make things, fix things. A doctor operates with hands. If he's got good hands he can save a life, take a tumor off a brain and save a life. They are marvelous things, hands. Only one thing wrong with them. They tell on you. You can tell what a man is by studying his hands and the way he uses them. They take a fingerprint and your own hand can put you in the chair. My hands scare me sometimes. It's almost like they got a brain of their own. Sometimes it seems like they hate me, these hands. It's like they do what I want them to do only because I got a stronger will. But they wait for a chance to cross me up—to do what I don't want them to."

I watch him closely, wondering when the pills will take effect.

I say, "How about it, Abie? Can I talk you out of quitting the bottle?"

He shakes his head. "Nobody has to talk me out of it now, Harry. It's just like I told you. I'm finished with it after tonight. No more booze. Finish! I been thinking. Jeez, I think what could happen to me rolling around like a peahead! You know I know a hell of a lot. They see me lushing, some people might get ideas I'm turning weak. They might get somebody to put a hole in me."

"Who would want to do that?"

"Louis! Whistle!" he says suddenly, a panicky look on his face.

"That's crazy," I say. "Now you're talking crazy again."

He looks at me, reassured. "Yeah, that *is* crazy, ain't it? Me, the Bug—Abie the Bug, who done so much for the club, getting hit in the head by his own people! Crazy. Man, that booze is really getting me down. Why would the club want to hit me anyway? Hell, we're partners. We're a like a family."

"Sure."

Fear begins to creep back in his face. "But sometimes things can happen." He looks over at me a moment searchingly. "Harry, I want to make a confession to you. Would you get sore? Will you promise not to get sore at the ol' Bug if I do?"

"Sure, I promise."

"Remember that time they made you with the murder car over in Chinatown?"

"Yeah?"

"And the bulls worked you over in that back room?"

"Yeah, what about it?"

"This bull that worked you over—Benedict—he had orders to do it. Our orders. He's in the club." He grins at my surprise. "You didn't know that, did you?"

"No. But why was he ordered to beat me up?"

"To see if you could be made to talk before you got to the D.A. We knew the D.A. would sweat you. We figured if a good beating couldn't make you talk, the D.A. couldn't crack you neither. Jeez, it's getting hot in here!"

"What would have happened if I had talked under the beating?"

"You never would've made it to the D.A.'s office, Harry. There were guns along the route. And Benedict knew just the route to take you."

I get a prickly feeling down the back of my neck. "Well, I didn't know Benedict was one of us, but I *did* know I'd get it if I talked."

"Don't be sore, Harry. You see, we—we didn't know you then. A thing like that couldn't—couldn't happen to you today. We know you now so we wouldn't worry. It couldn't happen to me, either. We know us. I been faithful all my years in the club. Okay, wanna take my case, for instance? I shot an Uncle Max. Okay, take that for granted. It's a legal case. I hit a lot of bums in my time. They were quiet, you know. Even if they thought I was dogging it or getting weak, they'd never—Why, Louis and them would talk to me first. Sure, try to reason with me, and I'd listen to reason fast. And if I didn't listen to reason, why, they'd only run me outa town. But they wouldn't—Naw, they just wouldn't do that, would they, Harry? *Harry!*"

"What is it, Abie?"

He is looking at me in a strange way. Tears begin to roll down his cheeks. "Something's happening to me. What's happening to me?" He blinks.

"Take it easy," I say.

Suddenly, he screams again, *"Harry!"*

I jump to my feet. "What? Shut up!"

He looks but his eyes do not see. They are filled with terror and hurt. "Harry, the *whisky*—aw, yuh hit the ol' Bug. Why, Harry, why? I said I'd straighten out. Don't let me die, please! Harry, where are you? Har—"

He falls back across the bed. He is out cold. I move fast. I want his Italian gun. I search around the room. I look in his bureau. Two drawers are filled with nothing but gloves—bundles and bundles of white, silk gloves! I look in the closet. I find the gun on the shelf behind a shoe box. I move Abie around on the bed so that he is stretched full-length. I turn on all the gas jets on the stove, wipe around for prints and go out quietly and quickly.

Downstairs, I see Madden up the street standing on the corner. He is watching me intently, eager for my call. I dismiss him. He grins and salutes me a cocky goodbye. When he disappears around the corner, I know I am free of him forever.

But I am alone and lonely now. It is impossible to hide. I must face what is real, and reality has the feeling of doom. I woke from the nightmare that was Madden, but there can be no waking from one that is real.

I stretch out on the sofa, puffing on a cigarette and listening to the radio. Jack Benny is horsing around with Rochester. It is funny, but laughter has become hard for me. Or was I always this way, and I am just beginning to notice it? Ma sits in the big chair, reading the newspaper.

She says, "What a shame about Mr. Pinkwise!"

"Yeah."

"But why do they have to make such a fuss?"

"What do you mean, Ma?"

"It's here in the paper. The coroner's jury found him a suicide, but the police are still suspicious. They find him with a stomach full of sleeping pills and the gas turned on, and yet they want to say it's something else. Why is this?"

"Aw, that's the cops for you, Ma. They're always looking to frame somebody."

"Stop talking like that," Ma says with annoyance.

I look at her. "Like what?"

"That language—'looking to frame somebody.' You sound just like one of those hoodlums."

I shrug. "It's just a turn of speech, Ma." Turn of speech. Iris! I have not seen her for weeks now. What must she think of me?

"Well, turn of speech or not, I don't want you talking like that around the house."

"Okay, okay."

Jack Benny has gone off the air. A gangster story comes on I get up and dial to another station where there is music. I lie back down on the sofa.

"And the terrible things they said about Mr. Pinkwise! Harold, they just couldn't be true, could they?"

"What?"

"That he was a murderer."

"If he was a murderer they would've had him in the electric chair long ago. You know that, Ma."

"Yes, but of course, they would have had to prove it first."

"Sure. And nobody could prove anything like that about him."

"Harold, you know, I never was quite sure what kind of work you and him did for Mr. Varga."

"Numbers, Ma. We just collected the numbers."

"Indeed? And so much money just for collecting numbers, my!"

"There's plenty of money in numbers. Everybody plays them."

Why is she asking so many questions? Ma has something on her mind. She is building up to asking me something. I think I had better cut her off the first chance I get.

"Did the police question you about Mr. Pinkwise's death, Harold?"

"Sure. They asked me when I'd seen him last—stuff like that."

"And what did you tell them?"

"Oh, for Pete's sake!" I jump up off the sofa. "I'm going out for a walk!"

"Oh, no, Harold! Don't go out. I want you to sit with me tonight."

"Well, if you're going to give me the third degree I'm going out!"

"Third degree? Why, I wasn't—"

"You're asking so many questions. What are you asking so many questions about Abie for?"

"Was I asking so many? Well, I wasn't aware. . . . All right, sit back down, I won't ask any more. I'm sorry, my dear. I didn't mean to upset you."

I sit on the sofa. "There are other things to talk about."

"Yes. I didn't realize—I forgot that you two were good friends, and that it might upset you to talk about him. Forgive me, my dear. We'll talk of something else."

I hesitate a moment. I decide to lie down again.

"What about that girl, Harold? Whenever are you going to bring her to the house?!"

"You really want to meet her, huh, Ma?"

"Of course. Didn't I tell you?"

"Well, I haven't seen her in a couple of weeks, but I'll bring her around the next chance I get."

"Why don't we plan for it? How about bringing her to the house for dinner next Sunday?"

"Okay, I'll ask her. If she's got nothing doing I'll bring her Sunday."

"Don't forget to ask because I will prepare . . ."

"Sure, Ma."

## 4

The heat is on!

Red Murphy talked on Georgie Whistle and the Bug. They cannot touch the Bug now, but Georgie Whistle is on the lam, and the police are searching everywhere for him. Business is shut down tight. No numbers, no banks, no protection, no whores, nothing. The mob is temporarily out of action. Nobody but Georgie is running yet, but we try to make ourselves scarce around the neighborhood. Louis wants me to stay close to home in case he needs me. There is so much excitement today I almost forget to invite Iris for dinner Sunday.

I go over to her house. The old woman opens the door. She groans when she sees it is me. I am offended.

"I won't bite you," I say. "I just want to see Iris. Is she here?"

She backs away from me and calls over her shoulder, "Iris!"

Iris steps into the kitchen from the bedroom, a folded sweater over her arm. "What is it, Grandma? Oh, it's you, Harold! Come back here—I'm in the bedroom."

I cross the kitchen and follow her into the bedroom. Neatly stacked clothes are sorted out on the bed. Two empty suitcases are on the floor.

"What are you doing?" I ask.

She shrugs, a look of consternation on her face. "I can't decide. I don't know what to do, Harold."

"What is it?"

"I got a letter from my brother, Bunny. He's doing pretty good out in California. He sent us train fare. He wants me and my grandmother to come out and live with him and keep house for him. I can't make up my mind."

"I'll make it up for you. You can't go."

"Why?"

I shrug. "I don't want you to."

She gives me a sharp look. "Do you really care? I haven't seen you in almost three weeks. Not even one word from you! I'll bet you never even thought of me once in all that time."

"Well, yeah, I'm sorry about that, Iris. But I've been pretty damn busy, believe me. When the Bug died I had to take over all his work and everything."

"What about *before* he died? He's only been dead a week."

"Well, yeah. Okay, I'm sorry about that, Iris. Please forgive me. I guess you sort of slipped my mind."

"Slipped your mind! Well, I like that! You have a girl, you say you love her, and you don't see her for three weeks because she just slipped your mind! You don't love me, Harold, and you know it."

"Well, okay, maybe I'm not so sure about this love business, but I like you a hell of a lot, Iris, please believe that."

She sighs heavily and sits on the bed. "I'm not so sure I love you, either, Harold. Maybe I'm just mistaking compassion for love."

"Either one is good enough for me."

"But not for me. Harold, I think I will go out West."

"No, I don't want you to go."

"Why?"

"Because I just *don't*, that's all!"

"Now that there's no Madden to make you rape, you can always take your veil to a prostitute."

"Don't say that!"

"That's why you're here now, isn't it? Just to use me?"

I am angered. "No, Goddamn it! That's just how much you know! If you want to know something, I came here to ask you for a date Sunday. I also came to tell you that my mother wants to meet you. How do you like that?!"

She gives me a startled look. "You told your mother about me?"

"Sure. And she wants me to bring you to the house for dinner Sunday. Does that sound like I just want to use you? Would I want you to meet my mother if I just considered you a whore?!"

She is impressed. She smiles and her eyes brim with tears. She throws her arms around me.

"Oh, Harold!"

"What the hell, just because I didn't see you for a couple of weeks is no reason to—to go running off to California. What do you want me to do—lie to you? I told you I'm not sure about love, but I like you. I like you for more than that other business."

She begins to dry her eyes. "Yes. All right, Harold, I believe you."

"That's better. Now, how about it? Will you come to dinner Sunday?"

She laughs suddenly. "Yes! I know now is the time I should play hard to get, but I'm taking no chances with you."

"Why should you play hard to get? You're not hard to get."

The smile goes quick. She looks at me sadly. "Now, why did you have to spoil it by saying a thing like that? You are right, Harold. For you, I'm not hard to get. But you'd better watch out or you'll win the grand prize for the world's worst Casanova."

"I'm no lover-boy, I admit. I wouldn't know how to make love if I tried."

"I believe you—absolutely!"

I look close at her. "Are you kidding me?"

"I was never more serious in my life."

"Well, all right. I'll call for you Sunday around one o'clock. We'll see a show first and then go on to my house. Okay?"

"All right. I'll be ready."

"And you're not going to California now, are you?"

"You don't want me to go?"

"No, I told you."

She thinks for a moment. "Well, I'll stay at least until Sunday."

"I don't want you to go at all."

"But my brother needs me there."

I am getting angry again. "And I need you here!"

"Harold, could you please try to tell me, if you don't love me and if you're not using me, just why is it that you need me here?"

"Because maybe *I am* in love with you!" I shout furiously. "How the hell do I know? I've never been in love with anybody before!"

I curse and rush out of there.

Iris is getting too damn fresh with me. What does she want me to do—get on the radio on a coast-to-coast hookup and shout out my feelings for her? To hell with that. I will not be that weak.

# XXIV

*A*FTER SUPPER, I take my shoes off and stretch out on the living-room couch. A singer's voice comes drifting out of the radio:

*"Where is the girl that I used to meet*
*Down where the pale moon shines?"*

I begin to think of Iris and her soft, black eyes. Sudden static smothers the singer's voice and kills a mood. Ma comes into the room. She goes over to the radio and fusses with the dials.

"Something's wrong with it," she says. "It doesn't play right any more. It goes off and on as it pleases. And the static!"

"I'll send a man up to look at it tomorrow."

The static goes. Ma turns the volume down low and sits in the big chair. She takes out her knitting and sighs heavily. "Oh, dear! I wonder what your father is doing tonight?"

"Forget about him," I tell her.

"I should. I know I should. But it is not an easy thing to do. Oh, he was not always the way you remember him. There was a time he was good. Oh yes. The thing was—it used to be he was so *honorable* . . . never betray, such a noble, loyal man. That was the big thing I loved so much about him—his honor and his faithfulness. And then suddenly one day he changed, and he was the complete opposite. He became a lying, cheating thing without respect for his family or himself."

"What happened to change him, Ma?"

She looks up at the ceiling thoughtfully, her brow wrinkles. "I'm not *sure* really, but I know it was a dreadful, horrible thing. He behaved terribly."

"Did he run around with other women?"

"Other women, yes. But it was not so much that. If that were the only thing, let me tell you, I could have cured him of *that* quick enough. I may not look it now, but in my younger years I was more than a match for any vamp who had her eyes on my man!" Suddenly she looks embarrassed. She smiles a little. "Oh, how shameful I must sound to you, Harold!"

"Oh, no, Ma, I believe it," I assure her. "To me, you are still the prettiest lady in the world."

She smiles with pleasure. "Why, thank you, Harold. What a nice thing to say! But as I was saying, it was not just other women. It was just the—crowd he was with. He ran around with a bunch of bachelors, you know, wild and irresponsible. I suppose he envied their freedom."

I look at her tired, sad face. I wonder. "Ma, were you ever *really* happy in your life?"

"Yes, there were times."

I am doubtful. "When? Tell me when was the happiest time of your life?"

"The happiest time? Oh, that's easy. Easy, because it stands out so big. The happiest time of my married life—of my whole life— was when I was pregnant with you. There were times when I carried you, when I didn't want any part of your father or anyone else. I would go off alone to a dark room and sit. You would kick once in a while at those times, and I would stroke myself gently to calm you. Oh, it was such a delicious, delightful time, you growing and living inside me, even though it was a feeling of being completely alone in the world—just my baby and me. It was like we shared a great secret together—the secret and wonder of creation, it was like. It was as if no other woman in the world but myself could have a baby, and I was guarding my secret with jealousy. And your father! During that time, your father was the—Oh, he was the sweetest, most attentive man in the whole world wide! He wouldn't allow me to do a thing for myself, not a *thing*. Anybody would have thought I was an invalid or something, instead of just being with child. Oh, I don't mean that being with child is nothing—a simple, easy thing—because it isn't. It is a very serious business, and many women die in childbirth." She coughs suddenly and looks up from her knitting. "Harold, dear, would you get my bottle of tonic from the medicine chest?"

Her words have depressed me. The interruption is a relief. I slip into my shoes. "Stomach bothering you again?"

"A little."

"I wish you would see a doctor."

"The tonic helps."

I get up and go to the bathroom. I open the medicine chest. I am startled stiff. I stare with confusion. The shelves are stacked with nothing but bottles and bottles of Moreland's Tonic! Endlessness stares out at me making me feel I have been trapped. I am overcome with horror at the billions and billions of pictures merging endlessly into themselves, into nothingness, pulling me into them in order to smother and drown me forever. I am dizzied and furious with this maddening thing that makes a weird point and goes running off. I want to smash every last bottle on the floor. I slam the door shut!

She knits.

"Oh, yes, that was the happiest time. But your father, oh, that man just treated me as if I were completely helpless. After coming home from work, he would make supper for both of us and do all the housework. He wouldn't even let me bathe alone. He came into the bathroom and washed me himself. I used to pout, but I loved every bit of it. I loved every wonderful, romantic moment of my pregnancy. So much so that I—that I almost wished those nine months would never end. And that's what the doctor said. He said it jokingly, of course, but it was funny, him saying it just the same. You see, you were a breech, you know. A breech is when the baby— Well, never mind, but it is a difficult birth. And when the doctor started having trouble delivering you, he looked at me lying there and shook his finger playfully at me and said, 'Katherine,'—oh, I remember just like it was yesterday—he said, 'Katherine, it looks like you just don't *want* to give this baby up.' And it might have been true, too. It might have been true, I mean, as a kind of premonition— because it was after your birth that your father started to misbehave.

"Harold, have you ever noticed that whenever a person close to you dies, it always rains? I have never known it to fail in all my life. Well, right after you were born, it rained and rained for days on end! It struck me then that a death had happened close to me.

Not the death of a loved person, but the death of—of a *beloved time*."

## 2

We come out of the Paramount movie palace at six-thirty. I help Iris into the car, and we start for my house. Iris is very quiet and looks upset.

"What's the matter?" I ask.

She smiles shyly. "I'm nervous."

"Why?"

"About meeting your mother. I hope she likes me, Harry. Do you think she will?"

"Sure."

"What's she like?"

"Oh—ordinary. No, not ordinary. She's something special to me."

Iris laughs. "Everybody's mother is."

"I guess so."

"How do I look? Do I look okay?"

"Sure."

"Do you like my hair fixed this way?"

"Yes."

"A lot of information I get out of you!"

"Well, what do you want me to say—you look lousy?"

"If I do."

"Well, you don't. Okay?"

"Yes."

We ride along in silence. I turn the car around onto Carlton Avenue. I pull up to the curb and park in front of the house. We climb out. Iris looks up and down the street as I lock the car.

"This is a nice neighborhood around here. I didn't know you lived up here."

"Not always. We used to live in a little rattrap on Myrtle."

I take her arm and we go into the hallway. Iris stops at the stairs.

"What's the matter?"

"I'm *scared*, Harry! Are you sure I look all right?"

She looks at me with big, anxious eyes. I see that she really is worried. I smile and pat her reassuringly.

"What are you scared of? Ma wouldn't hurt a fly—let alone a nice little girl like you."

"That's not why I'm scared. I'm scared she won't like me."

"Don't worry, she'll like you. Come on."

I take her arm again and we go upstairs to the apartment. I unlock the door and lead her inside. All is quiet.

I call down the long hallway, "Ma, I'm home!"

We start down the hall to the living room. Ma's room door is closed. She calls from inside as we go by.

"Harold, is that you?"

"Yes, Ma. I just got back."

"Is your friend with you?" she asks sweetly.

"Yes."

"Oh, that's fine! Take her into the living room. I'll be out in a few minutes."

I lead Iris into the living room. "Sit down and make yourself comfortable." Before I can stop her, she picks out the big chair to sit in. The springs scream and the left leg falls off. I catch Iris before she falls to the floor. "Not this chair. I should've told you. Sit on the sofa." She goes to the sofa. I bend over and stick the leg back into place on the chair. I am embarrassed. "I'm sorry. I asked Ma to get rid of it, but she won't."

"It's all right."

"It's one of those crazy chairs. You have to know how to sit down in it. Me and Ma know how to do it."

Iris looks around the room. "It's very nice in here."

I shrug. "The furniture is pretty old, but Ma keeps a nice house."

"I think the furniture is nice, too. We have hardly any at all in our living room."

"Maybe that's why you think this stuff is nice."

"No, we once had nice things—before my father died. Is that a mahogany table over there?"

"I don't know."

"We had a mahogany dining set once. The company took it back when we couldn't keep up the payments."

"I wish someone would take this stuff!"

"You really don't like it, do you?"

"I hate it. Want me to turn on the radio?"

"All right. Who plays the piano? You?"

"No. Ma plays."

"Good?"

"Pretty good. She sings, too. She used to study."

I switch on the Atwater-Kent. I begin to tune in a station when Ma's voice turns me around.

"Well, good evening, my dear!"

I am startled. I hardly recognize her. She is standing in the doorway wearing a red, satiny dress that reaches all the way down to her ankles. She has lots of rouge, lipstick and powder on her face, and her graying blond hair is all done up in curls. There is a triple row of imitation pearls around her neck and rings and bracelets on her fingers and arms. It is not that she does not look nice, but she looks strange and old-fashioned. She stands there smiling sweetly at me. I only stare at her with my mouth wide open, not knowing what to make of it.

She stretches her arms out to me. "Well? Aren't you going to kiss your mother?"

I come out of it. As I cross the room to her I wonder what Iris is thinking, and I become embarrassed again. I go to kiss Ma's cheek, but she takes her hands and guides my lips to hers. She is full of perfume!

"That's better," she says. She looks around at Iris on the sofa. "Well, now! Is this the young lady you wanted me to meet?"

"Yes, Ma—this is Iris."

Ma offers her hand to Iris. "How do you do, Iris. I'm very happy to meet you, yes."

"I'm very happy to meet you, too, Mrs. Odum."

"Why don't you call me Kate, dearie. It's so much more cozier. Will you do that?"

"If you want me to."

"Yes. We want to get along well, don't we? Yes, we do. And we'll never become very warm and friendly with all these formalities."

Ma moves away and sits in the big chair opposite Iris. Iris looks very uneasy. I want to give her courage. I go over to the sofa, smile at her and sit down beside her. Ma's eyes suddenly cut into me like a knife.

"Come over here beside me, Harold!" she says.

I get up and go over beside the big chair. "What's the matter?"

She takes my hand and rubs and rubs it against her cheek. She smiles over at Iris. "Forgive me, dear Iris, but you've had him to yourself all day. Won't you permit him this one little grace—to stand beside his mother's chair?"

Iris smiles weakly, but does not answer. I ease my hand out of Ma's grasp and sit down on the arm of her chair.

"I'm hungry, Ma. Is supper ready?"

"Yes—but be patient, my darling. Do let me and Iris acquaint ourselves a little first. Now, Iris, are you in love with my Harold?"

Iris hesitates a moment. "Yes."

"My, but you are forward! To say it just like that—to his mother."

"Well, you asked me, Mrs. Odum."

"Harold tells me he is not in love with you."

"That's what he *says*."

"What do you mean by that? Do you have reason to believe he *is* in love with you?"

"Well, I don't know . . ."

"You don't *know*! You don't *know*?! Well, my girl, you can't be very clever, not knowing about a thing like that. Or perhaps you *are* very clever in your own little way. . . ."

"No, I'm not very clever at all."

"Yes. A clever girl would know for sure whether a man is in love with her, no matter what he says. Don't you think Harold's love is a thing you ought to be sure about before wasting your time, as you are doing now?"

I look at Iris. I am surprised at what I see in her eyes. There is spark and fight there. I am pleased by this and a little amused. She is standing up to Ma. She stares straight and hard at her with unblinking eyes.

Iris says steadily, "I don't believe I'm wasting my time with Harry, Mrs. Odum."

"You don't, indeed?!" Ma says. "Well, I can tell you right now—No, never mind. Never mind. It is not right for me to say. It is for Harold to say whether or not you are wasting your time. Isn't that true, Harold?"

"Ma, why bring that up now. We were starting out to have a nice evening."

"And so we will. I have a nice roast in the oven, a tossed salad, apple pie—a wonderful supper. And I've prepared it all for you and your friend. But it is not fair, Harold. It is not fair for you to have her here under illusions about the way you feel. It is not fair to have a girl on a hook like this—to play with her. A young girl has deep feelings, and you are not to play with them like toys, my fine young man! I am your mother and I love you, it is true, but I will not stand by and let you make a fool of an innocent young girl. You must tell her how you feel, one way or the other. You must tell her in the beginning so she will know where she stands."

"But he has told me, Mrs. Odum."

"Told you what?"

"That he *doesn't* love me."

Ma smiles. "Well, then, my dear—"

"But I don't believe him."

"You don't *believe him*?!"

"I don't believe him because I know how hard it is for Harry to admit feelings of love and affection for a girl. I know this very well about him."

"Nonsense! I say you are talking nonsense because I'm his mother and I know him a great deal better than you do!"

"I know Harry the way you never could have known him."

"What do you mean by that?"

"It's not my business to tell you. Harry will tell you if he can."

Ma is silent. She stares hard at Iris. Iris stares right back at her. I sense something terrible boiling up in Ma. I want to change the subject quickly. I get up from the arm of her chair.

"Can't we find something else to talk about?" I ask.

"Did you hear what she said, Harold? Did you hear? She says she doesn't believe you."

"I heard her."

Ma looks up at me. "And what do you say to that? Just what do you say to that?"

"Nothing!"

Ma looks up at me, surprised. I try not to look at her.

"You have nothing to say?! You don't love a girl, and she says she doesn't believe you and you have nothing to say to that? Why, that is complete nonsense, Harold!"

I am annoyed. "What do you want me to do? I can't force her to believe me."

"Yes, you can. You can tell her, right here and now and in no uncertain terms, that you don't love her. I insist that you do it right this minute."

I do not know what to say. I think on it.

"Well, Harold?"

"I don't know, Ma."

She gives me a piercing look. She says very slowly, "You don't know what, Harold?"

"If I tell you, will you stop talking about it?"

"If you wish . . . I suppose so."

"Well, I don't know whether I'm in love with her or not."

"But you told me you *didn't* love her!"

"Yes, and maybe it was true then. But now—well, I don't know about it now."

"Then you think you might be in love with her now?"

"Yes—maybe."

"Oh!"

"I said, *maybe*, Ma. Gee, you don't have to act like—"

"Oh, I'm not acting like anything at all. It's just that—"

"Now you're going to be sore or something."

"Angry at *you* Why, Harold, I'm delighted! I'm really *delighted*. It's just that—Well, you told me, in all good sincerity, that you didn't love Iris, and I thought—"

"It's *maybe*, Ma. *Maybe* I love her."

"Oh, you're in love with her, all right. That's all very plain enough. Yes. Well, and I am delighted. I'm so happy for you, really, Harold, I am. Why, didn't I tell you just last week that I wanted you to find someone?"

"Yes, you did, Ma."

"Well, then!" She turns sorrowfully to Iris. "Oh, I'm so terribly embarrassed. Iris, dear, you must please forgive me. But I was under the impression that you were—you know the sort of girl—a pickup, I think they call them nowadays. Harold misled me into believing there was nothing but the most casual relations between you. Why, I never would have spoken to you in the manner I did if I had known you were the girl of his choice. Harold is a fine boy. He is the finest in all the world. And I'm sure any girl he chooses for his own must be equally fine. Oh, my dear girl, couldn't you find it in your heart to forgive me? Please?"

Ma begins to cry. She takes a little handkerchief and dabs at the corners of her eyes. I put my arm around her shoulders.

"No, no, I'm all right," she says, gently pushing me away.

Iris says, "Really, it's nothing to be upset about, Mrs. Odum."

Ma gets up and sits beside Iris on the sofa. "Then you forgive me, Iris?"

"Of course, Mrs. Odum. It's nothing."

Ma kisses Iris' cheek and holds her hand. "There. Well, now, now we all understand each other and I know we will get along fine. There'll be a lot for you and me to talk about in the coming days, Iris. And there are a lot of things I'll want to teach you, such as—how to make his favorite dishes and things like that."

I am annoyed. "You sound like we're getting married!" I say.

"Well, that seems to be the object of courting."

"I'm not getting married to *anybody!*"

"Look at him, Iris. Aren't men pitiful things?! We have them and they never realize it. They never seem to know what hit them until after the wedding."

They laugh together like little girls. I feel out of things. I am peeved at this. I feel like a piece of meat they are looking over in a butcher-shop window. Ma whispers something to Iris. They both look at me and giggle.

"What's all that about?" I ask.

"Secrets! Girls' secrets," Ma says, shaking a finger at me. She turns to Iris. "Dear, would you like a cocktail before dinner?"

"All right, yes."

"Harold, I have a bottle of whisky in the kitchen but I forgot to get a bottle of ginger ale. Would you be a good boy and run down to the store and get a bottle?"

"Aw, I don't feel like it, Ma. Can't we drink it straight?"

"Straight whisky might be all right for men, but not for girls."

"But I'll have to go all the way over to Vanderbilt for it."

"Well, you have your car—ride over."

I grunt and start out. As I go down the hall, I hear Ma saying to Iris, "Did you ever see such a lazy boy in your life?! You're going to have your hands full, Iris."

I drive over to the candy store on Vanderbilt and buy the ginger ale. As I start out I notice a short, fat guy smoking a cigar coming out of the phone booth. This makes me think of the Bug and his uncle, which in turn makes me wonder if anything new has turned up concerning the Gooney Package. I decide to phone Louis.

A woman answers the phone. I think it is Margie.

"Is Louis there?"

"Who is this?"

"Harry."

"Which Harry?"

"The Cat."

"Bastard!" It *is* Margie. I laugh. She goes. I wait.

"Hello, Harry?"

"Yes, Louis."

"Listen, Harry, there's a bug on the wire. Don't use no dirty words."

"Got you."

"Where you calling from—home?"

"Candy store. I just called up to find out how every little thing is. Anything new turn up?"

"Yeah. I'm glad you called up. I just heard they found him."

"Georgie?"

"Yeah. They got him down Gold's office now."

"What happens now?"

"What else? The big frame-up! The bulls know we're clean.

They're trying to get a whipping boy for that crime commission, that's all. I got nothing to hide. I don't think Georgie has either. Some sorehead in Sing Sing is trying to get a parole, so he starts lying on Georgie. He says Georgie was in something with him. Balls! Georgie is clean as a newborn baby. Me, too. Where do we come off associating with bums like Red Murphy? It's a big frame for the politicians, that's all. This is the thanks we get for being legit all these years."

"Yeah," I agree for the audience. "Is there something I can do?"

"Yeah. We won't let them get away with this frame-up. Tuesday I'm gonna make a meet with B.M. and some lawyers. Meet me over the office Tuesday around four or five in the afternoon. You know the place?"

"Pine?"

"Yeah."

"Okay."

"What are you doing now?"

"I've got Iris over the house. She's having dinner with me and Ma. Say, but if you need me now—"

"No, no, stay! Have a nice Sunday. How's the mama?"

"Fine."

"Good, good. Give her my regards. See you Tuesday, kid."

"Okay, Louis."

We hang up.

It is strangely quiet as I walk into the apartment. I go down the hall to the kitchen. Ma is busy setting the table with the roast, gravy and vegetables. She does not look at me.

"Here's your ginger ale, Ma. Where's Iris?"

Ma sighs. "She left rather suddenly, Harold. Now, let's see, what did I do with the gravy ladle?"

"What do you mean, she left suddenly?"

"Just what I said." Her eyes search around the kitchen. "Now, what in the world happened to that spoon?! I know I had it only a moment ago."

I am puzzled. "Is she coming back?"

"Who? Oh. I don't think so, Harold. Ah, here it is—in the big pot!"

I cannot make it out. I open the refrigerator to put the soda in. I am surprised to find two bottles of ginger ale already there.

"Ma, you *have* ginger ale!"

"Of course, I have. I bought it last night."

"Then why did—" Suddenly I understand. I am furious. "Ma, what did you say to her?"

Ma turns on me, snarling viciously. "She's a slut, that's what she is. A filthy, conniving little slut, and you had a nerve to bring her into this house!"

"But, Ma, you—"

"Oh, I know what you have been up to in the bed with her. I know what her filthy kind are forever plotting and scheming for. Well, she will not get her dirty claws into you, my fine young fellow. I've put an end to that disgusting bit of business, once and for all!"

"You insulted her, Ma. You shouldn't have done it!"

"Yes, I told her what she is and what she wants from you, and I will do worse than tell her the next time, but there will be no next time, you can believe you me."

"I'm going right now and apologize to her."

I rush out into the hall. Ma follows me.

"Harold! Don't you dare leave me to go to her!"

"I'm going to apologize, I tell you."

"You don't apologize to filth!"

"She is a *nice* girl. I invited her here and you insulted her. What does that make me? I owe her an apology and she's going to get it."

"Don't you dare leave me and go to her!"

"I'm not leaving anybody."

"You're betraying me. Yes, you are. Just like your father, you're betraying me for filth."

"Let go of me. I'm going!"

"Very well. It's either her or me. If you go, don't ever come back. It's either her or me. If you leave me to go to her, I *curse* you. I put a mother's curse on your head!"

I stop, turn. "*What?*"

"Yes, go if you can."

My anger gives way to fear. Ma has a terrifying look on her face. I have never seen her like this before. Her eyes are wild and hard. Her mouth is twisted and her teeth clenched. I back away as she moves slowly toward me, spitting strange words at me, her hands weaving through the air.

> "Go down, go down, my pretty youth,
> But you will not come up.
> Tangled mind will twist and turn,
> And tangled foot will follow.
> You will go down, my pretty one,
> But you will not come up again.
> So tangle, tangle, twist and turn,
> For tangling webs are woven."

"Ma, what is the matter with you?!" I shout.

"You will know soon if you go to her. Yes, you will know soon enough. Now, go if you can!"

I am afraid to go and afraid not to. I turn quickly away from her terrible face and run into my room, slamming the door behind me. I sit on the bed in confusion. What is happening? Has Ma suddenly gone crazy? She is like a witch. She has become a witch before my eyes. It is dark in the room. I turn on the lamp. What is the fear in me? Why do I tremble this way? My heart pounds. What is it? What is it? What is it?

I lie across the bed on my back and stare at the ceiling. I try to think it out. I love her, she loves me. How could she become so furious over nothing to curse me like this? How could she ever dream that I would leave her old and alone in the world? My heart aches. I am in agony.

But, maybe she has been drinking the whisky. Yes, it *must* be the whisky. She is not used to it. It has made her wild and drunk.

Yes, it was all because of the whisky. Soon she will calm down. Soon it will all go away, and she will come to me speaking soft and sweetly and tell me to come eat my supper. And all this heartache will be passed, and things will be right again with us, as they should be and always will be. Yes, it is all right. Please, call to me, Ma. Please call to me soon.

Suddenly the lamp goes out and I am in darkness. She has disconnected the plug in her room!

I find myself *screaming* in the dark.

**XXV**

I AWAKE, TIRED AND IRRITABLE. I recall last night. At once I am depressed again. Through the window I can see it is a cloudy day. I wonder whether Ma is out of bed yet. I crack my door open and peep out into the dimly lit hall. I hear Ma moving around in the kitchen. I smell bacon frying and coffee blurping on the stove. I am famished! But I am afraid to face Ma. Is she the same as last night or has she changed? What will she say or do to me? I know I could not bear to see again her face of last night. I do not know what to do.

I go to the bathroom and wash. I hear Ma singing in the kitchen. This is hopeful news that she is in a good mood. Now it will not be so hard to face her. Right away, I will tell her how sorry I am about last night, and everything will be all right again. I am heartened. I return to my room and dress quickly. I cannot find my shoes in the dark room. To hell with them. I can find them later. I keep my slippers on and hurry down the hall to the kitchen.

The table is set for two. Everything is nice and sparkling clean in the kitchen. Ma, in her housecoat, is at the stove. She turns to me as I enter. I look at her, contrite and uncertain.

"Good morning, my pet!" she says cheerfully. "I thought you were going to sleep all day!"

Ah! I am relieved. I go to her, kiss her check. "Ma, I want to tell you how sorry I am about yesterday."

She pats my face affectionately. "Of course, you are, my dear. And I forgive you completely. How stupid of me to curse you! I should have known all along that you didn't realize what you were doing."

"Ma, if I ever do anything to hurt you I'd die. I'd want to be dead."

"Why, it's impossible to imagine—you deliberately doing anything to hurt me. But this should be a lesson to you. Now you have seen for yourself how a—a mere slut can cause trouble between us."

"Well, it will never happen again."

"I'm sure it won't, Harold. And I know I have your solemn promise that you will never see her again."

"Never see her again?"

"Yes."

She looks intently at me. Her eyes begin to harden. I avoid them. "I mean, well, what do you mean by not seeing her again?"

"Taking her out, talking with her, things like that. You must break off all friendly relations with her."

"Even saying hello to her on the street?"

"Yes."

"But, Ma, she's not really *too* bad."

"For you she is bad. You must break off all friendly relations, Harold."

I hesitate.

Ma says, "You must understand, Harold, the only reason I forgive you is that I know that you will do this. I know that you are a good son and will recognize what is right."

She has given me the choice again, Iris or her. Me and Ma have suffered all through the lean days together. She stuck with me in her youth when she did not have to stick. It would be disgraceful to forsake her now when her hair is gray and her face tired. And what is Iris to me but a love beginning? What has she ever done for me but to rid me of Madden, and I am not so sure things are not worse? Damn Iris! My mother comes before the whole of the world.

"All right, Ma, I promise you. I'll break off from Iris completely."

"Of course, you will. Now, sit down and have a nice, hot breakfast!"

I must hang around the house all day, in case Louis has to get in touch with me. I look through the newspapers to see if there is any mention of Georgie Whistle. There is none. I go the phone and dial Louis' house number. I hear the ringing and wait. I wonder if Iris is working there today? The phone rings and rings and rings, but no one answers. I hang up.

I stand in the kitchen doorway, watching Ma iron clothes. She smiles at me.

"You don't have to do that," I say. "What's the matter with the Chink's?"

"Oh, these little things I like to do myself."

I take an apple from the refrigerator and munch on it.

Ma asks, "Who were you trying to phone?"

"Louis. Nobody answered."

"When do you go back to work?"

"I'll find out tomorrow when I see him."

I go into the living room. I pick up a magazine and flop on the sofa. I try to read. It bores me. I throw it aside. I think of Iris. Was she always so pretty as she is now? I do not remember. I wonder what she is thinking and feeling today? But why think of her? Forget it.

I get up off the sofa and turn on the radio. Static. I turn it off again. I am restless and bored. I can find nothing to interest me. I go to the window and look out at the empty street. It is a dark, dreary day with rain falling now and again. Why do I still feel so depressed? It is like the end of the world is nearing.

I go to the bathroom to pee. I notice one of Ma's tonic bottles sitting on the sink with the cork off. I have not had any of this stuff since I was a little bit of a kid. I have forgotten the taste of it. What is it like? I sniff at the mouth of the bottle. It smells like wine. I taste it. It is wine—sherry wine! I have an idea. I open up the medicine chest and sniff at all the tonic bottles lined up there. It is what I thought. They are all filled with sherry wine. This is Ma's little trick. All right, so she drinks on the sly. Let her. It does not bother me now. I do not believe anything can penetrate the numbness I feel.

I go back to the living room and lie on the sofa again. I pick up the magazine. It is still a bore. I throw it aside. Iris comes to mind with her moist lips and dark eyes. There is a fluttering, weak feeling in my chest. Goddamn it, forget about her. I turn over on my side and try to sleep.

Ma comes into the room with her knitting bag.

"Oh, stay right where you are!" she says. "Now is my chance to get at those blackheads on your face."

She puts her knitting down and places my head in her lap. She begins to squeeze. It stings.

"Are there many?" I ask.

"Not many. But enough to get attention. Hold still."

"It hurts!"

"Oh, don't be such a baby!"

"Isn't there an easier remedy than this?"

"Not a better one. My mother knew of a good one from the old country. Sheep's urine. You bathe the face with it."

"Ugh!"

"Keep still!"

The phone rings. I jump up. "I'll get it. It must be Louis." I go over to the phone by the door and pick it up.

"Hello?" I say.

"Hello, Harry?"

"Yeah?"

"This is Iris."

I get a jolt. I do not know what to do. I look around at Ma.

"Who is it?" she asks.

"It's Iris. Shall I talk to her?"

"Well, yes. Take this opportunity to tell her you won't see her again. Break off with her now. But don't be rude. Be gentle. After all, she is a young girl in love. Be firm, yes, but gentle."

Iris says, "Harry, can I see you? Can you meet me someplace?"

"No, I can't, Iris." *What did Ma say to you? I am sorry, Iris. I apologize to you on my knees!*

"Why can't you meet me?"

"Because I don't want you to be my girl any more. Is that clear? Let's just call it quits now."

"But *why*, Harry? Can't you tell me why?"

"Damn it, I don't have to give you reasons!"

Ma whispers, "Gently, Harold, *gently!*"

"Is your mother there?"

"Yes."

"Is that why you're talking this way?"

*Yes, Iris.* "What's she got to do with it?"

"Do you know what she said to me yesterday?"

"I don't know and I don't care."

"Harry, I love you, Harry."

*I love you, too, Iris.* "Well, I can't help that."

"Harry, I need you and you need me. I can help you."

"What do you mean?"

"Harry, your troubles—you know, like with Madden? I think it's got something to do with your mother. Don't you realize what—"

"You're nuts!" *Tell me, Iris. Help me.*

"Harry, I *must* talk with you someplace. I just can't let you go like this."

"Can't you get it through your head? I don't want to talk to you. I don't ever want to see you again. Get that?"

"You're parroting. You're just saying what she wants you to say."

"Okay, let's finish the talk. I'm gonna hang up." *Don't let me, Iris.*

"Then I'm going away, Harry, right away, if I don't see you. Me and Grandma are taking the train for California."

"Go ahead. What's it to me?" *Don't go! Oh, please don't go.*

"And you don't care at all?"

"Why should I care?" *I do care, Iris. Don't go. I love you, I love you.*

"We'll try to leave tonight—if I don't see you."

"Have a nice trip." *Oh, God, Iris—so far away! Don't leave me, don't leave me!*

"Harry, are you sure you mean what you're saying to me?"

"Sure." *Not a word of it, my love. Not a lying, cheating word of it.*

"Well, then, I guess this is goodbye. . . ."

"Guess so." *Don't go, please, I beg you. Fight with me, Iris. Help me fight for love that has come too late. Please, Iris, don't leave me, don't leave me!*

"I love you, Harry."

"That's tough!" *I love you, too, Iris. And you are holy and pure and sweet and the only thing that is good and clean in my life. Don't go, Iris. Don't go!*

"Goodbye, Harry."

"Okay. See you around, kid." *Goodbye love, hope, warmness, two-oneness, holiness. Goodbye Harry and Iris. Goodbye world. Goodbye every Goddamned thing.*

I hang up. "Well, that's that!"

"Yes," Ma says. "Now, that wasn't so very hard to do, was it?"

"It was a cinch, Ma."

I go over to the window and look out at the sad, gray day. My numbness increases. My eyes blur. I rub them clear.

Ma says, "What would you like for lunch, Harold? I think I'll fix you something very special. What would you like? Anything your heart desires."

My heart's desire.

## 2

I drive over to B.M.'s office at 70 Pine Street to meet Louis. I get off the elevator on the eighth floor. I walk down to the end of the hall to the office. As I enter a pretty girl looks up at me from the desk.

"Yes?"

"I'm here to meet Mr. Varga. Is he here?"

"Are you Harry Odum?"

"Yes."

"Yes, he's here. He's in conference with Mr. Gompers just now, but I'll tell him you're here." She pushes a button on the little box on her desk and speaks into it. "Mr. Gompers? Mr. Harry Odum is here to see Mr. Varga." A voice answers through the box, but I cannot catch what it says. She clicks it off again and smiles at me. "He'll be right out."

"Thanks."

The inner office door opens, and a youngish-looking guy comes out. He just stands there in front of the door, giving me the cold once-over, up and down, up and down. He is probably one of B.M.'s guns, but he just looks like a fresh punk kid to me . . . one of us fresh, punk, doomed kids.

Louis comes out, the punk steps aside. Louis looks at him.

"Go back inside, Leo. He wants to talk to you."

The punk goes back into the office. Louis looks excited. He is hurriedly wiping sweat from his face. He comes quickly over to me and takes my arm.

"Come on," he says. "I'll talk to you out in the hall."

We go outside. He looks up and down. The hall is deserted. He takes me by the arm and walks me slowly down the hall.

"We're in trouble," he says.

"What's happening?"

"The roof's gonna fall. You'd never believe what happened. B.M.'s going crazy. We're all going crazy."

"What is it?"

"Georgie Whistle is trying to make a deal."

"*What?!*"

"Shh!" He turns me around to walk back up the hall. "The dirty son of a bitch is trying to make a deal to save his own neck. If they'll let him out clean, he'll talk on everybody. Not just the Gooney Package, but the whole works. Everything he knows!"

"How do you know?"

"Our man in Gold's office."

I get the feeling of being trapped. But this is an old sensation to me. It does not panic me any more. "What do we do now?"

He goes into his pocket and hands me a fat roll of bills. "Get out of town right away. Take a plane to Florida. Hole up in the

Pennant Hotel, where you and the Bug stayed that time. I am flying down there later and I'll meet you there tonight. Sit tight until I get there. Okay?"

"Sure, Louis."

"Okay, now, hurry and beat it."

Suddenly Louis has disappeared back into the office, and I am standing alone and confused in the hall. What will I do? I cannot leave Ma alone, and I know she will not come with me. But Louis has given me orders. I must decide quick because things have become very urgent.

I get on the elevator, thinking on it. Laughter and gay talk comes to my ears. There are three other passengers in the car. There is an elderly, dignified man, a young woman and a strange young man. They are all well dressed and seem to be in a good mood. From the conversation, I learn it is a family group, father, son and daughter.

"Don't listen to him, Helen," the elderly man says. "Your brother is just in another of his teasing moods."

"I'm not teasing. I really mean it, Dad. We ought to keep her here with us a couple of more months."

"And what would my husband do?!"

"Without you, my dear girl. He'll do without you."

The girl laughs. "Hear him, Dad? The nerve!"

I look casually over at the young man. His face is turned full toward me. Suddenly I'm fascinated!

"Have you anything to read on the plane?" the father asks.

"Yes, Proust."

"Good Lord!" the brother-son says. "Are you going by plane or a rowboat?"

The girl laughs. "I've been digging at *Remembrance* for years now. The only time I have to read is when I take a trip. I imagine it will take me another ten years of trips to finish it."

"Look out it doesn't finish you first," the brother tells her.

I stare at this strange young man. I cannot take my eyes from his face. What is it? Do I know him? Have I seen him somewhere before? His eyes meet mine, linger curiously a moment, then back to his sister.

"Well, I suppose we'll have to wait another couple of years for a visit out of you."

"Nothing of the kind," she says. "I'll be here with Jim for the holidays."

The elevator stops. I get out first, but I walk slowly toward the exit, hoping the group will pass me so that I can watch them. On the street, I pause beside my car. I watch them as they cross the street to a dark roadster. They stand there laughing and talking. The elderly man kisses the girl, waves goodbye and merges with the throng of people coming out of office buildings. The boy and girl get into the roadster and pull out. I get into my car. I follow them.

I know what it is. I hate him. He is a complete stranger to me, but hatred for him cuts like a knife through me. I hate him and I want to take him. It is a crazy, senseless thing, but that does not make any difference to me. I will look for the chance, and I will take this strange, young man.

We are out in the suburbs. The roadster up ahead bobs along at a lively clip. I see no houses along this way. There is only the greenness of trees and bushes. I hear the sound of an airplane.

I think: He is taking her to the airport. He will come back alone. An idea begins to form.

Far up ahead of the roadster, I see the airport sitting on the horizon. I stop my car. The little roadster seems to suddenly pick up more speed and pierces ahead in the distance. I turn the car around. I back off the road amidst bushes and trees. I cut the motor off, lean back in the seat and light a cigarette. I wait.

I see the roadster far up the road coming back down. I pull my car up on the road and park across it, blocking the way. I wait.

A horn blows vigorously. The roadster comes to a halt.

"Hey, you're blocking the road, mister. What's the matter with you?"

I look over at him and smile. "What's your hurry?"

"Well, I'm in no hurry, but I know you have a lot of damn nerve if you're sober. Come on, pull that thing out of the way."

I had planned no further than this. I do not know what to do next. I try to think of something. I do not want to frighten him. I try to look pleasant. "I'm sorry but I can't. Something's wrong with my motor."

His eyes squint suspiciously at me. He stands up in the car, puts one hand on a hip and shakes his finger accusingly at me. "You're a liar! I saw you pull it out on the road from a-way back there. Who do you think you're kidding? Now, come on, good-looking, wiggle your ass back off of there."

Strangely his words suddenly frighten me. But I know what the score is with him now. Now I know what to do.

"Okay," I say, "don't get excited. I'll pull off in a second. But what's your hurry?"

He sits back down in the car. He looks at me with growing absorption. "And what's your big idea?" Suddenly, "Say, haven't I seen you somewhere before? The elevator! Weren't you in the elevator with me in an office building about an hour ago?"

I smile and shake my head. "I followed you."

"You did?" He smiles curiously. "Why?"

"I don't know—something about you, I guess. I like your looks."

He looks at me with meaning. "Well, I must say, the feeling is mutual."

Automobile horns honk at us. There are other cars from the airport behind us. A voice shouts at us, "Hey, you guys, get moving or pull off the road! Come on!"

"Let's pull over to the side," the young man says.

I pull my car halfway off the road. He does the same thing behind me. The other cars go by. I start to get out of my car, but I see that he is already out of his and coming toward me. I remain behind the wheel and push the car door open. He comes up, puts one foot on the running board.

"This is a nice car you have here," he says.

I agree. "It was a gift."

"Really? You must have nice friends."

"Yeah, sure." I light up a cigarette. I offer him one.

"No, thanks, I don't smoke."

He looks me over. I give him plenty of time. I look around the countryside. "Pretty cool for September, isn't it?" I ask.

"Yes. We'll have an early winter. Say, have you anything on your mind? Are you interested in anything?"

"Like what?"

"Action. A little action."

"Oh, I don't know. . . ."

"Well, either you are or you aren't. Make up your mind. I didn't get out of my car to listen to you talk about how cool it is for September. I'm a delicate girl, and I can't stand the stress and strain of such talk."

"Okay. I'm in the mood for some action."

"Now, a question arises. We're out here on the open road—and we also have two cars. I just don't know how—"

"I can back mine off the road again and get in yours. We'll go somewhere and you can bring me back."

He looks at me with keen, bright eyes. "Why, you fascinating dog, you! You had it planned all the time, didn't you? Played it so cute, too. All right, back yours off and get in with me."

I back my car off the road again. I lock it and walk out on the road. He sits behind the wheel of his car with the door open, waiting for me. I climb in beside him. We start rolling down the road.

"You know, I usually don't do this kind of thing," he says. "Some of them do, but I just don't like these casual pickups. But you made it so impossible to resist. Good Lord, following me all the way out here from Pine Street!"

"I couldn't help it," I say truthfully.

"Where shall we go?"

"There's lots of secluded places along here. Turn off into the first real good one you see."

He slows the car down. "Well, how about right over there?"

"Okay."

He cuts off the road into the high bushes. He drives slowly deep into them until we are well hidden from the road. Darkness is falling.

"You know," he begins, "when I first saw you looking at me that way in the elevator, I knew right away you were 'in the life.'"

"Sure," I say as the car comes to a halt. I feel for my gun.

I look at his dead face on the floor of the car. It is shocking that he looks so much like me. And so now I know. Now I know what I have been bidden.

I pull up onto the road and drive back to where my car is parked. I drive the roadster into the bushes, get back into my car and cut out.

The fever begins. . . .

I take the steps to Iris' apartment three at a time! I am frantic and eager. I knock at the door. Hoping, hoping! There is no answer. I bang at the door, louder, louder. There is still no answer. I twist the doorknob. I shove and pound furiously.

"Iris! Iris!"

Across the hall a man opens the door. He is chewing on a piece of meat. Meat.

"Ain't nobody there, mister."

"What?!"

"They moved. Gone clear across the country, they did. Her and the old woman."

Meat.

"What?"

"They left town, I said. Gone out to live in California."

Meat. Eating a piece of meat.

"California?"

"Yes. They left yesterday."

Meat, meat, meat, meat!

I go downstairs to the street. I go to the whorehouse on Hudson Avenue. No one answers. I am drunk with passion. Try one more. The Spanish house, Big Lola's. I pound on the door. It opens. I start in, but Big Lola blocks the way.

"What do you want?"

"A girl."

"No one's here. Don't you know? We been raided. Go away."

"I want a girl!"

"There's no one, I tell you. Go away!"

I start to move in. She slams the door shut in my face. I pound on the door again.

"Go away or I call the police."

I turn away in despair and go back downstairs to the street. My breath comes fast. I lean against the wall of the house to rest, but this goading thing inside will not let me stay. There is nothing to do but go home. I look desperately around for Madden. What am I doing? There is no Madden. I do what I do. I can no longer deny it. This is reality, sex is real! I do what I must do. Hatred cancels my crime, passion consumes my fears. And I know now what has been the horror of reality for me.

I make my way home. It has been asking for a long, long time.

**I** AM THE SHEIK OF ARABY

"Harold, what is the matter with you? You don't look well."

*I am the Sheik of Araby*

"You look ill. Are you ill?"

*I am the Sheik of Araby*

"What are you mumbling about? I can't hear you. You haven't been drinking, have you?"

*I am the Sheik of Araby*

"Come, let me give you a spoonful of tonic. You'll feel much better. Then I'll fix you something to eat. I have a surprise for you— some nice crisp Bermuda onion rings."

*I am the Sheik of Araby*

"Of course, you've come home. Isn't this your home, where you belong? What on earth are you talking about? You look so strange, Harold."

*I am the Sheik of Araby*

"Surely, you must be drunk. What *are* you talking about?"

*I am the Sheik of Araby*

"What do you mean, he's dead? He's not dead."

*I am the Sheik of Araby*

"Interfere—interfere with who?"

*I am the Sheik of Araby*

"Oh, my God, have you gone crazy?"

*I am the Sheik of Araby*

"*Who* did you finally kill? *Who?*"

*I am the Sheik of Araby*

"Go to your room at once. Do you hear me, Harold? I will not listen to this nonsense any longer. Go to your room at once!"

*Your love belongs to me*

"What?!"

*Your love belongs to me*

"No!"

*Your love belongs to me*

"Yes, but I didn't mean—"

*Your love belongs to me*

"Because I told you. Because of what they are, scheming, conniving sluts. I wanted to protect you. It is my duty to protect you from them. You're the only thing I have in the world. Do you think I would let them—"

*Your love belongs to me*

"It is a terrible lie—a vicious, filthy lie. And how dare you say such things to me? Have you forgotten? I am your mother—your mother. Do you realize what you are saying? No, I forgive you. I am your mother and I must forgive you. You are drunk and you don't realize. You have been drugged by those wicked people. I knew it was a mistake to let you work there. Come, Ma will undress you and put you to bed. Yes, I have seen your father like this—coming in crazy drunk. I cared for him, so I must care for you. It is the duty of a wife and mother."

*Your love belongs to me*

"Now, I just won't listen, Harold, I just won't *listen*!"

*Your love belongs to me*

"You despicable thing—how dare you? Oh, God in heaven, what did I ever do to deserve this sin? My own son, my own son! You are filthy and despicable. I am your mother and you are my son. I will not hear another disgusting word of it. Go to your room at once. Go—before I am forced to call the police against my own child!"

*Your love belongs to me*

"And after all I've done—that you should say these things to me. After all I've suffered and endured. I brought you into the world. I nursed and nourished you. When your father deserted us, I sacrificed and slaved and broke my back alone to keep a roof over our heads and bread in our mouths. When your father left, I could have abandoned you. Lots of women leave their children. I could have abandoned you and become a singer with a future. But no, I sacrificed it all for you—to stick with you, to give you all my love and devotion. And this is the thanks I get. This—this unheard-of—!"

*Your love belongs to me*

"What are you *saying*?!"

*Your love belongs to me*

"Never mind going to your room. Get out. Get out of the house altogether. I don't want you under the same roof with me. Get out—get out. Go—*hide* yourself, Harold, my darling!"

*The stars that shine above*

"Don't say that about your father!"

*Will light our way to love*

"Let go. Stop shaking me!"

*The stars that shine above*

"He was *not* homosexual! He was, well, he was just weak, that's all."

*Will light our way to love*

"Yes, I loved him. I loved him more than life itself."

*The stars that shine above*

"Yes!"

*Will light our way to love*

"Yes."

*At night when you're asleep*

"Oh, I'm so confused. . . ."

*Into your tent I'll creep*

"But you are not even a man yet. Oh, God, what am I saying? You are my son. Harold, please have mercy."

*At night when you're asleep*

"Harold, my baby, I love you. Don't do this thing to me. I am weak. I feel so weak because—I feel so sorry for you now, my poor, sick baby."

*Into your tent I'll creep*

"Don't say that. You will make me—I might—*surrender!*"

*At night when you're asleep*

"What are you going to do?"

*Into your tent I'll creep*

"Wait—no, no. But it is against all reason, Harold. It's against all morals of God and men. You are forcing me. Do you realize you are forcing me?"

*At night when you're asleep*

"Yes, then you will have to force me. I will not of my own free will because it is wrong."

*Into your tent I'll creep*

"No, no—I'll run into your room and lock the door."

*At night when you're asleep*

"No, I won't come out—not until you've changed. I'm afraid of you. I'll stay in this womb until you've changed.

*Into your tent I'll creep*

"Oh, you wild boy, you've broken the lock. Let go, now. No, no, please be a good boy. Stop, I must go."

*You'll rule this land with me*

"Very well, then, if you must—but not here. In my room! But you are forcing me. You must carry me. Remember, you are forcing me into this."

*You'll rule this land with me*

"Oh, Hap! Hap! You've been away so long!"

*I am the Sheik of Araby*

# 2

She cries, whimpers. I do not care. I hate her.

I must bathe. I go into the bathroom and fill the tub. The whimpering does not stop. It comes in through the cracks and invisible holes in the walls, pleading to me. I do not care. All I feel is anger.

I get into the tub, plenty of soap and scrub. I scrub, scrub, scrub, but it is impossible. I cannot wash myself away.

The crying and whimpering stops. There are little bumping noises outside. I do not care.

I dry myself. It is strange that nothing comes off on the towel. My head feels hot and tight. I will go out and get some air. This house is stifling!

I get dressed and come out of the bathroom. My mouth is dry and hot. I need water. I go into the kitchen. The woman is here flying around in the air. She looks at me. Her face is old and ugly. I go right past her to the sink without saying anything. I drink two big glasses of cold water slowly. It feels so good going down my dry, tight throat. I start out. I pause before I pass the woman again. I look up into her twisted face. I am not afraid any more.

"You are *dead*," I say to her.

I go down the hall and out to the street.

I walk slowly through Fort Greene Park. The sky is clear and the moon is full and naked. A night breeze cools my forehead, and I have a feeling of giddiness as if I have been drinking.

I feel fine! I have such a wonderful feeling of being free, I want to run about and roll on the grass like a happy puppy. I am glad she is dead. I am glad she is dead because I hate her. I hate her for what she has done to Ma and me and Hap. I hate her for all the misery and heartache she has caused us all. Now, we are free of her forever. Me and Ma will go away somewhere. We will pack a few things, just a few things, and me and Ma will catch a train somewhere. I will take her away from this place and the memory of that wicked and vile woman. We will go away somewhere and start all over again. We will forget the past.

I start for home again.

* * *

I enter the front door. The house is quiet.

I call, "Ma, I'm back again."

I go down the hall. I am eager to tell her of my plans. She is not in her bedroom. The bathroom door is open, and she is not in there. She must be in the living room. I look in. She is not there, either. Where can she be? She must have gone out. I go into the kitchen.

I am startled—frightened! There is a woman hanging from the ceiling light by a cord around her neck. It is . . .

"Ma! Ma!"

It is a long, black nothingness I come out of into a hazy, dreamlike kitchen. I lie on the floor, breathing heavily. I have cried myself out. The muscles of my stomach ache. I sit up slowly and wipe the wetness from my face. I look up at her casually. I feel nothing. She is unreal, like everything else is unreal except the hurt I feel. Slowly I climb to my feet. . . .

I cut her down from there. I hold her tenderly in my arms, my face against hers.

"Oh, Ma!"

I carry her into her room. I put her on the bed. I untie the cord from around her neck where it has cut deep into her flesh. I look at this brutal thing that has taken the life of my mother. It is part of the extension cord that carried light to my room. Angrily I throw it away, smashing it against the wall. I look at her face. It is twisted in suffering. I look around the room for something to cover her with. I see nothing. I look in a bureau drawer . . . tiny knitted clown suits, with brass buttons running down the front. Hundreds. The drawer is packed full with them! I close the drawer quickly against this sameness that has haunted me all my life. I do not open the other drawers in fear this thing will jump out at me again. I get a coat from the closet and gently place it over Ma. I go out, closing the door softly behind me. This is the end.

A bell is ringing. Phone? The doorbell rings, rings.

I go down the hall and open it.

"Who is it?"

"It's me."

"Who?"

"Me, Ding Dong. What's ud matter, Harry, don'tcha know me?"

"Oh, Ding Dong. Come on in."

I go back down the hall. There is whisky in the kitchen. Maybe a drink will help me. Ding Dong follows.

"The Owner sent me, Harry. He wanted me to make sure you left town. But you ain't gone, Harry!"

I go into the kitchen, open the bottle and take a drink.

"Everybody's frantic. Georgie Whistle is shootin' off like the Fourth of July. He's talking on the club. The mob has brung in outa-town guns to pick off witnesses before the cops collar 'em. I hear the cops are looking for you, Harry. That's why the Owner wants to make sure you are outa town. But you ain't gone, Harry. You're still standing here!"

"No. I'm not going anywhere."

"But you gotta, Harry."

"Why?"

"Because maybe the mob will get ideas about you. They might thunk you're waiting around to talk, too. Gee, Harry, I like you. I don't want them to get idea like that about you, I swear to my mudder."

Good old Ding Dong. I pat him on the shoulder. "Don't worry. Louis knows better than that."

"But, jeez, them guys don't take no chances, Harry."

"I don't give a damn. Anybody who comes here for me, I'll blast them right through the front door, cop or gun. I'm not leaving this house—never!"

"Harry, are you crazy, Harry? You want me to tell him *that*!"

"Who?"

"The Owner."

"I don't care. Get out of here, Ding Dong, and leave me alone."

"*Please*, Harry!"

"Get out!"

He goes. Who? Ding Dong. Was he really here or did I imagine it? What is dream and what is not? My head begins to hurt. I take the bottle and go down the hall to my room. I click the lamp, no light comes. I remember now there is no cord. I lie across the bed on my back in the darkness.

She is gone forever. I am numb with despair. Finished, forever gone. What a strange and terrible feeling! Alone, alone. All is sadness and gloom. I am alone and lost in the world. I feel so sick.

I open my eyes. Where am I? The rising fear dies quickly, as I realize this is my room and I am safe. But I am not safe here. Ma is no more. She is dead. It is impossible. That cannot be so. It is impossible. I take another drink from the bottle. The room is still and dark. . . .

*"Harold . . ."*

*The room is so dark. I strain my eyes to see the form moving toward me. It moves close to the bed. A hand strokes my face.*

*"Harold, dear?"*

*"Ma, is that you?"*

*"Of course, it's me, my baby."*

*"Oh, Ma!"*

*What grand relief! Happiness overwhelms me. I sit up and pull her to me. I embrace her with all my might. I kiss her over and over again.*

*"Why, what on earth is the matter?"*

*"I thought you had left me."*

*"Leave you? How silly. Why, how could I ever do such a thing? You are all I have and cherish in the world."*

*"I know. But I thought you had gone. It must have been a dream."*

*"A bad dream, Harold!"*

A dream? Dreaming again. Am I really all alone now without anyone? Everyone must have someone. Who have I?

*I find Varga and the Bug in the back room of the barbershop, where they are watching the girls count up the numbers take. I call*

*them aside and tell them about Ding Dong. Varga chews on his*
*cigar a moment, squinting at the floor. Now he looks at me.*

*"This kid ain't no friend of yours no more," he says. "The only*
*friends you got now is me, Georgie Whistle and the Bug. And don't*
*you ever forget that!"*

Louis! He is the one I have. He is the boss. He will tell me what
to do. I will go to him. I will tell him about Ma.

*"Tell him what about me, Harold?"*
*"Don't you know?"*
*"I don't think so."*
*"About what the old woman did to us."*
*"Oh, I really don't think I remember. I'm afraid you'll have to*
*tell it to me all over again, dear."*
*"All right, but not now. On the way. Get dressed and pack a*
*few things. But remember, only a few things."*
*"Where are we going—on a picnic?"*
*"On a trip. Florida."*
*"Florida! Oh, how wonderful."*
*"Hurry, now. We'll leave before the old woman gets back."*
*"Where will we live in Florida?"*

The hotel. What hotel was it? I cannot remember. Never mind.
I will phone B.M. He will tell me where I am supposed to meet
Louis. I will not take any clothes with me. I will just take my gun.
I might need it.

*"Well! I'm all ready, Harold."*
*She looks very young and gay and pretty.*
*"You look nice," I say. "You look just like a little girl."*
*"Why, thank you. What a nice thing to say!"*
*"Come on, we must hurry."*
*"Yes. And don't you forget to tell me about the old woman on*
*the way."*
*"I won't. Come on."*
*"How are we going—by train?"*

* * *

How? B.M. will tell me the best way. I go to the phone and dial his number. I wait.

"Hello?" a man's voice says.

"Mr. B.?"

"Who is this, please?"

"Harry."

"The *Cat*?!"

"Yes. I—"

"One moment. I'll—"

"Wait—I just want to know how to reach Louis."

"He's still here. He's right here now. Wait, I'll put him on."

I wait an anxious moment.

"Harry? What the hell's the matter with you?"

"Louis! I'm so glad I found you."

"You're still here. I told you to heel. What the hell kind of a message is that you sent back by Ding Dong?"

"Ding Dong? What message?"

"What do you mean, 'what message'? Ding Dong is standing here right now. He just come from your house."

"I didn't see him."

He talks to somebody away from the phone. I can make out only a few words of what he says. He comes back to the phone. "Harry?"

"Yes?"

"You been drinking. What are you trying to do—pull an Abie the Bug on me?"

"Louis, I am *not* drunk. I swear to God I'm not!"

"Then, what's the matter with you? Why didn't you heel out when I told you?"

"Something terrible has happened. You got to help me, Louis. I'm miserable."

"What is it? What's the matter?"

"My mother. Ma—she's dead, Louis."

"Dead? What did you say—she's dead?"

"Yes."

Away from the phone: "He says his mother's dead." Into the

phone: "What happened? Well, wait a minute, you can tell me all that later. I'm sorry as all hell, kid, but you realize it's important you get outa town right away."

"Yes, I want to. I want to go with you, Louis."

"Fine, fine. That's the attitude, kid. Now, listen, the boys will take care of the funeral and everything for you. Keep your chin up. I don't want you to worry about nothing, understand? Everything at home will be taken care of for you. Now, I want you to meet me at La Guardia Airport in an hour. Know how to get there?"

*"We cannot go in the car, Harold. We'll have to take a taxi."*

"We'll take a taxi, Louis."

"We? Who's we? I thought you was alone."

"No—my mother is here. She's coming with me. She wants to come."

"Your *mother*? I thought you said she was dead!"

"Yes, she is."

"And she's coming with you?"

"Yes. I don't want to leave her here. She won't be in the way, Louis."

"Just a minute." Away from the phone: "The kid has flipped or something. He says—" Silence. Wait. Into the phone: "Hello, Harry? Listen, kid, take it easy. Where are you now?"

"Home."

"Okay, now listen—try to keep your head. Everything's gonna be fine. I want you to stay right where you are. I'll send Ding Dong over there with a car to pick you up and drive you to the airport. Okay?"

"Okay."

"Now, you wait right there. Ding Dong will be over in about fifteen minutes. I'll be at the airport to meet you. Keep your chin up and sit tight till I see you."

"Yes, Louis, yes."

We hang up. I am shaking all over. I go back to the bedroom. I sit on the edge of the bed and pick up the bottle of whisky.

*   *   *

*"Are you going to drink again, Harold?*

*"Where have you been and what is the matter with you? You've been drinking. Oh, my God, my baby is drunk. Somebody has made my baby drunk O God what is the matter with you?*

*"Oh, I don't know what is going to happen. What did I ever do O God to deserve this? What did I do to anyone? Why must I have all this trouble? Why am I always betrayed? All I ever did was to try to live a decent Christian life. All I ever did. But look at me. Look at us. Struggle, struggle, all my life. Tried to make a decent marriage, a decent home. Try to bring up a child. But what do I get for it? Betrayal and heartache. You will turn out to be just like your father. But who have I to blame but myself? Mama told me. Stay away from that boy. He is no good. Stick to your singing. Stay away from him and you'll be a great singer, marry him and you'll be nothing. It's true—I had a beautiful voice. I did look like Helen Twelvetrees. I still do when I fix myself up, yes, I do, and you know that very well. I could have been famous if I hadn't married your father. I could have been married a much better man. Mr. Mizner, my voice teacher, wanted to woo me. He even proposed. Oh, how I used to agonize that man! He had money and he would have given me everything I wanted."*

*"I don't want to hear about him."*

*"He was a handsome one, too, this Mr. Mizner."*

*"I don't want to hear!"*

*"Such gorgeous curly, black hair and broad shoulders like a movie actor."*

*"Ma, I told you I don't want to listen!"*

*"Why, what's the matter, Harold?"*

*"Nothing."*

*"Yes, there is. Look at me. Why don't you look at me? Why, Harold, how sweet—I do believe you're jealous!"*

*"I am not!"*

*"You are!"*

*"Please stop it, Ma!"*

*"Oh, very well! But anyway I just wouldn't listen to anybody. That Hap! I would die for him with his sweet talk.*

"Now take the rest of your clothes off and get into your bed. Oh no, there is no light in your room and I'll need light to put on the cold towels. Go get in my bed. You'll sleep there tonight, and tomorrow I'll put the lamp in your room. Here, I'll help you. Come on, you naughty, naughty boy. What a shame! Did anyone see you? What will the neighbors say to see such a young boy coming home drunk. What a disgraceful thing!"

R-r-i-n-g!

"Take your underwear off, too. You will sleep better naked. Ashamed? Why, Harold, don't be silly. I have never heard of anything so silly in all my life. I am your mother, my dear boy, and I'll have you know I saw you before you saw yourself. Now, take off those shorts without further nonsense. That's it.

"My, what a baby you still are! But I can see already that you will develop a nice build like your father. You will be something then, to look like your father with his strong, manly body! And you are not weak."

R-r-i-n-g! !

"Get under the covers, all the way. Now lay still. I'll go get the cold towels."

Somebody is ringing a bell!

R-r-i-n-g! !

What?

The doorbell is ringing. I get up from the bed and go slowly down the hall. I open the front door.

"Who are you?"

"It's me, Harry—Ding Dong. What's the matter, don't you know me?"

Ding Dong. The face comes forward out of the fog into the light.

"Ding Dong?"

"Sure. What's the matter ud you, Harry. You drunk?"

"No. How are you, Ding Dong?"

"Okay. Didn't the Owner tell you he was sending me for you with the car?"

"I don't know. Where's Louis?"

"We'll meet him at the airport. I got the car downstairs. Come on, I'll drive you."

"I'll get my hat."

Ding Dong. Sure, I remember Ding Dong. My pal, Ding Dong.

*"Poor Arnie," Ding Dong says.*

*"Yes. He was my best pal," I say. "Now I'm all by myself."*

*"That Arnie! He sure was a swell, tough guy, all right."*

*"A pisserroo!"*

*"What did he do to get sent up?"*

*"I don't know."*

*I stretch and get up from the curb. I don't know what to do.*

*"Where you going?" Ding Dong asks.*

*"I don't know—home, I guess."*

*I start down the street. Ding Dong runs after me.*

*"Hey, Harry, can I be your friend now in Arnie's place?"*

*"I don't care."*

*He spits through his teeth. "Thanks, Harry. You're a pisserroo!"*

Ding Dong gets behind the wheel of the car. I climb in beside him.

Ding Dong says, "We find out Georgie Whistle didn't really sing yet. He's still trying to make ud deal. He wants to come out clean if he talks on something. But the D.A. don't like it, him coming out clean."

"I didn't come out clean."

"What?"

"I said I took a bath and didn't come out clean."

"Oh. Jeez, I sure was sorry to hear about what happened to your old lady, Harry."

"The old lady?"

*"Yes, you remember, Harold. You were going to tell me what the old woman did to us. You said you would tell me on the way."*

*"I said it and I'll say it again. If the old woman had left me and you and Hap alone, everything would have been okay. You were right, Ma—they use the sex thing, that's what they use, the sex thing. The way it was, I couldn't do anything until I killed him and put him out of my way. But every time I killed him he turned out to be Arnie, or Brownfingers, or that Chicago guy. Oh, but I finally got him, Ma—that last one, that strange young man. He looked like somebody else, but I knew who he really was. He couldn't fool me this time. And so I killed him. I killed him dead. And that's when I found out what she was up to with the sex thing, how she had trapped me with it. She was really out to destroy me, because my face and his face are the same. This is the mystery, Ma. Do you see the mystery?"*

*"Yes, I see it. And I see you never listened to my lesson. I warned you long ago of the evil of such a wicked woman. I warned you never to go near them. I wanted it to be just you and me together. We could have been so happy—just the two of us. But you wouldn't listen. You wouldn't listen to a mother's weeping heart. Now, we are lost, Harold—forever lost."*

*"No, we're not! Don't say that, Ma. We'll be together from now on."*

*"No, Harold. It's too late."*

*"No, Ma!"*

*"Goodbye, Harold. I must go now."*

*"No, Ma—come back! Come back!"*

"Take it easy, Harry."

"What? Where's Ma? Who are you?"

"Ding Dong." He turns and speaks to the back of the car, "What ud you make of this?"

I look around. There is someone sitting in the back seat, grinning at me.

"Who are you?"

"Leo," he says.

The car is not moving. We are surrounded by trees and darkness.

"Where are we?"

"Flushing."

Something is terribly wrong. I am afraid. I am afraid and I feel so lost and alone.

"Where's Ma? Where's Louis?"

Suddenly Ding Dong is screaming into the back of the car, "What are you waiting for, Leo? *Shoot him, Shoot him!*"

"What dream—"

E-X-P-L-O-S-I-O-N!!